# DARK BRINGER

## LORD OF EVERFELL
## BOOK 1

# KAT ROSS

*DARK BRINGER*

First edition

Copyright © 2025 by Kat Ross. All rights reserved.

Map by the author.
Images courtesy of Adobe Stock.

This story is a work of fiction. References to real people, events, establishments, organizations, or locales are intended only to provide a sense of authenticity and are used fictitiously. All other characters, and all incidents and dialogue are drawn from the author's imagination and are not to be construed as real.

Paperback ISBN-13: 978-1-957358-21-5
Ebook ISBN-13: 978-1-957358-20-8

*For Laura*

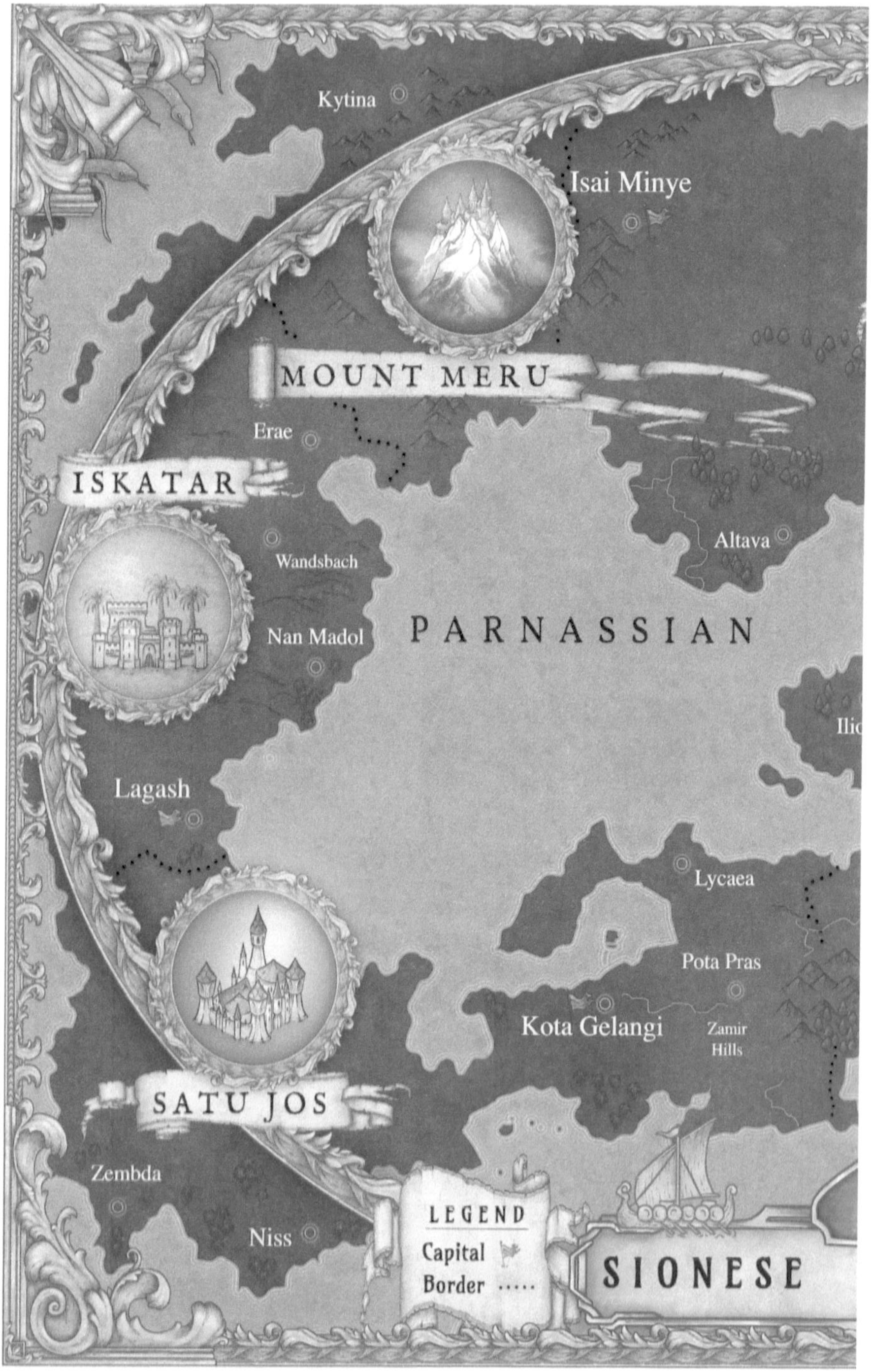
Kytina
Isai Minye
MOUNT MERU
Erae
ISKATAR
Wandsbach
Nan Madol
Altava
PARNASSIAN
Ilic
Lagash
Lycaea
Pota Pras
Kota Gelangi
Zamir Hills
SATU JOS
Zembda
Niss
LEGEND
Capital
Border
SIONESE

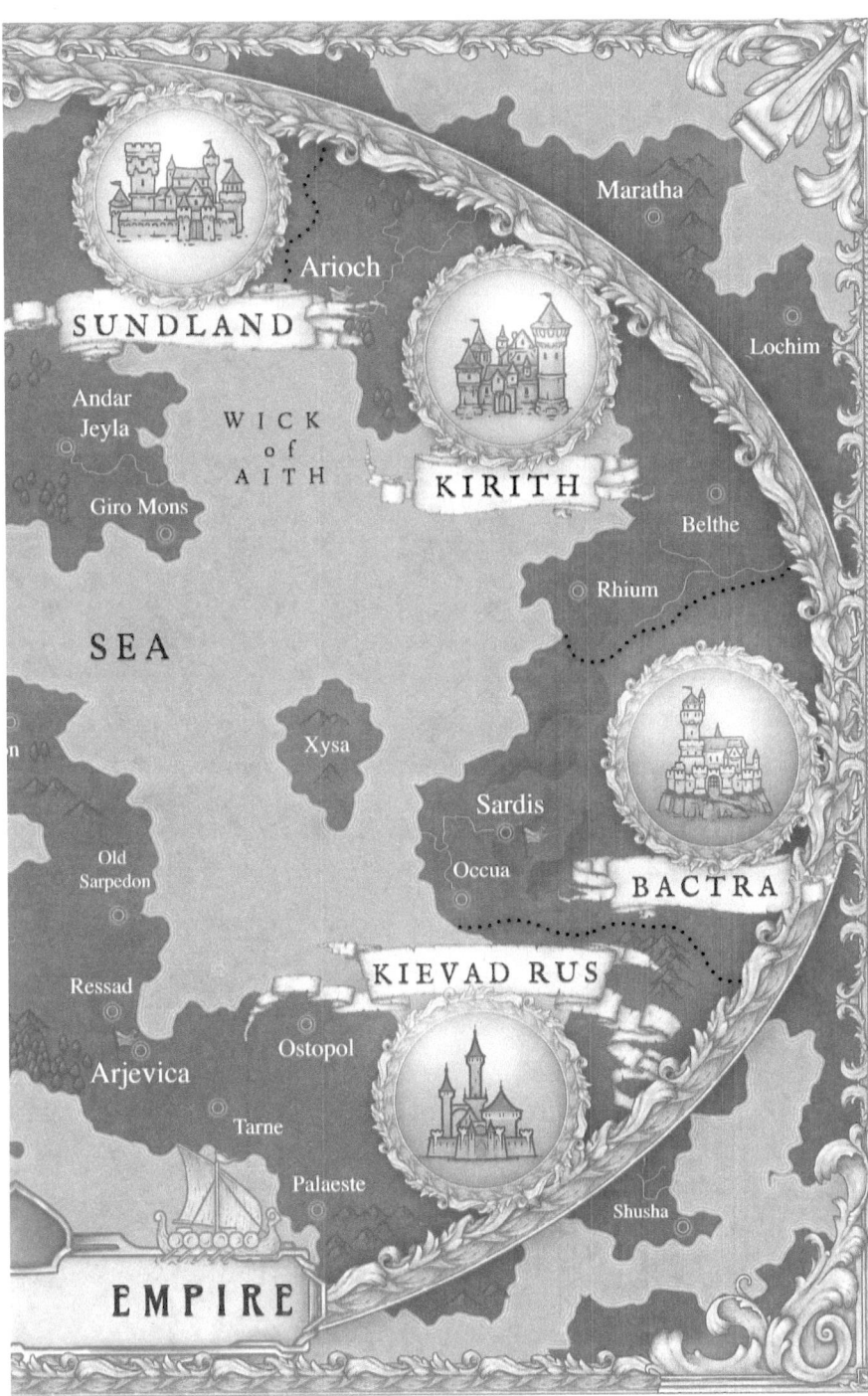

"What is dark within me, illumine."

John Milton, *Paradise Lost*

# PROLOGUE
## MOUNT MERU

T he cells faced east so prisoners could watch the legions drilling in perfect unison on the plaza below, golden armor dazzling at sunrise. Alluin Westwind was the only occupant. It was the nature of angels to be obedient—their father had made them so—and few broke the laws of Sion, fewer still the first commandment.

Witches and angels shall not procreate.

Adamantine chains bound his wings, but that was nothing to the agony of yearning for his lover and their child. Over the hundred days and nights that Alluin awaited judgment, he'd thought of little else.

It was snowing hard when the seraphim came for him.

They were imperial officers with intricately enameled breastplates and scarlet brocade along their sleeves. He stood as they flew through the open arch of his cell.

"It is time," the female said. She had brown eyes and wings a shade darker with bars of green along the primaries, iridescent like the breast of a hummingbird.

Alluin allowed each of them to grip an arm. The officers bore him through the snow, circling ever higher. He mentally rehearsed the argument he would present to their father. How he had tried to stay away from her. Had fought to remain aloof. But the spark that ignited when they first met had only grown brighter over the years, until neither could resist any longer.

Who had they harmed? No one! The child would go to the cyphers. As long as she never bedded an angel, there was no need to worry.

And she would not, Alluin assured himself. Cathrynne was a sweet, docile child who did as she was told.

Wind tore at his thin garments as they flew above the shining towers of Mount Meru, the angelic capital in the far north. Snatches of song rose from the Chorale, angelic voices joined in blissful harmony. The sound made him tremble. Why was he not dutiful like the others? What had planted the seeds of unrest? Was he flawed? Or was the law itself wrong?

His mind swam with confusion—but not regret. He would not regret a moment of their love.

Other angels glided between buildings, but none deigned to look at him. He was an outcast. Beneath notice. At last, his keepers banked sharply, and the tallest peak of the Sundar Kush loomed ahead. The place of judgment sat atop this peak, a square platform open to the sky. It had a single wall of dark gray stone flanked by two squat, crenellated towers. There was the suggestion of a door in that wall, a faint outline, but Alluin had barely a glimpse of it before the seraphim dropped him without ceremony upon the icy ground.

He landed on his knees, chains rattling, and fixed his gaze on the symbol of the empire—a triangle within a circle—hewn into the rock.

"Rise," a deep voice commanded.

Alluin expected to see Valoriel, but when he lifted his head, it was not their father who stood over him. Valoriel had wings of burnished gold, but this angel's were black as midnight. He wore a magistrate's robe, also black, its severity interrupted only by a violet cincture around his waist. Coal-black hair curled at his nape. He would have been pleasant to look upon were his face not so dour.

Alluin had seen Gavriel Morningstar from afar once or twice at the Chorale. He had heard tales of his pure heart and keen intellect. None did justice to the archangel's physical presence. It was almost as unnerving as their father. The air felt suddenly thin.

"You are Alluin Westwind, a census enumerator stationed at the Angel Tower in Arjevica?" Gavriel asked.

"Yes, Lord Morningstar," he managed. "Where is . . . where is our father?"

"Valoriel is away from Mount Meru." Gavriel's wings unfurled like living shadows, then settled once more. "I stand as regent in his stead."

A flicker of hope kindled. Perhaps the man known as Light-Bringer would prove more merciful.

"Let us commence with this disciplinary trial." Gavriel ignored the guards, his unwavering attention fixed on the prisoner. "You stand accused of consorting with a witch in violation of every law and custom of this land."

There was no point denying it; he'd been caught fleeing her bedchamber. But this was no impulsive tryst. They had been acquaintances for years before Hysto opened her heart to him. Then he had pined for her every moment they were apart. He knew each curve and dip of her body as well as his own. The sound of her laughter was sweeter than the Chorale. The time they'd had together was the happiest of his life.

Meeting Gavriel's stern gaze, Alluin could find words for none of this.

"The charge is true," he said at last. "I love her. We have a daughter together."

For eleven years they had managed to keep her parentage secret. Eleven years of stolen visits, of watching her grow from afar, pretending to be merely a friend of the family when all he wanted was to claim her as his own.

"If you decree it, I will remain here at Mount Meru for the rest of my days and never see them again," Alluin said, the words hollowing his heart. "Return me to the cells. But I beg you to grant them leniency. The fault is mine."

Gavriel's expression didn't change, but something cold flickered in his eyes. "The fate of your lover and her child are not mine to decide. It is yours that concerns me this day. You have violated the first law of Sion. Angels shall not mingle their blood with witches." He leaned forward. "Worse, you produced a child. A cypher, cursed to bear a monster."

Alluin raised an imploring hand. "But she won't," he said with desperate urgency. "She would never—"

"Repeat her mother's mistake?" Gavriel interrupted. "Let us hope she has more sense." He studied the symbol carved into the rock, his face growing contemplative. "Do you understand how the empire works, Northwind?"

"Yes," Alluin replied hoarsely.

"Explain it to me."

He swallowed with a dry throat. "The circle is Sion. It stands for unity among the children of the Divine Trinity. Valoriel created the angels. Minerva, the witches. Travian made the mortals. We are all cousins." His shackles clinked softly as he gestured. "It is represented by the triangle. Three together."

"And?" Gavriel stared at him with a touch of impatience.

"I . . . " He trailed off, uncertain what his inquisitor wanted.

"We are the base of the triangle," Gavriel said sternly. "The foundation. All rests upon our virtue and wisdom. If we falter, if we question the will of our father, then the ley, the lifeblood of this world, of magic, will be corrupted. Our cousins will sink into anarchy. Perhaps even into evil. Do you not grasp this?"

"I do, my lord," Alluin replied. "But I love this witch with all my soul. With every breath and thought and deed. Have you never loved someone thus?"

Angels were not expected to be celibate. They married each other or took human lovers. The first was encouraged, the second tolerated. Only witches were forbidden because of what the union might birth—the draconic race called Sinn. Fierce predators that had killed thousands before they were driven into the far reaches of the empire.

Gavriel's dark brows knit together. "What does that have to do with your crime?"

"I only ask that you consider the circumstances," Alluin said. "I would die for her. Perhaps that means nothing to the law, but you are a man. You must have passions and desires."

The Morningstar's face turned even grimmer. Alluin knew he had crossed a line, but there was little to lose now.

"Why are we sent into the world if we are forbidden to love whom we choose? We are all children of the Trinity. So my child is a cypher. She will grow up to serve the empire, as we do. She will become a shield and use her power for good. Where is the harm?"

Gavriel regarded him for a long moment. "Your arguments are irrelevant to this inquiry." He could not keep the scorn from his voice. "You knew what would come of the liaison. You knew the inevitable consequence. Yet you pursued it regardless, and for many years. If your daughter ever lies with an angel, her child is certain to wreak death and destruction unless it is killed at birth. Even if she does not, you have condemned her to the life of a cypher, to be feared and ostracized. Your selfishness knows no bounds."

Alluin's hopes withered.

"By the authority of Valoriel, the Summerlord," Gavriel said with the formal cadence of judgment, "I sentence you to two hundred years on the Plain of Contemplation."

Alluin had some idea that even if he never spoke to them again, he could watch from afar. Could reassure himself that they were well. But in two centuries, both Hysto and his daughter would be long dead, their bones ground to dust, their fates unknown.

"Why don't you save the trouble and kill me now?" he said bitterly.

Sarcasm seemed lost on the archangel. "Execution is not the proscribed punishment for witch-angel unions," Gavriel replied evenly. "The penalty is to be cast down for a term commensurate with the severity of the trespass. As it stands, you will have adequate time to consider your actions."

"You could show mercy, my lord," Alluin pleaded, rebellion draining away. "You are regent. You have the authority."

Gavriel frowned. "How is mercy merited here? You are a shepherd turned wolf, and for that you deserve no lenience."

"Wolf?" Alluin protested. "I am no wolf. She loves me!"

"You are deluded." Gavriel sounded weary of the entire proceeding. "If our father were standing in judgment, the sentence would be even longer. Count yourself fortunate he is away."

One of the seraphim officers handed Gavriel an oblong box of twisted wood. The archangel opened it and withdrew a black cylinder. He winced as it touched his skin, as if the contact caused him pain. Alluin felt a twist of dread. Even his guards looked uneasy, yet at Gavriel's nod, they dragged Alluin to the wall at the far edge of the platform. Lord Morningstar followed, gripping the black rod in his left hand.

"What is that?" Alluin asked hoarsely.

"The Rod of Penance," Gavriel replied. "It opens the way."

As if responding to its name, the thing flickered with ley power. But it held no life; this ley was a dull hue Alluin had never seen before. Lines of black light traced the great doors as they slowly swung wide to reveal a sheer drop. The clouds banked below the peak began to churn, lightning forking in their depths. A wave of terror crashed over him. This was no mere banishment—this was something else entirely. He struggled against the chains binding his wings.

"Alluin Westwind," Gavriel intoned, "I hereby judge you guilty of disobedience and treason, and banish you to . . ."

The rest was a buzz in Alluin's ears. An image of his daughter's face flashed before his eyes. Her fair hair belonged to him, but she had her mother's full lips and delicate brows. Cathrynne would be a great beauty someday—and a powerful witch, like all of her maternal line.

Was she weeping now? Alone and frightened after being torn from her family? He would give anything to hold her in his arms again. To smooth away her tears with kisses. To tell her how sorry he was.

"Wait!" he cried. "Please, Lord Morningstar, I beg you—"

Gavriel turned away, his mouth set in harsh lines. He gestured curtly. The guards heaved, and then there was nothing beneath Alluin but swirling snow. The last thing he saw before the clouds engulfed him was Gavriel's silhouette, the Rod of Penance extended over the void.

Then there was only grey mist, thunder rolling all around, and the certainty that wherever he was going, it was not a place from which he would ever return.

# CHAPTER I

# CATHRYNNE

## TWENTY YEARS LATER

T he old man drew on his cigarette and squinted through the haze.

"Strange noises," he said, tobacco-stained fingers gesturing to the house across the street. "Over there."

Cathrynne Rowan gave an encouraging nod. "That's what you said in the call, sir. Can you be more specific?"

He shrugged. "Sure, yes. Like thump. Very strange noises. All time of day and night." His Sundland accent was thick as butter. *Verra string nozzes.*

Her partner, Mercy Blackthorn, shot Cathrynne a skeptical look and mouthed the words *"feuding cats."*

Mercy was a strapping woman with a frizzy ginger mane and a dozen visible scars. Cathrynne was shorter and slightly built, with fair, chin-length hair and pale, creamy skin that gave her a fragile look. Men, in particular, tended to underestimate her.

Not that Cathrynne thought Josua Micarran was wasting their time on purpose. He seemed like a kind gentleman and had dressed up for them in a checkered suit that was probably the height of fashion forty years ago. A crumpled pack of Scholars poked out of the breast pocket. He had no shoes on, just black socks.

"Who lives over there?" Mercy asked.

Micarran exhaled twin plumes of smoke through his nose. "Mother, father. One boy. Six years."

"Surname?"

"Nilsson."

"Have you seen them recently?"

"Not for three days." He looked the cyphers up and down, taking in the whips coiled at their belts, the ravens tattooed on their hands. "You help them. You are witches, yes?"

"Hmmm, more or less," Mercy replied. "Thank you for reporting it, sir. We'll go have a look."

Lark Hill was a mellow neighborhood near Faraday College, mostly young families and student lodgers. Lately, it had seen an influx of migrants from Sundland. Cathrynne and Mercy seldom came out this way. Trouble was far more likely to arise in the rowdy student bars of Arioch's Old Quarter.

They crossed the street and paused at the curb to study the house. It was a mirror image of Micarran's. Yellow and white trim, well kept. The grass was shaggy and still damp from the morning rain.

"If anyone hurt that child," Cathrynne said in a low voice, "they might run into a wall or two before I manage to arrest them."

Mercy shot her a sidelong glance. "You don't need another complaint. They already take up a whole drawer."

Cathrynne snorted. "Felony won't care."

The head of the cyphers, Felicity Birch, tended to look the other way if someone deserved rough treatment. Cathrynne called her Sister Felony, though never to her face.

"One day you'll go too far," Mercy remarked placidly.

"I meant *by accident*. If they trip over a rug or something."

Her partner's eyes gleamed. "Yeah, that'd be a shame."

It was no secret how Cathrynne Rowan felt about men who hit their wives and parents who beat their children. About a third of the calls involved some variety of those crimes. The rest were drunks and thieves, occasionally murderers. Cathrynne didn't like them either, but they didn't get under her skin in the same way.

"Maybe the family went on a trip," Mercy said as they headed up the flagstone walk.

All the curtains were drawn tight. No movement. No *string nozzes*. Yet Cathrynne felt a twist of unease.

"Maybe," she said, her gaze catching on a carved wooden angel lying in the grass. Its wings were painted sky blue that shone with flecks of silver in the fading afternoon light. She picked it up.

"I've seen ones like this in the window of that fancy toy shop on Carlyle Street," she said. The paint had been rubbed away around the middle, right where a small fist might have clutched it. "The boy treasured it. So why was it left out in the rain?"

Mercy's face turned grim. She banged on the front door with the side of her fist. "Cyphers! Open up and let's talk!"

No one did.

Cathrynne circled around to the backyard. Wet grass dampened her boots as she backed up for a better view. There was a light burning on the second floor. A faint glow through the curtains. She returned to Mercy. "Looks like someone's at home," she said. "Since a minor child is involved, I say we have enough to go in."

Mercy nodded. "You take the front."

The door was locked, but it felt flimsy when Cathrynne jiggled the knob. No need to waste a projective gemstone. One solid kick and the door crashed inward just as Mercy battered down the back.

Cathrynne stepped into a mud room with winter coats on pegs and a line of boots and shoes. Most were large, a few boy-sized. She moved into the living area as Mercy's heavy footsteps clomped down a darkened hall. They met in the middle and looked around.

Every stick of furniture had been pushed against the walls. A green velvet settee lay tipped on its side. Chairs were stacked haphazardly. Lamps had been shoved under an end table, along with an assortment of toys. The carpet was rolled up, revealing four black scorch marks on the wood floor, each about six inches long.

Mercy sank to her heels and examined the floor as Cathrynne wandered to the rolled-up carpet, poking it with her cudgel. A faint charred smell hung in the air, like someone had burned supper. Her gaze flicked to the stairs. No irate homeowners appeared to investigate the intrusion.

"Let's take a look," she said.

They climbed the stairs. The upper story had two bedrooms, one big, one small. Beds unmade but no sign of a struggle. A lamp in the boy's room was left burning—the glow Cathrynne had seen from the yard. He had a cute sleigh bed with angel-print sheets. The kid had a thing for angels. There was also a dresser and a toy box and a miniature table and chairs. A stuffed bear sat in one of them, its black button eyes shining in the pool of lamplight.

They found nothing unusual in the bathroom or den. The rugs and furniture all seemed to be in their proper places. Downstairs, the kitchen sink was full of dirty dishes. Some were old and crusty. Others looked more recently used.

Cathrynne and Mercy returned to the living room and pondered this mystery.

"They could be getting ready to move," Mercy said. "Or they're staying somewhere else while they get the floor refinished." She sounded relieved. "That would make sense."

"Yeah. But then why didn't Micarran see the tradesmen coming in and out?" Cathrynne wondered.

"It's odd, I'll admit. But this was done deliberately." Mercy chewed her lip. "Separation, maybe? They have a fight. One of them takes the son—probably the mother. He drops the angel on the way out and they're in a hurry so she won't let him go back for it." She glanced at the front door. "Meanwhile, the father's at a bar drowning his sorrows with a bottle of cheap and nasty."

Without warning, the hair on Cathrynne's arms bristled. A prickling, crawly sensation tightened her scalp. Three symbols appeared, hovering over Mercy's head: a golden key, a sailing ship, and a coffin.

Her foretellings came rarely. Not even Mercy, her best friend for twenty years and partner for ten, had a clue that Cathrynne was a seer. It was her deepest, most terrifying secret. A power that would end with her bricked up in the kloster for the rest of her days if anyone discovered it.

But when the visions did come, she'd learned to pay attention. Cathrynne blinked, reading the symbols before they faded. The Key meant a door. The Ship meant travel. The Coffin meant death. Those were the broad meanings. But together, in that particular order, they meant something else, the way words formed a sentence.

Her gaze swept across the bare floor, the heaped-up furniture. It wasn't a domestic spat or a family packing to move house. Nothing was organized, just shoved out of the way to clear the space . . .

If not for the vision, she wouldn't have fit the pieces together —not fast enough. But she did now. Her mouth went dry.

This room was being used to force.

There was a field behind the chapter house for the same purpose, but it was much larger, fenced off, and guarded day and night so no one would accidentally wander inside. Forcing was how the strongest witches traveled, bending natural law to vanish from one place and reappear in another. But they needed a designated area—always open ground—or they risked materializing inside solid objects.

And if a person happened to be standing there when the witches arrived . . .

The air thickened. Cathrynne felt it in her teeth, a rising vibration.

"What's up?" Mercy's hand dropped to her cudgel.

She didn't know. Why would she? Neither of them had ever forced, it wasn't a power taught to lowly cyphers. They weren't even supposed to go near the field at the chapter house. But Cathrynne had snuck over there a few times when she was younger, just to see what the magic looked like, and she had the same feeling now, her ears popping as the pressure changed.

A box was forming in the middle of the Nilssons' living room. It resembled a giant shimmering bubble but square instead of round. There was no time for words. Cathrynne took four quick strides to the center of the room, to the scorch marks left by previous forcings. She grabbed her partner and dragged them both backwards.

An instant later, a clap of silent thunder shook the house. Cathrynne felt it through the soles of her boots. Two figures appeared where Mercy had just been standing—a man and a woman, both with the silver eyes of witches.

For a heartbeat, everyone froze. Mercy was staring at her cudgel. It must have been at the edge of the forcing zone because the stout wood was severed in half, the end cauterized.

"Stay right where you are," Cathrynne warned. "Do not move!"

The female witch was older and heavyset with a blotchy pink neck. Her gaze flicked to their hands. When she saw the raven tattoos, she looked relieved. "Just cyphers," she muttered.

A new spell began to coalesce. It involved receptive magic that Cathrynne didn't understand, but she felt sure it was nasty.

Mercy was faster, igniting a lump of topaz. Like all projective stones, topaz was ruled by fire and had quite a kick. The female witch was flung backwards, crashing into the stacked furniture. Mercy dove after her, leaving Cathrynne with the other witch. He had a long dour face and frosty eyes.

Mercy was now behind him. Cathrynne didn't want to hit

her with the backwash of a spell, so she went for her whip instead, flicking it at his neck. If he'd been human, it would have coiled around him like a noose, at which point she would have yanked his face into her knee, breaking his nose and maybe a few teeth. But he was a witch, so the lash bounced off an invisible shield.

"Too slow," he said.

A wave of force rippled across the room. It lifted her up bodily and sent her sailing down the hallway. *A hot ride.* That's what Mercy called going airborne. Cathrynne landed hard on her tailbone and skidded several cubits. The witch advanced, his lips curved in a mocking smile.

"Show me some of that infamous cypher blood! Is it really violet? I've always wondered."

She scrambled back as the hall plunged into darkness. The kind of pitch black that feels like drowning. Her pulse rammed into overdrive. She couldn't see. Couldn't breathe.

It wasn't real. She knew that. But knowing didn't stop the rising panic. She'd been claustrophobic since childhood, terrified of darkness and confined spaces. She threw her arms out and they banged into the walls. The narrow hallway felt like a coffin.

Cathrynne made a grab for her gem pouch as the witch threw another projective blast down the hall. It was like being caught in the bristles of a giant broom. She tumbled end over end until she hit something hard enough to see stars.

"They don't teach you anything useful, do they?" the witch taunted, his voice drawing closer. "You can't penetrate illusions. You can't shield yourself. The High Council doesn't trust you with fuck-all. You're just muscle for hauling away human garbage."

Laughter echoed through the darkness. That he was right didn't make it any better. She shook off the dizziness, trying to orient herself. Off to the left, she heard furniture breaking. Mercy and her witch were going at it hammer and tongs.

Cathrynne had a sudden image of Josua Micarran standing

on his front porch, smoking a Scholar and muttering about *string nozzes.*

"At least I have a job," she rasped into the blackness. "I'm not a criminal. And when I arrest you, you won't be coming back anytime soon. I hear the Iskatar prison camp is so hot, your piss evaporates before it hits the ground."

The witch chuckled. He was dragging something along the wall, pausing now and then to tap it on the wainscoting. It sounded like the cudgel she'd lost when he threw her across the room.

"How'd you find us?" he asked. "I bet it was that nosy geezer across the street." The scraping stopped for a moment. "He's supposed to be dead. I'll correct that oversight once I'm done with you." He drew a meditative breath, like he was mulling his options. She could feel his eyes crawling over her.

"Where are the Nilssons?" she asked.

Another chuckle. "If you're good, maybe I'll show you."

The footsteps stopped directly in front of her. She could smell him, sweat and a metallic tang.

"You're wrong," she said, "by the way."

"About what?" He sounded genuinely curious.

"I do know some magic."

"Well, go on, cypher," the witch said, amused. "Make your move."

Cathrynne bit her lip. Then she blindly groped for her gem pouch. It had gotten twisted up around her side. The cudgel came down, whistling as it cut the air. White-hot pain radiated up her left arm. She screamed, tears springing to her eyes.

"Oops," he said. "Did that hurt?"

Every cypher had a raven tattooed on the back of her dominant hand. It identified her if she ran away (which seldom happened), and it exposed her weak point. Disable her dominant hand and she couldn't cast a projective spell.

Cathrynne had expected him to break her fingers. Unfortunately for him, she was among the one percent who were ambidextrous.

She gritted her teeth. The wave of agony receded a little. "Gods yes," she gasped. "Does this?"

Her right hand sprang open, revealing the ruby she'd palmed while he was busy laughing at her. The witch drew a sharp breath as she unleashed the projective fire inside the stone. Scarlet light shattered the darkness. His eyes bulged as the force hit him in the chest. One moment he was standing over her, the next he'd gone through the living room window in a spray of glass.

Cathrynne held her mangled fingers to her chest. They were throbbing like live coals, but the suffocating darkness was gone. She limped back to the living room. Mercy was kneeling on the unconscious female witch.

"Now *that* was a hot ride," Mercy said with admiration. "He made it all the way to the lawn."

She started stripping her prisoner of every gemstone and piece of metal. Rings, bracelets, hairpins, buttons—anything the witch could use to cast ley when she woke up.

"She got in a few good licks," Mercy said. "But I clocked her and she went down. I don't think she's used to getting punched in the face."

Cathrynne glanced through the broken window. The male witch had cleared the porch and lay on his back in the front yard, twitching weakly. She wondered why they had chosen this house. What they needed it for. And where the Nilssons were.

"Hey," Mercy said, "you're bleeding."

Cathrynne touched her face. Felt sticky wetness.

*Show me some of that infamous cypher blood. Is it really violet?*

Yes, it was. The high ley content of angel blood gave it a blue tint. Witch blood—like humans—was red. Mingle them and you got violet. Now she had a nosebleed, a sign of the visions that she tried to hide whenever it happened.

"It's nothing," Cathrynne said, swiping a sleeve across her face. "Caught an elbow."

She turned away before Mercy could ask any more questions and headed outside. All along the street, neighbors were emerging from their houses, drawn by the spectacle. Josua Micarran watched from his own porch. Cathrynne waved and he lifted his cigarette in salute.

The witch groaned as she came near. He had dozens of small cuts from the glass, but none appeared life-threatening. A group of boys stopped their bikes at the edge of the yard. One nudged his friend, looking down the block. "It's the Jennies," he whispered with a note of awe.

An automobile slid up to the curb, all gleaming copper and sleek lines. The model was a Jentzen Mirage, hence the nickname. Two witches got out, wearing long white coats and sour expressions. The White Foxes had arrived.

Cathrynne yanked the gem pouch from the downed witch's belt before straightening to face them. There were orders of the White Foxes in every province, but George Claymond and Audrey Hayes headed the Arioch division. They hunted down rogue witches and viewed cyphers as disposable attack dogs.

George was burly and soft around the edges, with rings stacked on every finger. Audrey was famine-thin and favored dark maroon lipstick. Mercy called them Lump and Crump. It was funny, except that they were both very strong in lithomancy and utterly ruthless. Rumor had it that between them they'd killed a dozen rogues.

"Give me that, Rowan," Crump said in a peremptory tone, extending her hand.

Cathrynne turned over the gem pouch. "There's one more witch inside. They were using the Nilssons' house as a forcing zone."

Crump studied her, expressionless. "Do you know why?"

"We're not sure yet—"

Cathrynne cut off as a second car arrived, disgorging four more White Foxes. They fanned across the lawn and surrounded the male witch. Receptive gems ignited as they cast shields around him.

"Oh, that looks nasty." Lump eyed Cathrynne's hand with false sympathy. "Maybe you should sit this out."

Crump shot him a vexed look. "It's a little late for that, George." She stepped closer. "Why didn't you notify us? This sort of thing is well beyond your jurisdiction."

Lump clucked his tongue. "You could have been *killed*. Pure dumb luck you weren't."

Cathrynne tried to leash her temper. "We were investigating a noise complaint. We had no idea there were witches involved until they . . ." She was about to say "forced straight into us" but that might provoke questions about how they'd avoided dying. "Came back," she finished lamely.

Crump pursed her lips. "We'll need a full report, Rowan. Every detail."

"Sure," Cathrynne said. "As soon as I'm done."

"What?"

"The family. I need to find them." She studied Micarran's house, then tipped her head back and gazed upward. The houses were identical. Both had small attics. She turned and walked inside.

"Get back here, Rowan!" Crump shouted.

Cathrynne ignored her. Let the White Foxes take credit for arresting the witches. She didn't care about that. But the Nilssons were a human family, which *was* her jurisdiction. She darted around the Jennies who were questioning a long-suffering Mercy and headed for the stairs. Cathrynne paused on the second-floor landing, woozy from the pain in her left hand. *Minerva, please let them be alive. Especially the kid.*

She didn't expect the witch goddess to answer. Minerva hadn't been seen in centuries. But Cathrynne still prayed to her on a regular basis and now seemed like a good time.

There had to be a way up to the attic, something she and Mercy had missed the first time. It wouldn't be inside the bedrooms. But maybe the linen closet? She opened the door and started running her good hand over the shelves. On one side, it went straight through. She felt a dusty draft on her face. Illusion.

She stepped through the false shelving to find a dark, narrow staircase. "Hello?" Dread pooled in her stomach at the silence that followed. But then she heard a muffled thump. It could be another witch, so she readied a projective garnet. But when she reached the top, she found the Nilssons tied up on the floor, rags stuffed into their mouths.

"It's all right," Cathrynne said, moving quickly. "You're safe now."

The terror in their eyes changed to desperate hope. She struggled with the knots one-handed, freeing the father first so he could help the others. Soon they were crying and hugging each other.

"They dragged us from our beds three nights ago," the mother sobbed. "Said they'd kill Jakob if we called out or tried to escape."

The boy stared at Cathrynne with glassy eyes. His lips were chapped, and she wondered if the Nilssons had been given anything to eat or drink.

Then she remembered the wooden angel in her pocket. She gave it to Jakob, who clutched it tight. "I threw him out my bedroom window," he whispered. "So he would fly for help."

She smiled. "That was good thinking."

"They kept coming and going," his father added hoarsely. "Once, we heard them talking about the port. Timetables and deliveries."

That's when Cathrynne noticed a pile of new-looking crates against the wall. She hadn't paid much attention because the light was dim and she'd been focused on the Nilssons. But now she felt a strong resonance in her blood. She moved to the nearest crate and pried up the lid. It was filled with raw gems, all hot with ley.

"Well, well." George Claymond's voice boomed from behind. "Quite a haul."

She turned to find Lump standing in the doorway. He eyed the trunks with triumph but little surprise. "We'll take over from here," he said with a crocodilian smile. "You should go get that hand looked at."

"I will, thanks," Cathrynne said.

She nodded at the family and turned to leave. It would have changed a great number of things if she had. But then he said something unfortunate.

"There's a good girl," Lump remarked in the same tone one might use with a faithful dog.

Cathrynne stopped. She turned around. "I was just thinking about something, George. How did you get here so fast?"

The smile vanished. "What are you implying?"

"Oh, I'm not implying anything. I'm saying it straight. Maybe you knew that the witches who've been hitting the gem vaults at the port were hiding out in this house. But they're dangerous, and they've been forcing, so you waited for us to go first, just in case."

Lump turned red. "That's an outrageous accusation," he spluttered. "I won't dignify it with a response." His small eyes grew hard. "But nor will I stand for such an insult from the likes of you. I'll give you one chance to retract it, Rowan." He brandished a be-ringed finger. "One!"

She shook her head and helped the Nilssons down the stairs. The mother gave Cathrynne a sympathetic look. Medics had arrived, and they took charge of the family.

Mercy stood on the lawn, watching the prisoners get loaded for transport. The chapter house had brick and wood cells that didn't use any metal, not a single nail. The woman was still out cold, but the male witch shot Cathrynne a filthy look.

Crump must have gone inside because Cathrynne didn't see her. But two other White Foxes stepped into her path. "We were told to hold you for questioning," one said sternly.

Cathrynne held up her purple, swollen fingers. The Jennies winced in unison. "Can't you just give us a ride to the chapter house? I'll tell you whatever you want to know on the way." She cupped her nose, which was still trickling. "I think I might be going into shock."

They glanced at each other, then nodded. Not all Foxes were heartless.

Once in the back seat, Cathrynne grinned at Mercy. Then she crossed her legs, sat back, and proceeded to bleed all over the white leather upholstery.

## CHAPTER 2
# ACROSS THE PARNASSIAN SEA...

T he hour before dawn was a moment of pause in the cheerfully corrupt and deeply superstitious city of Kota Gelangi.

Even the hardest-drinking merchant princes had staggered home, and the politicians and gossip-mongers were yet to rise from their beds. As Tristo Arpin bumped a handcart over the cobbles of Rua Capitolana, lamps winked out and wings fluttered above, swarming in clouds as dense and black as a gathering storm.

The bats provided his livelihood, which was removing the guano that splattered Liberty Square. His sons, who were a great disappointment, called it shit-scraping. Tristo liked to remind them that there were worse ways to earn a living—just ask the poor souls who toiled in the mines.

The three men paused before the steps of the popular assembly. Everyone called it the Red House for its brick façade. Directly across the square sat the limestone offices of the gossip-mongers, whose broadsheets could be relied upon to deliver scandals, sexual indiscretions, and the crimes of the day, preferably violent.

They set to work. For a while, the rhythmic sluice of water

and scrape of stiff bristles on stone were the only sounds. In the gray light, Tristo's broom caught a paper idol blown from one of the shrines—a sinuous form with painted blue scales and a bit of scarlet felt glued to its mouth. For a tongue, he supposed, or flames.

He was a city man and had never seen a Sinn. Prayed he never would. In his grandparents' time, the draconic monsters had burned large swathes of Kota Gelangi. The creatures never returned to the capital, but they still plagued the mines, and people feared and worshipped them in equal measure.

Tristo picked up the soggy idol and returned it to the nearest shrine. It was just paper, but best to be respectful with such things. As his gaze drifted upward to the copper dome of the Red House, he noticed something dangling from the spire. Something that hadn't been there yesterday.

Tristo shaded his eyes, squinting at the object. On holidays, the provincial flag of Satu Jos would fly from the dome, a flame rising from a forge encircled by iron ingots. But it was not a holiday, and this was no flag. As he stared, a crow landed on it. Then another.

"Finish here," he said, thrusting the broom into his eldest son Gil's hands. "I'll be back."

"What is it?" Gil asked, but Tristo was already crossing the square. The night watchman had worked there for two decades and Tristo knew him well. He went around back to a door with a brass plaque that said *Mail & Deliveries.*

After half a minute of vigorous pounding, it was answered by an elfin, balding man in a blue jacket that was buttoned crookedly. "Arpin," he said in surprise. "Do you need to use the necessary room?"

"No," Tristo replied. "But something has caught upon the spire."

Dimas cupped a hand around his ear. "Did you say caught fire?"

The watchman had been going deaf for years, but his nephew

was a delegate's aide and made sure he kept his job. Tristo repeated himself, speaking slowly so Dimas could read his lips.

"Is it a bat?" Dimas asked, looking worried now. Bats were a protected species in Kota.

"Not a bat," Tristo said firmly. "Bigger."

The watchman stood aside. "Arpin, you'll come with me to check, won't you?" He winced. "My knees."

Tristo didn't want to. Surely it was just an empty flour sack, or perhaps a large paper idol caught by the wind. Yet the shape of the thing bothered him. And the way it didn't move in the wind, as if it was *heavy*.

No, he didn't much care to take a closer look, but Dimas was blinking at him hopefully, so Tristo came inside. The corridor smelled of expensive carpets and polished wood. Dimas led him past smiling portraits of past consuls. They reached a nondescript door and beyond it, a winding staircase that spiraled upward through the heart of the building.

"A long climb," the watchman warned, lighting a lamp.

Tristo's legs ached from hours on his feet, but morbid curiosity pulled him forward. They ascended in silence, breath puffing. Through narrow windows, he glimpsed the awakening city, coaches and carts rolling down avenues, smoke rising from kitchen chimneys, shrines coming alive with morning supplicants.

The stairs seemed endless, and they paused several times to rest. At last, they emerged onto a landing with a door leading outside.

"The dome gallery," the watchman explained, unlocking the door with a key. "Mind your step."

A narrow railed walkway encircled the copper dome. Kota Gelangi spread out beneath them, stone and terra cotta broken by green parks and a muddy brown ribbon of river. On another day, Tristo would have marveled at the view. But his eyes were drawn upward, to the spire that rose another fifteen cubits above them. And to what hung from it.

For a few seconds, he could not make sense of what he was seeing. Then Dimas was noisily sick, startling the crows. They exploded upward with raucous protests. When Tristo saw what they had perched upon, what they were doing, his stomach twisted, bile rising in his throat.

"Travian's bones," he breathed, pressing a fist to his mouth.

"We must inform the authorities," Dimas said weakly. "The vice consul, the witches . . ."

Tristo nodded, not trusting himself to speak. He stumbled back towards the stairs, Dimas following. By the time they stepped outside, the square was filling with gawkers. As Dimas went to fetch help, a group of smartly dressed gossip-mongers came running over, notepads in hand, shouting over each other.

"Is that what it looks like?"

"Who's up there?"

"Hey, you clean the square every day, don't you?" A big phony smile. "I remember you!"

Tristo regarded the eager group. Not one had ever glanced his way before, let alone bid him a polite good morning. He drew a steadying breath as his sons reached his side. Gil whispered in his ear, and Tristo nodded. It was a terrible thing, but such opportunities came once in a lifetime.

"How much will you pay for my story?" he asked.

A spirited negotiation ensued. The winning offer, from *Kota Confidential*, was more than six months' wages. Tristo tucked the dragha bank notes into a pocket of his apron and followed the scribbler to the edge of the crowd. She had shiny black hair and a stain on her cream-colored blouse.

"Spilled my kopi," she said when she noticed Tristo looking. "First off, do you know who it is?"

Tristo nodded. "The dead man is Consul Barsal Casolaba. I saw the chain of office around his neck."

The notepad dropped to her side. Her eyes widened, drawn past his shoulder to the spire. "Murder or suicide?"

"He was naked and impaled upon the Red House spire, so I

would say murder." Tristo wondered if he should have asked for more money. The other scribblers were casually drifting closer, pretending not to listen.

She made a shooing motion at them. "Get lost, I paid for an exclusive." She waited for her rivals to slink away, then turned back to Tristo. "What else? I need details. My readers want to know *everything*."

He swallowed, voice sinking to a whisper. "The worst part . . . Well, his eyes were burned from the sockets as if he'd seen the Great Serpent herself!"

# CHAPTER 3

# GAVRIEL

"Well, Morningstar?" Consul Cyranthe Dagan regarded him through her half-moon glasses. "Will you agree to look into the matter? You are Sion's chief magistrate, after all."

A short woman with curling white hair and quiet resolve, she was the highest-ranking human in Kirith. Fifteen minutes ago, she had turned up unannounced at his residence to inform him that Barsal Casolaba was dead and this was somehow Gavriel's problem.

"The answer is no," he said firmly. "I'm far too busy with other matters to travel at the moment." He glanced at his desk, where a stack of papers awaited signature. "Besides which, violent crimes are investigated by the cyphers."

Cyranthe was unruffled. "I expected you to refuse," she replied, "but as you well know, this is a politically sensitive case. Casolaba had enemies in high places, and one of them impaled him upon the spire of the Red House! All of Kota Gelangi woke up to the gruesome sight. The murder must be solved quickly or it will erode confidence in the Assembly, and perhaps the empire as a whole."

Gavriel wandered to a shelf of legal texts bound in black and gold, selected a volume at random, and pretended to immerse himself. "So, who is on this long list of enemies?"

"The opposition party in Kota's Assembly, for one," she answered. "The witches, for another. Neither trust the other side to conduct an impartial investigation."

"I'm sure they can reach a compromise."

From the edge of his eye, Gavriel saw a crooked smile cross her face. "They already did. *You*, Morningstar."

He closed the volume and ruffled his wings. "That is unfortunate as I must decline."

Cyranthe leaned forward, a small silver orrery swinging from her neck. Before she was elected consul, she chaired the astronomy department at Grunewold College.

"Gavriel," she said with uncommon urgency. "You are known throughout the empire to be impartial, showing neither fear nor favor in your judgments. You care nothing for influence and less for money. Only a just result. There is no better man for the job."

"I am not well liked in many quarters," he pointed out dryly.

"Which only proves my point," Cyranthe countered. "Whether or not people like you, your name is unimpeachable."

He moved to the window, his reflection ghosting against the glass. "Why then," he asked, "do you think that flattery will sway me?"

Cyranthe rose from her chair. Her reflection joined his in the window. "Just *listen*," she said. "Already the whispers have begun that agents from Kievad Rus had a hand in Casolaba's death. There are interests that would fan these flames into civil war. Is that what you want?"

"Obviously not." He moved to the hearth. The flames had dwindled, much like his enthusiasm for this conversation. "Are you certain the witches would not perceive my presence as impinging upon their authority?"

Cyranthe's eyes gleamed with triumph—she believed she was winning. "The witches asked for you specifically. So did the deputy consul, the ambassador from Kievad Rus, and the leaders of both the Freedom Party and the Miners' Union." She sounded bemused. "In fact, you are the only thing they seem to agree on."

Gavriel did not care what any of them wanted. Kota Gelangi was sure to be a vipers' den, and he had no desire to risk his reputation. "My docket is full at the moment," he said firmly. "Please convey my sincere apologies."

"Of course, you must do as you see fit." Cyranthe cleared her throat. "But . . . oh, never mind. I'm sure you don't care."

A final ploy. He suppressed a sigh. "Just tell me."

She donned a regretful expression. "I'm afraid word has leaked to the scribblers that you accepted the commission."

He froze. "What?"

"If you refuse now, it will be a grave insult to Satu Jos." Cyranthe tossed a broadsheet on his desk. "Don't scowl like that, Morningstar. It wasn't I who did it."

He scanned the newsprint. It was the usual blather, but Cyranthe was right. A "high-ranking anonymous source in the Assembly" claimed his arrival was imminent. "They presume much," Gavriel muttered.

"And yet the fact remains that you are needed," Cyranthe replied. "For the good of the empire."

Rain coursed down the library windows, blurring the view. He weighed his options. The scribblers—those ink-stained gossips whose fortunes were built on half-truths and innuendo—would have a field day if he denied the story, framing it as a change of heart. Perhaps even cowardice. Gavriel told himself that he was above such things, yet the prospect of his name being dragged through the mud rankled.

"Whoever did this thinks they're clever," he said, "yet they may regret the decision."

"Oh?" Cyranthe arched a brow.

"Someone will regret it, I can promise you that." He straightened his broad shoulders. "I will make an initial assessment. Three days, that is all I can spare." He held up a hand as she started to speak. "But only if I have freedom to call any witness I choose, as well as full access to Casolaba's papers."

"Of course," Cyranthe agreed quickly. "I will send a message." She moved toward the door, then paused with her hand on the knob. "Time is of the essence . . ."

"Yes, yes," he muttered impatiently. "I will leave straight away."

Cyranthe departed, passing Edvin Yarl in the doorway. He had been Lord Morningstar's secretary for four decades, and though the years had bent his back and silvered his curly hair, the keenness of his gaze had never dimmed.

"What was that about?" he inquired, clutching a diary to his chest with his right hand. Yarl's left sleeve was pinned at the elbow, a reminder of an old encounter with the Sinn.

"Clear my schedule for the next four days," Gavriel said. "I'll be taking a brief trip to Kota Gelangi."

"Very good, sir. Er, why Kota Gelangi?"

Gavriel gave him a grim smile, feeling a ripple of anticipation despite himself. "Barsal Casolaba is dead, Yarl. Brutally murdered and hung from the dome of the Red House."

Yarl's brow twitched—the equivalent of a shocked gasp from anyone else. "How tragic."

Gavriel was barely listening, his gaze drawn back to the embers glowing in the grate. Consul Barsal Casolaba had been corrupt to the bone—everyone knew it. His death would not be mourned by many, except perhaps those who had benefited from his machinations. But murder was murder, and Gavriel would find the truth of it. In fact, he was starting to look forward to watching the various powerful factions squirm beneath his questioning.

"Sir?" Yarl's voice broke through his thoughts.

"Pardon, what?"

"Do you mean for me to accompany you?"

"Yes, I am certain to need you," Gavriel replied.

Yarl swallowed. "I don't suppose we'll be traveling by sea?" he asked hopefully.

"I fear not." Gavriel spread his wings with sudden vigor. The coal-black feathers spanned the width of the library. He clapped Yarl on the shoulder. "There isn't time. We must get there while the trail is still fresh. But don't worry, it'll be a short flight."

The color drained from his secretary's face. Yarl disliked travel by air. It was his one weakness, this man who faced down angry petitioners and navigated political intrigues with unfailing composure.

"Very good, sir," he said, his voice faint.

"Pack what you require for three days," Gavriel instructed, moving to his desk to send a few urgent letters. "We leave in an hour." He couldn't resist a small jibe. "I suggest you bring an extra set of undergarments. I hear it's quite cool in the hills this time of year."

Yarl shot Morningstar a look that, from anyone else, might have earned a reprimand. "I shall pack accordingly." He paused, then added with unexpected passion, "And I am certain you shall get to the bottom of this heinous crime posthaste, sir!"

## CHAPTER 4
# GAVRIEL

G avriel savored the rush of wind as he soared above the astronomical observatory, its telescopes reflecting the late afternoon sun. Around it clustered the six colleges that made Arioch the greatest hub of learning in Sion.

Faraday with its million-volume library, whose copper roof had long ago turned a dignified blue-green. Bartolomeo with its acres of lawns and botanical gardens where students gathered between lectures. Grunewold and Whitworth with their fiercely competitive rowing teams. The Merry Sharp Institute with its distinctive yellow brick dormitories. And Kirith Polytech, newest among them, whose clean modern cubes contrasted with the city's medieval bones.

Students in dark robes hurried through the quads far below, some juggling stacks of books, others deep in lively debate. They came from every corner of the empire, drawn by the promise of knowledge and enlightenment. Some would stay for a lifetime, others would carry what they learned back to distant cities.

Arioch had changed little over the centuries of Gavriel's long life. Sleek automobiles purring through streets alongside carts and coaches were the main difference. As Kirith's archangel, he wanted only to protect this repository of knowledge and invention for as long as he could.

Yet for all the venerable prestige of the universities, Angel Tower remained the tallest building in the city. You could stand on almost any street corner and see its golden cupola, a reminder that while the provinces enjoyed a degree of autonomy, Mount Meru was the final authority.

Gavriel angled towards the fourteenth-floor landing platform, where the doors of the north gate stood open. The guards made a starburst with their fingers as Gavriel alighted on the platform, followed by seraphim carrying Yarl and the luggage.

"Have a safe journey, Lord Morningstar," said one.

He nodded curtly and strode through the gate. Inside, the tower opened into a hollow atrium where hundreds of angels went about the business of running the empire. Records of births and deaths, tariffs and tax revenues, agricultural production, provincial decrees, treaties, laws, and other documents—all were held in a vast repository.

Certain angels known as enumerators counted every human, witch, and cypher for the census. Since it was conducted every five years, the work never ceased and there were always rivers of paperwork flowing between the provinces and Mount Meru.

When they spotted Morningstar, the hum of activity ceased at once. Heads turned, voices hushed, as their archangel flew upward in lazy spirals. Gavriel could not instantly move from one place to another by forcing, as the witches did. But the Angel Towers of each provincial capital, seven in number, were all connected with liminal ley.

Ley was the animating force of Sion. Every living thing from earthworms to whales held a spark of it, and when a creature died, that spark would sink back into the vast ocean of ley at the center of the earth. It was the source of the witches' power and ran hot in Gavriel's own blood—although he could not work magic himself.

Liminal ley was the most subtle and peculiar type, flowing

along the boundaries where one thing ended and something new began but neither state was yet fully present. It was the gap between past and future, light and dark, here and there. Gavriel knew scholars in Antioch who had studied the liminal ley for their entire careers and still barely understood it.

Only the gods did, and they were the ones who had directed the construction of the Angel Towers.

Gavriel landed in the round chamber at the very top, where six archways stood equidistant from one another. Some showed views of shifting sand, others of snow and ice. Gavriel chose the one that led to Kota Gelangi. He paused at the threshold to lay a steadying hand on Yarl's shoulder. "Nearly there."

Yarl swallowed and gave a firm nod. The seraphim to either side stared straight ahead.

"Take care with him," Gavriel warned them, and stepped through the arch.

There is a certain unease one feels upon entering a liminal space. It is both familiar and uncanny. They are not places one ought to linger in, and Gavriel beat his wings hard, plunging into a fine mist. He flew blindly until he spied the golden glimmer of another tower, a twin of the one he had just left. He angled his wings and made for the open archway. A glance behind showed the seraphim and Yarl following.

Gavriel flew through the arch, folding his wings as he alit. Haniel, the archangel of Satu Jos, was waiting for him.

He had not seen her in some time, but she looked the same. Like a young woman just past the cusp of maidenhood, with waist-length fair hair and eyes the shocking blue of a glacier. She wore a silvery gown with fine embroidery at the neck. Her wings were white as a swan's breast.

Gavriel bent a knee. "Permission to enter your city?"

"Of course." She inclined her head. "Welcome, brother. We are honored to accept the aid of the esteemed Morningstar at this difficult time."

Gavriel couldn't tell if Haniel was being sarcastic. She didn't look honored, but she rarely expressed emotion. Although he had known her for centuries, he'd never understood her. She was the most aloof of the archangels. Her policy, if she had one, seemed to be to stay out of human and witch politics entirely and focus only on bureaucratic tasks.

Gavriel knew he was lucky to have Cyranthe Dagan as his consul in Kirith. They didn't always see eye to eye, but Cyranthe was honest and did what she thought best for the province. He could not imagine dealing with a consul like Barsal Casolaba.

Well, he *could*. Gavriel simply would not stand for the man's corruption. But Haniel was tolerant to a fault.

"I hope you will stay with me during your time here," she said. "I've had rooms prepared."

Before Gavriel could answer, the two seraphim arrived carrying his secretary between them. Yarl's natural complexion was brown, but Gavriel sensed a green undertone. He claimed liminal travel gave him indigestion.

Haniel's bow lips tightened. "I do not wish to be ungracious," she said, "but the towers are for angels alone, Gavriel. I am certain that we have had this discussion before, yet you insist on violating the prohibition."

"A thousand apologies, sister," Gavriel said, turning to his secretary. "Master Yarl, would you be kind enough to go ahead to the Red House and inform them of my arrival?"

Yarl composed himself with admirable speed. "Of course. I shall request a full dossier on the consul's recent activities."

"And arrange for the usual accommodations while you're at it."

Yarl nodded and closed his eyes as the seraphim gripped his arms once more and spiraled down through the hollow core of the tower.

"The usual accommodations?" Haniel echoed. "Tell me you are not taking quarters among the humans, Gavriel. I've had rooms prepared at my residence for you."

This, too, was an ancient dispute.

"A kind gesture," he said, "but you know my answer. I require solitude when adjudicating cases."

"But it would be far simpler to stay with me."

Gavriel met her gaze, which was somehow innocent and calculating at the same time. "I'll be here for three days, no more. You'll receive a copy of my report before I depart."

"So brief a sojourn?" She affected indifference, yet he caught a flicker of relief.

"I did not wish to come at all," he said sharply. "Three days will suffice."

"Very well." Haniel picked up the thread of her previous argument. "But I've said before and will say again, bringing humans through the arches taxes them severely. You should not do it. The poor man."

"And yet he survives," Gavriel replied. "Now to the matter at hand. What are your thoughts?"

She paused as a cherubim flew into the chamber bearing a tray with a pot of hot kopi, the sweet, muddy beverage popular in Kota Gelangi. Gavriel accepted a cup, gazing through the archway leading to Mount Meru. It was hidden by clouds, but he had a sudden longing to see his father. What counsel would Valoriel offer? Surely that it was another sign of the empire's slow decay.

"Consul Casolaba was neither an honest nor a good man," Haniel said matter-of-factly once the cherubim had departed. "Of course, few humans are."

"That doesn't justify his murder."

She made a noise of dismay. "Did I say such a thing? I am merely warning you that you have a very large haystack to comb through. Barsal Casolaba behaved more like a king than a consul. He used his influence to reward his allies and ruin any who stood in his way. The only surprise is that he managed to survive this long."

Gavriel sipped his kopi. "Give me the short list, Haniel."

She proceeded to name the Miners' Union, spies from

Kievad Rus, certain factions among the witches, and even the deputy consul, who had been angling for Casolaba's position for years.

"That's not counting the dozens of other violent enemies he must have acquired among the city's underworld," Haniel reported with some relish. "But I am certain you will get to the bottom of it."

Gavriel could not stop himself. "Why did you permit his corruption, Haniel? Isn't there something you could have done?"

She regarded him with pity. "First of all, the humans are Travian's children. He ought to manage them."

"Travian has been gone for centuries," Gavriel reminded her.

"Nevertheless, it is not my place to overstep." She adopted a prim expression that irritated him no end. "My role is an administrative one. And even if I cared to get involved, who should I have replaced him with? They are all the same. Grasping for wealth, pleasure, power—whatever eases the pain of their brief and pointless lives."

"Some, yes. But I disagree that they are all the same," Gavriel said quietly.

"You are entitled to your opinion. But I do not envy you this task." Haniel set her cup aside untouched, her voice honeyed again. "Should you require anything, brother, anything at all, you need only ask."

GAVRIEL FELL through the hollow core of the tower, its levels passing in a blur. At the twelfth floor, he snapped his wings open and arrested the descent. The guards at the east gate touched their breastplates in a salute as he passed through.

Kota Gelangi was three hours earlier than Kirith, but it was the southern winter and dark had fallen by the time he reached the Red House. Liberty Square was mostly empty, but a young man waited with Yarl at the top of the steps. He wore a maroon coat with diagonal brass buttons and clutched a leather valise.

"Lord Morningstar," he said with a nervous bow. "I am Levi Bottas, aide to the late Consul Casolaba. I've been assigned to assist in your investigation."

Bottas was in his early twenties, with side-parted black hair and a clean-shaven, artless face.

"You can begin by showing me the consul's office," Gavriel said.

"Of course. It's on the second floor."

The entered the Assembly and started up a marble staircase.

"How long did you work for Casolaba?" Gavriel asked.

"About a year and a half, sir. I came from Niss last spring."

He'd heard of it. A small resort town on Satu Jos's southern coast. "What brought you to the capital, Bottas?"

He cleared his throat. "My uncle runs the Sapphire Bay Hotel. He's, er, a generous donor to the Freedom League. When I expressed interest in politics, he arranged an introduction to the consul."

Nepotism, Gavriel thought with disgust. Like every other appointment in this city.

Other than a pair of watchmen, who stood straighter and looked alert when they saw Morningstar, the halls of the assembly were quiet. They made their way down a corridor. Bottas produced a ring of keys. "The consul's office has been sealed since the discovery of the body, by order of the witches," he said. "Shall I . . .?"

The door had been taped with the symbol of the Morag, head of the witches' High Council. Gavriel examined the seal closely. Satisfied that it was intact, he nodded and Bottas removed the tape.

"Give me the keys," Gavriel said.

Bottas handed them over, and Gavriel unlocked the door. "This will serve as my base of operations. I require interviews with anyone who had contact with Casolaba in the week before his death."

"I'll prepare a list," Bottas said.

The consul's office occupied a corner overlooking Liberty Plaza. It was cluttered with items ranging from a gold-enameled humidor for Casolaba's imported cigars to ochre Lagashi pottery and rare artwork. All gifts from his benefactors, no doubt.

Above the desk hung a portrait of the dead man. Middle-aged, jowly, with a white beard and receding hairline. The swell of his coat suggested a prodigious appetite.

"Who discovered the body?" Gavriel asked.

"A man named Tristo Arpin. He sweeps the square every morning and spotted it from below. Arpin alerted the watchman and they climbed the stairs to the dome. *Kota Confidential* printed an exclusive. I hear they paid a handsome sum for it." Bottas opened his valise and unfolded a broadsheet with the screaming headline, *His Eyes Were Burned Out!*

Gavriel quickly devoured the article. He had not known that particular grisly detail.

"Shall I add Arpin to the witness list?" Bottas asked.

"Since he has given such a detailed account to the scribblers," Gavriel said dryly, "that won't be necessary for the moment. Where is the body now?"

"Er, I'm not sure. The morgue?"

"Is that a question or an answer?" Gavriel snapped.

Bottas swallowed. "I shall find out straightaway, sir."

"What about this watchman? The one who was on duty. Did he hear or see anything?"

"I'm afraid not. He made a statement, it's in the file. But he's rather hard of hearing, sir. And his eyesight isn't very good."

"You have a deaf and blind watchman?"

"Not *completely*. Er, his cousin is a delegate's aide."

"Of course." Gavriel sighed. "I'll want a complete list of everyone who was in the Assembly building yesterday, their arrival and departure times, and any unusual visitors in the past month." He set the broadsheet aside. "We will commence the interviews with senior staff and lawmakers now."

Bottas looked embarrassed.

"Is there a problem?" Gavriel asked.

"No, sir, but—" He hesitated. "It's past the sixth hour. Everyone is gone for the day."

Gavriel stared at him. "Their consul has been murdered. They demanded my presence. And now they've left for supper?"

Bottas shifted uneasily. "It is how things are done here, Lord Morningstar."

Gavriel drew a slow breath and tamped down his fury. "So it is. I had forgotten." He fixed Bottas with an icy stare. "But you will go nowhere until I dismiss you."

"Of course not, sir." He handed over a book. "I retrieved Consul Casolaba's appointment diary from his residence. And I can give you a preliminary list of his close associates."

"Good." Gavriel turned to Yarl. "I'll want records of criminal cases with his name on them, both as complainant and accused. And you should go to his home and fetch his banking records, his will, and a summary of assets."

"His wife may object, sir," Bottas ventured.

"His wife has no choice." Gavriel opened the first dossier and set to work.

For the next several hours, he sifted through Haniel's haystack while Bottas and Yarl came and went, fetching more documents. The picture that emerged was of a vindictive, petty, greedy man whose corruption was matched only by his success in evading punishment. Bribery, witness tampering, and extortion were among the various charges, none of which resulted in conviction.

"What great fortune!" Gavriel muttered acidly. "Accusers who recant or disappear, evidence that goes missing, judges who suddenly reverse themselves and rule in his favor."

"His patronage extended throughout the city," Bottas admitted. "From the docks to the fire brigades."

"And where were you the night he died?" Gavriel asked, looking up from the records.

"In my flat sleeping, sir. Like most people at that hour." Levi Bottas looked frightened, but that didn't mean he was guilty. Anyone in his position would be worried.

"Do you know whom he might have met with?"

"I don't, sir, I'm sorry. His last appointment of the day was at four-thirty. I attended him and we left the Assembly together."

"Who was it with?"

"Primo Roloa. The head of the Freedom League."

"I know who he is. What was discussed?"

"Just the usual end-of-the-day meeting. They talked about some upcoming bills and went over the expected vote tallies."

"You shall write a statement detailing every word that was said, to the best of your memory."

Bottas stared at him like a cow over a fence.

"Now, please," Gavriel barked.

Casolaba's aide drew a breath and leapt up to fetch some blank paper. "Certainly, sir."

The sixth hour became the ninth, then midnight. Bottas brewed a strong pot of kopi. The wheels of the empire's justice tended to turn slowly, but Gavriel could not afford to waste a moment. His reputation depended on it. If someone in Kota Gelangi thought they could commit murder and escape the reckoning, they were badly mistaken.

---

DAWN WAS CREEPING over the rooftops when Gavriel closed the last ledger. Yarl, who had been dozing with his back straight as a board, stirred and blinked owlishly. Levi Bottas was still awake, but he looked bloodshot and rumpled, his maroon coat dangling from the back of a chair.

"You're dismissed, Bottas," Gavriel said. "Go home and

return in four hours. We shall commence with the interviews at nine sharp."

Bottas bowed, obviously relieved to be cut loose. Gavriel and Yarl gathered a few essential documents and locked the consul's office behind them. It was a pleasantly cool morning. Gavriel wondered if Tristo Arpin might be sweeping the square, but no one was about. Perhaps the man had taken his bounty and gone on a seaside holiday.

It was almost funny. Gavriel had expected to find a city in mourning, but Kota Gelangi seemed to greet Casolaba's demise with a shrug. Which, he supposed, was entirely in keeping with a province where fortunes might be won and lost in a single day.

The biggest mining operations were owned by a handful of old witch families and their human surrogates. They were the lions, but there were plenty of scavengers who fought over the leavings. Likely Casolaba had done someone dirty, expecting he'd be untouchable—but this time he was wrong.

Above the two men, dark ribbons of bats streamed through the sky, returning to their roosts after a night of hunting. Yarl peered up at the infamous spire atop the Red House. "If only they could speak," he murmured.

"Indeed." Gavriel's lips curved in a rare smile. "I would subpoena them as witnesses and our crime would be solved by lunchtime."

They headed down the broad avenue leading from the Red House to the district where visiting dignitaries, members of the assembly, and various special interests kept houses.

"I'm afraid I couldn't secure your usual residence," Yarl said. "It was occupied by a delegation from Iskatar." He paused. "The broker suggested an alternative. It was all I could find at such short notice."

"Our stay is brief," Gavriel said. "I'm sure it will serve."

The house stood at the end of a cul-de-sac, four stories of pink stone faced by a fountain with frolicking stone nymphs.

The inside was worse. Gilt mirrors, red velvet upholstery, and nude statuettes plated in gold.

"Did you rent a brothel?" Gavriel asked.

"It belongs to Councilor Adnan Virek," Yarl explained, "who is currently serving a term of house arrest in his second residence. He was convicted of perjury in an unrelated matter."

Gavriel shook his head. "If the scribblers discover I am staying here, they shall turn it into a scandal."

"Which is why I dismissed the household staff. The broker promised discretion."

"And I'm sure you paid well for it. No matter, this will suffice." Gavriel softened his tone. "Get some rest. We have a long day ahead."

Yarl nodded. "Sir."

They parted ways, and Gavriel wandered through the house. Virek apparently collected glass figurines of the Sinn, for they were everywhere. It was a peculiar local custom, keeping idols of the monsters that laid waste to their mines on a regular basis. He picked one up, studying the long tail and fierce teeth.

Some experts claimed the Sinn were a throwback to the primordial deity Valmitra, whose form was serpentine when she came to this world. Gavriel could not say if it was true. But something in the mingled blood of angel and witch had created an entirely new species, draconic and bent on destruction.

There were Sinn in Kirith, but they were the forest-dwelling kind, rarely seen. Their desert cousins were much larger and more aggressive. He had spotted a few from the air during his travels throughout the empire, but they never came near. He was not certain he would have survived the encounter if they had.

Gavriel climbed the stairs to the rooftop terrace. Kota Gelangi was more spread out than Kirith, the buildings lower. All except for the Angel Tower, which stood white and gold against the lightening sky.

He sat on a stone bench, clearing his mind in preparation for the day. After a few minutes, a soft scuff made Gavriel turn. Yarl stood in the doorway leading to the stairs, his tall, rather gaunt figure silhouetted against the interior darkness.

"Up so soon?" Gavriel said. "I thought I told you to rest."

Yarl's silence was disconcerting. What if he was suffering a stroke? The thought of losing him provoked a rare moment of self-doubt.

*I shouldn't have made him work through the night. Shouldn't have brought him through the archway without considering the strain.*

Yarl was in his seventies now. How swiftly the years had flown by! Gavriel feared the inevitable day his secretary would retire. Edvin Yarl was loyal and efficient, certainly, but he was also Gavriel's closest companion—his *only* companion, in truth.

The time would come when he was gone forever. Gavriel knew this. It was the curse of a long life to feel the pain of loss again and again. Now, he silently vowed to all three gods that he would better care of his friend until that day came.

"Edvin?" He rose and took a step forward. "Are you unwell?"

The sun crested the distant hills, washing across the terrace. Yarl's features were rigid. A counterfeit mask of the man Gavriel knew. Too late, he grasped the truth.

*Illusion.*

The figure raised a hand and a hammering force struck Gavriel's chest. He slammed into the waist-high wall enclosing the terrace. There was the snap of bone cracking. For a heartbeat, he teetered at the edge.

Then he was falling. His broken wing flared with agony as he tried to slow his descent. The left extended, beating uselessly against the air, as he plummeted toward the marble fountain below.

# CHAPTER 5
# CATHRYNNE

The chapter house of the witches of Arioch sat in the heart of the city where the six colleges came together. It was enclosed within a high brick wall hidden by climbing roses. They smelled sweetest at dusk, just after a spring rain, and Cathrynne always associated them with coming home.

A statue of Minerva, the witch of Sion's divine trinity, stood at the main entrance. Her marble gaze fixed upon all who entered, one arm raised to cast a spell. The statue was twelve centuries old—which is how long it had been since anyone last saw her.

The original chapter house had grown over the years into a sprawling compound that encompassed living quarters, meeting halls, smithies, the forcing ground, classrooms, the seers' kloster, and other functions. It was part of Arioch's Old Quarter and had the same baroque limestone architecture as the surrounding colleges.

Cathrynne's left hand throbbed fiercely, so she was glad the White Foxes drove straight to the infirmary. She got out, feeling a moment's satisfaction at their looks of disgust when they saw the bloodstained backseat, and then Mercy was steering her through the doors.

A new, modern infirmary was being built on the east side. In the meantime, a makeshift clinic occupied the ground floor of a former gem storehouse. Inside, it smelled of alcohol and harsh cleaning products.

A witch named Angus Valinger was on duty. His mournful face softened when he saw them. "Ah, my two favorite repeat clients. Back so soon?"

"You're not laying a hand on me," Mercy warned. "I have enough scars already, thanks."

He laughed. "Come now, Blackthorn. How many times have I stitched you up?"

"Too many. Just look at me. I'm a patchwork quilt."

He arched a brow. "Are you saying it's my fault that you keep getting in brawls?"

"No, but you could take a few sewing lessons. A blind butcher would do a better job—"

"Enough banter," Cathrynne interrupted, holding up her hand. "Can you fix this?"

"Ouch." Angus led them to a surgery in the back and examined her, his touch gentle despite Mercy's ribbing. "You're lucky it's a simple fracture."

She ground her teeth as he manipulated the bones into alignment. Then he wrapped the fingers in a bandage, leaving the thumb free.

"Best I can do. Try not to use it for a few weeks," Angus said.

"Not a problem." Cathrynne flexed her right hand. "I can still give a hot ride with this one."

"You should have seen the last one," Mercy put in. "It was *glorious.*"

Angus shook his head. They left the infirmary and went to report to Felicity Birch, a.k.a Sister Felony. It was the dinner hour and most cyphers and witches were eating in the dining halls—separate, of course.

"I think I might be in trouble," Cathrynne confessed as they crossed into the cyphers' territory. There was no sign or outward indication, but the buildings got a bit smaller and shabbier.

"Lump and Crump?" Mercy guessed.

Cathrynne nodded glumly. "Mostly Lump, though I don't think Crump is happy with me either. I accused Claymond of setting us up."

Mercy grimaced. "Bet that went over well."

The sinking sun cast long shadows as they crossed the grounds. As always, Cathrynne's gaze drifted to the top of the tower that stood in a wooded area at the far edge of the grounds, distant from other buildings. The seers' kloster. Its windows were four-inch slits. Once you went in, you never came out—not until they carried you out in a pine box.

Seers were both mad and dangerous, or so the witches claimed. They mostly talked gibberish, though an occasional genuine prophesy might emerge. Telling the difference was next to impossible.

Cathrynne had no idea why her own talent was different. Why she saw symbols instead of the future. Why she wasn't stark raving yet, when most seers didn't make it past their teens before they were found out. But the end result would be the same. The witches would never let her roam loose if they knew what she could do.

Mercy followed her stare. "Courage Hazel just got sent up."

Cathrynne didn't know her well, but she recalled a quiet, kind girl who fed the pigeons that strutted around outside the mess hall. "How did it happen?"

She always asked this question. Someday, she might be the one getting sent up. She was obsessed with the early signs. If she knew them all, maybe she could recognize them in herself and run away while she was still rational enough to plan ahead. It was usually strange behavior, outbursts, a distancing from the real world as the visions took hold. Courage had always struck her as normal, which was even more terrifying.

"I'm not sure," Mercy said. "Poor woman. She's only nineteen."

They were quiet for a moment, regarding the kloster through the trees. Cathrynne blew out a breath. "Do you think I'll get suspended?"

"It's all thrice-damned nonsense," Mercy replied, which wasn't an answer.

They walked in silence. Cathrynne ruminated about being stuck in her cramped barracks for weeks on end. She couldn't escape the memories of being eleven years old and trapped in a coach with two White Foxes for weeks, taking the long way round from her childhood home to Kirith because the winter storms wouldn't permit a sea passage.

Besides hunting down and arresting rogue witches, the White Foxes also sniffed out cypher children. They had chapters in every province, and were the most powerful and secretive order within the witches.

Cathrynne told herself everything would be okay. After all, they'd helped to catch some of the most-wanted witches in the empire. She'd nearly convinced herself of this until they reached Felicity Birch's office, where George Claymond and Audrey Hayes were on their way out.

Audrey's dark red lips parted in a vicious smile when she saw them.

"Enjoy your freedom," she said. "It won't last long."

---

"Mum," Cathrynne and Mercy said in unison.

They stood at attention while the head of the cyphers looked them over. No one knew her exact age, but she was *old*. Too old to bother with the dress code. Felicity Birch wore whatever she liked. Today, it was wide gray slacks and a blue cable-knit sweater.

"You were damned lucky," Felicity said. "Those witches have

killed three cyphers. Two at the port in Arioch, one in Bactra. Plus a customs official. He was probably dirty, but still. Good job."

The wall behind her desk had a small plaque for every cypher who had died in the line of duty, which was quite a few.

"Thank you, mum."

"Don't thank me yet. Get in here and close the door." Felicity lowered her voice. "The White Foxes are pushing hard for both of you to be punished, and this time they won't back down."

"We were just doing our job," Mercy protested. "They ought to be thanking us."

"And yet they're not." Felicity shook her head with exasperated fondness. "It was foolish to antagonize them, Cathrynne. You know they don't like you. They never have. In their view, you were found too late. They prefer us to be molded from birth."

Cathrynne was the only cypher without a grace name. She'd refused to answer to "Serenity" when she first came to the chapter house at age eleven. After a year of punishments failed to wear her down, Felicity had finally conceded, allowing her to keep her given name as long as she changed her surname to Rowan.

"That's hardly my fault," Cathrynne muttered.

"No, but your lack of diplomacy, not to mention self-preservation, is a pain in the ass," Felicity retorted. "However, I have an idea that will buy us time for things to cool down." She braced her hands on the desk. "Pack your bags. I'm sending you both on an assignment abroad."

"Where are we going?" Cathrynne asked, bewildered and anxious. Mercy enjoyed travel and often spent her leave in exotic locales, but Cathrynne never left Arioch. Not in two decades. Both ships and carriages felt confining.

"Kota Gelangi," Felicity replied.

Her heart sank further. The capital of Satu Jos was across the Parnassian Sea, a journey of two weeks. The direct route was faster, but most ships hugged the coast since the aquatic Sinn preferred deep water.

Cathrynne frowned. "Why?"

"Lord Morningstar needs protection," Felicity said. "He's investigating the death of Consul Barsal Casolaba. You do know about that?"

Cathrynne never read the gossip rags, but she vaguely recalled hearing about a consul's death. Illness, wasn't it? Or poison?

"You mean the one who got impaled," Mercy said.

*Impaled?*

"Yes, that one," Felicity agreed. "Morningstar just arrived in Kota yesterday and someone has already tried to kill him. Presumably the same person who murdered the consul."

There was a shocked silence. Such a thing was unheard of. Archangels embodied the might of the empire. It was almost as insane as assaulting the god Valoriel himself.

"Who would dare?" Cathrynne wondered.

"Someone desperate to avoid capture, I imagine," Felicity said. "He wasn't hurt too badly. Apparently, he fell from a roof and broke a wing. Whoever did it got away. The assailant used illusion to get close. They masked themselves as his secretary, Edvin Yarl."

"So it was a witch?" Mercy exclaimed.

"Careful now," Felicity warned. "Such a spell requires skill but little strength. There are plenty of human weirdlings with enough witch blood to cast an illusory cantrip. Until we know for sure that a witch did it, it's not a matter for the White Foxes. He's refused their aid anyway. He also refused local protection. Understandably, I suppose."

"So you're sending *us*?" Cathrynne asked, still confounded at this turn of events.

"I wanted to send a dozen cyphers, but he'll only accept two," Felicity replied briskly. "And despite your recent blunder, you're the best I have. Besides which, it will get you away from

Lump and Crump. Don't bother denying it, I know what you call them . . ."

Cathrynne's scalp prickled. Felicity's voice dimmed, replaced by a buzzing in her ears. *Not now. By the three gods, not now.*

But she couldn't stop the visions once they began. All she could do was stay calm and pretend everything was fine. Her gaze flicked across the images hanging in the air over Felicity's desk. Quickly memorizing them and then looking away since it wouldn't do to sit there gawping at nothing like a freak.

The Dark Rider. Stars. A pair of doves, their beaks touching. The Crossroads.

The vision faded within seconds. Sometimes she knew right away what it meant. Sometimes, like now, she was unsure. The Rider usually foretold a message, and Stars could certainly be Gavriel Morningstar. But the rest . . . Perhaps it would come clear later.

Cathrynne touched her nose. A single drop of violet blood smeared her fingertip. She scrubbed it on her trousers. Thank the Trinity, Felicity wasn't looking at her.

"When do we leave?" Mercy asked.

"At once," Felicity replied. "Morningstar doesn't like to be kept waiting, and whoever did it might try again." She fixed them with a serious look. "Behave and do as you're told. This is a golden opportunity to redeem yourselves."

"So we're travelling by sea?" Mercy asked.

Cathrynne knew the answer. There were thirty-six pictures in her repertoire of visions. One was The Ship, and it had not appeared.

Felicity gave them a tight smile. "Not quite."

\* \* \*

The forcing ground lay beyond the training quads at the farthest edge of the compound. It was contained by a wrought-iron fence covered with caution signs. Felicity waited at the center of the muddy yard. At her side stood a small woman with fierce white brows like a bird of prey. Ninnoc, an old crony of Felicity and one of the few full witches to befriend a cypher.

Ninnoc smiled warmly at Cathrynne and Mercy. "So these are our troublemakers? They look capable enough."

"Oh, they're plenty capable," Felicity said. "It's their judgment that concerns me." She fixed them both with a dour look. "The witches of Kota will provide you with gems. Get yourselves straight to the Red House. And be respectful to Lord Morningstar. If you win his favor, the Foxes can't bring you back. The archangel of Kirith outranks them."

Cathrynne did not want to leave Arioch, and she most definitely didn't want to be hurled through space with unnatural magic. But she grasped that she'd been offered a way out and resolved to do whatever it took to stay in the Morningstar's good graces.

Ninnoc reached into her gem pouch and selected two stones. Obsidian in her right hand, moonstone in her left. One imbued with projective ley, the other with receptive ley. Exactly what you were never supposed to blend together.

"Stand close together and don't move," Ninnoc instructed. "If you need to sneeze, do it now."

Cathrynne stared at the patches of scorched earth. Some were fused into a glassy, tubular structure called fulgerite, forged by the union of unspeakable forces. Everyone knew the stories. Witches who lost a limb when the box fractured. Others who never turned up at all.

"A bit closer now," Ninnoc said encouragingly.

Cathrynne and Mercy squashed themselves together so tightly that Cathrynne could count the beads of sweat on her partner's eyelashes. Felicity nudged their luggage into the forcing zone. She gave a firm nod, then took six steps back.

"Minerva keep you," she said.

The stones in Ninnoc's hands ignited. A low vibration traveled up through the ground. Then a silent thunderclap. The world lurched sideways. For a bad moment, Cathrynne's body began to stretch as if she were tied to four mules, each running in a different direction—

Then everything snapped back into place. She landed hard on her back. A vile oath, muttered quietly, signaled the arrival of Mercy. The sky was a deeper blue than Arioch, the sun hotter. Instead of mud, the forcing ground was clay baked hard as stone. A witch in a loose, ankle-length robe stood at the fence. His black hair was gathered into a topknot.

"You must be Cyphers Rowan and Blackthorn," he called, politely ignoring their rough arrival. "The Morag is waiting."

Cathrynne sat up, heart drumming. The Morag? She was the head of the High Council. The most powerful witch in Sion! How did Felony fail to mention that they would be called to see her?

It could only be because Felony hadn't known. Which didn't bode well.

Cathrynne shot Mercy a wary look as they shouldered their bags and followed the witch into a low, thick-walled building of sandstone. Inside, the air was cooler and smelled of dry, peppery spices. He led them to a set of ancient, elaborately carved wooden doors and pushed them open.

"The cyphers from Kirith," he announced, then stepped aside to let them enter.

The room held little furniture, just a low table and overlapping rugs in a mandala pattern. Isbail Rosach, the Morag of Sion, sat cross-legged on the floor with a few other witches, separating gems into piles. Sunstone and amber, beryl and moonstone, olivine and peridot.

The Morag looked younger than Cathrynne had expected, but witches aged slowly, and the strongest might reach two hundred years or more. She had long, dark hair worn loose around her shoulders, with only a few threads of silver. Like all witches, and cyphers, too, her eyes were a metallic pewter. Scars wound from her left cheek down her neck and into her robe.

Lithomantic spell burns. Cathrynne could tell that much from the stellate pattern.

"Let me be clear." Her voice was low and gravelly. "You are not wanted here. Were the choice mine, I would assign cyphers from Satu Jos to guard Lord Morningstar, but he has stubbornly refused to accept anyone outside his own province."

Cathrynne tried not to wither under her stare. Mercy wore the bland, unflappable expression she had perfected from years of breaking up bar fights.

"I assume you are trustworthy or Felicity Birch would not have sent you. You will shadow him wherever he goes and report to me on the investigation. Everything he discovers, everyone he speaks with. You might serve Morningstar, but you are under my command, make no mistake about it. Is that perfectly clear?"

"Yes, mum," they answered.

"I will have your things brought to Lord Morningstar's residence. You will stay there as long as he remains in this city." She stared at them hard. "If any harm befalls him, if a single feather of those infamous black wings is ruffled, the fault will be yours and yours alone. We cannot afford any more fiascos. Is *that* clear?"

"Yes, mum."

"Good. Morningstar is at the Red House. You may proceed there directly. Do you know the way?"

"I do," said Mercy.

Isbail tossed them each a bag of gemstones and made a gesture of dismissal. "I expect your first report tomorrow."

"But how will we slip away?" Cathrynne wondered. "If we're guarding him night and day?"

"I am certain you will think of something," the Morag replied grimly.

They backed out of the room. When the doors closed, Cathrynne exhaled a taut breath.

"That went well," Mercy said, as the male witch escorted them out. "How much worse can Lord Morningstar be?"

Kota Gelangi was dirtier than Arioch and hot as blazes. The sticky smell of ripe fruit hung in the humid air, and everywhere Cathrynne looked, she saw stone alcoves cluttered with paper monsters. A man in a fine robe approached one, knelt down, and furtively left a handful of figs.

"I see why it's called the City of a Thousand Shrines," Cathrynne remarked as they bulled through the midday crowds. "They really do worship the Sinn."

"Well, most people have relatives scratching out a living as rockhounds," Mercy said. "Or they work for the witches who own the big mines. Either way, the Zamir Hills are infested with Sinn and the papers say they've been getting bolder. Attacking in broad daylight. I guess they hope that if they pray hard enough, the Sinn might start listening."

"I wish Minerva would listen," Cathrynne muttered.

Mercy shot her a sharp glance. "You don't know that she isn't. Now, we're almost there. Brace yourself, because Morningstar won't be easy to please. I've heard stories about him."

"Like what?" Cathrynne knew the archangel of Kirith existed in the same way she knew gravity existed. She believed it was real, but she didn't think about it much. And she certainly never expected to meet it in person.

"To be blunt," Mercy said in a low voice, "he's a bit of a prick. High-handed, arrogant, and critical of every little thing."

"And he's an angel," Cathrynne said. "I'm shocked."

Mercy didn't laugh. "We're serving two masters now. The Morag wants us to spy on the Morningstar, but if he finds out, it's straight back to Arioch."

"Then we just have to make them both happy," Cathrynne said. "How hard can it be?"

Mercy snorted. "The eternal optimist."

They cut through an open-air fruit market, rounded a traffic circle clogged with various conveyances, and the Red House appeared, occupying one side of a square. Guards in scarlet uniforms flanked its wide entrance. They directed Cathrynne and Mercy to the second floor.

A crowd milled around outside the dead man's office. A few seraphim, three tense-looking witches in flowing robes, and more uniformed guards. The door opened, and an elderly man emerged. His face was deeply lined, his eyes bloodshot.

"Are you the cyphers from Kirith?" he asked.

Mercy nodded. "I'm Cypher Blackthorn. This is Rowan."

"Come in, come in." He turned to the waiting crowd. "The rest of you are to disperse on the orders of Lord Morningstar."

The angels frowned. One stepped forward. "We need but a moment of his time—"

"Now!" a deep voice barked from inside the room. "All of you, out!"

The angels looked unhappy, their wings stiffening in affront, but they stalked off. The witches followed, eying Cathrynne and Mercy with resentment before disappearing down the stairs. The secretary led them inside and closed the door.

Lord Gavriel Morningstar sat behind a desk, his right wing bound against his body in a sort of sling. He looked up as Cathrynne entered and their gazes caught. His eyes were a tawny golden-green, the only color against his tanned skin and black magistrate's robe.

Angels were always comely and Gavriel Morningstar was no exception. He had clean, masculine features, with a winsome dent at the center of his chin and thick coal-black hair that matched his brows and wings. But his jaw was unshaven and he had a rough, commanding quality that made her breath turn shallow.

*Archangel.* There were only seven in the empire. Each wielded immense power. Not magic, or he wouldn't need cyphers to protect him, but political power. And this one certainly had raw magnetism to spare.

Cathrynne dragged her eyes away before he noticed her reaction. Morningstar had more authority than ten consuls. More even than the Morag. And he'd send her back to Arioch if he didn't like her.

"Thank you for coming," he said crisply. "I regret the need for it, but there is nothing to be done about that. What are your names?"

"Mercy Blackthorn, Lord Morningstar."

She swallowed. "Cathrynne Rowan."

His eyes settled on her once again . . .and lingered. "I asked for two cyphers," he said softly.

"I am a cypher," she replied.

"Then why don't you bear a grace name?"

At least the hundredth time she'd been asked that question. "I do, in a way," she hedged. "Cathrynne means *pure* in the ancient tongue of Bactra."

He studied her, his expression unreadable. "So you are originally from Bactra?"

"No, I am Kirithi."

A partial truth. She'd lived in Kirith for twenty years. That the first eleven were spent in Kievad Rus didn't count.

Morningstar looked as if he might press further, but then weariness crossed his face. "As long as you keep me alive long enough to find Casolaba's killer."

"That I swear to do," she said.

"Good." He drummed his fingers on the desk, the corners of his finely carved lips turning down in a grimace. "I originally intended to conduct an initial inquiry of three days, but I have decided to remain in Kota Gelangi until the case is solved. I will not be intimidated."

That didn't seem to require a response so she said nothing, but Cathrynne was secretly thrilled. It could take weeks to catch the culprit. Let Lump and Crump stew in their own juices.

She looked around the office, assessing it for weaknesses. The large windows overlooking the square were an immediate problem. She turned to the secretary, Edvin Yarl. "Can we have drapes installed? An assassin on any of those rooftops across the way would have a clear line of sight."

Yarl blinked. "Certainly, Cypher Rowan."

"And the corridor needs to be kept clear at all times," Mercy added, "unless someone has an appointment with Lord Morningstar. Tell the guards not to admit anyone unless they're authorized."

"Indeed. I shall do so immediately." He gave them a tired smile. "It is a relief to have you here. I don't want to insult our hosts, but I trust my own compatriots from Kirith more."

Cathrynne liked Yarl. You could tell right away how someone felt about cyphers by the way they looked at you. His gaze was direct and unafraid.

There were mounds of paperwork on every surface. She noticed a list of names on a side table and reached for it. Morningstar's head jerked up.

"Don't touch that," he snapped.

She withdrew her hand and met his flinty gaze. "Sorry."

"Don't touch *anything*. You may stand by the door," he instructed, turning back to his papers. The cyphers from Kirith had ceased to exist.

She and Mercy exchanged a look. *A bit of a prick*. Yes, that described Gavriel Morningstar perfectly.

# CHAPTER 6
# GAVRIEL

He ran down the witness list for the tenth time, trying to gather his thoughts. He had never needed bodyguards before and he didn't care for it. They were a distraction when he needed all his faculties focused on the case.

At least Mercy Blackthorn looked like a proper cypher, tall and solid. But he wasn't sure what to make of her partner, the one with the strange name.

He had to admit that Cathrynne Rowan's silvery hair and eyes made a striking combination with her sweet, delicate features. Never before had Gavriel seen a cypher whose angel blood was so pronounced. He could more easily picture her singing in the Chorale at Mount Meru than wielding the whip and cudgel at her hip.

Against his will, he kept sneaking glances, the witness list entirely forgotten now. She wore the uniform of the cyphers, a snug bodice and breeches that revealed a shapely form. Her left hand was bandaged. He wondered if she'd lost a fight in some seedy tavern before coming here. Of course, he was recovering from an injury himself. He decided to be charitable and give Cathrynne Rowan the benefit of the doubt.

"Lord Morningstar." Levi Bottas poked his head in. He wore a dark suit with a black cravat knotted at his throat.

Rowan blocked his path, one hand dropping to her cudgel.

"It's all right," Gavriel said. "He's Casolaba's aide. I'm expecting him."

Bottas eyed the two cyphers with trepidation.

"This is my new security detail," Gavriel explained. "Now, have you located the body? I shall want to examine it myself."

Bottas grimaced as if bracing for a storm. "That will be difficult, my lord, since he's been cremated."

"Who ordered that?" Gavriel snapped.

"The widow, sir. She said it was the consul's wishes."

"Is she unaware that there is a criminal investigation underway?"

"No, sir. But no one had given the morgue any explicit orders to hold the body, so they released it to her yesterday. She was adamant that her husband didn't want to be gawked at if he passed away. Her words, sir."

"How convenient. Then we must confirm the account of the street sweeper, as he was the last to view the body. Yarl, I will leave that to you." Gavriel turned back to Bottas. "What about the other witnesses? Don't tell me they're all on holiday."

"No, sir," he said quickly. "In fact, the first on your list is waiting outside. Assemblywoman Luzia Bras."

She was the head of the Miners' Union, the main opposition party in Kota's Assembly. The Miners' Union and Casolaba's Freedom League were old foes, making Luzia Bras a prime suspect.

"Show her in," Gavriel said.

The cyphers at the door stood back, though they looked ready to pounce at the slightest threat. Luzia Bras strode into the office with the brash confidence she was famous for in the Assembly. She wore a leather jacket and trousers and carried herself with the authority of someone used to commanding a room.

"Lord Morningstar," she said, taking in the injured wing. "I heard what happened. It's outrageous. Killing that pig Barsal is one thing, but now they've crossed the line!"

Gavriel suppressed a smile and gestured for her to sit. "For the record," he said, "you've come voluntarily to discuss Consul Casolaba's murder, is that correct?"

Her laugh was loud and genuine. "I didn't know it was optional. But I've nothing to hide. Sure, I despised him. So did a lot of people. He had no friends, Lord Morningstar." Bras's dark eyes flicked to Bottas with undisguised contempt. "Only flunkies and rivals."

Yarl's pen scratched against a fresh ledger, recording every word.

"You speak bluntly of a man whose body is barely cold," Gavriel said.

If she knew Casolaba had already been cremated, she gave no sign of it.

"And I'll say the same over his grave." Her lip curled with contempt. "The pig grabbed my ass right in the Assembly chamber when I first came to the Red House as a junior delegate. He treated the women staffers like concubines, and sold out the miners to the gem conglomerates every chance he got. His death improves the province."

Gavriel did not bother to dispute this assessment, which he privately thought was accurate.

"I saw the harassment complaints," he said. "All of them were eventually dropped."

Luzia Bras snorted. "After Barsal paid off his accusers. Or threatened them." She gazed at him frankly. "What more can I tell you?"

"Where were you the night of the murder?"

"At home." She glanced at Yarl with a smirk. "Write that down, and make sure you note that I would not be ashamed to kill such a man if I could get away with it. He deserved everything he got. But it wasn't me."

Gavriel wondered if she was bold enough to toy with him. Yet the woman's hair was streaked generously with gray and deep laugh lines bracketed her mouth. She must be in her sixties. Could she have carried Casolaba's body up to the spire? And considering that Gavriel himself was attacked with lithomancy, the culprit was likelier to be a witch.

The witches had a non-voting delegation that observed the Assembly proceedings. Any one of them might have lured Casolaba inside after the building closed.

"Can someone verify your whereabouts?" Gavriel asked.

"My children are grown, and I kicked my worthless husband out years ago." She shrugged. "Ask my neighbors if you want. I was home by eight. I'm not as young as I used to be. I need my rest."

Gavriel let her go. Primo Roloa entered next, bringing with him the scent of tobacco. The acting consul, formerly Casolaba's deputy, fidgeted in his seat, fingers twitching for the cigarette he'd just extinguished.

"This is a terrible business," he said. "A terrible business. The Freedom League pledges full cooperation. Whatever you need."

"I appreciate that." Gavriel folded his hands on the desk. "Your relationship with Consul Casolaba, was it cordial?"

"Entirely." His fingers drummed the armrest. "We had our disagreements, naturally. That's politics. But we maintained a united front for the party."

"And the night of his death?"

"I was at a fundraising dinner until well past midnight. Hundreds of people saw me there. I made a speech." He loosened his collar. "A political function we hold annually. Important for maintaining relationships with the biggest donors."

Gavriel nodded to Yarl, who made a note to verify this claim.

"Did Casolaba have enemies who would wish him harm?" Gavriel asked, curious only as to whom Roloa would choose to name.

A nervous laugh. "The consul's position makes enemies by its nature. But murder?" Roloa shook his head. "Unthinkable."

"I would ask you to be more specific."

Roloa blew out a long, wheezing breath. "The Miners' Union, obviously. Bunch of thugs. Everyone knows it."

"Did he have any late meetings planned the night he was killed?"

"None that I'm aware of."

"Would you be willing to surrender your weekly diary?" Gavriel asked.

Roloa opened his valise and took out a small book. "I expected you'd ask that. Here it is, Lord Morningstar."

Gavriel flipped through the pages and saw nothing of interest. But of course, Roloa would hardly write anything incriminating in a diary.

"Thank you for your time," he said. "We'll be in touch."

Roloa flashed a relieved smile. "I have every confidence you'll catch this rogue, Lord Morningstar. The people of Kota Gelangi deserve no less."

THE AMBASSADOR from Kievad Rus was the last interview of the morning. An uncommonly tall man named Tamarkin Volkov, he was graying at the temples, with cropped hair and prominent ears.

"This is ludicrous," he declared before Gavriel asked a single question. "To insinuate that Kievad Rus had any involvement in this heinous crime is slander of the highest order."

"I fear we've begun on the wrong foot, ambassador," Gavriel replied. "This is an interview, not an inquisition. I must speak to everyone who knew the man, surely you grasp that."

Volkov sniffed, but deigned to sit down. "We have nothing to gain from Casolaba's death."

"There are several mining disputes currently in arbitration between your province and Satu Jos."

He waved a dismissive hand. "Those are legal matters, as you must well know, Lord Morningstar. The Assembly had nothing to do with them. And to be perfectly candid, we preferred Casolaba to his deputy. Barsal could be reasoned with."

"Bribed, you mean."

The ambassador sighed deeply. "If you're looking for suspects, I suggest you start with the witches. Who else could hang a man from the spire?"

*And burn his eyes out*, Gavriel thought.

"I am examining every angle," he said. "Now, perhaps you can tell me where you were the night of the murder?"

---

WHEN THE FIRST batch of interviews were concluded, Gavriel rose and stretched his uninjured wing. "I fear we are no closer to the truth than when we began, Yarl," he said. "Let us verify the witnesses' alibis. You and Bottas can do that."

A pair of workmen arrived to hang the drapes. Gavriel reluctantly abandoned the desk to make room for them.

"Have you visited the scene of death?"

He turned. Cypher Rowan was looking at him expectantly.

"Both the witches and the Assembly guards examined every inch of the dome," Gavriel said. "They found nothing besides the body."

"I just wonder why he was displayed so publicly." She bit her full lower lip, frowning. "They could have slit his throat and dumped him in an alley, but they wanted the whole city to see their handiwork."

Gavriel lifted his gaze from her mouth, distracted. "Your point?"

"It just seems as if someone was sending a message. I could

escort you up to the roof." She hesitated. "Unless you have something more important to do."

His first instinct was to refuse. Rowan's advice was unsolicited and doubtless a waste of time. But his current approach had yielded little progress, and the workmen were now hammering.

"Very well," he said reluctantly.

She approached Levi Bottas, who hovered at the door. "How do we access the dome?" she asked.

"There's a stairwell at the end of the corridor." He eyed Gavriel's bandaged wing. "But it's quite narrow."

"I'll manage," Gavriel said.

Bottas found an elderly guard, who led them to a nondescript door. He unlocked it and stepped back. "It's a long climb," he warned.

"How many people have a set of keys to that door?" Gavriel asked.

"All the senior watchmen," he said, a bit defensively. "At least a dozen of us. And I don't think the locks have been changed in . . . oh, ages. These stairs predate the current building. When they rebuilt after the Great Fire, they incorporated the old tower. It was the only part still standing."

The stairwell was indeed narrow, forcing Gavriel to angle himself to the side. His broken wing throbbed in protest as it brushed the wall, but he refused to admit weakness in front of Rowan. She seemed to think he was some desk-bound bureaucrat.

He expected her to tire, but she climbed the tight spiral steps without pausing for breath. Light filtered through embrasures, illuminating dust motes that swirled in her wake. At last, it opened onto a landing. Far below, through an ornate iron lattice, he could see the main floor of the Assembly Hall. Above stretched the vaulted ceiling of the dome.

"Is this where they found him?" Rowan asked.

"No. He was suspended from the spire itself." Gavriel

pointed to an exterior door. "The killer must have gone through that way. It would have to be someone strong enough to carry the body up all those stairs."

She tilted her head, considering. "Or maybe they didn't take the stairs at all."

He gave her a dark look. "Are you implying an angel did this?"

"Have you ruled that out?" Her gaze had an uncanny directness.

"No seraphim would murder a human," he said dismissively. "Their loyalty to the ideals of the empire is absolute."

"Not all of them," she replied. "If that were true, I wouldn't exist."

Gavriel had no ready response. She was right, of course. Every cypher was living proof that an angel had strayed from his vows. The thought made him uncomfortable.

"Let us have a look," he said brusquely, "since we came all this way."

They stepped through the door to a railed walkway that circled the outside of the dome. An iron maintenance ladder curved up to the spire. The view was sweeping and they stood for a moment in silence, the wind whipping Rowan's fair hair about her face.

"Well, that's interesting," she said.

"What is?"

"You can see the chapter house of the witches quite clearly. And the Angel Tower, too. Maybe the killer wanted to send a message to all the great powers of this city."

Her observation was astute. The murder wasn't just an assassination, it was a warning. But to which power? And from whom?

"I think you're right," Gavriel admitted. "They went to a great deal of trouble getting him up here, not to mention the risk."

She looked pleased. "I've investigated a few murders, though not like this one. But unless it's a drunken brawl, the place the body is left usually has significance—to the killer, at least."

Rowan's smell enveloped him. It was tantalizing, an alchemy of sweet and bitter. The climb had brought a delicate blush of color to her cheeks, and she stood close enough to discern the varying shades of gray ringing her irises.

"Well, shall we go down?" she asked.

He nodded, aware that he'd been staring. "Yes. I've seen enough."

Each step of the descent jarred his broken wing, but his mind was elsewhere. Reluctantly, Gavriel admitted that visiting the scene had been worthwhile. The message of the murder was clearer now, even if its author remained a mystery.

---

HE SPENT the remainder of the day immersed in Casolaba's letters, searching for direct evidence of a motive. Yarl filed them into dossiers as he finished with them, occasionally making notes on matters that warranted further investigation. Gavriel found nothing overtly incriminating, but the pattern suggested a consul who played all sides against the middle.

The new blinds had been drawn tight and all the lamps were burning. Outside, the city buzzed with rumors, but inside there was only the rustle of paper and scratch of Yarl's pen. Gavriel rubbed his temples, feeling the beginnings of a headache.

"These banking records don't align with his official salary," he muttered.

"Consul Casolaba had many private consulting arrangements," Yarl remarked dryly.

Gavriel grunted. "I also see regular payments for a flat on Rua Alva. We must look into that—"

A sharp click drew his attention to the far corner of the office. "Now this is interesting," Mercy Blackthorn announced with triumph in her voice. A section of wood paneling had shifted.

"What is it?" Gavriel asked, rising from the desk.

"A secret door." She pushed it open, revealing darkness beyond. "Quite clever. The mechanism's built into the decorative molding."

"Where does it lead?" he asked, peering past her broad shoulder.

"Let's find out," Rowan said.

The two cyphers disappeared into the passage. They returned a few minutes later. "It's a stairway," Blackthorn reported, "leading down to a side entrance, completely concealed from view. Anyone could enter or exit the consul's office without passing through the main lobby."

This changed matters considerably. "So our killer could have entered this way on the night Casolaba died," Gavriel said.

"And from the office, it's just a short distance to the stairs leading up to the dome," Rowan pointed out.

He turned to Yarl. "Summon Levi Bottas."

When the aide arrived, he professed shock at the hidden door. "I—I had no idea," he stammered. "I swear it, sir!"

"You were his chief aide," Gavriel pointed out. "You must have spent a good deal of time in this office."

"Well, yes, but he was a very private man." The words tumbled out in a rush. "There were meetings I wasn't permitted to attend. He didn't confide in me. I just took notes and ran errands. But Acting Consul Roloa was Casolaba's deputy for many years before I arrived. He must know about it!" He raked a hand through his dark hair, causing it to stand on end.

"Calm yourself, Bottas. I am not accusing you. Why don't you bring us all some kopi?"

The flustered aide departed.

"He's lying," Rowan said. "The whole lot of them are."

Gavriel arched a brow.

"I could beat the truth out of him," she offered. "It wouldn't take long."

Blackthorn winced. Gavriel wondered if it was a poor jest, but Rowan looked entirely earnest. "The investigation would go a lot quicker that way," she added.

Gavriel turned to Yarl, who gave an amused shrug. "That is not how justice is administered in Sion," he said severely, aware that his reputation would be tarnished by even a whisper of what she had just said. "I fear you are ill-suited to this posting. Perhaps I should request someone else."

Her face froze. Then, a flurry of emotions. Embarrassment followed by regret and a flash of naked fear. "I apologize, Lord Morningstar," she said in a humble tone. "I spoke out of turn."

The abrupt shift intrigued him. There was very little artifice to Rowan; she seemed to voice whatever she thought.

"Very well. See that it doesn't happen again," he said.

Yarl cleared his throat. "It's growing late, sir. You should get some rest."

Gavriel eyed the papers yet to be sifted through. He was tempted to remain, but his broken wing was aching and he'd had little sleep in days now.

"The streets aren't safe after dark," Blackthorn said. "Too many vantage points for a hidden assailant."

"I'll arrange for a coach," Yarl said, moving toward the door.

It arrived promptly, its matched foursome of tawny caracals padding silently in their harnesses. Gavriel settled into the cushioned interior, while the cyphers took positions on either side. Yarl sat opposite, his diary open on his knees as he made final notes from the day's investigation.

As the coach pulled away from the Red House, Gavriel studied Rowan from the edge of his eye. Her methods were barbaric, but there was something bracing about her directness. In a world of half-truths and strategic omissions, it was a rare quality.

*I will keep her as my bodyguard*, Gavriel decided. *At least for now.*

## CHAPTER 7
# CATHRYNNE

T he townhouse Lord Morningstar was renting looked even nicer than a luxury hotel. He kept making remarks about how tasteless the décor was, but if he had to spend a week in the cypher barracks, he might not be so picky.

As promised, their luggage had been left in the foyer. Brass lanterns hung from chains, and two curved staircases swept upward to the second floor.

"You'll need to wait here while we check the house," Cathrynne said.

Morningstar sighed. "Is that necessary?"

"Someone tried to kill you last night," she reminded him. "So yes, it is."

He waited with Yarl while she and Mercy conducted a thorough search. The first floor had a cavernous kitchen with acres of gleaming stone countertops, a formal dining room, a paneled library that also served as a study, two closet-like rooms for the maids, and a glass-walled conservatory overlooking the rear gardens.

The next two floors held a total of seven bedrooms, each furnished in the style of a different province. Cathrynne liked the Iskatar Room best. There were real palm trees in pots on the terrace and a wraparound mural depicting the month-long games staged by that fiercely competitive province, where the pursuit of glory was life's highest calling.

The artist had done an incredible job. Cathrynne could have spent an hour studying the details, but the scene that caught her eye showed the archangel Raziel watching footraces from a red pavilion. He had deep brown skin and wore a white dashiki with a square, gold-embroidered neckline. Raziel's neck and wrists were slender and elegant, the slight curve of his full lips intriguing. Was that a smile?

Cathrynne wondered if Morningstar had ever smiled in his life, which in turn made her wonder how old he was. He didn't look more than thirty-five, but that meant nothing. Archangels aged at the pace of granite eroding beneath wind and rain.

She knelt to peer under the huge four-poster bed. No waiting assassins. Not even a speck of dust. But the guidebook on the side table looked interesting. Cathrynne leafed through it. Iskatar's capital, Lagash, was apparently famous for cheese and salt.

"I'm claiming this one," she said, checking the walk-in closet and pink marble bath.

"All yours," Mercy replied from across the hall. "I want Mount Meru if Morningstar hasn't taken it."

It was Mercy's dream to climb the Sundar Kush range. She was a decent mountaineer, but she said the Kush were the ultimate test. Dozens died there every year—just in the foothills.

The only other bedchamber that showed signs of habitation was the Kirith Room, which had obviously been claimed by Edvin Yarl since it smelled of his citrus hair pomade.

"I don't think Morningstar has taken a bedchamber," Cathrynne said when they'd finished searching the third floor. "Maybe he doesn't sleep at all." It wouldn't surprise her.

"Right. That leaves the roof," Mercy said.

They found the spiral stair leading up one flight and stepped out to a flat terrace with stone planters and a bench. A waist-high brick wall enclosed the roof. At the far side, purple and white wildflowers burst from a crack in the slate tiles. They bloomed in thick profusion—but only in that one place.

"I bet that's where he bled," Mercy whispered. "Angel blood has so much ley, odd things happen when it's spilled."

Cathrynne walked to the edge, careful not to step on the flowers, and leaned over the wall. It was a long drop down to the street below. Enough to kill a human and probably a witch. Even for Morningstar, it must have been agony.

"Here's a question," she said. "Why didn't they finish him off? There he is, lying broken in the street, no one about. You'd never get a better chance."

"Keep your voice down," Mercy hissed. "He might hear you."

She glanced at the stairwell. "All the way up here?"

"Yes! Angels have very acute senses." Her face said, *And you can't afford to offend him again.*

"Right." Cathrynne mouthed an apology. "All clear!" she announced loudly.

Mercy sidled closer. "I agree," she whispered. "Maybe the attacker was interrupted."

"Maybe." Cathrynne still thought it strange that someone ruthless enough to hoist Casolaba onto a spire and leave him there for the crows would balk at cutting Morningstar's throat, or whatever it took to kill an archangel.

They flipped a coin to decide the watch. Cathrynne lost, taking first shift. By the time they went downstairs, Morningstar had disregarded their order to stay put and sequestered himself in the library. Yarl told them to take any of the bedrooms they liked. He bid them good night and retired, followed soon after by Mercy.

Cathrynne hadn't eaten since breakfast. She rummaged through the kitchen, which was stocked with copper pans of every size and ingredients that all required cooking. After twenty years of mess hall chow and street food, recipes remained a mystery. Finally, she discovered a bag of chips in the pantry. She padded down the hall and knocked on the library door.

"Enter," came Morningstar's clipped voice.

He sat at another desk—apparently, his favorite place in the world—reading through stacks of documents under a pool of lamplight. "What is it, Rowan?"

"I can't leave you alone," she said.

"I'll be fine," he replied testily.

She glanced at the windows facing the street. "Anyone might come through those. We can't take the risk."

After a long pause, he sighed in defeat and gestured to an armchair. She sat down and tore open the paper bag. He looked up with a pained expression as she popped a chip into her mouth. Cathrynne wished she had eaten them in the kitchen first, but it was too late now.

"I won't get crumbs on the carpet," she mumbled, "if that's what you're worried about."

His gaze flicked to her feet. "You already have, but I will not begrudge you sustenance."

She smiled. "That's kind of you."

He examined her suspiciously, then returned to his papers.

Cathrynne ate the chips as quietly as possible. He did not look up again, though a muscle ticked in his jaw. When she crumpled the bag, it sounded like a building collapsing. She tossed it at the wastebasket next to the desk, missed, and was forced to go over and retrieve it.

"I hope you enjoyed your meal," Morningstar muttered venomously.

"I did, thank you."

He gave a curt nod. She returned to her chair and settled back to watch him work. Were all archangels so self-important? It seemed like a lonely existence, though he probably liked it that way.

After a while, he looked up again. "I plan to be here all night. It will be quite tedious to have you sitting there watching me the whole time." He glanced at the floor-to-ceiling shelves. "Perhaps you'd care to read a book?"

"I don't read books."

"That doesn't surprise me," he murmured, returning to his document.

"Why not?" She had no idea what he thought of her and was genuinely curious.

He set down his pen. "I only mean that you seem like more of a . . .physical type."

She thought of Mercy. "You mean nature hiking?"

He shrugged a wing, exasperated.

"Oh, I don't climb mountains," she said. "I just break legs."

He seemed unsure if she was joking. When he buried his nose in the papers again, Cathrynne allowed herself a tiny smile.

---

MERCY RELIEVED her at three a.m. Both women were cranky and tired when dawn broke and Yarl informed them that they were heading back to the Red House. The three-hour time difference with Arioch made it feel like the middle of the night. Naturally, Morningstar looked as fresh as if he'd slept on the clouds wreathing Mount Meru.

As before, he sat at the dead man's desk—the Magistrate's Throne, Cathrynne thought of it—while Yarl recorded witness testimonies in a big book. A parade of delegates and staffers shuffled in throughout the morning. None admitted to knowing anything about Casolaba's death. None seemed grieved by it.

"Did you notice any unusual visitors in the days before the murder?" Morningstar asked a round-faced clerk with who worked in an office a few doors down.

"No, my lord." The clerk's eyes darted to the smirking portrait of Casolaba and then to the window, as if seeking escape.

Lying, like the rest of them.

"And what was your personal opinion of the consul?" Morningstar pressed with an almost evil glint in his eye.

"He was always friendly. An effective leader," the clerk replied primly.

Lies, lies, and more lies.

Cathrynne's knees were stiff from standing. Her eyelids drooped from boredom. Just as she considered how much trouble she'd be in if she dozed off, the door burst open and Levi Bottas rushed in, his cheeks pink and hair poking out in all directions. "Sir, you must come down to the Assembly chamber."

Morningstar's jaw tightened at the interruption. "Why?"

"Just come!" Bottas beckoned urgently.

He rose with a flinty expression. Cathrynne trailed his billowing black robes down the stairs, Mercy and Yarl behind her. The Assembly occupied a large oval room with tiered seating above the main floor. A gallery circled the chamber where spectators could observe the proceedings. Bottas led them past a bunch of scribblers with pens and notepads who eyed Gavriel appraisingly.

On the floor below, Luzia Bras stood at the speaker's podium, hands gripping either side. She seemed to be enjoying herself. "I won't compare Primo Roloa to a whore," she declared, "since that would be an insult to the hard-working prostitutes of this city—"

Shouts erupted from the benches of the Freedom League.

Luzia raised her powerful voice above the din, "—who are more honest, sincere, and forthright than the acting consul, and certainly give better bang for your copper than he ever could!"

The scribblers in the gallery burst into laughter, as did the opposition benches. Primo Roloa merely shook his head, an indulgent, slightly contemptuous smile on his face.

"The Miners' Union demands a snap election to choose a new consul," Luzia continued, slamming a palm against the podium. "The people deserve better than a puppet whose strings are pulled by the mining conglomerates!"

More shouts, both in support and protest.

"And while I have the floor," Luzia's voice hardened, "I demand an investigation into the death of a boy from my district found floating in the river yesterday with a burn mark on his back from lithomancy!"

The chamber fell silent before exploding into chaos. A woman in silver robes—the non-voting witch representative—jumped to her feet. "That accusation is offensive and baseless," she cried. "There is no evidence whatsoever that a witch was involved!"

Delegates shouted at each other from every corner. Roloa banged a gavel, demanding order with little success. It was getting ugly. Cathrynne shared a look with Mercy. They were about to usher Morningstar from the chamber when Luzia Bras looked up at the gallery.

"Lord Morningstar!" she called. "Will you investigate this boy's death? Or do you only care about crimes against the powerful?"

He froze, then stepped forward, the center of attention. "I have no mandate to do so," he said stiffly, his voice carrying through the chamber. "My commission extends only to the death of Consul Barsal Casolaba."

The muttering grew angrier. "Justice! Justice!" someone shouted from the Miners' Union benches. Others took up the cry.

Cathrynne scanned the gallery, aware of how exposed they were. Too many entrances, too many people. "We must go," she murmured. "Now."

For once, he didn't argue. They left the gallery with shouts still ringing behind. Once they were in the corridor, Morningstar rounded on Levi Bottas. His face was a livid white. Cathrynne had never seen him so angry. "You set me up," he growled.

Bottas quailed. "I had no idea what she planned, I swear! Luzia Bras just told me to bring you. She said she had evidence related to the murder and intended to present it before the Assembly."

Morningstar briefly closed his eyes. Then he gave a mirthless laugh. "I've been outfoxed. And you, Bottas, were her cat's paw. Do you know anything about this dead boy?"

He hung his head. "It's the first I've heard of it."

Morningstar spun on his heel and strode from the building, pausing on the marble steps. The setting sun caught his dark wings, picking out flecks of green and blue like the plumage of a grackle.

"Shall I call the coach, sir?" Yarl ventured.

"I wish to fly," he growled, "but I cannot. At the least, we will walk. I need fresh air."

Cathrynne felt sorry for him. How terrible to have such a gift and yet be grounded. They returned to the nearby townhouse in silence. Once there, Gavriel retreated to the library, shutting the door behind him. Yarl announced that he would make them all supper.

Mercy dropped onto a couch upholstered in sea-foam satin. "By Minerva, what a mess. I'm not sure Bottas is as innocent as he pretends. First, he has no clue about the hidden passage leading to the consul's office. Then he lures Morningstar into the Assembly chamber for a public flogging and claims it was all Luzia Bras's idea."

"You think they're in cahoots?"

"They could be. Bras has something to gain from the death. Now she can call a snap election. She might even become the next consul." Mercy idly flicked the end of her whip. "But I can't see why Levi Bottas would help her."

"Sex, money, power," Cathrynne said. "Take your pick."

"Maybe it's all three," Mercy speculated. "Maybe Bottas likes older women. She said she kicked her husband out. She seduces him, then pays him to get rid of Casolaba and promises him a position in the new government. Levi Bottas was perfectly placed to get close to Casolaba. The consul would never have seen it coming."

"That makes sense," Cathrynne said, "except that his eyes were burned out and I can't see Bottas doing that for no conceivable reason. Plus, whoever attacked Morningstar used illusion. Neither Bottas nor Bras are witches. If they had a smidgen of witch blood, we'd see it in their eyes. A thin ring of silver or a grayish cast. Neither has it, I checked."

"Yeah. Too bad, it was a nice theory." Mercy glanced at the library door and lowered her voice. "Toss a coin for who has to go in there?"

---

THE DELICIOUS AROMA of frying chickpeas and garlic filled the townhouse. Cathrynne found Yarl in the kitchen, managing several saucepans one-handed. A linen cloth draped over one shoulder.

"The table is set in the dining room," he said, "but there's still time to freshen up before supper."

"Is that a polite way of saying I look dirty?" Cathrynne asked. She caught her reflection in a copper pot. Hair like a haystack, smudges under her eyes. "Never mind, don't answer that."

She went upstairs to change. When she returned, she was surprised to find both Mercy and Morningstar seated at the long dining table. He'd shed his magistrate's robe and wore a white shirt with the sleeves rolled up, revealing strong forearms.

"A proper meal seemed sensible after the day's trials," he said almost cheerfully, pouring wine for the table.

Cathrynne shot Mercy a look of amazement. Mercy replied with a modest shrug. A minute later, Yarl bustled in with a platter of rice with roasted vegetables and flat bread. Everyone murmured thanks and dug in.

"So," Mercy said, "how did you two meet?"

Morningstar glanced at Yarl. "Shall we tell the tale?"

Yarl set down his napkin. "It's hardly remarkable."

"I disagree." Morningstar swirled his wine. "I tried to hire Master Yarl decades ago when he was a graduate student at Faraday College. A professor friend recommended him. I had gone through several secretaries and was struggling to fill the position."

"Six in one year, if I recall," Yarl added.

The corner of Morningstar's mouth twitched. "Yarl had just returned his dissertation, demanding points be taken off for a grammatical error that the teaching assistant had missed. My friend said he might actually be more irritating than I am."

Cathrynne choked on her wine. Her eyes watered, but she managed to swallow. "Fine," she croaked. "Go on."

Morningstar was staring at her, which only made it worse. "However," he continued, "Yarl refused my offer."

"I had other interests," Yarl explained. "My area of research was Sinn physiology and behavior. I was passionate about pursuing field work."

Cathrynne went still. She glanced at Morningstar, but he had looked away.

"After graduation," Yarl continued in an animated tone, "I spent years traveling to every corner of the empire, studying the various species in their natural habitats. My first published article was on the dwarf mosswing of Kirith. Beautiful creatures with scales like autumn leaves."

"You've actually seen one?" asked Mercy, the avid hiker.

Yarl nodded. "In fact, I am proud to say that my research helped promote conservation efforts. They're protected by law in Kirith now."

"As they should be," Mercy replied firmly. "Damned poachers nearly drove them to extinction, selling the claws and teeth for quack potions."

"Indeed," Yarl said gravely. "It was a terrible crime." He brightened. "I also studied the ringed skimmer found in marshlands. It mostly eats frogs. The spiny thresher and mottled shellback are both deepwater species. Those I only saw from afar. It wasn't easy to convince a vessel to get close." He leaned forward. "The great northerns of Sundland are the second-biggest. They delve through ice and snow and build tunnels that go for miles."

"Which are the biggest?" Mercy asked.

"The blue emperors, of course," Morningstar put in. "Glorious beasts with scales of molten silver and tongues like sapphires. They're the ones that burned Kota Gelangi to the ground."

The boyish enthusiasm in Yarl's eyes dimmed. "I was one of the few to document their migration patterns. But then I got a bit too close. My own fault. I was young and terribly brave, and I'd gotten lucky for long enough that I was convinced of my own invulnerability." He touched his pinned sleeve. "It cost me my left arm from the elbow down."

"Wow," Mercy said. "I'm sorry about that."

"Thank you, but I consider myself fortunate," Yarl replied. "Others who have met great northerns never lived to tell of it." He paused to swallow a gulp of wine. "After the accident, I could have taught at Faraday, or any other university of my choice. But I wanted a fresh start. So I wrote to Lord Morningstar, who hired me at once."

"I was still in need of a secretary," Gavriel said dryly. "And my professor friend was right. We were perfectly suited for each other."

Yarl winked. "That professor changed careers herself. She is now the consul of Kirith."

"Cyranthe Dagan?" Mercy exclaimed.

"The very same."

She grinned. "Now, that *is* a good story!"

"I still keep up with the literature," Yarl said wistfully. "Much has been discovered in the last forty years, although we still know little about how they communicate or why they are so hostile. I had proposed that their aggression was a response to *ours*, but that provoked a firestorm of criticism." He grinned. "No pun intended."

Mercy began bombarding Yarl with questions. Did the aquatic Sinn breathe flames, and if so, could they do it underwater? Were the desert varieties truly growing immune to magic? Could a blue emperor derail a train if it wanted to?

Yarl answered each query with exhaustive detail. Morningstar added anecdotes of his own, having encountered various Sinn species during flights across the empire.

"Cathrynne? You look pale."

Mercy's voice broke through her reverie. She forced a smile. "Thank you, Yarl, for a delicious meal. I'm just tired. Still adjusting to the time difference, I guess. Leave some dishes in the sink, I'll do them in the morning." She turned to Mercy. "Can I have second watch?"

"Sure," Mercy said gently.

Gavriel's eyes met hers. Something in his level gaze suggested he understood her reticence.

"I regret that either of you must lose sleep over me," he said. "So don't worry about the dishes, I shall wash them myself." He pushed his sleeves above his elbows and began collecting plates.

Cathrynne relaxed a bit at the sight of a haughty archangel bussing the dinner table. Then she nodded to them all and went upstairs. Once in her bedchamber, Cathrynne unwrapped the bandage around her left hand. Three of her fingers were still eggplant purple, but the swelling and pain were minimal. Her angel blood made her heal twice as fast as a witch—which was still faster than a human.

Cathrynne took a long, hot bath. Then she rewrapped her hand and lay down on the canopy bed, enjoying the ambience of the Iskatar Room. She fancied that it smelled of warm cardamom and fragrant smoke from water pipes. If she concentrated hard enough, she could hear the roar of the crowd as the winners knelt to receive laurel wreaths.

At least the artist hadn't painted any blue emperors or great northerns darkening the skies. No reminders of the monsters her womb would produce if she ever . . . Well, it didn't bear dwelling on. She and Mercy were different that way. Cathrynne did not like to think about the Sinn, nor to talk about them.

The quiet murmur of conversation downstairs made her drowsy. It reminded her of the dinner parties her mother used to throw with lots of fabulous people, witch and human. Another thing Cathrynne rarely thought about anymore.

After a while, she drifted into disturbing dreams.

A boy floated in water, a wine-colored birthmark branding his pale, bloated cheek. His eyes opened and the river around him darkened with blood.

The scene shifted to a windy hilltop. A witch with a scarred hand held up a card. It bore an image of The Scythe, one of the thirty-six symbols she saw in her foretellings. A harbinger of violent change. A reaping.

"He comes," the Morag said, her voice harsh and guttural. "God-killer. Dark-bringer."

She stood in front of a kloster. Cathrynne saw dirty faces pressed to the windows. They were staring at her, lips moving, though she could not hear their voices.

Isbail Rosach laughed grimly. "It is the end of an age. The Summerlord will fall. And you, Cathrynne Rowan, are the Witch of Winter." The Morag reached out, seizing Cathrynne's jaw in a bruising grip. "He comes!"

She woke with silk sheets tangled around her legs and the taste of river water in her throat. Trembling, Cathrynne whispered a prayer to Minerva. Then she switched on all the lamps and waited for Mercy to fetch her for second watch. What the dreams meant, she didn't know. Only that sleep would not return this night.

# CHAPTER 8

# KAL

S

he kept her head down as she hurried along Rua Capitolana, the collar of her peacoat flipped up to hide the ship tattoo on her neck—an impulsive decision from happier days that only made her stand out.

Blustery morning rain had left the gutters choked with wilted paper idols. No one touched them, not even the street rats who scrounged coins cleaning the sidewalks in front of shops. Everyone knew it was bad luck.

Kal could write a damned *book* on bad luck. How she wished they had never gone into that abandoned mine. Durian would be with her right now, arguing about whose turn it was to brew a pot of kopi over the campfire. They'd watch the sun rise and then they'd go searching the canyons for Sinn artifacts. Collectors paid big money for a scale or claw.

Instead, she was stuck in Kota Gelangi and witches were hunting them both.

Seven days had passed since Durian went into the river. A week of repeating the same desperate mantra: *He's alive. He knows how to swim. We'll find each other.*

Kal's gut tensed as the crowds parted for a tall witch walking his caracal. The massive cat padded beside its master, its green eyes sweeping the street. He wasn't one of the pair they'd tangled with, but maybe they were all looking for her now.

*Travian's bones!*

Kal almost panicked but forced herself to keep walking. If she crossed the avenue, she'd just draw attention to herself.

*Act casual. Don't make eye contact.*

She turned to a shop window, catching a glimpse of her bouncy halo of dark brown curls and long, rangy stride. The caracal's ear tufts twitched as she passed, but the witch didn't pay much attention to her. She released the breath she'd been holding only after rounding the next corner.

Ten more minutes and she reached Liberty Square, with the Red House on one side and ornate office buildings on the other. They had rooftop billboards advertising the city's gossip rags. *Kota Confidential, The Provincial Gazette, Rumor Has It,* and *The Daily Mumble.*

Kal slipped into a park next to the square, which offered the best view while providing cover. It was her and Durian's meeting place. If they were ever separated, they'd come to the monument dedicated to the Trinity, wait until sunset, and repeat daily until they found each other.

The bronze statue sat atop a slab of black marble in the center of the square. Valoriel stood on the left, broad wings unfurled, gazing outward with stern authority. Durian referred to him as the "tasty beefcake" of the Trinity, which was true but almost certainly some kind of heresy.

Beside the father of the angels, the witch goddess Minerva held a pick in one hand and a handful of gems in the other. And on the right, Travian, sire of the humans.

Unlike the other gods, whose forms were unchanging, Travian was sometimes depicted as male, sometimes as female. This particular statue was long-haired and androgynous. Travian strummed a lute, face caught in a moment of sardonic amusement, as if they alone understood some cosmic joke.

Durian had been raised in the Cult of the Bard, a loosely

organized offshoot that claimed Travian had never left Sion and was still around, walking among his children in disguise. Durian was an avid believer, unlike Kal, who cared less about absentee gods and more about getting out of Pota Pras. But every day, she had prayed to Travian to keep an eye on her best friend. To help them find each other.

She sat down against a tree whose leaves were turning to autumn gold. There were hardly any trees in Pota Pras so she couldn't say what kind it was. That's the sort of thing Durian would know. His mother had moved around a lot when he was young, and he loved to tease Kal for being a provincial rustic, while he was a sophisticated man of the world.

From her vantage point, she could see anyone approaching the monument from three directions. If witches came, she'd know they had caught him and she'd run before they saw her. But she still hoped Durian would show up eventually. He was smart. He knew how to hide. His limp might slow him down, but he'd make it.

She hadn't slept properly since their escape, managing fitful dozes under the bridge, one ear alert for footsteps. Her stomach cramped with hunger. The last of her coin had purchased a heel of bread two days ago. But she refused to leave Kota Gelangi without him.

A juggler set up near the monument, tossing bright red balls in a widening circle. A crowd gathered, children shouting with glee as he added a sixth to the rotation. Kal scanned their faces, searching for Durian's sandy hair and birthmark, but he wasn't among them.

Hours passed. The sky deepened to cobalt. The juggler counted his coins and departed. She watched the last of the daylight fade and the street lamps wink on, all at the same time.

Disappointment crashed down. Durian wasn't coming. But tomorrow, she promised herself, tomorrow he'll turn up. She could hear his voice in her head as he told some crazy story. Bitch, you'll never *believe* what happened to me . . .

She retraced her steps to Rua Capitolana, merging with the evening crowds. She didn't see any witches. But as Kal paused at a corner, waiting for a gap in the traffic, she overheard two men in silk hats and billowing qandrissi pants talking.

"Casolaba had it coming. Too many fat fingers in too many pies."

"Maybe so, but do you want the Miners' Union in charge? They're threatening to strike again and that's never good for business."

"The Freedom League is positioning Primo Roloa to take his place." A snort. "Assuming he isn't the one who had Casolaba eliminated."

Kal didn't follow politics, but even she knew that Barsal Casolaba was the consul of Satu Jos. She stepped over to a brightly-lit kiosk at the next corner and scanned the headlines.

*MORNINGSTAR GROUNDED! Will shocking attack on magistrate stall murder probe? High-ranking sources express doubts . . .*

Kal picked up the paper and read the first few paragraphs. The consul had been found hanging from the spire of the Red House. An archangel had come from Kirith to investigate, and someone had hurled him from a building and broken his wing. There were no arrests yet in either crime.

As she turned the page to keep reading, a smaller article caught her eye: LUZ CRIES FOUL ON DROWNING! *The head of the Miners' Union is demanding answers in the tragic death of a young rockhound pulled from the Bessemer River five days ago . . .*

The newsprint blurred. Blood thundered in her ears. A mistake. It had to be someone else.

Her frantic gaze skimmed the newsprint. The authorities wouldn't release his name until the family had been notified, but he was said to be from Pota Pras—

"You buying that?" asked the boy running the kiosk.

Kal shook her head. She replaced the broadsheet with fingers that felt detached from her body. The world around her continued its noisy, oblivious orbit. Hers had just stopped spinning.

A heavy, dense pain crouched on her chest like someone had buried a pick there. She made herself turn and walk away.

Kal paid no attention to where she was going. Random memories cropped up. Durian at thirteen, new to the neighborhood, sheepishly knocking on her door the first time his mother locked him out. At sixteen, drawing elaborate maps of the places they'd travel to someday. At twenty-two, his green eyes wide with wonder as he examined the mysterious stones.

Eventually, Kal looked up to find herself back at the bridge spanning the narrowest stretch of the river. For the last week, she'd slept in a nook where the foot met the embankment. Once she was safely in her hideaway, she dropped to her knees and dug the kaldurite from her coat pocket. She loosened the drawstring and took out one of the stones. It glowed evilly in the semi-dark, shifting from blue to red to violet. Cold, so cold it burned.

Kal stared at the black water rushing beneath the bridge, remembering another river, this one deep underground, its calm surface reflecting the beams of their electric torches.

---

SHE'D NEVER LIKED the abandoned Clear Creek Mine. Twelve men had died there in a tram accident and she felt sure it was haunted. The entrance gaped like an open wound in the hillside, timber supports rotting at the edges, warning signs bleached by the sun.

But when Durian had rousted her from her bed at dawn, alight with the fever of discovery, she'd agreed to check it out. Now, standing at the mouth of the tunnel, she wondered if desperation had driven them both mad.

"We agreed never to go past the first collapse," she reminded him. "It's too unstable. And you promised—you *swore* on

Travian's name—that you'd never go exploring underground alone."

Durian turned to her, the sandy flop of hair not quite concealing the port wine birthmark that covered one sharp cheekbone. His smile was unrepentant. "You're missing the big picture."

"The big picture is our corpses mummifying down there if we get trapped."

"Bitch, you sound like my mother." He rifled through his pocket. "Have a look."

Kal held the rock up to the morning sun. A rough garnet, about the size of her palm, with several reddish seams. Worth a decent amount, but not a trip into the city. Not for one. "Where'd you find it?"

"Just a little way in. I'm sure there's more." He waggled an eyebrow. "Maybe a lot more."

Kal handed it back. "You risked your scrawny ass for this?" But even as she scolded him, she felt the familiar pull of possibility. You never knew when the big strike might come. They hadn't found anything worth selling in weeks. She sighed. "Define *a little way in*."

"I found a new passage where the main shaft collapsed." His eyes were pleading now. "Come on, we're already here. I need you, Kal. We stick together, right? This could be it."

They stared at each other, the unspoken truth hanging between them: they were running out of time. The mines took a piece of you. A little bite, every time you went down, until they'd eaten you whole. Kal knew thirty-year-olds who looked fifty. Bent and battered, with dirty creases that never went away. Even the ones with brown skin like her looked somehow pale underneath, spending most of their lives in the dark.

And they all had the cough. Every time you slammed that pick into the wall, it kicked up fine particles of dust. They filled your eyes and nose. In time, they'd turn your lungs to stone, too.

She did not want to end up that way.

"Fine," she said. "But if anything looks shifty, we get out."

Durian's whoop echoed off the buttes. Kal shook her head and pulled a torch from her pack. "Lead the way, dumbass," she said.

The first mile was easy enough, following a main shaft they'd explored many times before. Old tram tracks ran down the middle, steel rails pitted with rust. When they hit the cave-in that always marked their end point, Durian pointed out a new tunnel.

"Check it out," he said. "Someone's been busy."

Kal examined the opening. The rock looked melted, not hacked. When the Sinn delved new tunnels, it sometimes unearthed new seams. A lucky few had made fortunes in the defunct mines.

Durian lit a match and held it to the gap. The flame wavered.

"There's air coming through," he said. "Might even be another route back to the surface."

Kal considered the tunnel. It meant Sinn activity, but that was a risk they took every time they hiked into the Zamir Hills.

"How far to the garnet field?" she asked.

"An hour, tops," Durian replied with his trademark cocky grin.

The passage was wide and smooth-bored. Every hundred cubits, they stopped and turned off their torches to listen for telltale sounds that meant they weren't alone. There is no darkness like the darkness underground. It has *weight* to it. Kal heard nothing but silence, so they kept going, the circles of light casting long, misshapen shadows along the walls. Her grandfather, a lifelong rockhound before the lung rot killed him, always said the dead kept watch in the deep places.

Then she heard trickling water ahead. Another wider tunnel bisected the first. They forded a shallow river and came to a section where the ceiling had partially given way. Navigating the dark shaft beyond would require dropping to hands and knees.

"This is where I turned back," Durian said, pointing to a spot on the rugged ground. "I found the garnet over there. Figured it got knocked loose. But you can feel the draft. I think there's a bigger cavern beyond this. Anything could be in there!"

"That's the problem," Kal said, staring at the dark hole. "Anything could be in there."

Durian flipped the hair from his face. "No risk, no reward."

The crawl through the final passage was the worst. So tight in places that Kal feared they'd become wedged forever in the earth's grip. But Durian's hope was infectious, pulling her forward.

About thirty cubits in, the strap of his pack caught on a sharp protrusion. He wiggled and cursed until she ordered him to hold still. She managed to squeeze up past his legs and work it free. Then they were through, scrambling into a chamber that made Kal's breath freeze.

"Travian wept," she whispered.

The cavern was unremarkable save for what littered its floor. Hundreds of stones, scattered across the ground like seeds cast by a farmer. In the torchlight, they gleamed with vivid color: blue, scarlet, and violet. The weird part is that they weren't even rough. All the stones looked cut and polished. Just lying there for the taking like some lazy afternoon daydream.

"Serpent's eye!" Kal cried, scooping up a teardrop-shaped stone. She squinted into its luminous depths. Serpent's eye was worth a fortune. A cache this size would be enough to buy a merchant cutter three times over.

Durian danced a lopsided jig. One leg was shorter than the other, twisted after a childhood fever, and he always joked that he'd fit in perfectly with sailors and their rolling gait. "Told you!" he crowed.

Kal took a closer look. "Hold up, I might be wrong. The colors aren't banded. The facets shift in the light."

Durian examined another stone, muttering to himself as it morphed from blue to violet to red in his palm.

"Plus, it's cold," Kal added. "I've heard serpent's eye is warm to the touch."

They stared at each other. Kal's mind raced. New gems were rare, especially ones this unusual. It might be worth as much as serpent's eye—or even more.

"We need a name for it," she said, gathering more stones from the ground and filling her pouch. "Something that sounds *expensive*."

Durian grinned. "What about kaldurite? Kal and Durian."

"Kaldurite," she repeated, testing the word. "Well, it's better than durkalite."

She laughed, the sound bouncing around the chamber. In that moment, all the years spent in darkness scrabbling and digging and hacking were worth it. This was the strike they'd prayed for—enough to put the Zamir Hills behind them forever. Kal imagined standing on the deck of their own vessel, running ahead of a fresh salt wind. The start of something vast and blue and limitless.

Durian lifted her up and spun her around until they both fell to the ground, dizzy and cackling hysterically.

"Bitch," he shouted, "we're rich!"

---

THE RIVERBOAT SHUDDERED against the current. Kal sat at the stern with Durian, two fat purses of kaldurite stones in their laps. Each time they opened the drawstrings to peek inside, the gems caught the sunlight, shifting from blue to scarlet to violet.

They'd left most of the find intact, taking two samples to sell in Kota. It wasn't by choice. All their stupid laughing and yelling had drawn attention. When they'd felt the tremors of an approaching Sinn, the two of them had hightailed it out as fast as they could crawl.

But Kal felt confident no one else would come along and poach their fortune. The Clear Creek Mine was in a remote area far from any train depot. In their years of exploring it, she'd never encountered another rockhound.

"Once we sell this batch, we'll go back for the rest," Durian said. "And next time we'll play it cool. In and out like little mice, girl."

"Stop touching them," she whispered, swatting his hand away. "You'll wear the shine off."

He laughed, that ridiculous bray that had earned him the nickname "donkey" from the other kids. "That's not how these beauties work." He leaned back, stretching his bad leg out before him. "I'll buy the first round when we celebrate tonight."

"Yeah, well, you owe me," Kal said, but she was smiling. His optimism had always been infectious, a balm for her more practical nature.

The boat docked hours later at the bustling quay of Kota Gelangi. They got off with the crowd, Durian's limp pronounced after sitting so long. The gem brokers' district lay fifteen blocks inland, a maze of narrow streets with shops watched by hired muscle. Most of the brokers were weirdlings—humans with just enough witch blood to sense the ley.

As always, they headed for Doña Lisi first. She gave fair prices, never trying to undercut them as most brokers did with young rockhounds. Her tiny shop smelled of sandalwood, the walls lined with locked display cases.

"It's my favorite speculators from Pota Pras!" She greeted them with a smile, adjusting her magnifying eyepiece.

Durian produced his mining license, a clay disc stamped with a nine-digit number. Kal hovered behind him. They'd chipped in together to buy one since they didn't come cheap, and you had to have a license to sell gems to a broker.

Doña Lisi copied the number into a ledger. "So what have you brought me today?"

"We found something special," Durian said, unable to keep the excitement from his voice. He placed three of the kaldurite stones on the velvet pad she kept for examinations.

The old woman's eyebrows rose slightly as she picked up the first stone. "Brilliant color," she murmured. She held it to the light, then placed it on her scale. "Good weight."

"It's not serpent's eye, is it?" Durian blurted. "I mean, we think it might be a new gem."

"We shall see," she replied, reaching for her testing tools. Traders used various instruments to assess gems, but the most important was a simple ruby—one hot with ley power—that would resonate with any other hot stone. Doña Lisi used a set of calipers to hold the ruby over the first kaldurite stone, then the second, then the third.

She eyed them regretfully. "I'm sorry. There's no resonance. None at all. These stones are empty."

Durian shook his head. "No, no. That's not possible. They came direct from the earth."

All raw gems held ley. It was only depleted by lithomancy.

"Then they were in a dead zone." Domina Lisi shook her head. "It happens sometimes. Areas where the ley runs thin, or stones that formed improperly. They're pretty, yes, but without resonance . . ." She gave them a pitying look.

"How much?" Kal interrupted, her voice flat.

"For cold gems? I can offer you six draghas apiece. Enough to make decorative pieces. But they're of no use to the witches, and you both know that's where the real money is."

Durian's face crumpled. They'd hoped for a hundred per stone. Maybe two hundred. He handed over the raw chunk of garnet. "What about this?"

Doña Lisi tested it. "Now this one is hot. I can take it off your hands for, oh . . . fifteen dragha?"

"But we found it in the same place," Durian protested. "So it wasn't a dead zone." He eyed her with suspicion.

Kal reached for the gems. "We'll try elsewhere," she said, stiffly.

Doña Lisi shrugged. "Suit yourself." She closed the ledger and returned to polishing a chunk of agate.

They walked from broker to broker. Each yielded the same result: the stones were striking but held no ley. By mid-afternoon, they stood on a street corner, hungry and dejected.

"We need enough for a hostel," Kal said. "Let's try the jewelers."

They'd never dealt with jewelers, who only bought cold stones. In the end, they chose one at random called D'Amato's. The proprietor was middle-aged and paunchy, with thinning dark hair. It was combed over his bald spot with scented pomade. Kal thought he had soulful eyes, like a friendly dog.

"These are unusual," he said grudgingly, examining the kaldurite. "I haven't seen this color shift before. No ley, of course, but the aesthetic quality isn't bad."

"Not bad?" Kal exclaimed. "Look at them! They're exceptional."

He arranged five stones in a row and eyed them critically. "I suppose I could create a pretty necklace with these. Twenty-five for the lot."

"Forty," Kal countered.

D'Amato laughed. "Thirty, and only because I'm in a good mood."

It was a fraction of what they'd hoped for, but enough for a bed and ale to drown their sorrows. Durian glanced at Kal, who nodded reluctantly.

"They came from a larger deposit," Durian added as he handed over his mining license and filled out the requisite forms. "We could bring more."

Kal shot him a warning glance. They'd agreed to lie about where they found the kaldurite. The Clear Creek Mine might be abandoned, but it was still owned by a wealthy witch family, or a conglomeration of them. Better to say as little as possible.

But the words were already spoken. D'Amato's eyes gleamed. "I'd be very pleased to see more," he said, handing over the bills. "Very pleased indeed."

They found a cheap hostel near the river and spent the

evening at the bar. Durian, who was never down for long, managed to convince her that they'd picked a bad sample and the others would be brimming with ley.

"It doesn't make sense, does it?" he said. "I mean, why would they be empty?"

Kal stared into her glass. "Who knows? It also doesn't make sense that they were just lying out like that. Not in a seam. Not raw. It's like someone dumped them there."

"But no one goes down there."

"The Sinn do."

"So what, they stashed a bunch of old rocks in that cavern?" He twirled a finger. "Bitch, you're losing it."

Morning brought clear skies and fresh determination. They left the hostel early, walking along the riverside Corniche. The plan was to try a few brokers they'd missed the day before, but they'd only gone a short way before two witches in long white coats approached from the opposite direction. Kal knew they were witches because of the way the sun turned their eyes into mirrors.

The woman had spiky blood-red hair and piercings all over her face—lips, eyebrows, nose, both ears. The man was big with dark beard stubble and a heavy brow. When he smiled, she saw that his front teeth were capped with silver.

"Good morning," he said, moving to block their path. "We'd like a word."

His accent was pure Kievad Rus. Kal heard it all the time in the hills, which straddled the border.

"Um, about what?" she asked, her stomach fluttering.

Were they in trouble? Did someone figure out they'd been trespassing at Clear Creek? But only she and Durian knew. They'd put fake coordinates on the jeweler's forms.

"We heard you found something interesting," said the pierced witch. "If you've got any left, we'd love to buy them from you. We'll pay a good price."

A warning buzzed in Kal's head, but Durian looked thrilled. "How good?" he asked.

"How about fifty per stone?"

"Sure! We still have a bunch." He reached for his pouch, but Kal laid a hand on his arm. The offer made no sense.

"Why would you pay so much for depleted gems?" she asked.

Durian jabbed a hard elbow, which she ignored. The witches would know the moment they touched the stones that there was no ley inside. And they must know that anyway.

"We're always interested in new varieties," the man said. "To study. But we'll need to see them first."

"Durian—" Kal hissed, but he'd already handed the pouch over.

The woman opened it with caution as if there might be a scorpion inside. Her face gave nothing away as she studied the stones. But then she did an even more peculiar thing. She didn't toss the purse back or tuck it into a pocket. She set it down on the street, next to her white boots, as if she didn't want to touch it.

"Tell us exactly where you found these," she said, "and we'll complete our transaction."

Kal scowled. You never gave up the exact location of a claim, not for anything.

"That's not part of the bargain," she said.

The male witch's glinting smile evaporated. He raised a fist and Durian floated off the ground. A sudden wind whipped the sandy around his face, which wore a look of sheer terror.

"I'll ask again. Where did you find these?" the woman demanded.

Without thinking, Kal reached down and pried up a loose paving stone. She hurled it with all her might. It clipped the witch on his beetled brow. Durian dropped to the ground, gasping. Kal grabbed his hand and dragged him down the Corniche. It was deserted except for a dog-walker across the river.

"I can't—" Durian panted, his bad leg twisting.

"You can!" Kal gripped his hand tighter. "We're not far from the market—"

An invisible force tore him from her grasp. Time slowed as Durian sailed over the stone embankment and into the river. He went under and didn't come up. The witches sprinted down the Corniche. The man was bleeding and furious, the woman livid.

"You idiot," she snarled. "We need them alive. Get the girl!"

Kal took off like a jackrabbit as chips of stone exploded from the walls on either side. Each moment, she expected to be hurled into the river like Durian. Yet somehow none of the spells seemed to hit her. She ducked into a side street, then another and another, zigzagging through smelly stalls. The fish market. Kota's morning crowds were thickening now, and a glance behind showed no white coats.

Only when she was certain she'd lost her pursuers did she slow to a walk, lungs burning. Her fingers found the pouch hidden in her pocket. The witches had Durian's kaldurite, but not her share.

What did they want a bunch of worthless empty stones for anyway?

And Durian . . . Guilt stabbed her. It was her fault. She should have just let them have it.

Kal skulked through the shadows, trying to decide what to do next. She couldn't go to the authorities and file a complaint, demand a search of the river.

The witches *were* the fucking authorities.

## CHAPTER 9
# GAVRIEL

T he scribblers had found a new angle to their tedious narrative, one that struck uncomfortably close to home. Gavriel read the latest edition of the *Daily Mumble* with mounting irritation.

MORNINGSTAR'S JUSTICE RESERVED FOR THE RICH AND
POWERFUL ONLY?

Even as Kirith's archangel dedicates his prodigious ener-gies to solving the high-profile murder of Barsal Casolaba, the recent death of a young speculator fails to merit similar scrutiny. When asked at the Assembly whether he planned to open a second inquiry, Lord Morningstar blithely replied that it was beyond the scope of his commission. Perhaps he should tell that to the grieving mother, who languishes in the gritty mining town of Pota Pras with no answers regarding her young son's demise . . .

It was absurd.

And precisely the sort of accusation that would gain traction among the public. Gavriel folded the offending broadsheet and placed it atop the pile he'd already scanned. All touted variations on the same theme.

"It's an obvious angle for the opposition to exploit," Yarl remarked, "especially since they are demanding a new election. The consul's death commands your full attention, while a poor boy from the mining country lies forgotten. It plays well to their base."

"It's inaccurate!" Gavriel exclaimed. "I do not have an open-ended invitation to look into every suspicious death in Satu Jos! This is a matter for the witches."

"They've been implicated in the boy's death," Yarl replied dryly. "No one will believe their investigation is unbiased. I agree that the timing is unfortunate, but you cannot simply ignore this new development, Lord Morningstar."

It made Gavriel even more vexed that he was right. "What do you suggest?"

"Perhaps it would be prudent to have one of the cyphers from Kirith look into the matter? Only to determine if there's any truth to the claims that lithomancy was involved. If so, you can go on the record recommending a special tribunal. Let Luzia Bras lead it."

Gavriel considered the various angles but could find no flaw. Yarl's solution was masterful. "Yes, that will work. My cyphers aren't local and thus will be deemed impartial. Make it appear like a discreet inquiry, but ensure that the scribblers are aware. Then we kick it back to the Assembly." He regarded his secretary with great fondness. "We must ensure you live another fifty years as I could not go on without you."

Yarl looked both pleased and weary at this prospect. "Which one shall we send, sir?"

Gavriel was tempted to rid himself of Rowan for a day or two. She had a way of watching him with silent intensity that he found distracting. But of the pair, Rowan was the loose cannon. She had a habit of saying whatever was on her mind. If the gossip-mongers cornered her, she might blurt out anything.

That would be a disaster. He needed to carefully manage every aspect of the investigation from here on. If his reputation were tarnished, Gavriel feared that the last glue holding the empire together would dissolve.

"Mercy Blackthorn will do," he said.

"Very good. I have another lead for you, sir," Yarl added, "regarding the payments for that flat on Rua Alva. Apparently, Casolaba had a mistress. Her name is Gia Andrade. Shall I summon her here?"

Gavriel hesitated. That was his usual practice. But the scribblers had been lying in wait outside the Red House to ambush him that morning and the gods only knew what might leak if they got hold of her.

"No, I shall go myself. Excellent work, Edvin."

Yarl nodded and fetched the cyphers, which took but an instant since they were standing outside the door.

"Cypher Blackthorn," Gavriel said, "I would like you to visit the morgue and examine the boy's body. Determine if there is any evidence of lithomancy and gather whatever details you can. His name, where he came from, et cetera."

A flicker of surprise crossed her bluff features. Clearly, she had assumed he didn't care.

"I can do that, Lord Morningstar," Blackthorn said.

She headed for the door with Yarl, who had prepared documents with Gavriel's seal that would give her access to the morgue. The man was nothing if not efficient.

"Cypher Rowan, you will accompany me to an address on Rua Alva. We shall leave immediately." He removed his magistrate's robe and hung it on a coatrack. Underneath, he wore his usual starched shirt, waistcoat and trousers. It was late autumn, but the days were still balmy. "Is there a problem?"

She was staring at him with a mutinous look in her eye. "With all due respect, Lord Morningstar, you're all over the broadsheets. Appearing in public would cause a tumult."

He gave her a thin smile. "Would it?"

"Yes, it would. I can't go alone, since that would leave you unattended. So you should either summon her to the Red House or send Yarl."

"Summon *her*? I have not mentioned the purpose of the visit, so I can only assume you were listening at the door."

She opened her mouth, then shut it again.

"Yarl has other duties," Gavriel said, unused to explaining himself. "And the mistress is more likely to talk if we catch her unawares, before she has time to concoct a story. Isn't that how you would conduct an investigation, Rowan?"

She faltered. "Well, yes, But you're a special case." She studied him like he was some zoo specimen, biting her lower lip. "I'd cast an illusion around you, but I don't know how."

This surprised him, though he knew little about cyphers. "Why not?"

"We're blunt-edged weapons," she said, a wry twist to her mouth. "We are not taught the subtle arts. So you must see that it would be madness to proceed with this plan."

"Then it was not a cypher who attacked me on the rooftop," he murmured. "I can rule them out entirely."

"Yes, but that's hardly my point!" She continued to protest as Gavriel opened the hidden panel and they took a dusty, dark staircase down to the side exit.

"Just trust me," he said gently.

She fell silent but regarded him with skepticism. Gavriel focused on the raw power in his blood, directing it to the light-waves bending around his form.

"Your wings," Rowan exclaimed. "They've disappeared! But I thought angels couldn't work the ley."

"I cannot," he admitted, "not like witches do. But I can use it to make a glamour. My brother Michael calls it *laying scales upon their eyes*. It is one of the powers granted to archangels. I can conceal my true form when necessary. Shall we proceed?"

She scanned the street and seemed satisfied. The scribblers

were all camped out by the main entrance. "I assume you know the way?"

He nodded and they fell into step together. He'd been alone with her once in the library, but that was different. He'd been working, with a large desk between them.

Gavriel cleared his throat. "Have you been to Satu Jos before?"

Rowan shook her head. "It's my first time."

"How do you find it?"

"Fine."

"The kopi is good," he remarked, a bit desperately.

"Hmmm."

She was a veritable font of conversation. "Did you know," he said, "that there are no buildings older than a hundred and thirty years? That was the time of the Great Fire, when the Sinn came from the Zamir Hills and burned Kota Gelangi to the ground. The old city had wooden structures that turned to ash in an instant, so afterwards they rebuilt with brick . . ." Gavriel trailed off.

Rowan was ignoring him, her gaze flicking between the rooftops and the shadowed rookeries between buildings.

"You don't like to speak of the Sinn," he observed.

"What? I don't care. Talk about whatever you like."

Gavriel realized that while no one gave him a second glance, Rowan drew wary looks and a few warding gestures. He wondered how it might feel to inspire fear simply by existing.

"Never mind," he said. "Er, what happened to your hand?"

"A witch broke it," she replied absently.

Rowan didn't elaborate and he gave up. They left the downtown behind and walked along the Corniche, a riverfront promenade with cheap hostels crowding the side streets.

"Is it true that you turned down the aid of the White Foxes?" Rowan asked.

He glanced at her. "Who told you that?"

"Felicity Birch."

"Yes, it's true. I much prefer cyphers."

"Why?"

The frankness of her gaze made him decide to answer honestly. "I don't care for their tactics. Nor their history."

When the Sinn had first appeared in Sion, no one knew where they came from. Eventually, it was discovered that the monsters were the result of mingling witch-angel bloodlines for two generations. The Morag at the time, a grim woman named Amfreide Karadas, created an order to find infant cyphers and kill them before they could breed. These hunters become known as the White Foxes because their coats blended with the snow in the northern provinces where the order was founded.

It was a long time ago, but Cathrynne Rowan seemed well aware of all this. Her mobile face went very still. Gavriel silently chided himself for mentioning it.

"Minerva finally made them stop," Rowan said quietly. "If it weren't for her, I'd be dead. I haven't forgotten that."

"Nor should you," Gavriel agreed. "It was an abominable practice. Had I been alive at the time, I would have put a stop to it myself."

Rowan smiled at him. It lit up her entire face. Gods, but she was lovely. He felt a strange wistfulness and crushed it ruthlessly.

They walked in easy silence for a while, the river a glittering serpent on the right. At the sixth pedestrian bridge, Gavriel guided her across to the residential neighborhood of Nove Octaver. It was named after the date of another infamous Sinn attack, but he decided not to tell her that.

Rua Alva was a quiet street with well-kept buildings divided into flats, each with flowerbeds in front, though they were withered now from the chilly nights. The address he sought had an archway with a locked wooden gate. Peering through the slats, he glimpsed an interior courtyard with potted trees and a small fountain.

Gavriel rattled the gate. "Good day!" he shouted. No answer

came. "Well," he said with a sigh, "I suppose we must wait until someone comes along. Or return another time—"

Rowan's bootheel struck the gate. It flew open with a splintering crack.

"You do realize this is criminal trespass," he said with a scowl.

"But it was broken when we arrived." She looked up at him, guileless.

Gavriel disapproved of her cavalier attitude toward the laws she was sworn to uphold. But the gate stood open and he was eager to learn what Gia Andrade might know about Casolaba's death.

"I shall do the talking," he said sternly.

They climbed the stairs to the second floor and found number five. Before he could stop her, Rowan banged hard on the door. Silence stretched, then footsteps.

Gia Andrade was in her middle years with thick, curling black hair and a generous figure. She wore a belted dressing gown embroidered with silver birds at the hem. Heavy kohl smudged her eyes.

"Did the landlord send you?" she asked in a flustered tone. "I told him I'd have the rent next week . . ." The words faded as she noticed Rowan's smoky eyes. "Go away," she snapped. "I have nothing to say!"

"Just a few questions," Gavriel said quickly. "It won't take long."

A naked, bearded man with a hairy belly appeared behind her. He tried to slam the door, but Rowan's boot slid into the crack. She forced the door wide quite easily, even with a broken hand, and Gavriel reassessed his initial impression that she was weaker than her partner.

"You heard Gia," the man snarled. "Piss off, witch!"

Rowan moved like a striking adder. Gavriel watched in amazement as she reached through the door, seized the man's flaccid member, and used it as a handle to yank him into the hall. Another well-placed kick to the rump and he half-tumbled, half-slid to the foot of the stairs, cursing vividly all the way. When he got to his feet, she held up her hand in warning. A gem nestled in her palm. The man swiftly retreated.

Gavriel feared that Gia Andrade was about to receive similar treatment and lifted the glamour. When she saw his wings, her eyes rolled back to the whites. He caught her before she hit the floor and carried her inside.

The flat was small but clean, decorated in the local style with a rug in intricate repeating medallions, bright cushions, and a backgammon game in progress on a table. A sulky-faced cat darted away as they entered, streaking into the next room to hide under a rumpled bed.

"That was savage of you, Rowan," Gavriel admonished as she checked the other rooms and found them empty.

"He was obstructing an investigation," she called over her shoulder.

"But still, did you really need to . . . Never mind." He gestured to a decanter on a side table. "Pour a glass of that pear brandy."

She frowned. "How do you know it's pear brandy?"

"I can smell it."

"Stoppered? From across the room?"

Gavriel nodded impatiently. She looked impressed and poured a finger of the amber liquid into a glass. He tipped a few drops between Gia's parted lips. Her eyelids fluttered, then flew wide.

"You are . . ." she whispered.

"Gavriel Morningstar, archangel of Kirith," he confirmed. "You can answer my questions truthfully now, or Cypher Rowan can bring you to the Red House for questioning there."

Gia shot an anxious glance at Rowan, who leaned against the doorframe.

"Of course, my lord, if I had known . . . please forgive my rudeness." She sat up and drew her dressing gown tighter with trembling hands.

"There is no offense," Gavriel said. "When did you last see Barsal Casolaba?"

She took a hefty gulp of brandy and coughed. Color returned to her cheeks. "The night he died."

"What was his manner?"

"He seemed nervous," she admitted. "Preoccupied. But excited, too."

"Did he say why?"

Gia hesitated. "He'd found something. A new kind of gemstone that was beyond priceless. He said it would change everything."

Gavriel's interest sharpened. "Those were his exact words? That it would change everything?"

She nodded firmly. "But he wouldn't tell me more. After we .. . engaged in a tryst, he left to meet someone. It was after midnight by then. Before you ask, he didn't tell me who." Her eyes filled with tears. "The next day, I heard what happened to him. I swear, Lord Morningstar, that is all I know."

He searched her face for deception and found none. "Did he mention his aide? Levi Bottas?"

She looked puzzled. "The boy from down south? No, not that night. Barsal thought he was a bit dense, to be honest. He only hired him because his uncle gave a lot of money to the Freedom League."

"What about Primo Roloa, the deputy consul? Or Luzia Bras?"

She shook her head. "He'd complain about them sometimes. That's all."

Gavriel asked a few more questions, but she knew nothing more. They left the flat and descended the stairs. Gia's naked visitor lurked behind one of the potted palms, hands covering his groin. He crouched low when he saw Rowan, peering between the fronds with apprehension.

"You can go back up now," she told him in a friendly manner.

He waited for her to pass, then scurried up the stairs, bare buttocks wobbling. Gavriel did his best to remain aloof, clamping his molars together. Rowan did not make a jest. She was scanning for hidden assassins ahead.

Outside, rainclouds gathered, threatening a downpour. It would be a wet walk back to the Red House, but Gavriel felt pleased with their progress. Rowan might be heavy-handed, but he had her to thank for his first real breakthrough. Had he come alone, he would still be standing outside the gate.

"Finally, a lead we can use," he said giddily. "Casolaba's death must be connected to this gem, and whoever he met must be the killer. I'm afraid it is looking more and more like the witches are behind it, but I must follow where the evidence takes me."

Rowan gave him a half-hearted nod and halted at the curb. The cobblestoned street was deserted, yet she stared intently into the distance.

Gavriel followed her gaze. "What is it?"

She didn't reply at first. Her pupils were huge. Then she said, "Something isn't right."

The hair on his nape stirred as he watched a line of violet blood trickle from Rowan's nose. A second later, Gavriel heard the rattle of wheels. A coach rounded the corner, drawn by four caracal cats. They were running flat out, the muscles of their flanks bunching and lengthening.

He took a startled step back. The coach bore down, veering towards the curb. Then Rowan flew into him and they both went sprawling into the flowerbed. She twisted at the last moment to ensure he landed on top, sparing his injured wing.

Their faces were inches apart. Her scent, the one that had been distracting him since the moment they met, even from across a room, grew dizzyingly strong. Smoky vetiver and the earthbound stillness of oakmoss, with a hint of almond blossoms.

Gavriel wrenched his gaze away, turning his head in time to see the coach thunder through the space he had occupied a moment before.

His heart pounded, partly from the near miss, mostly from her warm body beneath him. His left knee pressed between her legs, and he had a powerful urge to take a strand of her pale hair between his fingers and test its softness. To caress the smooth skin of her cheek. How plump her lower lip was, like a ripe summer berry—

It must have only been a few seconds before she pushed him off and chased down the coach. Still stunned, Gavriel pulled himself together and followed. The whey-faced driver stood at the end of the block stammering apologies. When he saw a cypher and angel approaching, his terror redoubled.

Rowan ignored him and strode up to the snarling cats. She allowed them to sniff her hand, then scratched them beneath the chin. Their tails stopped lashing. One began to purr, a calming rumble.

"Since you nearly ran Lord Morningstar down, you may take him to his residence," she said in a colder tone than Gavriel had ever heard her use.

The driver was happy to oblige. "I'm terribly sorry, my lord," he said, wringing his hands. "They went wild. I've never seen such a thing. Normally, my girls are the sweetest darlings. Perhaps they caught the scent of a rat . . ."

Gavriel assured him that he did not blame the caracals. Rowan, stone-faced, gave the address of the townhouse on Boulevard Dos Safiras. As the coach started off at a normal pace, she said softly, "There's a residue of ley on those cats. Someone riled them up."

He had guessed as much. "How did you know?"

"Most people with witch blood can sense the lingering magic of a spell."

"That's not what I mean," he said evenly. "How did you know the coach was aimed at me?"

She avoided his gaze, looking out the window. "I heard the wheels. It was moving too fast."

Gavriel doubted this. He had heard nothing until it was too

late and his hearing was keen. But he decided not to press. Rowan looked grim and unapproachable. She furtively wiped the blood from her lip, angling her body away from him.

What troubled him more than her obvious lies was his own undeniable physical reaction to her. Even now, he longed to close the distance between them and sit by her side.

Gods, the scent of her.

His jaw tightened. The pressure of the investigation must be getting to him. Gavriel vowed never to indulge such mad thoughts again—and to keep his distance from Cathrynne Rowan.

# CHAPTER 10
# CATHRYNNE

The caracal-drawn coach bounced across a patch of uneven cobblestones. Cathrynne stared into the blurry darkness, replaying the moments before it had nearly crushed Morningstar beneath its wheels.

Never in her life had a vision come with such force and clarity.

She was stepping off the curb when her scalp began to tingle. The neat rows of houses vanished in a blink. In their place she saw The Dark Rider, The Fox, and The Crossroads. Each symbol layered with meaning, but together the message was clear. Something was coming—something dangerous—set in motion by a cunning mind. And it would shift the future on its axis.

She had reacted without thought, throwing them both into the flowerbed. The blazing heat of his body had been an unwelcome surprise. He carried himself with such detachment, yet his skin had felt feverish through the heavy fabric of his clothing.

How thick his lashes were against the tawny green of his eyes, like one of the big cats. He had gazed at her with a softness she had never seen before.

Shock, no doubt.

Most people created tiny ripples in the ley, their lives a single raindrop on a still pond. But Morningstar's influence was more like the turbulent wake of a steamship, or the pull of the tides.

It was clear that he did not believe her explanation.

Cathrynne returned to berating herself. One more slip and he would realize she had the power of foretelling. She would be immured in a tower for the rest of her life, reduced to babbling through a slot in the wall. Just another mad oracle entombed in stone.

*Next time,* she thought furiously, *I'll let him get whatever's coming to him.*

Morningstar seemed to sense her dark mood and made no attempt to engage her. The silence stretched between them, taut and palpable, until the coach jolted to a stop in front of the rented townhouse. He reached for his billfold, but the driver rushed to stop him. "No, no, after that unfortunate accident, it's the least I can do."

"The fault wasn't yours," Morningstar replied.

"Even so, even so." The driver bowed, leapt into the seat, and departed with as much haste as he could without giving offense.

Inside the house, Mercy and Yarl were sharing a fragrant pot of kopi in the conservatory. Rain streamed down the wall of glass windows.

"I've got news about the dead boy," Mercy announced as they entered.

Morningstar shook the damp from his wings and dropped into a chair. "Go on."

"His name was Durian Padulski." She glanced at her notes. "From a town called Pota Pras at the edge of the Zamir Hills."

"Was it lithomancy that killed him?"

"I can't say for certain—any residue of the spell would be long gone. But I can tell you that he was dead before he hit the river. The papers got it wrong. Durian Padulski didn't drown. There wasn't any water in his lungs. Cause of death is undetermined, but the coroner found a burn mark on his back that could be from projective ley. You must have seen those before."

He shook his head. Mercy looked surprised. She unbuttoned her coat and pulled the collar aside. "Like this."

It was a classic projective pattern, like a star had been branded into her flesh.

Morningstar was quiet for a moment. "Pota Pras is a mining hub." He turned to his elderly secretary. "Gia Andrade—Casolaba's mistress—told us that he mentioned a new kind of gem. Something worth killing for. Now we have another death, possibly related to the gem trade. I'll admit the connection is tenuous, but it's worth investigating."

"Shall I go to Pota Pras and follow up with the family?" Mercy asked.

Morningstar rolled his shoulder with a wince. "I must go myself. They deserve that much."

"Then take Cypher Blackthorn with you," Cathrynne suggested, desperately hoping to avoid his company. "I can remain behind and trace his movements here."

Gavriel appeared grateful for the suggestion. Their eyes met briefly before they both looked away.

"I'll head to the wharf and inquire about riverboat schedules," Mercy said, throwing on her coat and heading out the door.

Morningstar stood quickly. "Yarl, if anyone in the Red House asks where I am for the next few days, tell them my broken wing pains me and I'm resting. No one is to disturb me."

"As you wish, sir."

"I have every confidence you can manage the investigation in my absence. If anyone refuses to cooperate, tell them they'll be charged with obstruction and whatever else you can think of once I return."

He vanished into the library. Cathrynne took up a post outside, deeply relieved. Tomorrow, he would be on his way to Pota Pras with Mercy, and she would be free of his horrid presence.

THE KITCHEN SMELLED OF HOME. Not her own—she'd forgotten what that smelled like—but warm and inviting. Cathrynne paused in the doorway, watching Yarl arrange fried mustard greens and oysters on a plate. Her stomach growled, a reminder that she hadn't eaten since morning.

Yarl looked up, his face creasing into a smile. "I thought you might be hungry. Please, sit."

She slid onto a wooden stool at the kitchen island. The oysters glistened in their crisp coating, and the mustard greens had been sauteed with garlic and pepper. Pure Kirithi comfort food.

"This looks divine," she said, picking up her fork. "You're a man of many talents."

"One doesn't live to my age without acquiring a variety of skills." He poured glasses of water from a clay pitcher. "I've found that Lord Morningstar rarely remembers to eat unless food is placed directly in front of him."

Cathrynne took a bite of the greens, savoring the bitter-sharp taste. Yarl leaned against the counter, watching her eat. "I must also thank you for saving his life today. He told me about the carriage."

The fork paused halfway to her mouth at the memory of Morningstar's breath tickling the hollow of her neck and his solid weight pressing her down into the flowerbed. She forced herself to chew and swallow. "Just doing my job."

Yarl's keen brown eyes studied her. "He's not accustomed to needing protection. I think it unsettles him." A rueful smile. "His brother Michael, the archangel of Sundland, is reputed to be fearsome with a blade. But Lord Morningstar never had an interest in learning the martial arts. He's more of an intellectual." Yarl paused. "Of course, he is quite fit. Flying requires immense strength, and Valoriel designed the angels to have aesthetically pleasing physiques."

She decided to steer the conversation to a safer topic. "Forty years is a long time to work for someone." *Especially a poxy prat, as Mercy would say*. "Do you think about retiring?"

Yarl chuckled. "I threaten to every now and again, but I believe I have another decade in me yet." He wiped down the countertop. "Who will look after him when I'm gone?"

The remark was made lightly, but she got the sense Yarl did actually worry about Morningstar. "He seems capable of looking after himself," Cathrynne said.

"In some ways, yes." Yarl folded the cloth. "In others, not at all. He forgets that not everyone views the world as he does. Time moves differently for him."

She couldn't help asking. "How old is he?"

"Over seven hundred years, I believe, though he rarely speaks of his age." Yarl touched his silver curls. "I was a young man with dark hair and a spring in my step when we first met. Yet Lord Morningstar hasn't aged a day."

She contemplated this as she ate. Angels were very different —that much she'd known. But watching everyone around you get old and die while you remained unchanged must be difficult. Perhaps that was why so many of them never left Mount Meru. It was easier to stay among their own kind.

"How long can archangels live?" she asked.

"I am not sure," Yarl admitted, "but they measure their lives in millennia rather than decades."

Cathrynne finished her supper in silence. Yarl tried to take her plate, but she shook her head. "You cooked. I'll clean."

He conceded with a smile and went to prepare a tray for Morningstar and Mercy, who had returned from buying their riverboat tickets and taken the first evening watch. Cathrynne soaked the pans in soapy water, her thoughts drifting. How strange it must be to watch civilizations rise and fall like the tide. No wonder he seemed so remote. Perhaps it was self-preservation.

As she rinsed the silverware, movement caught her eye. A

large crow alit on the windowsill and glared at her through the glass, red eyes unblinking. Cathrynne knew what it meant: a summons from the Morag. She recalled her nightmare and felt a centipede crawl up her spine.

*He comes.*

The crow launched into the sky with a caustic croak as Yarl bustled into the kitchen. "There's an almond trifle for dessert," he said with a wink. "It's my specialty."

Cathrynne patted her stomach. "I promise to save room for it, but think I'll go for a stroll first. Walk off those fried oysters."

He glanced at the window. The crow had vanished. "It's raining," he pointed out.

"I don't mind." She dried her hands on a towel. "It reminds me of Kirith."

"Just have a care." Yarl eyed her with grandfatherly concern. "The streets of Kota Gelangi can be dangerous after dark."

"I'm a cypher," she tossed over her shoulder. "The streets should be afraid of me."

As she left the kitchen, Cathrynne heard him laugh. The warmth of it followed her down the hall as she gathered her whip and cudgel and stepped into the rain. No bats tonight. The weather had taken a turn and it was cold enough to see her own breath pluming white in the misty drizzle.

She knew the way to the Red House by now. It was lit up at night, the notorious spire glowing against the clouds. She paused, trying to imagine how one might hoist a body onto it, then retraced the route Mercy had taken her the day they first arrived at the forcing ground.

A twenty-minute walk brought her to the chapter house. Welcoming yellow lights burned in its windows. She told her business to the witch on duty and was escorted to the Morag's chambers.

Isbail Rosach sat on the carpet deep in conversation with another woman, rangy and dark, with more scars than Cathrynne had ever seen. Not stellate scars. These were burns. She had fought the Sinn.

"This is Marvel Yew," the Morag said by way of greeting. "Head of the cyphers in Satu Jos."

"Mum," Cathrynne said with a respectful nod.

Marvel Yew gave no acknowledgment. She wore a uniform similar to Cathrynne's, but instead of the starburst symbol of Kirith, hers had a flame rising from a forge.

"Your presence is overdue," the Morag said tartly. "I told you to report to me yesterday."

"I'm sorry, mum. We've been busy."

She did not extend an invitation to sit. "What progress has Morningstar made in the investigation?"

Cathrynne knew it was possible that she was speaking to the woman who had ordered Casolaba's death and maybe even that morning's attack, but she wasn't about to deceive the most powerful witch in Sion—especially since she was such a poor liar.

"Casolaba's mistress told us that he discovered a new kind of gem. He said it was priceless."

The Morag's head cocked. "A new gemstone?"

"That's what she claimed. But she didn't know what it was, or who he was meeting about it."

"Go on."

"Lord Morningstar believes the consul's death is connected to the boy found in the river. Durian Padulski."

Her silver eyes gave nothing away. "Connected how?"

"Padulski is from a mining town in the Zamir Hills. If he was murdered, it's quite a coincidence."

"*Was* he murdered?"

"We can't say for sure," Cathrynne admitted. "Mercy Blackthorn saw the body. She said the burns could have been caused by a projective spell."

"Could have been." The Morag looked skeptical. "And he died before Casolaba?"

"Yes, by about four days."

"So what's the theory of the crime?"

"If Morningstar has one, he hasn't shared it with me."

"What is *your* theory, then?"

Cathrynne thought of the witches at the Nilssons' house. "Maybe the boy was involved in some kind of gem smuggling ring. He knows too much. Or maybe he steals from them. They kill him. The consul finds out and makes a fuss, so they kill him too."

Isbail nodded slowly. "Tell me, Rowan, does Barsal Casolaba seem like the sort of man to give an angel's purple piss about a rockhound from the hills?"

"No, mum. I suppose not."

"Don't look so deflated. There may still be something in it. What else? You're holding back."

"Not holding back, mum. Just haven't got there yet." She watched the Morag's reaction. "Someone tried to kill Lord Morningstar again today. It was right after we left the mistress. He was almost run down by a coach."

Isbail Rosach and Marvel Yew exchanged a quick, unreadable glance. "Was he harmed?" Isbail asked.

"No, mum. But someone used lithomancy again. I believe they enchanted the caracals."

Her face darkened. "Are you accusing *me*?"

Cathrynne swallowed hard. "Of course not, mum."

"It was I who requested Lord Morningstar's presence here," the Morag said. "Would I do that merely to kill him once he arrived?"

"No, mum."

Isbail Rosach drummed her rings against the desk. "What does Morningstar plan to do next?"

"Mercy Blackthorn is going with him to Pota Pras. I'll stay behind in Kota Gelangi to poke around and see what I can find out."

She looked up sharply. "I think not. You will accompany the archangel to Pota Pras."

Cathrynne tried not to scowl. "It's already been decided that Mercy will go."

Isbail fixed her with a cool stare. "You'll do as I say. I know of your troubles with the White Foxes in Kirith."

A queasy knot formed in her stomach.

"They have a chapter in Kota," she continued, "and they are aware of your presence. It would not be wise for you to stay here alone. Better if you disappear for a day or two."

"Maybe it was them who attacked Morningstar," Cathrynne blurted.

"Why?"

"Because they killed Casolaba and don't want him catching them."

"And they killed Casolaba because . . .?"

Cathrynne glanced at Marvel Yew, who had been observing the exchange in silence. It was hard to tell what she thought. Cathrynne plunged onward and hoped she wasn't leaping from a cliff.

"The new gemstone," she said. "They want it for themselves."

The Morag looked amused at this heresy. "I will concede that the White Foxes often behave as if they are a law unto themselves, but I have no grounds to accuse them of treason. Their order is under my authority. They are accountable to the High Council. And I have not heard even the faintest whisperings of a new gemstone."

"Well, I think it exists. You just don't know about it."

The Morag seemed to tire of her pertness. "What else?"

"Nothing, mum." She stared at the carpet to hide her mutinous scowl. "I will do as you say."

A snort. "Damned right you will." Isbail Rosach reached into her robes and took out a gem pouch, which she tossed over. "Freshly mined. Learn what you can in Pota Pras and report back when you return to the city."

Cathrynne tucked the pouch into her belt, partly mollified. Back home, she received a strict gem allotment each month. If she blew through them too fast, she was out of luck. "Thank you, mum."

The Morag waved her away. Cathrynne waited outside the door for a minute, but no one came to show her out, so she made her own way through the low-ceilinged corridors. She desperately did not want to travel with Gavriel Morningstar. What if another vision came? It was a choice she didn't care to face again.

Lost in thought, Cathrynne paid little attention to where her feet led her. She looked up to realize that she had taken a wrong turn and was in an unfamiliar corridor. There was no one around to ask for directions. She tried to backtrack and only got more lost. When she found a meeting room with large windows facing the outside and an unlocked exit door, she pounced on it.

In the rainy darkness, it was hard to tell which way the front gates were. As in Arioch, the compound was sprawling. She hurried down random pathways, head bent against the down-pour, which is why she didn't see the kloster until she was right in front of it. The tower was hulking and dark, without a flicker of lamplight. She knew it was the kloster because of the stench. It reminded her of a zoo. Of animal misery. She was turning away when a soft voice called to her.

Called her name.

It came from one of the bottom cells. Fingers curled through the bars, beckoning. Cathrynne hesitated. She wanted to quickly walk away, to pretend she had not heard, but this was a sister, after all. Something in her could not refuse. She approached warily. The girl's hair was matted into chunks, so filthy it was impossible to tell its natural color.

"Dark-bringer," she whispered furtively. "God-killer. He comes."

Cathrynne blinked away the icy rain. "Who is he?"

The girl's eyes were lucid. Sane, if appearances could be trusted. "I don't know his name. But when he falls from grace, you must not interfere. You must let him serve his penance, even if it lasts forever."

"Penance for what?" She was bewildered. "And why would I interfere?"

"Because you love him."

She shook her head, though dread curdled her stomach. "I love no man. So what you see will never come to pass."

The seer regarded her for a long moment. "I hope it is so," she said at last.

Cathrynne impulsively reached out and gripped the girl's fingers with her own, ignoring the terrible odor that wafted through the bars. "What is your name?"

"Julia." She swallowed. "Julia Camara."

A full witch, then, not a cypher.

The pouch at Cathrynne's belt was full of projective stones. She had an urge to pull the tower down, to reduce it to rubble. Her anger was big enough that she felt sure she could do it. "I'll get you out. Run as far as you can. They'll never know who did it—"

Julia drew back, alarm on her face. "No, no. I am safe here."

Cathrynne shook her head, tears stinging her eyes. Her bandaged fingers curled into a fist. "Please let me help you."

A ghostly smile touched the seer's lips. "We will meet again. Now go, Cathrynne Lenormand. Go, Witch of Winter. *Go!*"

She jerked her hand away and retreated into the dark cell. Cathrynne stood there for a minute, her blood racing. The girl knew her birth name. No one knew that except for Felicity Birch and the White Foxes who had dragged her from her childhood home.

She ought to call Julia Camara back. Demand answers.

Instead, she turned and walked away, feeling like a vile coward.

CATHRYNNE EASED the front door shut. The lamps were switched off save for a line of light spilling from beneath the library door. She kicked off her wet boots and left them on the rack, then padded across the floor in damp stockings. She was almost at the stairs when the library door opened and Morningstar emerged, looking rumpled and annoyed. Of course, his unruly black hair and creased shirt only made him more attractive.

"Where did you go?" he demanded.

"For a walk. Am I under house arrest?"

He scoffed. "In this weather?"

She lifted her chin defiantly. "Yes. I happen to like walking in the rain. Where's Mercy?"

"Making a pot of kopi."

Cathrynne heard whistling coming from the kitchen, along with the faint clatter of mugs.

"I'm not a complete fool," Morningstar said. "You must have gone somewhere."

"If you must know, I stopped by the chapter house to pick up more gems." She looked down the hall, wishing Mercy would emerge from the kitchen. "There's been a change of plans. I'll be escorting you to Pota Pras."

When she looked back, his hazel eyes had narrowed. "Isbail Rosach set you to spy on me, didn't she?"

"What? Don't be ridiculous."

He searched her face for an agonizing minute. Whatever he saw there made some of the suspicion soften. "You saved my life today," he said in a gentler tone. "I trust you, even if I don't trust the witches."

There must have been a window open in the library, for a cool draft swept the foyer. Cathrynne shivered in her damp clothes, aware of how little she deserved his faith. "Goodnight, Lord Morningstar."

"Goodnight, Rowan," he said with a slight bow, formal and

distant once more. "We depart early tomorrow. I'll thank you to be ready on time."

She watched him retreat into the library before climbing the stairs to the Iskatar Room. Whatever awaited them in Pota Pras, she couldn't shake the feeling that it was only the beginning of something far worse.

---

THE BESSEMER RIVER was swollen from recent rains, its muddy waters broken by the wakes of vessels of every size. Ring-billed gulls wheeled overhead, their cries piercing the din of shouting stevedores. Fish, tar, and hemp mingled in the cool morning air, the smell of port cities across Sion.

Morningstar strode along the quay beside her. He'd glamoured his wings, appearing human to anyone who glanced their way. With his gray tweed suit and black valise, he looked like a sleek, wealthy broker on his way to a business deal. Cathrynne wore her uniform of jacket, bodice, and snug trousers, with a whip and cudgel at her hip, but cyphers were a common sight in mining country. The same ancient covenant that had given the witches control over raw gems also compelled them to defend the human population against the Sinn.

Almost every witch and cypher in the province had served on the front lines at some point, which is why so many of them bore burn scars. It was entirely different from Kirith, where Sinn encounters were rare and never deadly.

Cathrynne, who hadn't left Arioch in twenty years, was ignorant of all this until Morningstar took it upon himself to give her a history lesson on the way to the port.

"The Bessemer is the lifeblood of Satu Jos," he droned in his magistrate voice, "linking the gem-rich interior to the coast. Countless barges ferry raw stones and metals to waiting ships bound for every province in Sion. In return, the ships bring equipment, food, and other necessities to the towns upstream.

Of course, with the advent of rail transport a century ago, much of that freight is now moved by trains."

"You sound like a geography primer," Cathrynne muttered, scanning the crowds for silver eyes. It had to be a witch who was trying to kill him. Maybe more than one.

He frowned. "What's wrong with that?"

She sighed. "Nothing. Which one is ours?"

"There." He pointed to a three-deck paddleboat with a red-painted hull. "The *Cinnabar Queen*."

It was an old vessel, not one of the new ley-powered ones. Steam billowed from the tall stacks, and its massive paddlewheel turned slowly, churning the brown water to froth. They joined the line to board. It was a mix of miners and brokers. No one gave Morningstar a second glance as he presented the tickets to the purser, who directed them to a second-class cabin on the top deck.

To Cathrynne's dismay, it was *tiny*, scarcely able to accommodate a single chair and bunk. Morningstar set his valise on the floor. His wings alone took up more than half the space.

"I'm going on deck," Cathrynne announced, dropping her bag.

"Suit yourself." He sat down in the chair, opened his valise, and pulled out a batch of papers.

Cathrynne made her way to the deck circling the second tier. It was crowded with passengers watching the city slowly dwindle behind. She found a spot at the railing and leaned against it, letting the breeze cool her face.

A young woman stood nearby, hunched in an oversized peacoat with the collar flipped up and a cap pulled low over her eyes. There was something both fierce and secretive about her posture. When she lifted her head to follow the path of a gull, Cathrynne glimpsed a tattoo on her neck. A sailing ship running with the wind, a froth of waves at its bow.

As if sensing the attention, the woman turned. Their eyes met. She flinched and skulked away, disappearing down the stairs to the lower tier. Cathrynne had never seen her before and chalked it up to a general dislike of cyphers.

She remained at the rail and watched lavish waterfront mansions drift past, their vast emerald lawns sloping down to private docks. Gardeners knelt in the landscaped gardens and uniformed maids served breakfast on stone verandas. Presently, the banks of the Bessemer grew wilder, dotted with the occasional village. The sun climbed, burning away the morning mist.

She wondered what kind of power Casolaba's new gem possessed that so many people were chasing—and dying—for it.

After a few hours, the growing chill drove her back inside, along with the guilty knowledge that she shouldn't have left Morningstar alone. If Mercy were here, she'd have him playing a game of cards and laughing.

Cathrynne found the archangel as she'd left him, nose buried in a sheaf of documents. "Take the bunk," he said without looking up. "I don't require sleep."

She nodded wordlessly and lay down, then stole a peek when he wasn't looking. He had rolled his sleeves up, revealing those strong, tanned forearms. A lock of dark hair spilled across his forehead, making him seem almost boyish.

But Morningstar was not a boy. He was an archangel, an irritatingly attractive one, and his presence, even absorbed in work, sucked all the air from the cabin. Thinking of him so close—and yet so unreachable—made her exhausted. The rolling of the riverboat didn't help.

She decided that it would be wise to steal a brief nap since they might be up quite late in Pota Pras and she hadn't slept much the night before, fretting both about the journey ahead and her disturbing encounter with the seer. She locked the cabin door, then lay down with her back to Morningstar, gazing out the porthole.

When Cathrynne drifted off, she saw a faceless angel with wings of flame, falling like a bolt of lightning from the heavens.

## CHAPTER II

# KAL

T he riverboat bumped against the wooden pilings of Pota Pras's quay, sending a shudder through the deck. Kal tugged her watch cap lower, tucking in stray wisps of her springy brown hair. There was no sign of the cypher she'd spotted earlier, but that didn't mean she wasn't being hunted.

She shuffled forward with the line of disembarking passengers as a train whistle pierced the morning air. The Zamir Hills Express, preparing for its journey into the heart of mining country. Once, that sound had represented opportunity. Now it was just another grim reminder of all her mistakes.

Four witches patrolled the wharf, their rings and bracelets winking in the late afternoon sun. A pair of caracals stalked beside them, fur rippling over muscled shoulders. The beasts stood waist-high to their handlers, alert and deadly.

There were always witches at the quay since a Sinn attack had burned two dockside warehouses to the ground last year. They watched the skies, not the passengers, but Kal's skin still prickled as she walked past them.

In her mind's eye, she kept seeing Durian hit the river and not come up. If they knew his name, they'd know her name, too, and where she came from. But she couldn't run far without identity papers. She also needed her savings, the stash she'd been hoarding since she was ten and sold her first find, a Sinn tooth that was bone-white and as long as her hand.

Thank Travian she'd had the sense to buy round-trip tickets when they left Pota Pras. Otherwise, she would have been walking for days to get home.

*Home.* Her heart lurched. How could it be home without her best friend? Her fellow oddball and dreamer, who insisted that anything was possible. Part of her refused to accept that he was gone. It was another boy they'd found. Kota Gelangi was a huge city.

The crowds thinned, dispersing into the dusty streets. Kal blended with a group of miners. Three steps later, a shoulder collided with hers, hard enough to make her stumble.

"I beg your pardon," said a deep voice with a crisp Kirithi accent.

Kal looked up into a pair of golden eyes ringed with green. The man was tall and darkly handsome, with broad shoulders and coal-black hair. His clothes were fine, so he must be one of the agents who worked for the mining conglomerates.

The cypher from the riverboat stood behind him. Kal nearly shit a brick.

She muttered an apology and tried to move past, but he gripped her sleeve, the pressure light but inescapable. "I'm a stranger to Pota Pras," he said. "Perhaps you could assist me?"

One of the witches had turned to watch them. Kal desperately wanted to get away.

"Sure," she said with false cheer, "where to?"

"I'm looking for Elisabetta Street."

Kal didn't react through sheer force of will. "You a scribbler?" she asked, eyeing his hands. No ink stains.

He shook his head. "A friend of the Padulski family. Maybe you know them?"

Durian's mother had no friends besides the other cleaning

women she worked with, and a few from the Cult of the Bard. Certainly none who dressed like this man.

"Sorry, I don't," Kal said. "But I can give you directions to Elisabetta Street." She pointed in the opposite direction from Durian's house. "Five blocks that way. Turn left past the concrete air attack shelter, then right at the school. About a mile or so. It's near the tannery."

Let him smell that poxy stench while he figured out the right way.

"I'm most obliged." His wolfish eyes lingered on her face. There was an intensity to him, a sense of hidden power that made her teeth ache.

"Happy to help," she chirped brightly, and slipped into the crowd.

Kal counted to twenty before glancing over her shoulder. The man and the cypher were actually following her directions, and the witches with their caracals had moved on. Relief made her giddy. She walked fast, turning at the first corner. When she was alone, she squeezed her pocket, feeling the hard lump of the kaldurite stones.

In and out. Go home, grab her savings, and disappear again— this time for good.

THE HOUSES GREW SHABBIER the farther she got from the downtown landing, but it was a familiar route. Kal knew the places where wild columbine poked through cracks in the sidewalk, where she and Durian would pick cherries in summer. The buckled asphalt where she'd tripped and skinned her knee when she was nine.

A gang of kids stood in a weedy lot, arguing over the rules of some game. Kal nodded at three men lounging in folding chairs outside the tobacconist's shop. They were smoking and talking about the special election. Whether the Miners' Union would finally get a majority in the Assembly.

People in Pota Pras hated the witches, but they hated Casolaba's Freedom League even more.

When she got close to Elisabetta Street, Kal cut through backyards. She knew the dogs and they didn't bark. Five more blocks and she was home, a single-story cinderblock box with a basement bunker in case of Sinn attacks.

The neighborhood, which everyone called the East Side, had been built as worker housing by the Carvajal mining company. A witch family, of course. Witches owned *everything* in Pota Pras. The Carvajals had twelve daughters and named the streets after them. All the houses looked alike except for the little touches added by the people who lived there.

Kal's house had green shutters framing the windows and a birdhouse she'd made herself and mounted on a pole that doubled as one side of the laundry line. There were usually clothes flapping from it in the steady, dry sirocco winds, but today it was bare. Not a good sign.

She watched from cover for a while, trying to figure out if it was safe to go inside. She didn't want to wait too long because the rich man and his pet cypher would be figuring out she'd bamboozled them right about now and heading back this way. Plus, the last riverboat left at dusk, and she couldn't risk being stuck here overnight. It was much easier to hide among the surging throngs of the city.

At last, she slunk to the back door, opened it a quarter of the way, just before the hinge creaked, and slipped inside. The moment she closed and latched the door, a floorboard groaned just outside the kitchen. She grabbed a cast-iron pan from the stovetop.

Kal held her breath, edging toward the doorway. A shadow moved across the wall. She raised the pan, pulse thundering, and stepped around the corner—

"Whoa!" A familiar figure stumbled back, hands raised. "Take it easy, sis!"

Kal lowered the pan. "Bastian? You scared the shit out of me!"

Her elder brother stood before her, dark braided locks spilling down his back, horn-rimmed glasses slightly askew. He should have been in Kirith poring over astronomy charts, not facing her with fear and relief battling in his eyes.

"What are you—" she began, then felt her breath whoosh out as he pulled her into a crushing hug.

"You're alive," he whispered. "After what happened to Durian, I thought . . . I was so worried!"

Kal inhaled the familiar scent of floral soap they all teased Bastian about, her throat closing with grief. "So he really is . . . I'd hoped . . ."

The tears she'd held back for two days burst, and she wept on her brother's shoulder. He held her just as he had when they were kids and she was upset about something, stroking her back and planting kisses on the side of her head.

"Why aren't you at Faraday?" she sniffled when the worst of it had blown over. "Term's not done yet."

Bastian was the smartest of the Machena brood. He'd won a full scholarship to study abroad in Arioch.

"Festival of Caelum the Wanderer," he explained. "It's a big deal. All the schools close except for Merry Sharpe. We get a month off." He pulled back, expression darkening. "But that doesn't matter. What happened, Kal? The cyphers brought Durian's body back yesterday."

Her shoulders tensed. "Where is everyone? Mom and Dad? Jett and Jinx?" Those were her twin brothers, both younger by three years.

"On a two-week surveying gig. They left before . . . before everything happened. I haven't been able to reach them." Bastian pushed his glasses to his forehead. "Witches came looking for you, Kal. They asked questions all over the East Side."

"Witches?" Her pulse ticked up a notch. "When?"

"A few days ago."

"How many days exactly? It's important, Baz."

He frowned, calculating. "Six. I'd just gotten home."

Kal's mind raced. That was *before* Durian's body was pulled from the river.

"What did they look like?"

"Well, they weren't regular witches. In Arioch, people call them Jennies. White Foxes. One had these, like, metal teeth. Freaked me out."

Kal swore. "The jeweler," she said. "D'Amato. They must have tracked us through him." She slumped. "Everyone knows the witches have eyes in the gem district. We were so stupid, Baz. We thought we'd found something valuable."

"What was it?" Bastian asked, leaning forward.

Kal reached into her pocket and showed him one of the stones, its facets gliding from blue to violet to deep red as it caught the light from the window. He gave a low whistle.

"Serpent's eye?" he asked.

"That's what I thought, too, but there are subtle differences. We named it kaldurite. But when we took the stones to Kota, all the brokers said they were empty of ley. Worthless except as pretty baubles."

Her brother frowned. "That's weird."

"We needed money so we sold a few to a jeweler named D'Amato. Durian let slip that there was more. D'Amato must have told the witches. They found us the next day." She swallowed a hot lump. "Durian handed his stones over. They had no reason to hurt him, except they did anyway. When we tried to run, they used a spell. He went flying into the river . . ."

Her voice cracked. Bastian held her again until the tears stopped. "I'm so sorry, Kal. But you can't stay here. They'll find you."

"I know." She wiped her eyes, jaw firming. "I just came back for my savings and my identity card."

He nodded grimly. "Make it quick. I'll pack some supplies."

Kal found a shovel in the toolshed and dug near the fence line. The rusted kopi tin was about half a meter down. Inside lay every coin and bill she'd saved for better days to come. When she went back inside, Bastian handed her a rucksack.

"Sandwiches," he said. "Assorted other shit. Take this, too." He held out their father's old Bluekiller pistol.

Of course, it couldn't actually kill a blue emperor. Nothing did. It might slow one down though, if you landed a lucky shot, so miners were among the few to be granted carry licenses.

Kal hesitated. "Guns don't work against witches. They can use anything with metal against us."

"I know. But it's not just witches you need to worry about," Bastian countered. "There are desperate people in the world." He looked sad and worried.

Reluctantly, she took the pistol, along with a box of .38 bullets, wrapping them in a rag before tucking it into the big pocket of her peacoat. Then she hurried to the room she shared with the twins and stuffed a few clothes into the rucksack.

"Where will you go?" Bastian asked.

Before she could answer, a low keening sound, like an animal caught in a trap, drifted through the window. Kal knew what it was immediately.

Durian's mother. He lived next door.

*Had lived.*

"They're having the remembrance," Bastian said in a quiet voice. "The procession starts tonight. I plan to go."

When you died in Pota Pras, friends and neighbors would gather at your house to say goodbye, drink, and celebrate your life. Then everyone would trek to a place deep in the hills called the Valley of Bones, carrying your body with them. They'd unwrap your shroud and leave you out for scavengers, naked as the day you were born. The ley animating your consciousness was gone and now your body would follow.

Close relatives often stayed for a few days, camped in a cave. If a blue emperor came along and ate you, or burned your body to cinders, that was considered a great honor.

Unlike Kota Gelangi, there were no shrines to the Sinn in Pota Pras. People didn't put out diced fruit or folded scraps of paper.

They gave up their dead. The people they loved the most. The ultimate offering.

Now Durian would be given to the Sinn, too. Kal stared into space, struggling to process this. As usual, her brother read her thoughts.

"Don't go over there," he warned. "I've seen him, Kal. Just don't."

Her eyes brimmed. "I have to. I need to know he's really gone."

Baz shook his head. "His mother won't be glad to see you."

She managed a watery smile. "His mother was never glad to see me."

"Come here." Bastian pulled her into another embrace. "Pay your respects quick and get out of town. Make your way to Arioch. Find me at Faraday. I can sneak you into my dorm. We'll figure something out together." He frowned. "Maybe I should just go with you now—"

"No." She exhaled a shaky breath and hoisted the rucksack. "I'm glad you were home, but someone needs to stay and tell Mom and Dad not to worry. Love you, Baz."

"Love you too, sis." She felt his eyes follow as she crossed the street.

Durian's house was even smaller than Kal's, two rooms with cheap plywood flooring and very little furniture since the Padulskis had moved so many times after his father walked out. That's when Durian's mom had joined the Cult of the Bard. It preached three tenets: relish the pleasures of life, love freely, and lead a nomadic existence like Travian, never staying in one place too long.

Durian was two when his mom quit her engineering job and set off on a twenty-year odyssey around the Parnassian Sea. She took menial jobs to get by, which is when her drinking got worse. Even though she spent most of her wages on men and liquor, Lena Padulski was a snob. She believed her son was better than the grubby kids of Pota Pras and did everything she could to discourage his friendships. This infuriated Durian, since the Cult of the Bard also preached charity and kindness to strangers.

Lena Padulski's prized possession, the last thing of any value that she hadn't sold, was a velvet painting of Travian hanging on the wall above the busted couch, hair long and wearing a beatific expression.

The main room—half kitchen, half tiny living area—was crowded with neighbors. They eyed Kal with a mix of pity and curiosity as she slunk through the back door. The dining table had been draped with a white cloth. As the crowd parted and Kal saw what lay upon it, she knew Bastian was right. She shouldn't have come.

The body bore little resemblance to her friend. Its face was bloated and waxy, sandy hair combed straight back to expose the birthmark he'd grown it long to hide. He wore a too-tight brown suit she'd never seen before.

Durian would be so pissed if he knew what they'd done to him. Kal's jaw tightened as she reached down and adjusted the hair to be more the way he liked it.

He looked smaller. The spark of ley in him was gone, sunk down into the earth to join the source. She could almost hear him laughing. *Don't worry, bitch, someday I'll be reborn inside a fat diamond. Wouldn't that be cool?*

The clay disk of his mining license rested on the edge of the table. Kal had an urge to claim something of Durian's. A keepsake. Not to remember him by—there was no chance she would forget, not if she lived to a hundred—but just to hold in her hand. She glanced around, then slipped it into the pocket of her coat.

A sharp intake of breath made Kal turn. Durian's mother stood behind her, stinking of spirits, her eyes red-rimmed and furious.

"You!" she hissed. "What happened to my boy? He followed you to Kota Gelangi and you got him killed! What did you do?"

"I—" Kal began, throat dry. "I'm so sorry, Miz Padulski. I—"

Through the window above the kitchen sink, she saw the well-dressed man and the cypher from the riverboat coming up the walk. They'd found her.

Kal retreated toward the back door. "I'm sorry," she mumbled to Durian's mother. "I'm so sorry. But I have to go!"

# CHAPTER 12
# CATHRYNNE

S he felt a jolt of recognition the moment she entered the Padulski house. It was the young woman from the river- boat who'd sent them on a wild goose chase. The girl rabbited out the back door, but not before throwing Cathrynne a glare that could have chipped stone.

A dozen mourners packed into the small room turned to assess the two strangers who had just walked in. Their faces hardened when they caught Cathrynne's silver eyes. The long trek across town had taught her that witches weren't popular in Pota Pras.

Cathrynne started pushing through the crowd to catch the girl in the peacoat when a group of men blocked the way. All were big and wide with hands like shovels.

"Murderer," one growled. "Your kind isn't welcome here. Take your gentleman friend and get out, or his face won't be so pretty when we're done."

Cathrynne stared into blue eyes, glittery with drink. "Lay a finger on him," she said, "and I'll break your knees."

The man's lip curled. "There's six of us and one of you."

"Do you really want to do this at a wake?" she asked, easing her cudgel free. "Because I have no problem with those odds."

Before anyone could make a move, the room fell silent. The men stared past her shoulder, mouths slightly agape. She guessed what had happened before turning around; Morningstar had dropped his glamour. They shuffled back to give the midnight sweep of his wings a wide berth as he approached a thin woman in a blue dress. She had the same sandy hair as the boy on the table, and though her skin was gray and puffy, Cathrynne guessed she'd once been beautiful.

"Who are you?" she asked in a tremulous voice.

"My name is Gavriel Morningstar," he said gently. "I grieve for your loss and vow to do whatever I can to bring your son's killer to justice."

Gone was the cold, haughty creature Cathrynne had first met. His face was solemn as he sank to one knee and took her hand. A sense of peace, of reverence, spread outward like ripples across water. Cathrynne returned the cudgel to her belt, a bit awed. Clearly, he had powers she knew nothing about.

The woman clasped his fingers, silent tears streaming down her cheeks. "An archangel," she choked, "in my own house."

Morningstar turned to the gathered mourners. "Would you grant us privacy?"

The men who had been ready to do battle moments before now looked shame-faced. They nodded and filed into the back-yard, where people were cooking food on a brazier. Someone passed around a bottle, and they stood in a knot, stealing glances back at the house.

"Tell me about your son," Morningstar said.

Her eyes clouded. "I wasn't a good mother," she confessed, the words coming in a rush. "I left him alone. We fought all the time. But only because he was so clever. I just wanted the best for him. I told Durian he had to get high marks so he could go to college, but he was a dreamer. Had his own ideas."

Morningstar nodded encouragingly. "Children often do."

She didn't speak for a long moment. "He was marked by Travian." A hand rose to her cheek. "I told him that when he was born, the god came to see him in his cradle and was so pleased, he spilled a bit of wine. Durian liked that story." She smiled, lost in memory.

"Why did he go to Kota Gelangi?"

Her face darkened. "He said he'd found something valuable. That he was taking it to the gem brokers in the city. It's the last time I saw him alive."

"What did he find?"

She shook her head. "He was cagey. Wouldn't say. But that's usual. Don't want competition, do they?"

"Did he go alone?" Morningstar asked.

A bitter smile. "Durian never went anywhere without Kal."

"Who's Kal?" Cathrynne asked, a dark suspicion forming.

"Kalisto Machena." Her lip curled. "My boy's no-good friend. Always talking him into some new scheme. They had a crazy idea about buying a ship, becoming traders."

Cathrynne exchanged a look with Morningstar. "Where can we find her?"

"She was just here," the mother said, gesturing toward the back door. "She lives in the next house over."

What a thrice-cursed day this was turning out to be! Morningstar had Durian's partner in his grasp—literally—on the quay and they'd let her slip away. Now Cathrynne understood why she'd sent them to the wrong part of town. She was buying time to get away.

Cathrynne ran to the next house and pounded on the door. After a moment, a young man opened it. He was tall and slender with long, tight locks. Thick-rimmed spectacles gave him a scholarly air.

"Where's your sister?" Cathrynne asked, peering around his shoulder.

He feigned puzzlement. "Um, sorry, but I haven't seen Kal in weeks."

"Don't mess with me, she was just at the wake!"

He shrugged and stood back. "Feel free to look around. But she's not here."

Cathrynne stormed through the house, searching all four rooms and the basement crawl space. Empty, just as he'd said.

Kalisto Machena had rabbited again.

She returned to the front room, frustrated. "What's your name?"

"Bastian," he answered warily.

"Listen to me, Bastian. Your sister is in deep trouble, which I think you already know. If we don't find her soon, she could end up like her friend. So if you want to save her life, you'll tell me where she went." Cathrynne held his eyes, willing him to believe her. "I'm not one of the bad people. I'm trying to *catch* the bad people. Hear my accent? I'm from Kirith. You can trust me."

For a moment, she thought he might relent. Then his gaze flicked to the window, to the sun lowering over the Zamir Hills. "I'm sorry, but I have no idea where she is."

The door closed in her face. Cathrynne met Morningstar coming out of the Padulski home, his wings once more glamoured.

"No luck, I take it," he remarked as they fell into step, heading back toward the riverboat landing.

"The brother's covering for her."

"I'm surprised you didn't hang him upside down and shake the answers loose."

Cathrynne felt affronted. "He's a witness, but also just a kid. I would never do that."

He arched a brow. "So you have standards."

"Of course I do. Besides which, I have a feeling she's headed into the hills. If she's smart—which she must be since she's still alive—she wouldn't have told him where she was going anyway. Did you get anything useful from the mother?"

"She said that Kal and Durian often spent time at a place called Red Dog Camp. It's an abandoned copper mine."

Cathrynne nodded, fitting the pieces together. "So they find something valuable in an old mine. Take it to Kota Gelangi to sell. Durian ends up dead, and now Kal's on the run. Consul Casolaba was involved somehow. The question is, what did they find that was worth killing for?"

They reached the quay as the sun cast long shadows across the muddy water. Cathrynne found the harbormaster, a gruff woman with hands like tanned leather who informed her that the last boat to Kota Gelangi had just sailed, and the next wouldn't depart until the following morning.

"Kal Machena's not leaving by water," she told Morningstar.

He chewed this over. "Can you track her with lithomancy?"

Cathrynne sighed. "I think it's possible, but I don't know how to cast that kind of spell. Tracking would require receptive magic."

"You weren't taught?"

"No," she admitted. "Only simple projective magic. Enough to knock people around and break up bar fights." She touched her cudgel and whip. "Mostly, I rely on these." The flicker of sympathy in his eyes annoyed her. "My point is, Kal could be anywhere by now. Let's just wait for the next boat back to Kota."

Morningstar gazed at the distant hills. "I think we should have a look at Red Dog Camp. It's not far, out near the border. It's familiar. She might feel safe there."

A clammy eel slithered through Cathrynne's stomach. "That's a long shot," she argued. "And the border with Kievad Rus is dangerous."

"You don't strike me as someone who fears bandits, Rowan."

"It's not bandits I fear," she confessed. "It's the Sinn."

Understanding dawned in his eyes. "Of course, quite sensible of you. Yet I cannot give up so easily. Why don't you wait for me here? There are plenty of hostels."

Cathrynne was tempted to stay behind. Enjoy a hot bath and soft bed. But she was supposed to protect him. What kind of cypher would she be if she let fear rule her?

Besides which, Morningstar had sounded almost *relieved* to

abandon her in Pota Pras. What did he imagine might happen in the desert? Did he think she would hurl herself at him bodily again? It was ridiculous!

"No," she said firmly. "If you must go, I will too."

He studied her for a moment, then nodded. To her relief, he said nothing more about it. They bought dinner at a stall near the quay. Red lentils wrapped in flatbread that drew the interest of marauding gulls. After tossing them the scraps, Morningstar took a map of the region from his valise. They studied it while they made their way to the train station.

Fifty draghas bought two seats in a private compartment for the last train into the hills. Cathrynne searched the faces of the other travelers, but Kal wasn't among them. No surprise. The girl wouldn't let herself be cornered so easily. Most likely she'd struck out on foot.

They boarded just as the sun sank behind the mountains, facing each other on worn velvet cushions. The carriage lurched forward with a clatter of wheels, gathering steam as it left Pota Pras behind. Morningstar took off his coat, folding it on the empty seat along with his valise.

"I made a vow to Durian's mother," he said gravely. "I intend to see it fulfilled."

In his starched white shirt and gray pearl-buttoned vest, he looked like a wealthy broker, yet there was a dangerous, quiet edge to his voice. His tawny caracal eyes gathered the light of the sconces.

He would not stop, she realized. No matter where this investigation took them.

She could feel the fierce heat of his body warming the compartment like a banked hearth. Cathrynne turned to the window, pressing her forehead against the vast and limitless darkness beyond.

# CHAPTER 13
# KAL

S ix of Bastian's famous egg and paprika sandwiches. Two changes of underwear. One thermos of cold lemon tea. And a rusty tin stuffed with bills of various denominations, most of them low.

Along with the pistol in her pocket and the cursed gemstones, that was the sum total of Kal's possessions.

She'd told her brother that she had a plan, but the only plan was to get as far as possible from Pota Pras.

Kal set a steady pace she could keep up all night. She and Durian never wasted money on trains, not when the journey itself was half the adventure. He would limp along at her side, his deformed foot slowing but never stopping him, that flop of sandy hair bouncing with each step.

She belly-crawled up to a ridge. From here, she could see the places they'd explored together. Broken Boot to the west, the abandoned structures of Red Dog Camp just visible in the distance, and somewhere beyond, Little Thunder, where they'd found traces of agate and quartz but nothing worth selling.

Kal pressed a hand to her side, feeling the slight bulge where she'd hidden the kaldurite in the lining of her coat. She'd almost thrown the stones away. But if the witches valued them so much, they must be worth something. She just didn't know why yet.

*Bitch, we're gonna be rich.*

Kal adjusted her pack and picked her way down a narrow path. All her life, she'd been scheming to escape. Now, she'd give anything to turn back the clock and have her old life back. To have Durian back.

Well. She had to keep going.

Ilion was her best chance. The port city was a four-day hike if she pushed hard. From there, she could buy passage on a ship headed anywhere—Kirith, Old Sarpedon, even all the way to snowy Sundland. Change her name, disappear. Start over where the witches couldn't find her.

If such a place existed.

The landscape grew wilder as she continued north, a treeless badland sculpted by wind and rain into twisted spires. Buttes rose from the earth, their sides scored by centuries of erosion. Deep gullies cut between them, creating a maze that only the most seasoned prospectors could navigate.

Rockhunting was a cutthroat business. People set traps on streambeds using boards studded with rusty nails. Roads were often blocked with illegal gates, though she and Durian would just climb over. There were a million stories about buried treasure in the Zamir Hills, and they'd actually found rusty lockboxes a few times, but all were empty.

Now the last rays of sunlight caught the high pinnacles, making them gleam like the edge of a knife. Shadows pooled in the valleys and the temperature plummeted. Night fell quickly out here, a liquid chill that crept into your bones. Kal thrust her hands into the pockets of her peacoat.

When she reached a flat outcrop, she decided it was a good place to rest. She shrugged off her pack, wincing as she rolled her shoulders. The rock still held a bit of warmth from the sun. She took out a sandwich wrapped in wax paper and leaned against her pack.

"Thank you, Bastian," she mumbled through a mouthful of egg and paprika.

Her thoughts drifted to the pair from the riverboat. The cypher and the well-dressed man. He wasn't a witch. His eyes weren't silver. But there had been something about him. A commanding authority.

*How many people were hunting her?*

She took a swig from her thermos. She'd need to refill it tomorrow at one of the springs. Standing, Kal took her bearings. The cluster of stars called Amira's Hourglass was just visible, faint pinpricks of light in the deepening blue. As long as she kept it in front of her, she'd stay on course for Ilion.

The wind picked up, lifting springy curls from her forehead. In the distance, a hawk rode the thermals, wings rigid as it hunted for prey. She scanned the skies but saw nothing else.

Everyone in Pota Pras feared the Sinn, but in all her years of exploring, Kal had only seen them a handful of times. She and Durian had found their tunnels, yes—smooth-bored passageways through solid rock that no human tool could create. Yet the creatures themselves were elusive.

"Maybe they're not as common as people think," Durian had once said. "Or maybe they just want to be left the fuck alone."

Kal reached for her pack to get moving again when it slid across the ground, all on its own, and came to rest at the feet of the witch with all the piercings in her face. The other one with metal teeth stood beside her. He picked up Kal's pack and shook it upside down. The rest of Bastian's sandwiches spilled out, along with her life's savings. He eagerly tore the lid off the kopi tin, then scowled and upended it. Paper bills fluttered in the wind.

"Where are the stones?" the pierced witch demanded.

Kal slid a hand into her coat pocket, fingers brushing the pistol grip. Her heart was beating so hard she could feel the vibration across her entire chest. "I threw them away."

"Don't you lie to me. You'll take us to the exact place where you found them or I'll peel the skin from your body and feed it to you."

It didn't sound like an idle threat. For a heartbeat, Kal almost turned over the stones. Told them everything. But even if she did that, she knew they would kill her, just as they had killed Durian.

She backed away, buying time. "How'd you find me?"

The male witch smirked. "Do you honestly believe we weren't watching your house?"

Her chest froze. *Bastian.*

"Don't look at me like that, we didn't hurt your brother. What do you think we are, monsters?" He laughed, silver teeth gleaming in the darkness.

"Just leave me alone. I don't have any more!"

He ignored that. "We thought you might lead us to the mine, but my partner Ash here is tired of following you. She thinks it would be a lot quicker if you just take us there now. So what do you say, Kal?"

The red-haired witch, Ash, raised her hand, fingers splayed. Cold skittered across Kal's skin, raising goosebumps along her arms, but nothing else happened. With an angry snarl, the male witch started striding toward her. Without thinking, Kal drew the gun. She pointed it at him and squeezed the trigger. The crack echoed through the gullies. Her hand was shaking and the shot missed. She steadied the aim with both hands and fired again. This time he staggered, blood blossoming against his white coat.

She stared at that for a moment in shock. She'd never shot anyone before. But he was still fucking coming and her finger clenched convulsively on the trigger, firing again and again. Muzzle flashes lit the darkness in strobing bursts. When the hammer fell on an empty chamber, she turned and ran.

Constellations wheeled above in the high dome of the sky. Durian had memorized them all, pointing them out on clear nights when they camped in the hills. *The Ladder and the Throne. The Broken Feather. See it, Kal?*

Now she made him a silent promise. She would escape. She would survive. And someday, she would make the witches pay.

# CHAPTER 14
# GAVRIEL

He pretended to consult the map, but his gaze kept lifting to the cypher seated across from him. She was staring out the window, her right elbow propped on the armrest and her left hand, the broken one, resting on her thigh.

Although Rowan looked deep in thought, her expression was not fixed. A succession of tiny changes flitted across her features like gusts of wind across water. A slight smile, followed by a tightening of the lips and a crease across her brow as some new musing made her frown.

He would give much to know what she was thinking about—then reminded himself that such things were not his concern. When he had learned that she would be escorting him to Pota Pras, Gavriel had felt apprehensive and elated at the same time. So far, he had kept his head sharing close quarters with her.

And why not? In his mind, he had reframed the incident with the coach so that his racing pulse was due to a near brush with death, *not* a near brush with Cathrynne Rowan.

He did enjoy her company. She was far less predictable than most humans or witches he had met. He sensed hidden depths and found her bluntness refreshing. The revelation that she feared the Sinn, for example, was a natural impulse, but he suspected few of her sisters would admit to it. Gavriel had no disdain for cyphers. He admired their devotion to duty. It was entirely the fault of their angelic fathers—

The train jolted to a stop in a cloud of steam and hissing brakes. The depot was a tiny platform with a sign naming it Jarbidge Station. Gavriel surveyed the desolate hills silhouetted beyond the window, wondering if Rowan wasn't right. Finding anyone out here felt like a fool's errand.

She slung her pack over one shoulder. They joined a dozen miners who hunched against the biting wind. None spared them a second glance.

"Last stop before the Western Trail," the conductor called from the steps.

"When do you come back this way?" Rowan asked.

"Dawn tomorrow." He tipped his cap to her and climbed into the train as it pulled away.

Heavy machinery had carved parallel grooves into the earth leading toward a distant smudge of lights. The miners headed off down the rutted road. Rowan tugged her collar higher, blonde hair blowing about her face, as Gavriel consulted the map. He pointed to a faint track running northeast. "Red Dog Camp should be over those hills."

The moon was full and the sky thick with stars, illuminating the rugged landscape in a pale glow as they set off.

"Have you ever met the Morag?" she asked after several minutes of silence.

"Once," he said. "At a conference on the extractive industries hosted by Kievad Rus. She seemed like a formidable woman."

Rowan gave a low laugh. "Scary is more like it. She has loads of scars from fighting the Sinn."

"Most witches in Satu Jos do."

"How many Morags have you known?"

A slight smile touched his lips. "Many, Rowan. Yet sometimes I wonder how much longer the current system will last."

"What do you mean?"

He hadn't meant to broach the subject, yet he didn't mind speaking freely with her. "Only that I see all the tiny fractures running through Sion and watch them widen every year. The ancient balances of power are shifting. Take the Sinn, for example. They are malevolent, yet far more real to most people than the founders of this world."

"You speak of the triple god."

He inclined his head in agreement. "My father rarely leaves Mount Meru anymore. Travian and Minerva withdrew from public life an aeon ago."

"Do you know what caused the schism between them?" she asked.

"No. It was before my time and Valoriel will not speak of it." He paused. "There is speculation, of course."

Her eyes lit up. "Please tell me. I have always wondered." When he hesitated, she added, "Minerva is dear to my heart even though she has been gone for so long. The cyphers hold her closest, I think. She saved us."

Gavriel knew the gruesome history, how the infants had been killed. It was a dark time. He disliked idle gossip, but found himself softening. What harm could come from telling her?

"Have you ever heard of the Plain of Contemplation?" he asked.

Rowan shook her head.

"It is a place where disobedient angels are sent so that they may have solitude to learn from their mistakes." Gavriel knew this was a ridiculous euphemism and Rowan seemed to know it, too.

"Like the prison camp for witches in Iskatar?" she asked.

He exhaled a plume of white. "I suppose the purpose is the same. But I have never seen this place myself. It is not within the confines of this world."

She frowned. "How is that possible?"

"There is a fey device that opens a portal. It is called the Rod of Penance." He cleared his throat. "In any event, after the third Lagashi rebellion in which Kven separatists tried to establish an independent state, my father grew furious. It was a pitched battle, with great losses among the legions before they prevailed. He berated Travian for allowing humans too much free will. Then he suggested that a healthy fear of punishment—something more severe—would keep them in line."

"So Valoriel proposed that humans be sent to this Plain of Contemplation, too?" she guessed.

"That's what my sister Suriel claims," Gavriel admitted. "Travian refused and Minerva took his side. But my father would not relent. Eventually, they grew weary of his incessant arguing and simply left."

"Do you think it's true?"

Gavriel gazed up at the stars. "I would not speak ill of my father. His intentions are always pure. But I will concede that he can be quite stern. And stubborn. So this explanation is possible."

He glanced at Rowan. "In the end, Valoriel may yet be proven right. Humans outnumber witches ten to one, and angels a hundred to one. They are the brains and brawn that keep the empire running. I have great respect for them, but I suspect they will not suffer the yoke of Mount Meru forever. Someday, they will throw it off, and I fear the bloodshed that will result since our cousins are neither gentle nor forgiving when roused."

Rowan considered this. "Maybe so," she said at last. "But I am sworn to protect them regardless."

He nodded. "As am I. And who knows? Perhaps Travian will return and take matters in hand." Privately, Gavriel did not believe he would, but who knew the minds of gods?

The condition of the road grew worse the farther they went. Gavriel held his injured wing close as they scrambled up loose scree and navigated around deep crevices. At last, they crested a rise and saw the camp below.

It was a collection of shacks and rusting derricks that had a skeletal appearance in the darkness. They picked their way down the slope and found the main building half-collapsed, its roof caved in on one side. Wind whistled through broken windows. Gavriel ducked through the doorway. Footprints overlapped in the dust, but it was impossible to tell if any were recent.

Inside, mining tools lay scattered about. Anything worth taking was already gone. Pickaxes missing their handles, shovels caked with ancient mud, cracked lanterns, and empty crates. In one corner, a ledger book lay open. He examined the brittle pages. The last entry was dated fifteen years earlier.

They spent another hour searching the camp. Kal Machena was not there, and they found no signs of recent digging. It was past midnight by the time they finished. Clouds obscured the moon and it started snowing.

"We should return to the station," Gavriel said, frustrated at the waste of time. "We can wait for the train there."

Rowan shivered. "It's a long way. I vote we shelter here until the snow stops."

"If you prefer."

They went back inside the main building, which had been a barracks and still had rows of metal cots. Gaping holes in the roof allowed flurries to float inside. She huddled against the wall, arms wrapped around her knees.

"I didn't think to bring a bedroll," she admitted. "Mercy likes to go camping, but I never leave Arioch."

"Why not?"

Her jaw set and she averted her gaze. "I like it there."

Gavriel studied her sidelong in the dim light. He had a high tolerance for cold, much preferring it to the hot, humid days of Arioch's summer, but he was aware that humans and witches were more vulnerable.

At first, Rowan's angel blood seemed to warm her sufficiently. They talked about Kal Machena and where she might have gone. Rowan told him that she'd seen the girl on the riverboat, and that she had a sailing ship tattoo on her neck. This led to a discussion of the human proclivity for inking pictures into their skin, a practice found in all provinces.

Rowan unwrapped her bandage and showed him her hand. The bruises had faded enough to make out the raven on the back, which she said marked her projective hand. Then she grinned impishly and confessed that she could cast with both hands, a rare talent among both witches and cyphers.

The night wore on and the chill deepened. Rowan fell silent. When she stopped shivering, he began to worry. It had happened with Yarl once, when Gavriel was foolish enough to bring him to Mount Meru. Yarl's speech slurred and he grew lethargic. Alarmed, Gavriel had flown him to a doctor in Isai Minye, the nearest human city, who informed him with disapproval that the cold and altitude had nearly killed his secretary.

The Zamir Hills were not nearly so high as the Sundar Kush, yet he recognized the signs. Without allowing himself to consider the implications, Gavriel unfurled his uninjured wing and folded it around Rowan's shoulders like a blanket. She looked surprised, then grateful.

"Better?" he asked.

She nodded and blew on her fingers. "You're not c-c-cold at all, are you?"

"I was raised where the air is so thin you would struggle to draw breath."

The wind picked up, howling through the abandoned camp. But he could see that she was reviving. She stretched her legs out and braced her palms against the floor.

"So you never leave Arioch," he said. "What are your favorite places in the city?"

"Well, there's a bar called the Wandsbach Lounge in the Old Quarter. I'm sure you've never been there. It's a cypher hangout, mainly. Run by a Kven from Iskatar. I like the fake palm trees." She thought for a moment. "There's also a very good tea shop near the chapter house. It has sixty-seven specialty cheeses."

"So many?"

Rowan laughed in delight. "Yes, sixty-seven! It's on Dean's Court. Go there if you don't believe me."

"I have my doubts," Gavriel said with mock severity. "List these alleged cheeses."

"Oh, I can't remember them all. But here's a few I've tried." She ticked them off on her fingers. "Cascaval and vorag. Stinky mancha, which is the proper name and entirely accurate. Herbed sheep's milk kedem from Petrosaca, lovely for spreading on toast. What else? An anise and pear-flavored Solway that's not for everyone, but if you're adventurous, you must taste it."

She went on for a bit more, then ran out of steam. Or cheeses, he thought in amusement.

"Well, I can't claim to be surprised," Gavriel remarked, "since they insist upon adding cheese to everything in Kirith."

She studied his face in that direct way she had. The dark sweep of his wing rose up behind her head. He could feel her blonde hair tickling the alulae feathers, which were exquisitely sensitive.

"And what do you do for fun, Lord Morningstar, when you aren't buried under paperwork?"

"Call me Gavriel. I am informal with my friends."

Her lips parted in surprise. Then she gave him that sunny, beaming smile. "Only if you call me Cathrynne."

His heart beat faster. "Very well. I like the astronomy tower with its brass telescopes. And the opera house because it reminds me of the Chorale. Have you ever been there?"

Her brows drew together. "The Chorale? I've never heard of it."

Of course she wouldn't. It was the glass and crystal basilica at Mount Meru where the seraphim praised the ley with their voices, but as a cypher, she might live her entire life not even speaking to an angel.

"I meant the opera house," he said. "Everyone dresses in their finest clothing and they fill the hall. It has beautiful gilded balconies with private boxes. You can hear the sounds of the orchestra warming up in the pit, and then the lights go down and the singing begins."

Rowan—Cathrynne—looked enchanted, and he imagined how it would be to escort her to the opera on some fine summer evening when the wisteria were in bloom and the great Eve Olivero was singing the part of the witch Ulrica.

Gavriel had the wild urge to lean closer. To enfold her entirely within his wings, close enough to feel the whisper of her breath. They were alone. No one would know. But what would *she* do?

Crack his skull with her cudgel, most likely.

Silence fell between them. He felt compelled to say something. By the Trinity, *anything*.

"I have never spent so much time with a cypher." The words sounded stiff even to him. "You are . . . " *Intoxicating, fascinating, forbidden*. "Very competent."

She looked gratified. "Thank you, Lord . . . Gavriel."

Their gazes met—and caught. That deep, mysterious blend of oakmoss, vetiver, and almond blossoms washed over him. He read her expression easily this time. By the Trinity, she wanted him too.

A reckless impulse seized him, one he knew was mad yet felt helpless to resist.

The ley in his blood *craved* her. There was no other way to describe it. He had never felt anything like it before, not in seven hundred years of life.

He leaned forward before he could stop himself, one hand catching the soft line of her jaw. Her lips were close enough to feel the slight gust of air. Cathrynne's breath was sweet and innocent, like dew on green peaches.

He had not kissed a woman in a very long time. Gavriel stroked a thumb along her cheek. His head dipped, his mouth meeting hers. Gentle at first, testing.

He paused as she stiffened against him, but then her fingers threaded into his hair and she pulled him closer. The last bit of his resolve came unmoored. His teeth grazed her rapid pulse as he trailed kisses down her throat. Cathrynne gasped, head falling back. He unbuttoned her coat with one hand, the other tugging her shirt free to caress the smooth skin of her hip. Heat flashed through his body, pooled low in his belly.

He knew it was wrong, knew the penalties for them both, but he was beyond caring. *Just once. Let me have her just once.*

Gavriel was about to lay her down on the downy feathers of his wing when the ground beneath them shifted. It was subtle—just a slight vibration—but Cathrynne stirred in his arms. "What was that?" she whispered.

Gavriel ruthlessly took hold of himself. "Merely the wind, I'm sure—"

The words died as another tremor came, stronger this time. Cathrynne pushed him back, her cheeks flushed. "That wasn't the wind!"

His gaze rose to the partly collapsed ceiling. The rest of the building looked as if it might follow suit with little encouragement. "There's seismic activity in this area," he said, still painfully aroused and trying to hide it. "I've seen the geological surveys. A major ley current runs along the border." With reluctance, he added, "We should get outside."

She cast him a flustered look and quickly gathered her pack. When they ducked through the crooked doorway, it was still snowing hard and drifts had gathered along the windward side of the building. The snowbank cracked and shifted as another tremor came.

"Is this normal?" Cathrynne demanded. She had a wild look in her eye.

"I've experienced such quakes before," Gavriel assured her. "They're only deadly if you're trapped in an enclosed space when they strike."

A strange shudder ran through her. "Then let us get away from camp."

She was turning to the road when a massive creature slithered from a fissure in the earth. Somehow, they must have over-looked it in the darkness. Gavriel had never seen one of the desert breeds from the ground before, only from the air. The size of it was staggering.

A blue emperor, named for the cobalt hue of its claws and tongue.

A flaming mane licked the ridges of its back, casting a red glow across the ground. It had two sets of ridged horns and a patch of golden scales from throat to chest. Six powerful legs, each tipped with razor-sharp claws, supported its massive body. A barbed tail covered in overlapping metallic plates lashed back and forth, gouging furrows in the frozen earth.

Gavriel found Cathrynne's hand, lacing their fingers together. *"Don't move,"* he whispered.

Whether this was the correct advice, he couldn't say. But avoiding its attention seemed wise.

The Sinn's head swung toward them. Its eyes were pools of molten gold, terrible and mesmerizing. Nostrils flared as it caught their scent.

They both dropped to a crouch as colossal wings unfurled. It launched from the ground and soared overhead, a river of flame streaming from its maw. The camp was briefly illuminated in orange light. When darkness fell again, it seemed thicker.

"Run!" Gavriel shouted, pushing Cathrynne in the direction of the road.

The Sinn banked in the air, its massive wings stirring up a blizzard as it came around for another pass. Together, they sprinted across the open ground. The beast roared, a sound unlike any Gavriel had heard before. Another blast of flame shot past, close enough to singe. They dove behind an outcropping as the intense heat turned the snow to billows of steam.

The blue emperor landed with a bone-jarring thud. It stalked forward, its long, scaled body undulating like molten quicksilver. The serpentine head reared back, preparing another blast.

Before Gavriel could stop her, Cathrynne stood to face the

creature. She held a ruby, its facets catching the Sinn's fiery mane. Gavriel sensed the volatile ley inside the stone. Felt it ignite, directed by her will. An invisible wall of energy rippled across the ground.

It had no effect. The Sinn roared again and slammed its tail down, reducing a ledge to a heap of rubble.

Cathrynne dropped the depleted gem. "Close your eyes," she said grimly, fisting another stone from her pouch.

Ley flared again. A cloud of sandy grit rose up. Gavriel wanted to shield her from the monster with his own body, but her voice demanded obedience and he could feel the power within her surging, boiling. She was a cypher and this was her business.

He curled his good wing around himself. A maelstrom buffeted him on all sides, obscuring everything beyond a few cubits. All he could see was Cathrynne, flaxen hair whipping around her face and a sapphire glowing like a cold moon through her fingers. Her eyes blazed with the same light as the gem.

Gavriel heard an angry shriek from the Sinn, but he could not see what it was doing.

The storm lasted half a minute or so, though it felt longer. When the wind subsided and the dust had settled upon them both like a shroud, the blue emperor was gone. Only deep grooves in the earth marked where it had stood.

"Did you kill it?" he asked in amazement.

"No. It flew away." Her chest heaved with effort. "Blinding it was the only thing I could think of." Cathrynne rounded on him, a tempest still raging in her eyes. "We're leaving this cursed place tonight, Morningstar, even if I have to walk all the way back to Kota Gelangi!"

# CHAPTER 15

# KAL

*I shot a witch.*

Kal still couldn't quite believe it. Guns never worked against witches. It was the metal. They threw a spell at you and made the mechanism misfire. Her father said that was why the witches let miners carry sidearms. They were no threat. The witches still had the upper hand.

But Kal had seen the red stain blooming against the white of his coat. Watched him stumble back. It made her queasy, but she hoped he was dead.

The other witch—White Foxes, Bastian called them—with the piercings in her face had given chase, but Kal was faster. She'd slipped into an old mine entrance, a gap in the hillside no wider than her shoulders, invisible unless you knew exactly where to look.

Now the darkness embraced her as she moved deeper into the tunnel, breath coming in short, ragged gasps. At least the battery-operated torch was in her pocket, not her pack. Once Kal reached a safe distance from the entrance, she paused to click it on. Shadows jittered across the ceiling as she slowed to a walk.

Her savings was gone, scattered in the wind when the witch

dumped her pack. With a sinking heart, Kal remembered that her identity card was in there, too. She couldn't get across any borders without it, and now she had no money to buy a fake card. Not that she had any idea where you could get such a thing.

But she still had the Blue-killer pistol and the torch and the kaldurite. Plus Durian's mining license. She kissed it for luck and replaced it in her pocket.

When the tunnel shrank to a crevice, she bit her lip, then dropped to hands and knees. Rough stone scraped her palms, but no way was she going back. The new plan was to get as far as she could underground before surfacing again.

Between the vast network of old mining tunnels and the new ones made by the Sinn, you could go a long way without ever seeing the sun. Kal plunged onward, praying that she wouldn't hit a dead end. Thankfully, the shaft finally widened and met a crossing passage. She took that one, and then another, doing her best to avoid the tunnels that sloped downward. By the Trinity, she was thirsty. Sometimes you could find a trickle of water down the walls, but these mines had none.

She was at another intersection, pondering which way to choose, when a distant rumble echoed through the tunnel. Kal held her breath, counting the seconds. The sound didn't repeat, but that meant nothing. The desert Sinn only made noise when they burrowed through rock. If they were moving through an existing tunnel, they could be surprisingly quiet.

Once, she and Durian had come across the remains of some miners caught unawares. The sight had haunted her for months.

She kept going, always choosing the widest tunnels and the ones that didn't lead deeper into the earth. If she could walk upright, she did. But if there was no other option besides crawling, she did that.

The battery in her torch started to dim. If it died altogether, she knew this labyrinth would be her tomb.

*Just keep going forward.*

Her stomach twisted with hunger, but it was the thirst that worried her. She'd gone days without food before, but water—that was a much bigger problem. Time to find a way out.

Except she hadn't a clue where she was.

The stirrings of panic fluttered in her chest as she kept hitting dead ends. Places where rubble filled the shaft or a seam had simply petered out. The torch dwindled to a sickly yellow glow. She decided to turn it off and use the walls as guides. The thick, impenetrable darkness made her chest tighten, but it was better than knowing the battery was dead for good.

When Kal stumbled into a low cavern, she nearly toppled into the pool at its center. Only the splash at her feet warned her to stop. Her heart raced. If she'd submerged the torch . . . It didn't bear thinking about.

She flicked it on long enough to see clear water. The sight of it broke something inside her, and she fell to her knees. Her hands trembled as she cupped them, bringing the tepid liquid to her lips. It tasted of minerals, but she drank greedily. Then she sat on her haunches, flicked the torch on again, and looked around.

The cavern stretched into darkness, the torchlight too frail to penetrate its depths. Water bubbled up from beneath, forming a lake wide enough that she couldn't see the far side. The sides of the cavern were high and jagged. The only way forward was to wade through.

She held the torch in one hand and the bundle with the gun in the other, raising them over her head. The surface wasn't bad, but the bottom water was bitingly cold, rising quickly to her waist. She gasped in shock and clenched her jaw.

*Just keep going forward.*

Halfway across, a vibration sent wavelets rippling across the pool. Kal flicked the torch off. She stilled in the blackness, water lapping at her ribs. Just the mines settling. The Zamir Hills straddled some of Sion's biggest leylines. A jolt every now and then was normal.

When the rumbles ceased, she pushed forward, her breath echoing off the cavern walls. She tried not to think about what might live in the lake. An ancient, patient creature that had waited years for some idiot to stumble into its lair . . .

"Stop it," she whispered. "Get a grip."

The water rose to her chest. She hesitated somewhere in the middle. If it got any deeper, she'd have no choice but to go back. She couldn't risk soaking the torch.

But luck turned her way. The next few steps brought her up a gradual incline. When she reached the other side, Kal stood dripping, her sodden coat a heavy weight on her shoulders. Then she flicked the torch on and almost cried. The passage beyond twisted like a corkscrew, descending deeper. Definitely dug by the Sinn.

She glanced at the pool but couldn't bring herself to retreat. She doubted that she could find her way through all the dead ends and cave-ins anyway.

Exhaustion made her sink to the ground. How deep had she gone? Were the White Foxes still searching or had they given up by now? She would rather face the witches again than be trapped wandering this stone maze. Alone in the black . . .

Splashes sounded behind her. Something was coming through the lake.

*Not alone at all.*

Kal unwrapped the pistol. She fired wildly into the dark. The hammer clicked down on an empty chamber. *Shit!* She'd forgotten to reload. Kal frantically thumbed the magazine release and crouched down. She fumbled the box of bullets from the dry bundle that she'd so carefully carried across the water, but her hands were shaking and they spilled everywhere.

Panting with adrenaline, she grabbed a bullet as it rolled away, pushed it into the magazine, and slammed the mag back into the pistol. Then she flicked off the torch, backing into the tightly corkscrewed tunnel. If she couldn't see it, maybe it couldn't see her.

One bullet. She'd have to make it count.

The splashing grew closer. Her heart slammed against her chest as she counted down.

*Three. Two. One.*

She flicked the torch on, aiming it into the cavern.

"Bitch, do you have to point that *directly* in my eyes?"

Kal blinked hard. A boy stood at the edge of the water, one pale, skinny arm shielding his face. But she knew that voice. That sandy hair and left foot twisting inwards.

The pistol wavered. "Get away from me," she whispered.

Durian lowered his arm, flashing the crooked, white-toothed smile that had charmed half of Pota Pras. Then he took a rapid step forward. "Boo!"

Kal recoiled and he burst into the braying donkey laugh that always made her laugh too, even when nothing was funny.

Like now. Not fucking funny at all.

Kal stared at him. Hallucination. Had to be. She'd lost her shit.

"You look awful," Durian said, squinting. "Seriously, could you lower the torch?"

She did, and then promptly burst into tears.

"Come on, girl. Keep it together." He limped over, wearing the same clothes he had on the day he died. Durian's city outfit. A long blue coat with diagonal brass buttons, which he claimed was the latest fashion, over baggy white pants. He was ridiculous about those pants. They had to stay *pristine*.

"I can't," she sobbed. *Not without you.*

She slid down the wall and ugly-cried. Durian sat next to her. He looked frighteningly real, even close up.

"What are you?" she managed. "A ghost or something?"

The question seemed to bore him. "I don't know. Just tell me what happened."

Kal drew a shaky breath. Then she crawled to the lake and splashed water on her face. When she turned around, Durian was still there. Waiting for an answer.

She swallowed. "Do you remember . . .?"

"Dying? Yeah, you can skip that part."

"Okay." She nodded. "Okay. Uh, well, I waited for you at the statue of the Trinity . . ."

She told him about reading the article in the gossip rag about a drowned boy, but that she refused to believe he was gone until she'd come back to Pota Pras.

"I stopped by your remembrance ceremony," she said.

"Good turnout?" he asked hopefully.

"Oh yeah," she lied. "There were about fifty people there. Your mom . . ." Kal grimaced.

"She blamed you, right?" He shook his head, the flop of hair bouncing. "Typical. What was I wearing?"

"Uh, like this brown suit . . ."

He swore. "Really?"

Kal nodded.

"Damn, I hated that old moth-eaten thing. Told her I'd never wear it again. I guess she got the last laugh." He donkey-brayed. "At least I'll be naked when they leave me for the scavengers."

"Could we talk about something else?"

"Yeah, bitch." He sobered. "How'd you end up down here?"

Kal told him how the witches caught her, and she shot one.

"You shot a witch?" Durian arched a skeptical brow.

Kal had given up trying to reject his presence. Maybe he was a spirit guide. Maybe he was a figment of her imagination. Either way, she felt glad he was with her.

"It's true, asshole," she said. "I swear it on the Trinity."

Something sharp poked her hip and she shifted. The kaldurite. She took it out of her coat lining. The pouch was soaked, but the gems inside threw off sparkles of blue, red, and violet as she laid them out on the ground.

"I think it's the stones," she said slowly. "That's what they do." She turned to face him, the revelation leaving her breathless. "They block the ley. *That's* why the witches want them."

Durian's green eyes gleamed in the fading light of the torch. "Go on."

"It's why I got away on the Corniche and you didn't. I kept my bag of stones. You'd handed yours over. The spells didn't *miss*. They just couldn't touch me."

"And it explains why they couldn't yank the gun from your hand, or make it malfunction," he added. Durian let out a whoop that echoed through the cavern. "We were right all along! These stones are worth a fortune."

"More than a fortune," she said, her mind racing. "Kaldurite evens the playing field. Takes away the witches' power."

"No wonder they're hunting you," he said. "If this gets out . . ."

"It would change the world," Kal finished.

They stared at each other in excitement.

"You're going to get filthy rich for the both of us, Kal," Durian said with a crazy grin. "Swear it to me."

She laughed. "I swear it on Travian's honor and all hope of his return."

That was the strongest oath she knew how to give him. Even though Durian and his mom fought constantly and agreed on almost nothing, he remained a devoted follower of the Cult of the Bard. He firmly believed that Travian was out there somewhere in disguise, watching over his children. Or having a good time at least.

"Better get moving," Durian said, jerking his chin at the twisted, downward-sloping tunnel ahead.

Kal nodded briskly. She took a moment to add three more bullets to the magazine, then rewrapped the box and the pistol. Stashed the kaldurite back in its pouch. Then she entered the sinuous, off-kilter tunnel, bracing her hands on the walls for balance.

The torch died soon after that, but Durian stayed with her, whispering encouragement and chivvying her onward with descriptions of the ship she would buy—a small, fleet caravel that could navigate the shallows with a minimal crew. Together, they would sail far away, somewhere the witches could never find them.

The tunnel gradually widened. After a while, she could see the walls again. Gray light filtered through an opening some-where up ahead. She must have walked all night. Judging by the ravenous ache in her belly, maybe more than one night.

Kal staggered the last stretch, lightheaded with joyful relief at her escape from the mines. It wasn't until she stood at the exit, staring down at a scrubby valley, that she realized her friend hadn't spoken in many minutes.

When she turned back, Durian was gone.

# CHAPTER 16
# CATHRYNNE

S he stared at the sluggish brown current of the Bessamer
River, thinking that she really ought to thank that beast
for stepping in before she made the worst mistake of her
life. She had kissed an angel and there was no point pretending it
would have ended there.

How she missed the cold, haughty Lord Morningstar! At
least he had been manageable. But Gavriel . . . The heat in his
eyes when he looked at her stole her wits. *Damn it all.*

The consequence of such couplings had been drilled into her
since the day she arrived at the chapter house in Arioch. If the
angel's seed took root in your womb, you could take a draught to
induce abortion, but that wasn't guaranteed to work.

Cyphers never survived the births. The Sinn clawed their way
out. Their own mothers were the first to die—but not the last.

Gavriel Morningstar was no ordinary seraphim. He was an
archangel. The seventh son of Valoriel, a god. What might their
union produce?

A terrible thought came. What if the Dark-bringer was *her
own child?*

Cathrynne gripped the rail, swallowing bile. The seer had

called her by name, had known exactly who she was. Every detail of that rainy night at the kloster was branded on her memory.

*When he falls from grace, you must not interfere. You must let him serve his penance, even if it lasts forever.*

A single day ago, Cathrynne could not have imagined Lord Morningstar falling from grace. He was the most devout of the angelic host. Rigorous, emotionless, and always correct. Yet at Red Dog Camp, she had glimpsed another man. One who came a hair's breadth from breaking his vows.

The word *penance* lodged in her mind like a splinter of glass. Gavriel had used that word himself. The Rod of Penance. He said it opened a portal to the Plain of Contemplation, which sounded pleasant but wasn't at all.

Cathrynne mulled over the vision she'd had in Felicity's office. The Dark Rider. Stars. A pair of doves, their beaks touching. The Crossroads.

Yes, she saw it now. The Dark Rider brought a dire warning. If she fell in love with Gavriel Morningstar, it would alter the course of many things—and not for the better.

Cathrynne retreated into silence for the rest of the trip back to Kota Gelangi. It wounded Gavriel. She saw it in the tightness of his jaw. The man who had bantered about cheese, who had held her hand and sheltered her with a wing—who had kissed with utter abandon—disappeared. In his place returned Lord Morningstar, high-handed and arrogant.

*Thank the three gods.*

"We arrive within the hour." The voice behind her was clipped.

Cathrynne didn't turn from the rail. "I know."

She sensed him lingering, perhaps waiting for more, but she kept her eyes fixed on the churning water below. After a moment, he turned away, the cabin door closing with more force than necessary.

"I TRUST the journey to Pota Pras was eventful?" Yarl asked as he greeted them at the front door of the manor house.

*You have no idea*, Cathrynne thought, dropping her pack in the foyer.

"Partly," Gavriel replied. "How were things in my absence?"

"Well, your return is timely," Yarl continued, following them into the drawing room. "Barsal Casolaba's funeral is scheduled for this afternoon. Your attendance is expected."

Gavriel looked annoyed. "I suppose I have no choice. When?"

"The procession begins at three. You have been allocated a position of honor behind the immediate family." He gestured to a stack of broadsheets on the table, all blaring headlines about the lavish funeral. "The city mourns."

"As well they should for such a paragon of virtue," Gavriel remarked in acid tones. "Where is Cypher Blackthorn?"

"She said she had an errand to run," Yarl replied.

"Do you know when she plans to return?" Cathrynne asked.

"I'm afraid not."

She cursed inwardly. She'd hoped Mercy could escort Morningstar to the funeral.

"Then I'll freshen up and change," she said, struggling for a neutral expression.

They parted ways without another word. In the Iskatar Room, Cathrynne stripped off her dusty clothes, washed her face, and donned a fresh uniform of silver bodice and jacket over snug black trousers. She combed the snarls from her hair and twisted it into a knot at the nape of her neck.

She emerged at a quarter of three to find Gavriel waiting in the foyer. He wore his severe black magistrate's robe, which only served to emphasize the breadth of his shoulders. They joined the crowds filling the boulevard. White bunting draped lampposts and balconies, the traditional color of mourning. The funeral procession wound through the city center, led by an honor guard bearing Casolaba's empty coffin on their shoulders.

169

Behind walked his widow and two grown children, carrying a silver urn that presumably contained the man's ashes.

Witches and cyphers patrolled the streets, but since Cathrynne felt certain one—or more—of them was the culprit, she took little comfort in their presence. She divided her attention between the crowds surging against makeshift barriers and potential assassins on the rooftops.

By necessity, she had to keep Gavriel closer than she liked. He did not complain and actually seemed to be enjoying her discomfort, which annoyed her even more. She deployed a frosty stare to ensure that no one came within arm's length, including the other dignitaries.

These included the ones with motives: the ambassador from Kievad Rus; Primo Roloa, head of the Freedom Party; and Luzia Bras, leader of the Miners' Union, who caught Gavriel's eye and gave him an approving nod. Cathrynne guessed Bras was well aware he had visited Durian Padulski's mother in Pota Pras.

"Where's Levi Bottas?" she asked, craning her neck. "I'd expect him to be here."

Gavriel looked around, but Casolaba's aide was nowhere to be seen.

"My sister Haniel is absent as well," Gavriel said, "but that is unremarkable. She disdains humans and Barsal Casolaba was no exception."

The procession followed Rua Capitolana to Liberty Square, where a temporary stage had been erected. One by one, officials climbed the steps to deliver eulogies for the consul. They praised him as a devoted public servant, a loving family man, a champion of the people.

"What a remarkable transformation," Gavriel murmured, his voice low but cutting. "Just days ago, those same people told me privately how much they loathed the man."

After the speeches ended, they followed the procession to a cemetery where mausoleums housed generations of Kota's luminaries. By the time they returned to the townhouse, Cathrynne was in such a foul mood that she wished someone would attack just so she could beat the tar out of them.

---

AT DINNER THAT EVENING, Mercy and Yarl continued their animated conversation about the Sinn, while Cathrynne pushed her food around the plate. Every time she looked up, Gavriel was watching her, though he'd glance away the moment their eyes met. Mercy took the first watch, and Cathrynne tumbled into bed, exhausted.

She dreamt of a featureless plain that stretched in all directions. It was a place of both scorching heat and dreadful cold. Frost glittered on the frozen earth, yet it was pocked with shallow pits in which hot ashes smoldered.

She walked and walked, until she perceived something on the horizon. When she drew closer, she saw it was a serpent coiled around a tower of black stone. The snake held a beating heart in its jaws. Red clouds streaked the sky, twisting into unnatural shapes.

Pain lanced through her chest as the snake's jaws tightened. The heart burst between its fangs, spraying the stones of the tower with violet blood—

Cathrynne jolted awake. Sweat drenched her nightshirt. She fumbled for the bedside lamp and switched it on. The clock on the bedside table read 3:33.

The middle of the thrice-damned night.

Around her, the house lay silent. Her racing pulse slowed and the nightmare faded, leaving vague unease. She switched off the lamp and lay back down. When she drifted off again, she didn't dream.

The next morning, Cathrynne found Mercy in the kitchen buttering a sesame cake.

"You look tired," Mercy said.

"And you're the one who stayed up all night," Cathrynne said wryly. "Have you seen him yet?"

Mercy shook her head. "He went to bed at around two. I kept a watch outside his door, but he hasn't come out." She patted her belly. "Got hungry, so I thought I'd grab something from the kitchen."

It turned out that Gavriel *did* sleep, though it wasn't very much. He'd taken the Sundland Room on the top floor.

Cathrynne bit into a cake. "I'll take over."

She climbed the stairs and sat down in the chair Mercy had stationed outside the Sundland Room. The hour grew later. The sun climbed in the sky. No sign of Gavriel.

Clearly, he was avoiding her. She didn't relish discussing what had happened at Red Dog Camp, but they needed to clear the air. It would never happen again. With any luck, he would find Casolaba's killer and they could go back to Arioch and never speak to each other again.

Cathrynne firmly ignored the traitorous ache in her heart at this prospect. She knocked on his door. Gavriel didn't answer, so she pushed it open. The room was dim, the curtains drawn. He lay atop the duvet, charcoal wings spread limply. His skin was ashen, dark hair plastered against his forehead. The nightshirt clung to his chest, damp with perspiration, yet when she touched his hand, it was cold.

"Cathrynne," he croaked, hazel eyes flickering open.

She gripped his fingers. "I'm here. Tell me what's wrong?"

He tried to speak but coughed instead, a dry, rattling sound.

"Yarl!" she shouted. "Come quickly!"

He appeared in the doorway, his face paling at the sight of his master. "I'll send for the healers at the Angel Tower immediately," he said, backing toward the door.

She helped Gavriel take a sip of water, then eased him back against the pillows. His wings trembled with the effort, the once glossy black feathers dull and lifeless.

The dream flashed through her mind again. She had assumed

that Gavriel was the serpent, shredding her heart in his jaws. But the clouds meant deception. A hidden antagonist creating chaos, fogging minds to obscure the truth.

Cathrynne cursed herself. She had been so preoccupied with her own demons that she'd been blinded to the real threat.

"Stay with me," he murmured, his fingers tightening around hers.

"I'm not going anywhere," she promised.

# CHAPTER 17

# KAL

She walked into Arjevica as the midday sun struck the gold cupola of the city's Angel Tower. She'd unknowingly crossed the border between Satu Jos and Kievad Rus in the mining tunnels, emerging south of a town called Ressad. From there, she'd hitched a ride with a lorry driver who had just delivered dry goods to one of the camps. The woman let her sleep in the empty cargo bed. She hadn't asked any questions.

Kal felt relieved to have made it so far, but she knew no one in Arjevica. The capital of K.R. was every bit as prosperous as Durian had claimed. Its boulevards stretched wide and straight, paved with white stone and lined with trees turning autumn gold. Sleek automobiles prowled the streets, and the buildings were tall and elegant. Even the air tasted cleaner.

Without money for a bed or food, she wandered randomly, hoping to snatch a piece of fruit from a stall. But Arjevica didn't have open-air markets like Kota Gelangi—or if it did, she couldn't find them. It was all grand avenues and fancy shops, and the owners watched her suspiciously from the moment she entered.

When night fell, she found a park bench across from a large building with illuminated columns and richly dressed people going in and out. She burrowed into her peacoat and tried not to drift off. At least it was a nice neighborhood. She'd be less likely to get robbed. But if anyone tried, she was ready.

One pocket held the loaded pistol, the other her pouch of kaldurite. The stones were worth a fortune to the right buyer, but she wouldn't make the same mistake as before. Witches had spies in every gem district. She couldn't just walk into a shop and try to sell them. No, she needed a plan. A smart one.

Problem was, she felt too hungry and exhausted to think straight. She dozed sitting upright on the bench, jerking into wakefulness every few minutes. When dawn came, she was more tired than she had been the night before.

"Sorry to bother you, miss, but are you alright?"

Kal looked up. A youngish woman stood over her, bespectacled and wearing a yellow headscarf. Her eyes were dark brown so she wasn't a witch.

"Fine," she replied, licking dry lips. "Just resting."

The woman smiled. "To be honest, you look like you could use a hot breakfast."

Kal wished she'd go away. The park was coming alive with people, but none of them even glanced at the filthy girl on the bench. What did this woman want?

Back in Pota Pras, she'd known a girl named Nina. When they were in their last year of school, a woman with red-painted fingernails and glamorous clothes came to town. She went around chatting up the prettiest girls. Kal didn't like her, but the woman never approached Kal anyway. People whispered that she was with a theater company in Kota Gelangi and traveled the province looking for fresh talent. Nina signed a contract with her and they left on the riverboat together.

Her family never heard from her again. When they went to the city and sought help from the cyphers, they found out that the theater didn't exist. Nina had vanished.

"I'm not selling my body," Kal growled. "So piss off."

The woman blinked. "You misunderstand. I teach at the

Lenormand School." She held out a hand. "Let us start over. My name is Manij."

Kal eyed the soft, plump hand but didn't shake it. "That's not a Rus name."

"Because I am Bactrian." Manij smiled. "I came to Arjevica seven years ago."

"Good for you." Kal folded her arms.

Manij's gaze was knowing. "The Lenormand School is for young women who have nowhere else to go. I thought you might fit that category."

"No, thanks," Kal said. "I'm doing just fine."

Manij shrugged. "As you wish. I'm walking there now, it's only a few blocks away. You can have a quick look from the outside first, if you like. But it's your choice." She glanced at her wristwatch. "I will be late for class if I linger."

Kal hesitated. A group of rough-looking young men lounged on a nearby bench. They were staring at her and elbowing each other. Their laughter had an ugly edge to it.

"I'll walk with you," Kal said, rising quickly to her feet. "Just to see."

She'd slip away if it felt wrong. The streets were busy enough now that Manij couldn't kidnap her in broad daylight. Plus, she had the pistol. Kal didn't want to shoot anyone, but just the threat might be enough.

They walked together out of the park. Kal felt the boys' eyes on her back. "So why did you move here?" she asked, probing for weaknesses in the woman's story.

"My sister was murdered by her husband," Manij said matter-of-factly. "I wanted to help women in bad situations, and a friend told me about the Lenormand School. It is their mission to offer sanctuary to any girl or woman who needs it, especially those who lack the resources to help themselves."

"I'm sorry," Kal said, wondering if the story was true. "How come you sound like a Rus, then?"

Manij glanced at her, amusement in her eyes. "Because I am

from the south of Bactra. Northern Bactrians have a Kirithi accent." She gave a wry smile. "Of course, people born and bred in Arjevica know immediately that I am not from here." She lowered her voice. "They can be quite snobbish about it, too."

They paused for a break in the morning traffic, then crossed the street.

"Anyway, the Lenormand School gives young women a second chance," Manij continued. "Some are fleeing violence at home. Others are running from something else. Whatever it might be, rest assured that is your business."

Kal cut her a sharp side look, but Manij's face was bland. "We teach practical skills to help students become independent. Our graduates are given jobs in Kievad Rus—or beyond if needed."

They turned a corner and Manij stopped walking. A high brick wall thick with ivy enclosed the next few blocks. Through wrought-iron gates, Kal saw clusters of stately brick buildings surrounded by trees and grass. No bars on the windows.

Young women strode along the pathways between the buildings, laughing and talking, books clutched to their chests. They wore identical uniforms—white shirts, gray skirts and black woolen leggings.

Kal didn't care for the wall. But the students didn't act like prisoners.

"I have to get to class," Manij said. "If you're interested, I'll drop you off at the admissions office. They can explain more."

Kal weighed her options. She had no money and didn't know a single soul in Arjevica. The White Foxes would not give up hunting her so easily, especially since she'd shot one of them. If she slept on the streets, she'd be easy to find—and easy prey for rapists and thieves. This school might be the safest place until she came up with her next move. She could always run away if she didn't like it. The wall presented no obstacle to a woman used to climbing the rugged Zamir Hills.

"All right," she said. "Thank you."

Manij squeezed her shoulder. "A wise decision." She unlocked the gate, led Kal through, and locked it again behind them. They walked through the grounds to a building with a brass plaque that said *Administration*. Inside, Manij waved at a receptionist and took her down a hall with polished wood paneling and large windows overlooking a grassy quad. Another door at the end was marked *Dean's Office*. Manij knocked once, then opened the door.

Kal's pulse spiked. Her vision tunneled.

A witch sat behind the desk.

"I found a young woman in need of our assistance," Manij announced, then turned to Kal with a bright smile. "Good luck," she chirped before bustling away down the hall.

The urge to run was overwhelming as the witch's pewter eyes took her measure. Kal reminded herself that she was immune to their magic now. This one showed no sign of recognition.

She didn't wear white, either.

"I'm Lara Lenormand." Her voice was cool and assertive. "What's your name?"

Kal squeezed her shaking hands into fists. "Kyra Navarra."

She'd picked her new name on the long lorry ride. Kyra for her grandmother. Navarra for Durian's favorite café.

"Please, sit down." A hand stacked with rings gestured at two matching armchairs facing the desk. Kal sat. The witch regarded her seriously. She was beautiful and pampered-looking, with shining brown hair and the flawless skin of rich people. Her clothes looked expensive too, a beige silk blouse with jeweled buttons.

"Well, Kyra," she said, "I want you to know that no one gets into these grounds without my permission. If you decide to stay, you will be safe here. But the choice is yours. You can walk out that door right now and no one will stop you."

Kal hesitated. She'd lost the White Foxes in the hills. They couldn't know which way she'd gone from there. It might be anywhere. And since she had crossed the border underground, there was no record of her arrival in Arjevica.

"I know you're scared," the witch said in a softer tone. "But you don't need to be. Not anymore."

A braying donkey laugh made her stiffen. Durian leaned on the edge of the desk, ankles crossed.

"The irony of *that*," he chuckled. "Bitch, you have to admit it's funny. But this is also the last place they'll look. It's like the fox hiding out in the henhouse." He stroked his chin. "Or the hen hiding out in the fox's den?"

Kal yanked her gaze back to Lara Lenormand. Clearly, she was losing her mind.

"I'll stay," she said in a small voice.

Lara smiled. "I'm glad. Welcome to your new home, Kyra."

---

THE DEAN ORDERED a tray of juice and raisin buns, and had Kal fill out a bunch of papers. She invented a new hometown and deducted four years from her true age, which was twenty-two. When she finished, Manij came back and brought her to the dormitory.

"This will be your room," Manij said, stopping before a door marked with the number 27. "You'll share with two other girls who are in class now."

Kal noticed that the door had no lock. Inside were three beds—two facing each other along opposite walls, and one tucked into a windowless alcove. All had identical white-painted frames. Next to each bed stood a narrow desk and chair, and against the far wall, three wardrobes.

The beds facing each other had belongings scattered beneath and on top—books, shoes, a half-folded sweater. The alcove bed was bare.

"That will be yours," Manij said, following Kal's gaze. "You'll find uniforms and other necessities in the wardrobe. The bathing facilities are at the end of the hall."

Not the worst place she'd slept in—not by a long shot.

"Tomorrow morning, we'll test your aptitude for different vocations," Manij continued, handing her a book with embossed gold lettering. "This is the Lenormand School Code of Conduct. Please try to read it by the end of the week."

Kal flipped through the pages. "The whole thing?" She wasn't the fastest reader.

"Start with the first section," Manij replied. "The rest can wait until you've settled in. Supper is served from six to eight in the dining hall. Your roommates will show you where that is."

Kal smiled, wishing she'd leave. "Got it."

When the door closed, she waited a few minutes to make sure Manij was really gone. She even opened the door and checked. The hall was quiet. Moving quickly, she lifted the mattress of her new bed and wedged the pistol and box of spare bullets between it and the boxspring. An obvious hiding place, but it would do for now.

The wardrobe had four white shirts, two gray skirts, three pairs of woolen leggings, and a jacket with the school crest—L.S. in twined script—emblazoned on the breast. She found a plush towel on the shelf above. The bathroom at the end of the hall was empty when Kal entered, her peacoat clutched to her chest.

Six showers lined one wall, each with a small changing area separated by frosted glass partitions. She chose the one farthest from the door and hung her coat on a hook so she could keep an eye on it. The kaldurite was hidden in the lining, and she wasn't about to let it out of her sight. Not with witches around.

She turned the brass fixtures and water rushed out, quickly heating to a steaming flow. Kal stepped under the spray and gasped. Back home, hot water was a luxury, heated bucket by bucket on the woodstove. She only bothered to do it for bathing in winter, or for washing *really* dirty clothes.

She used lemon-scented soap and shampoo from dispensers mounted on the tiled wall, watching the gray water swirl down the drain. When she returned to the room wrapped in a towel, the daylight was fading. The Code of Conduct lay on her bed where she'd left it. She picked it up and thumbed through the pages. The rules seemed endless.

No leaving the school grounds without permission. No breaking curfew, which was eight o'clock. No smoking, swearing, drinking, or fighting. She could almost hear Durian complaining that anything fun was banned, but he didn't show up. Kal wasn't sure if she felt relieved or disappointed.

The door swung open, and two girls walked in, their laughter cutting off when they saw Kal.

"You must be the new girl," said the short one. She had restless eyes that darted around the room and an aura of nervous energy. "I'm Elena." She set her books on one of the desks. "This is Gabi."

Gabi was blonde, tall, and statuesque. Both looked around Kal's age.

"I'm Kyra," she said.

Gabi eyed the Code of Conduct in her hand. "I hope you're not a snitch, because we don't pay much attention to the rules."

Kal snorted. "Definitely not."

They both looked relieved. Elena pawed through her school bag and took out a crumpled pack of cigarettes. She opened the window, lit one, and blew the smoke outside. "So where are you from?"

"Lycaea."

It was a port city on the northern coast of Satu Jos. Kal couldn't claim to be local because she couldn't fake the thick, throaty Arjevican accent. The minute she opened her mouth, people would know. To Kal, she had no accent at all, but Durian said she pronounced her consonants funny.

"That's a long way." Gabi eyed her speculatively. "Been running for a while?"

"A couple of weeks."

An awkward silence fell as they studied each other. Kal wished she'd gotten dressed before they came back.

Elena blew a series of smoke rings. "This place used to be a home for unwed mothers."

"Or any girl who annoyed her parents," Gabi added. "It was like a prison. Some say it's haunted by the ghosts of girls who died here, though we've never seen any."

Elena gave a nervous laugh and sucked on her cigarette. "Not to worry, that was twenty years ago. It got closed down after some scandals. Then the Lenormands bought it and renovated all the buildings. It's totally different now."

"Who are they?" Kal asked. "The Lenormands."

Elena shot her a dubious look. "You really don't know?"

Kal shook her head.

"They're the wealthiest witch family in Kievad Rus," Gabi said. "Nobody messes with them."

"Didn't you meet Lara?" Elena asked. "She wears a big emerald around her neck."

"That's the one who admitted me," Kal said.

"Lara's a massive bitch," Gabi said admiringly. "Once, this girl's father showed up and was standing out on the street by the gate, demanding they give his daughter back. Lara went out there, and when he wouldn't leave, she forced him to the middle of nowhere."

"Forced?" Kal echoed. "Like made him go?"

Gabi laughed. "Kind of. Forcing is when the witches make you disappear into thin air." She made a *poof* gesture with her fingers. "You come out someplace else."

Kal licked her lips. "They can do that?"

"The powerful ones like Lara can." Gabi kicked off her shoes and lay back on the bed, crossing her long legs. "Don't get on her bad side."

"We all just want to graduate," Elena said. "Find jobs and be free to live our lives. But everyone understands why security is tight. A few years ago, this asshole got inside the school pretending to be a delivery man and stabbed his ex-girlfriend. She had to go to the hospital."

"Shit," Kal muttered. "Did she live?"

"Yeah. The doctors saved her." Elena stabbed out her cigarette on the sill and tucked the butt into a small tin. "But Lara made sure he got a life sentence in the mines."

Kal had heard of that. Prisoners condemned to plumb the deepest, darkest shafts in the zones with high Sinn activity. Most of them didn't last long.

The man deserved it, but she didn't want to think about the mines. She chose a uniform from the wardrobe and excused herself to change in the bathroom. When she returned, her stomach was rumbling.

"Do you want to get some food?" she asked. "I'm starved."

Elena jumped up. "Sure! I'll show you the way. You coming, Gabi?"

The tall girl shook her head. "I have to study for a test tomorrow."

"Gabi's a genius," Elena whispered. "She just got admitted to the Merry Sharp Institute of Gemology in Kirith! The Lenormands are paying for everything."

Kal grinned, genuinely glad for her. "That's great. My—"

She about to say, *My brother goes to Faraday*, but stopped herself in the nick of time. She was Kyra Navarra from Lycaea now. Only child, now an orphan.

"My friend said that's a really good school," she replied instead.

Gabi nodded absently, deep in a textbook. Elena grabbed her jacket and breathed in Kal's face. "Do you smell smoke?"

"Um, yeah."

"Shit. I hope we don't run into any teachers." She made a face. "I should quit anyway. The cleaning lady who smuggled them in for me got fired last week. I'm almost out of cigs."

"They will kill you," Gabi said in her deadpan voice, not looking up from the book.

Elena gave a nervous whinny that reminded Kal of Durian

and herded Kal out the door. "We'll bring you something back, Gab!"

# CHAPTER 18

# CATHRYNNE

S he woke in an armchair, pulse galloping, the fiery afterimage imprinted on her eyes. It was the same dream as before. A faceless angel falling through blackness, wings trailing flame like twin comets.

"Cat." Gavriel shifted on the bed, sheets rustling as he murmured her name.

She leaned forward, stiff from hours of sitting vigil, and found his hand. It was ice cold. That alone told her something was very wrong.

"I'm here," she said.

Gavriel's green-gold eyes opened, dulled by whatever ailed him. The planes of his face looked more severe, shadows pooling in the hollows of his cheeks.

"How do you feel this morning?" she asked anxiously. "Worse?"

"Weak," he admitted, the single word clearly costing him effort. His mouth twitched into what might have been a smile. "But better now."

For days he had been like this, burning with cold, unable to eat more than a mouthful. They wrapped him in blankets, though he often threw them off in restless sleep. Other than the wasting, he had no other symptoms.

A knock made her tense, though she expected this visitor. Yarl had gone himself to the Angel Tower to fetch her.

"Enter," Cathrynne called, releasing Gavriel's hand.

The door opened and she tried to hide her surprise. She thought all archangels must be tall and imposing like Gavriel and his darkly handsome brother Raziel of Iskatar.

But the archangel of Satu Jos was small and youthful. She had waist-length snowy hair and alabaster skin. Her wings were also snowy white, making her sapphire eyes appear even more luminous in the dim light. Despite her petite stature, Haniel glided across the room with the grace of a being both ancient and powerful.

"Sister," Gavriel said, his voice stronger than it had been moments ago.

Pride, Cathrynne suspected.

Haniel's face betrayed nothing as she approached the bed. "Your secretary tells me you have not improved."

A seraphim healer had come from the Angel Tower the day before. She had found nothing wrong with him.

"I despise being ill," Gavriel muttered.

"You should have stayed with me," Haniel chided. "This manor you rented looks like a harem." Her gaze flicked briefly to Cathrynne. "It is beneath you, brother."

"Are you saying the décor is lethal?" Gavriel asked with a bit of his old spirit. "I'll grant that the gilt and marble is excessive, but the Sundland Room has rather grown on me."

It was the least lavish room in the house, with austere antique furnishings and wallpaper with a faded motif of snowflakes.

"You jest, but I am entirely serious." Haniel's cool gaze turned to Cathrynne again, settling this time. "Leave us, cypher. I will examine him myself."

Cathrynne decided that she did not like Haniel. And she was reluctant to leave Gavriel alone with anyone, even his sister.

Gavriel looked between them as the tension built. "Let Cypher Rowan stay," he said in a placating tone. "I don't mind. It is her job to guard me."

Haniel's lips tightened in displeasure. "As you wish." She moved to the opposite side of the bed and laid a palm against his forehead. She lifted the lids of his eyes, listened intently to his heart, and manipulated different parts of his wings.

"I fear there is a toxin in your blood," she said at last.

"What kind of toxin?" Gavriel demanded.

Her gaze grew puzzled. "I'm not certain. Perhaps you were infected in the Zamir Hills."

Cathrynne wondered if she was to blame. He had been pure before. Did the kiss corrupt him? Her fists clenched and she made herself loosen them.

Haniel produced a glass vial from her robes.

"What is that?" Gavriel asked.

"Meltwater from the snow at Mount Meru," she replied. "It has healing qualities."

Gavriel nodded and accepted a few sips. Haniel set the vial on the bedside table.

"See that he drinks the rest of it," she said, smoothing the dark hair back from his brow. The examination seemed to have exhausted his reserves. Gavriel's eyes closed again, his breathing turning shallow.

"He will recover," Haniel said serenely. "You should see improvement by morning. Have patience and let him rest."

After she left, Cathrynne sniffed the vial. It smelled like plain water. She returned to her chair, studying his face. He did not seem improved. The skin beneath his eyes looked bruised, the bones too prominent, as if something was consuming him from within.

ANOTHER WEEK CRAWLED BY, each day stealing more of Gavriel's strength. She measured time by the sharpening angles of his face. Haniel's promise had proven empty. He was fading faster now.

When she wasn't watching Gavriel struggle for breath, Cathrynne paced the bedchamber, wondering which of his enemies had found a way to break the unbreakable archangel.

"He's been poisoned," she said for the tenth time. "I'm certain of it."

"But when?" Yarl wondered. "And by who? I've prepared every morsel of food myself."

The scent of a bland vegetable broth filled the room, but even that made Gavriel turn his face to the wall.

"He was fine when we first got back from Pota Pras," Cathrynne said, chewing her lip. "It had to be afterwards."

"Casolaba's funeral?" Mercy suggested.

"I thought of that. No one came near him. I made certain of it."

"He seemed well until he retired that night," Mercy said. "Then he was sick by morning."

"Could someone have broken into his room?" Cathrynne asked.

"I don't think so. It's on the top floor, and I was outside the door all night. I made certain the windows were locked before he went to bed."

Yarl set the untouched broth on a sideboard. "That's what troubles me. By all logic, it seems impossible."

"Well, someone got to him," Cathrynne said. "I know they did!"

Gavriel stirred beneath the blankets. "I can hear you," he muttered, "talking about me as if I'm already gone."

She crossed to his bedside. "You're not going to die," she said firmly. "But you can turn that clever brain of yours to some use. Any ideas?"

Before he could reply, they heard voices outside. Yarl drew the curtain aside and peered out the window to the courtyard below. "It's the Morag," he announced. "With a delegation of witches."

Gavriel struggled to sit up, mouth setting in a stubborn line. "Tell them to go away," he growled. His gaze was pleading. "Please, Cathrynne. I don't trust them."

She didn't trust them, either. Any one of them might be the poisoner. But she was only a cypher, as low in the witch hierarchy as you could get, and she wasn't sure Isbail Rosach would listen.

Plus, she had ignored a series of red-eyed crows that came and pecked at the windows of the manor house. Isbail Rosach was probably quite annoyed with her.

"Stay and keep watch over him," she said to Mercy and marched down the stairs.

The Morag waited on the doorstep with an escort that included the enigmatic head of the cyphers, Marvel Yew, along with two White Foxes. Cathrynne felt sure she'd never met them before. One had rings in her lips, nose, and both eyebrows, each glittering with a small gem. The other was heavyset and unshaven. He had dark circles under his silver eyes and looked haggard. Cathrynne met their cold gazes, then addressed herself to the Morag.

"Please come in, mum," Cathrynne said, steering the group into the library.

"Where is Lord Morningstar?" the Morag demanded before the door had even closed. "He hasn't been seen at the Red House in over a week."

"He's indisposed at the moment, mum," Cathrynne replied.

"*Indisposed*," the Morag repeated. "Is he aware that the consul's aide, Levi Bottas, has vanished?"

"Ah . . ."

"Either Bottas is another victim, or he is Casolaba's killer and his guilty conscience has driven him to flee. But the man must be found. If Lord Morningstar is unfit to carry out his commission, we will appoint someone else to lead it."

She knew Gavriel would rather die than give up his appointment, as ludicrous as that might be. "He's not unfit, mum. Just suffering from a case of the flu."

"Then let the Morag see him," the female White Fox said. "Let Morningstar tell her himself that he is fit to continue."

Her accent was hard to place, just vaguely southern. "And you are?" Cathrynne asked.

She scowled. "My name is Ash Razum."

"How about you?" She turned to the other White Fox.

"My name is none of your business, cypher," he growled, flashing a set of metal teeth. This time, Cathrynne caught a distinct Kievad Rus accent. It was the same as the ambassador Gavriel had interviewed.

The Morag raised a quelling hand. "I would like to see Morningstar myself," she said. "To discuss these new developments."

Cathrynne held her gaze steadily. "That won't be possible, mum, as he is sleeping right now."

The Morag shook her head in disgust. "At the least, you shall tell me what happened in Pota Pras."

Cathrynne sensed the White Foxes pricking their ears up.

"We didn't make much headway," she said regretfully. "Lord Morningstar spoke with Durian Padulski's mother. She said he'd found something unusual in the hills and planned to sell it in the city, but she didn't know any more about it."

"What about *where* he'd found it?" Ash Razum exclaimed.

Cathrynne answered to the Morag. "She knew nothing."

"Perhaps the boy is a dead end." The Morag's lips pursed. "Lord Morningstar shall have one more day to *rest*. We shall return tomorrow for his response."

The delegation left. Cathrynne bolted the door and made sure the White Foxes had disappeared down the street before dashing up the stairs to rejoin Mercy and Yarl in the sickroom.

"They're gone," she announced, catching her breath.

Gavriel nodded wearily. "Thank you."

Cathrynne quickly related the encounter. It had given her an idea. "We need to go back to the beginning," she said. "The boy was killed first. By lithomancy."

Mercy nodded. "I saw the body. I'm certain of it."

"Which makes Bottas more likely to be a third victim," Yarl ventured.

"He must have known something," Cathrynne said. "Maybe even who did it. And the killer decided he was too much of a risk."

"So he was eliminated," Mercy said. "But what about Durian? If a witch murdered him, how did they know what he'd found?"

"Because someone told them," Cathrynne said. When she and Gavriel had visited Casolaba's mistress, she'd noticed cheap hostels along the riverbank. "Durian and his friend must have stayed somewhere when they came to the city. I'll shake some trees and see what falls out."

Mercy gave a grim nod. "Do what needs to be done." She glanced at the gaunt figure on the bed. "I'll watch over him."

———

CATHRYNNE SCOURED the hostels near the Corniche, asking questions of anyone who worked there. The first seven denied seeing a young man with a birthmark on his face, but at the eighth, the barkeep gave her a flat look.

"Don't want trouble with the witches," he said.

"All I need is information." She slid several gemstones across the bar. He hefted them in a palm.

"Those are hot with ley," she said. "Guaranteed."

His brows rose. The gems disappeared into his apron pocket. "They stayed one night. Couple of weeks ago. Didn't see them after, but I read about the boy in the papers. Shame, that." He paused. "Do you want to see the ledger? I got proof."

She shook her head. "It's okay. Did they talk about where else they'd gone in the city?"

"No, but they were sitting at the table next to Rafi." He nodded his chin at a huge man with a forked beard hunched over a glass in the corner. "Maybe he heard something."

Cathrynne thanked him and ordered another round of Rafi's favorite drink, which the newly rich and chatty bartender explained was called a Spiked Admiral, named after a horned species of desert Sinn. She brought it over and slid into the seat across from him.

"A present," she said, sliding the frothy glass across the table.

Rafi sneered. "Piss off."

Cathrynne unwrapped the bandage from her left hand and gave the fingers an experimental flex. The bruises were almost entirely faded. Angus Valinger had done an excellent job resetting the bones.

Rafi stared at the raven tattoo below her knuckles. The sneer turned to hatred.

"Listen, bitch, I have nothing to say—"

Cathrynne grabbed his beard and slammed his cheek down on the scarred table.

"You can't—" he spluttered.

"I'm not from here," she said softly, using an elbow to keep him pinned. "So I don't give a damn about your civil rights. File all the complaints you want. Now, quiet down and you can have that drink, plus another one."

He stopped struggling. "What do you want?" he asked from the corner of his mouth. It sounded like wuh-oo-un?

Cathyrnne eased up a little. "There were two kids in here a while back. One drowned. You probably read about it in the gossip rags."

He said nothing.

"You were sitting next to them. I want to know where they went, who they talked to."

He grunted. "Damn, psycho, just let me up."

She sat back. Rafi smoothed his beard and shot an affronted look at the bartender, who nodded.

"Look, all I heard was some jeweler on Beryl Street. They thought he'd ripped them off or something."

"Which jeweler?"

A shrug. "The kid didn't say a name."

She unhooked the whip from her belt and gave it an expert flick. The loud pop nearly made Rafi piss himself.

"D'Amico, okay!" he exclaimed. "Travian's bones, that's all I know."

"Thank you." Cathrynne stood up and dropped another gem on the table. She left him nursing his two drinks and asked the bartender for directions to Beryl Street. It wasn't far, but it stretched for twelve blocks and had dozens of jewelers. She couldn't find any called D'Amico, but inquiries confirmed that there was a jeweler named Simão Gomes D'Amato.

When he saw her through the front window and rushed to lock the door, she knew she'd found the right place.

"I've had a long day," Cathrynne said, forcing her way inside. "Don't make it longer."

"We're closed," he said, visibly shaking.

"Not quite yet you're not," she replied, pointing to the beaded curtain leading into a back room.

He retreated into a small, cluttered office, sweating profusely. She noticed a black telephone on the desk.

"I know that Kal Machena and Durian Padulski were here," Cathrynne said, "so don't waste my time denying it."

His complexion turned ashen. "I had nothing to do with that boy's death. It happened after he left!"

"Sit," she ordered. D'Amato slumped into a chair behind his desk. "Maybe you didn't kill Durian, but you tipped off the one who did. Am I right?"

He swallowed hard, eyes darting around.

"Whose payroll are you on?" she demanded.

"The Freedom Party," he said quickly—too quickly. "About

half the jewelers in the district reported to Consul Casolaba. We were supposed to keep an eye out for anything interesting or unusual. The rest spy for the Miners' Union. I mean, everyone does it!"

D'Amato held her gaze, aiming for outraged innocence. Cathrynne believed him, yet she sensed it was a partial truth.

"But that's not all, is it?" she said softly. "There's someone else you reported to. A little double-dipping."

Jowls wobbled as he shook his head. "No, no."

Cathrynne thought of Gavriel, fading away in his bed. She rose abruptly and grabbed D'Amato by the collar, dragging him across the desk. Stacks of papers avalanched to the floor. "Tell me about the gems. Why were they special?"

"The girl called them kaldurite! They look like serpent's eye, but they . . ." He trailed off, looking terrified.

She shook him, their faces almost touching. His hair smelled strongly of pomade. "They what?"

"They repel the ley."

She frowned. "How?"

"I don't know! They just do. I've hears rumors, but it's the first time I've seen any." His words came in a rush. "I bought a few samples. The kids left and I never saw them again, I swear!"

Cathrynne released him. "Show me the gems."

He shrank away. "I gave them all to Casolaba."

"No. You would have kept at least one for yourself. Because the other person, the one whose name you won't give up, is a witch. And you needed to protect yourself just in case."

The startled look on his face confirmed her guess.

D'Amato thrust a clammy hand into his pocket. "You can't use lithomancy on me!" he squealed.

Cathrynne's jaw set. "I don't need to."

The tussle was brief. She pried his fingers open and extracted a small gem that shifted from blue to purple to red as it caught the light. The moment it touched her skin, awareness of the ley vanished. It was like going blind or deaf. A critical sense was simply gone.

Nausea twisted her stomach. A wave of dizziness made the room spin. She dry-heaved, steadying herself against the edge of the desk. D'Amato seized his chance and darted past her, light on his feet for a paunchy middle-aged man. She heard the shop door open and close. The kaldurite slipped from her fingers.

Within a minute, the sickness passed. Once again, she sensed the ley in her pouch. The ley that coursed through her own blood, courtesy of her angelic father.

"Blessed Minerva," she said, staring down at the gemstone lying at her feet.

Everything made sense now.

---

CATHRYNNE HAD the feeling of being shadowed on her way back to the townhouse, but she saw no one. She'd wrapped the gemstone in a piece of velvet and stowed it in an empty jewel box. That seemed enough to dull the effect so she could carry it in her pocket.

She pounded on the front door until Mercy threw the bolt. Then she raced up the stairs to Gavriel's bedchamber. He lay so still she feared the worst, but when she touched his shoulder, he stirred slightly, then lapsed again into unconsciousness. His skin was gray.

"Found something?" Mercy asked.

Cathrynne tossed her the jeweler's box. She caught it one-handed and took out the stone—then flinched. "What *is* that?" Mercy threw it to the carpet, her mouth drawn down in revulsion.

"That," Cathrynne said, "is what's killing Gavriel."

"What's killing Lord Morningstar?" Yarl came in.

"It's called kaldurite," she explained. "A gem that repels the ley. Pick it up."

Yarl did so. He held the stone to the lamp, watching it shift from sapphire to ruby. "It's extraordinary," he said softly.

"Do you feel anything?" Cathrynne asked.

He frowned. "No."

"It must be because you're human. When I touch it, I feel a bit sick." She looked down at Gavriel. "But his blood is almost pure ley. We need to search his body."

"What if he swallowed it?" Yarl looked stricken.

"I think he would already be dead. Come, help me. It will be small, hidden somewhere against his skin."

They removed his shirt, which had laced vents to accommodate his wings. Gavriel was a strong man, his chest solidly built, but she could count his ribs. When Yarl removed his trousers, she and Mercy turned their backs. Minutes passed.

"I cannot find anything," Yarl said, frustration in his voice.

"Lay the sheet over him," Cathrynne said. "It must be there."

She heard the rustle of cotton. "Mercy, help me turn him on his side."

Together, they managed to roll Gavriel over. Beneath his shoulder blades was a second set of scapulae. His wings extended from those. Cathrynne ran her fingers carefully along each feather, starting with the small coverts and moving downward to the primary flight feathers, probing for anything foreign. Near the joint where wing met shoulder, nestled among soft down, she encountered something hard and smooth.

The moment she touched it, the ley vanished. She gasped and instinctively drew her hand back. Gavriel moaned.

"Careful," Yarl warned. "His feathers are rooted in the bone. Pulling one out is like pulling a tooth. I am not certain he can survive the shock."

She nodded and parted the feathers, ignoring the queasy feeling in her stomach when she touched the kaldurite. It was the size of a thumbnail, affixed to feathers and skin with a tarry adhesive.

"How did it get there?" Mercy asked.

Cathrynne worked the stone loose, picking it away from the adhesive. "Someone must have come in while he slept."

Mercy shook her head. "I told you, no one entered this room."

Cathrynne gave the stone to Yarl, who added it to the jeweler's box. Her fingers still tingled from the contact, as if she had brushed the scales of a dozing serpent.

"I woke up at three thirty-three exactly," she said. "I remember looking at the clock. Maybe I heard something."

At those words, Yarl seemed to age ten years in an instant. He sat down in the chair next to Gavriel's bed, staring at nothing.

"What is it?" Mercy asked, laying a hand on his shoulder.

He had not shaved in several days. A hand stole to his chin and rubbed the white beard sprouting there. "Haniel . . . She is an Angel of the Hours," he said.

"What does that mean?" Cathrynne had never heard the term.

Yarl glanced at the clock. It was five after nine. "She has great power at certain times of day. The mirror hours. Five fifty-five. Ten-ten. Eleven-eleven . . ."

"Three thirty-three," Cathrynne said, her gut sinking.

Yarl nodded. "For that minute, she can move through time and space as if it were frozen. If she came here, she might have walked right past us and no one would remember her presence."

Mercy muttered a curse. "Haniel examined him, didn't she? She probably made sure the kaldurite was still in place, still hidden."

Cathrynne eyed the open window. It was growing dark out. She stood up and closed the sash, then drew the curtains.

"Hanirl knew about the journey to Pota Pras, too, which neither of us had mentioned."

*Perhaps you were infected in the Zamir Hills.*

A cold worm of dread burrowed into her heart. If the archangel of Satu Jos wanted Gavriel dead . . .

"We need to get him out of this province immediately," Cathrynne said. "Haniel must have killed Casolaba too. Hung him from the dome when their partnership went wrong."

"I'll fetch a diligence," Yarl said, heading for the door.

Mercy shook her head in amazement. "Is there anyone—*anyone*—in Kota Gelangi who isn't part of this fucking conspiracy?"

## CHAPTER 19
# CATHRYNNE

The rooftop gave a wide vista of both the skies above and the streets below. Cathrynne crouched in the shadow of the wall, a chunk of antimony in her right palm. Bats swooped around her head, hunting insects, but she was watching for something larger and more purposeful—something like armored seraphim gliding through the darkness with murderous intent.

If Haniel knew the kaldurite had been found, she would try to kill Gavriel some other way. And this time she might succeed.

The first truly bitter night of the southern winter had arrived in gusting flurries of snow. Cathrynne's fingers were stiff as she examined Yarl's pocket watch: 9:55.

She blew out an impatient breath, watching the white fog dissipate. Ten-ten, the mirror hour when Haniel had the power to come and go unseen, was drawing near.

Yarl had left to hire a coach nearly an hour ago, heading to the train station where drivers congregated all night. What could be taking him so long? What if he had been captured? Interrogated?

Dire scenarios were filling her head when a large coach rounded the corner. It was a diligence, enclosed and sturdy, designed for long-distance travel. It halted before the townhouse and Yarl stepped out. He tilted his head, searching the roofline. Cathrynne raised her hand in a quick wave. Relief washed through her as she flew down the stairs.

Mercy waited at Gavriel's bedside. "He's no better," she said grimly.

The kaldurite had been glued to his wing for almost two weeks, devouring his strength. It made Cathrynne furious to think she had sat next to him all that time with no clue that the cause of his ailment was within arm's reach.

"It's not too late," she said stubbornly. "We can still save him. But we must get him out of Satu Jos." She glanced at the window. "Yarl found a diligence. He's waiting outside."

"Thank Minerva," Mercy said with quiet feeling.

Together, they positioned Gavriel on a makeshift sling made of a blanket. Cathrynne ensured his wings were tucked against his body. He was too fragile to withstand another shock.

"On three," she said, taking his shoulders while Mercy moved to his feet. "One, two—"

They lifted together, grunting with effort. Gavriel was still a big man. Add in his towering wings and he was not a light burden.

"Stairs will be tricky," Mercy muttered, backing toward the door. "You want to go first or shall I?"

"I'll take the lead." Cathrynne adjusted her grip. "Watch the frame."

They maneuvered him through the opening, Cathrynne walking backward. The descent down the stairs was a grueling exercise in coordination. Halfway down, Mercy's foot caught on the carpet, nearly sending them all tumbling.

"Careful," Cathrynne hissed.

"Trying," Mercy snapped back. "Not exactly a featherweight, is he? Ironic, that."

They reached the bottom landing, both breathing hard. The grandfather clock in the foyer read 10:06. As they shuffled across the entryway, the front door swung open. "Quickly," Yarl said, glancing at the sky. He lowered his voice. "I paid the driver well, but his courage may not last if questioned by seraphim."

The caracals turned their heads at Cathrynne and Mercy's approach, long, tufted ears twitching. The driver tipped his cap. "I am Lucio Tavora. I will get you across the border, never fear."

Years of working the streets had made Cathrynne a quick study of character. Lucio Tavora had a bluff, honest face and calloused hands from years of handling the reins.

"Thank you, Master Tavora," she said. "Perhaps you can help us?"

"Of course!" He leapt down from the bench. Together they maneuvered Gavriel's limp form through the carriage door and onto one of the long, cushioned seats. Mercy and Yarl climbed in after. Cathrynne hesitated, scanning the skies one last time.

No winged shapes eclipsed the moon. No shadows crept along the walls.

"Come, Rowan," Yarl called softly. "It's 10:08."

She joined them in the carriage, and the driver clicked his tongue. The team of six muscular caracals sprang forward, the diligence picking up speed as it reached the broad, straight avenue of Rua Capitolana.

"Where are we headed?" Mercy asked, bracing herself as they rounded another corner.

"Arjevica," Yarl replied. "We will bring him to his sister, Suriel."

"The archangel of Kievad Rus?" Cathrynne bit her lip, worried. "What makes you think this one can be trusted?"

"Suriel favors him," Yarl replied. "She is dangerous, but not to her brother. And she despises Haniel. There is no chance they are conspiring together."

"Why does she hate Haniel?" Cathrynne asked, somewhat mollified.

"I cannot say, but they are very different. Haniel shuns political intrigue—or pretends to—while Suriel thrives on it. And of course, their provinces are ancient rivals."

"Short of Mount Meru, another Angel Tower is the only place he'll be safe," Mercy agreed. "Kirith is too far away. But Arjevica is just over the border."

Cathrynne had not been to the Rus capital since she was taken from her childhood home at the age of eleven. She'd never expected to see it again, but getting Gavriel to a sanctuary where he could heal was all that mattered now.

Ten past ten came and went. She took out the pocket watch again and watched the minute hand creep around the dial, half-expecting the carriage door to swing open and reveal Haniel's grinning face. Or worse, to see nothing at all; to blink and discover Gavriel dead or vanished from the coach. But the mirror hour of 11:11 passed without incident, and the caracals continued their steady lope through the streets.

The diligence passed the diplomatic quarter, and then the fruit and vegetable market, its stalls shuttered for the night. Finally, they reached the outskirts of Kota Gelangi and the main east-west road that ran all the way to Bactra.

The next mirror hour—12:12—slipped by, yet Cathrynne felt no relief. Gavriel lay motionless, his breathing so shallow she could barely see his chest rise and fall. Heartsick, she took his hand. It felt frigid, and she chafed his fingers, tried to lend him her warmth.

Across from her, Yarl reached into his coat pocket and withdrew the jeweler's box she had taken from D'Amato. He lifted the lid and the kaldurite's chill sparkle filled the carriage. Just a tiny shard had nearly killed an archangel.

"We will give it to Suriel as proof of this murder attempt," he said, an edge of anger in his voice. "She will tell their father Valoriel, and he will see that justice is done."

THE ROAD to Kievad Rus wound through the southern reaches of the Zamir Hills, which were thickly forested. Sleet lashed the coach windows, turning the world beyond into a blur of shadow. It was the middle of the night by now, and they saw no other conveyances on the road.

Mercy seized her chance to doze off, but Cathrynne felt too wired to sleep. At each mirror hour—1:11, 2:22, 3:33—she braced for the worst. But Haniel never appeared. She must not know of their escape yet. Perhaps she was confident her ploy had worked. After all, the stone had gone undiscovered for nearly a fortnight. Another day or two, and Cathrynne felt sure it would have finished him.

But he was not meant to die in that bed. He had another destiny.

Her eyes glazed over and she saw Julia Camara's face through the bars of the kloster.

*"When he falls from grace, you must not interfere. You must let him serve his penance, even if it lasts forever."*

*"Penance for what? And why would I interfere?"*

*The seer's eyes held a glint of pity. "Because you love him."*

She tried to shake off the memory, but a small, terrible voice wondered if she was doing the right thing. What if Gavriel died before he committed whatever crime lay in the future? Would she spare the world the upheaval the Morag promised?

She rubbed her forehead. Too many tangled dreams. Too many visions she could not make sense of. But the man lying with his head in her lap was real. And she knew in her heart that she could not let him die, no matter what it cost.

Cathrynne counted Gavriel's labored breaths and tried to work through the events of the last week. The value of kaldurite was obvious. For an ambitious man like Casolaba, if he could get enough of it, he might make himself a king. There had been kings and queens in Sion once, very long ago. Cathrynne learned that in her history classes, though she'd never paid close attention in school.

Perhaps Casolaba and Haniel had been in league together, and then had a falling out. It was also obvious why angels would not want the existence of kaldurite to be widely known—it could kill them.

As for the witches . . . well, it would give one faction an edge over the other. Plus, if the witches failed to control the kaldurite supply, they could easily be defeated by a human army.

She thought of what Gavriel had said when they hiked through the hills to Red Dog Camp.

*I see all the tiny fractures running through Sion, and watch them widen every year. The ancient balances of power are shifting.*

Kaldurite, if someone possessed it in abundance, would more than shift that balance. It would overturn it completely.

"We're making good time despite the weather," Yarl observed, breaking into her dark musings. "We should reach the border before dawn—"

The coach slowed, then lurched to a stop. "What now?" Mercy growled, waking in an instant.

"Stay here," Cathrynne said. "I'll have a look."

She readied a projective gemstone in her fist. Then she opened the door and jumped down into frozen mud. Wind drove the sleet sideways, stinging her eyes. She walked to the front of the diligence, where the driver climbed down to meet her. Frost rimed the brim of his hat.

"We need to haul that out of the way," he said, pointing to a large tree branch blocking the road.

Cathrynne approached warily, but it wasn't a clean cut. The thick part of the branch looked jagged. Dead wood. The storm must have broken it off.

She was bending to drag it to the side of the road when she caught a faint whiff of char. One of the caracals growled low in its throat.

She knew that smell. It was the same one from the Nilssons' living room.

She threw a blast of projective magic into the trees. An

instant later, she was lifted up and hurled bodily against the coach. The impact drove the breath from her lungs. She lay there in the frozen mud, gasping silently, until a strong hand dragged her underneath.

"Poxy bastards," Mercy grumbled, hurling a spell of her own into the trees. She lay belly-down in the frozen mud next to Cathrynne. "It has to be the Jennies."

Cathrynne dug into her own gem pouch, seeking a particular stone. She knew them all by touch alone, and red jasper made her think of lions and archers. Like an arrow in flight, it kept its potency over long distances. Her fingers found a chunk and she threw another battering wave of ley into the trees.

"I think they forced here." Cathrynne whispered. "Got ahead of us and set a trap."

Another onslaught came from the forest. The coach rocked violently and the caracals yowled in their traces.

"One more direct hit and it might roll," Mercy warned.

Cathrynne thought of Gavriel and his elderly secretary inside the coach. The diligence was large and heavy. Once it tipped, they'd never be able to right it again.

"Hang on." Mercy ducked back into the diligence, emerging seconds later. "Get Morningstar across the border," she said. "I'll find you in Arjevica."

Cathrynne stared. "What? I'm not leaving you behind!"

Mercy grinned, her teeth white in the darkness. She held up the kaldurite, the stone shifting colors in the gloom. "What can they do to me?"

"I'll stay," Cathrynne insisted. "Give me the stone. You go with Morningstar—"

Another blast of ley knocked her back into the icy mud. She clawed her way up, ears buzzing and little jolts of electricity dancing along her skin.

Mercy stood untouched, her blue-gray eyes stormy. "Go, Cathrynne. Gavriel needs you. I'll catch up."

She strode to the branch blocking the road, grabbed it one-handed, and hurled it aside. Then she plunged into the dark woods.

Cathrynne didn't waste a precious second. She forced herself to stand and found the driver, who was hiding behind the bench.

"Road's clear," she whispered. "But we have to go *now*."

Lucio Tavora gave a frightened nod. He clambered back onto his seat, hands shaking as he took up the reins. Cathrynne jumped aboard as the caracals raced away. Lithomantic bursts lit the trees behind them. She watched the bend in the road recede through the sleet-frosted window.

Mercy would come out on top. She always did.

Cathrynne's jaw tightened. She felt sure it was the White Foxes, and the witches they recruited were always the strongest. The most merciless. She swore angrily and touched her split lip.

Yarl took a handkerchief from his coat pocket. "Here."

She pressed the linen against her mouth. "I shouldn't have let that jeweler escape. He must have run straight to his masters."

"Or they tracked us another way," Yarl agreed. "Mercy Blackthorn is a brave woman. I hope her gamble pays off."

"So do I," Cathrynne said.

———

Several hours passed. The coach slowed again and Yarl peered out the window. "The border," he said. "We're nearly there."

Cathrynne drew open the curtain. Dawn had broken. Through the window, she saw a suspension bridge above a river. Customs posts stood on either side, flags snapping in the wind. The Satu Jos banner—a flame rising from a forge—faced off against the rook standard of Kievad Rus.

A railroad trestle also crossed the gorge. A train had stopped and officials moved through the brightly-lit cars, checking identity cards. Cathrynne could see the passengers' bored, sleepy faces through the windows.

The diligence halted at the customs post and a guard in the brown uniform of Satu Jos peered inside.

Yarl leaned forward. "We have urgent business in Kievad Rus. This is a diplomatic mission."

The guard's face was impassive. "Even diplomats require transit papers with the proper seals."

"Do you not recognize Lord Gavriel Morningstar, archangel of Kirith?" Yarl demanded. "He requires immediate medical attention. We were waylaid by bandits on the road."

The guard's hand rested on his sidearm as he studied Cathrynne's silver eyes. "All the more reason to verify your identities." Two more guards appeared behind him. A nod and whispered word from the first, and the men went running off. "I'm afraid I can't allow you to leave Satu Jos without clearance from the Angel Tower in Kota Gelangi."

Cathrynne surveyed the post, calculating how fast she could incapacitate the guards before the shooting started. Not good odds, since she couldn't risk Gavriel getting hit.

Yarl's face darkened. "Listen carefully. I am Edvin Yarl, secretary to Lord Morningstar. If you prevent his passage, you will answer directly to Mount Meru. Would you like to explain to Valoriel himself why his son was delayed?"

The guard seemed unmoved.

"I can arrange for you to be personally escorted to the Summerlord's presence," Yarl continued. "I'm certain he would be fascinated to hear why a lowly border official thought his authority superseded that of an archangel."

A new voice cut through the tension. "What seems to be the problem?"

A woman in the navy uniform of Kievad Rus was approaching across the bridge. An officer's insignia gleamed on her collar.

"These travelers claim diplomatic status but have no papers, captain," the Satu Jos guard admitted grudgingly. "A cypher, a human, and an angel. One of them is injured. Who knows what mischief they've been up to?"

The captain's eyes flicked to the interior of the coach, lingering on Gavriel's slumped form. Recognition sharpened her eyes. "That is indeed Lord Morningstar, and Suriel is expecting him," she said. "I'll take responsibility for them. Kievad Rus welcomes the archangel and his party."

The guards exchanged glances, still uneasy.

"Unless you'd prefer to make this a more serious incident?" the captain added. "I can call Suriel herself—"

The men stepped back, defeated. "They can pass."

Cathrynne heaved a sigh of relief as the coach rolled forward again, wheels rumbling over the wooden planks of the bridge.

"Thank you for intervening," Yarl said to the Rus captain, who walked alongside.

She nodded. "Lord Morningstar is ill?"

"He needs his sister's aid," Yarl replied, keeping Gavriel's condition deliberately vague. "But she will be grateful. What is your name?"

"Captain Von Hahn."

"I will tell her."

Once they reached the other side and passed the rook standard, some of the tension leached from Cathrynne's shoulders. "A cypher named Mercy Blackthorn is following behind us," she said to Captain Von Hahn. "Will you see that she is allowed across the border?"

"I can do that." She eyed them all with reserved curiosity, as though she wanted to ask more questions—but might be better off not knowing the answers. "Shall I send word ahead to Angel Tower?"

"Yes, please," Yarl replied. "Ask them to have healers ready."

The captain gave a brief salute and waved them past the checkpoint. Cathrynne sat back. Mercy *would* come to Arjevica. And if she didn't . . . Well, Cathrynne would hunt those White Foxes to the ends of the earth.

THEY PAUSED ONCE to rest the caracals and wolf down a quick meal at a roadside inn. Gavriel's condition remained unchanged, but he didn't seem worse. It was dark again by the time they reached the Angel Tower. Cathrynne Rowan stared up at the golden cupola. In twenty years as a cypher, she had never set foot inside one.

"Here we are," Lucio Tavora said, his good humor returned now that they had reached their destination.

The man had not uttered a word of complaint, even after the harrowing attack on the road. Now he jumped down from his perch and opened the door with a bow.

Yarl untied his purse and took out a stack of dragha bills. "The remainder of your payment. And additional for the hazards you and your cats faced."

Tavora waved it away. "The agreed upon fare is sufficient, Master Yarl. There are always passengers looking for transport back to Kota Gelangi. I am sure to fill the seats."

"You're certain?"

"Quite." Tavora glanced at Gavriel's still form, his expression growing serious. "It was an honor to serve the Morningstar. Should you require my services again, you need only seek me out."

Together, the three of them eased Gavriel from the carriage. His wings dragged on the wet pavement, the onyx feathers dull. Before they'd taken a step toward the gate, it swung open. Four seraphim emerged, brusquely taking charge of Gavriel. In the moonlight, their faces were like living statues, devoid of compassion or any emotion at all.

"Wait," Cathrynne said, a flutter of panic rising in her chest. "I should—"

"Let them," Yarl murmured, as Tavora clucked his tongue and drove off.

She lowered her voice to a bare whisper, remembering

Mercy's warning about angelic hearing. "I don't trust anyone but you, Edvin."

He squeezed her hand. "The feeling is mutual. But only his own kind can save him now."

They followed the seraphim into the tower. It had pearly walls that seemed to glow from within. The central chamber soared upward, a dizzying spiral that made her head swim. The seraphim carrying Gavriel flew upward. Cathrynne and Yarl followed along a stairway that hugged the curving inner walls.

"Suriel is the oldest archangel living," he said softly. "She wields great authority. Haniel would not dare to cross her, and she certainly would not set foot within this tower uninvited."

Cathrynne nodded distractedly, trying to ignore the seraphim who had stopped to stare at the human and cypher invading their inner sanctum. For the sake of Gavriel's elderly secretary, she hoped they would not have to climb to the top. But at the third landing, a tall, golden-winged figure awaited them.

Suriel, the archangel of Kievad Rus, was as beautiful as her brother was handsome, like a statue cast from burnished dark bronze. She wore a simple white turban and gown of pale ivory cut to expose her smooth brown shoulders. Her shrewd eyes fixed on Gavriel, who dangled limply from the arms of the seraphim.

"What has happened?" she demanded.

The timbre of her voice made Cathrynne think of spiced rum and woodland mosses, with a seductive swirl of opium smoke.

Yarl bowed. "He has been poisoned, my lady."

"Poisoned?" Suriel's delicate brows knit. "With what?"

"A stone called kaldurite. It repels the ley."

The archangel's face hardened, but she did not seem shocked. "Come," she said.

They followed her into an octagonal chamber of naked stone and a few sparse furnishings. Suriel gestured for the seraphim to lay Gavriel on a backless sofa of dark blue velvet. "Fetch Asmod-el," she commanded. The angels flew off.

She knelt beside Gavriel, her gown pooling on the floor. "Who would have the temerity to do such a thing?"

Yarl swallowed. "I fear it was Haniel," he said.

Suriel's head snapped up. "Haniel? Are you certain?"

"No one else came in contact with Lord Morningstar for at least twelve hours before he fell ill," Yarl said. "She is the only one who could have entered his bedchamber unnoticed."

Suriel merely stared at him, and Cathrynne wondered what she was thinking.

"Very brief contact with kaldurite may be tolerable for angels," Cathrynne added, "but prolonged exposure leads to death. We're certain it was her who hid it within his wing feathers."

"Where is this stone now?"

"We don't have it anymore, my lady. Yarl gave it to my part-ner, Mercy Blackthorn. We were attacked in the forest by witches. White Foxes, I think. She stayed behind to fight them off."

Suriel's full lips pressed into a line. "So you have no proof of this claim."

"It is connected to the death of Consul Casolaba," Yarl said quickly. "And a boy from Pota Pras. Haniel might be behind those deaths, as well."

Skepticism tinged her voice. "Yet you were attacked by White Foxes?"

Yarl hesitated. "We did not see them."

"But they worked lithomancy," Cathrynne added.

"This conspiracy runs deep," Yarl said. "We are still wading through the shallows. But this latest attempt to kill Lord Morn-ingstar is without a doubt connected to his investigation."

Suriel studied Gavriel's ashen face, deep in thought. Finally, she turned to Yarl. "You will tell me everything that transpired since your arrival in Kota Gelangi." Her gaze shifted to

Cathrynne, cooling somewhat. "Thank you for bringing my brother to safety. But I will not permit a witch—or half witch—to remain in my tower."

Cathrynne had expected the dismissal, but it stung none-theless. "I understand," she said stiffly. "I'll report to the local chapter house." She paused. "Just tell me, can you save him?"

"I will do everything in my power," Suriel replied. "His will is strong. If anyone can return from the brink, it is Gavriel."

Yarl gave Cathrynne a small nod, his eyes communicating silent gratitude. Another seraphim appeared—presumably the Asmodel that Suriel had summoned. With a bow and last glance at the motionless body on the couch, Cathrynne turned and descended the spiral staircase alone. She had done her duty. It was better this way. There was nothing she could do to help him now, and to remain in his presence would only risk exposing the feelings she desperately wished would go away. Once Mercy turned up at the chapter house, they should both return to Kirith.

Yet the thought of Kal Machena out there somewhere, running for her life, made Cathrynne hesitate. It felt cowardly, abandoning the girl to her fate. She scrubbed a hand across her eyes. She was too tired to think straight. A good night's rest and she would decide what to do.

Outside, Arjevica's streets lay empty. It was warmer here than in the hills. Puddles of rain dotted the wide boulevards that ran outward from the Angel Tower like the spokes of a wheel. A seraphim at the gate gave her directions to the chapter house.

Funny how the city was both familiar and strange. Several times, she recognized a landmark—the ballet, for instance—but a few streets later, everything seemed foreign. The lanes grew narrower and lined with dark shops. She must have taken a wrong turn. The seraphim said it was only about a twenty-minute walk and she had been going for longer than that.

She was looking for someone to ask when the purr of an engine broke the quiet. Headlights swept the wet cobblestones.

The car slowed. When she saw it was a Jentzen Mirage, Cathrynne fisted a stone.

The car pulled alongside. The driver's side window rolled down. A male witch with short dark hair graying at the temples and blandly attractive features leaned out, one arm casually resting on the door.

"Get in," he said in a reasonable tone. "I'll give you a lift to the chapter house."

"Piss off." She kept walking.

The Mirage kept pace, driving slowly alongside. "We don't have to be on opposite sides of this, Cathrynne."

She glanced over at him. "Is that why you sent your thugs?"

He smiled. "I just want to talk. That's all."

At the end of the street, headlights flared as a second Mirage braked hard and skidded in sideways, blocking her path. The Kievad Rus versions of Lump and Crump emerged. Ash, with her candy-red hair and face full of jewelry, and her hulking metal-toothed partner.

Cathrynne backed away to keep them all in view.

Ash slammed the door. "I've got this, Kane," she snapped, then turned to Cathrynne. "Don't be stupid, cypher. Just get in the car—"

Cathrynne flicked her whip. It wrapped around the witch's ankle. With a yank, she jerked her off balance. Ash yelped and hit the ground hard.

The street erupted in bursts of ley. Cathrynne threw herself down as a gust of invisible force blew her hair back. She answered with obsidian, slamming Kane against the windshield hard enough to crack it.

He wasn't down long. Silver teeth flashed as he grinned, and then a shield snapped into place. The bastard didn't wear the caps as a fashion statement. Silver had protective qualities. She sensed sunstone igniting. A hammer of air knocked her backward. She twisted and managed to keep her feet.

Cathrynne lowered her head and charged. Kane dodged at

the last second and her cudgel glanced off his shoulder, drawing a pained grunt. But Ash was back, and so was the older male witch from the car. They swarmed her. Something struck her temple. Lights exploded behind her eyes, then she was being dragged across the road and stuffed into a small space. The trunk. Panic nearly made her black out.

The last thing Cathrynne heard was the screech of tires as the car sped away.

## CHAPTER 20

# KAL

S he gazed at her reflection in the bathroom mirror, barely recognizing the woman who stared back. Her curly hair had been bleached and frosted pink at the tips. Sparkly powders and creams made her brown eyes bigger and her lips poutier. She practically *glowed*.

The aptitude test had not gone well. Unfortunately, swashbuckling captain of a merchant ship wasn't on the list of careers. She could have aced the questions to be a gem broker, but it was too risky. Kal might be an expert, but Kyra Navarra didn't know a thing about mining.

Now, auto mechanic—*that* sounded interesting. But her math scores were too poor to qualify. Which made her fit for only one profession, according to the Lenormand School.

The beautician track.

Now she was stuck in classes about hair and makeup, surrounded by girls who whispered behind their hands every time her Pota Pras accent slipped out.

"You should've seen their faces when you asked for a *warshcloth*," Durian said, followed by his donkey laugh.

"Shut up," Kal muttered, looking around to make sure the bathroom was empty.

Durian grinned at her in the mirror. He came and went as he pleased, and she had given up worrying about it. Kal figured she was having some kind of mental breakdown, but a mouthy ghost was the least of her problems.

"Look," she said, exasperated, "the food is decent, the beds are clean, and I doubt the White Foxes will look for me here. That's enough for now."

"Is it though?" He tilted his head. "What if they *do* come looking? You can call yourself any name you want, but that tattoo won't lie."

She turned her head, checking her neck in the mirror. The upside of learning cosmetology is that she'd blended a foundation to perfectly match her medium-brown skin tone and cover up the ship tattoo.

"See?" she said. "It's hidden."

"Yeah, but one swipe with a wet *warshcloth* and you're screwed," Durian pointed out cheerfully. "Somehow, hanging around a place infested with witches just strikes me as a bad idea."

"I don't disagree," she snapped. "But to run, I need money. Which I had until those Foxes took it all from me!"

Her lips tightened as she remembered the witch upending the tin can with her life's savings. The wind must had blown it over half the Zamir Hills by now.

"Calm down, bitch." He flipped the hair from his eyes. "I'm just trying to help. There has to be *some* way you can get out of here."

The bell chimed, signaling the end of break. Kal straightened her jacket and freshened up her lip gloss. Part of her grade was based on personal appearance. "I want to see you all *shine!*" the teacher would tell them.

Durian was right. Even if she didn't get caught, two years of this shit was unthinkable.

She struggled to focus in her next class on brow styling and accidentally over-plucked her partner, leaving a bald spot, which did not go over well. Over the next few hours, she considered and rejected half a dozen plans.

She could run away anytime she wanted—that wasn't the problem. But she didn't have any marketable skills to get by in a big, expensive city like Arjevica. She didn't feel good about stealing and sucked at it anyway, so that was out. The smaller towns in Kievad Rus would be even worse. Fewer jobs and tight-knit communities where a stranger would be remembered if anyone came asking.

That evening in the dining hall, she pushed the food around her plate and listened in on the conversation at the next table. Two girls were whispering fervently, heads bent together.

"—dying for a smoke," one said. "Three weeks and I'm losing my mind. I think I've gained ten pounds."

Kal vaguely remembered her roommate Elena saying something about a cleaning lady getting fired for smuggling cigarettes into the school.

"My sister sent me money for my birthday," another girl said. "I'd pay double for a bottle of that cherry liqueur from Falin's."

They saw her looking and Kal hastily shoveled food in her mouth. But that night as she got undressed for bed, she mentioned what she'd overheard to her roommates.

"Everyone wants something," Elena said with a shrug. "But the gates are locked, the walls are high, and the wards trigger if anyone tries to leave."

"Wards?" Kal asked.

"You know, lithomancy," Gabi said. "A few years ago, girls were sneaking out to the clubs every weekend. They messed it up for everyone when they got caught. Now there's wards along the walls. They glow blue, but you only notice it after dark."

Kal felt a spark of excitement. "What if I could get things? Like from outside?"

Gabi and Elena swapped a dubious glance. "If Lara Lenormand finds out, you'll get expelled," Elena said.

"She won't. But I'd need to charge a commission for the risk."

"You won't get past the wards," Gabi said flatly, opening one of her engineering textbooks and settling in to study.

"We'll see about that," Kal said. "So, do you want anything? Or know someone who does?"

"Ciggies," Elena said immediately, as Gabi added, "Romashka chocolates. I'd give my left tit for a box."

By lights-out, Kal had a list and a wad of bills. As soon as the dormitory fell silent, she took her peacoat from the wardrobe and shrugged it on over her school uniform. It held her most precious possession—the stash of kaldurite stones in the lining.

"This is either genius or the dumbest thing you've *ever* done," Durian remarked as she eased open the window. He was sitting on the sill, arms folded and ankles crossed. "And that's a low bar."

Kal nearly retorted that *he* was the one who had egged her on, but Gabi and Elena were still awake. She gave them a wave and climbed out the window.

She shimmied down using cornices, lintels, and decorative brickwork for hand- and footholds. Kal had wormed in and out of vertical mine shafts since she was a kid, and it was even easier than she'd hoped. She jogged through the shadows to a deserted corner of the grounds and stood there for a moment, taking stock.

The wards were set along the wall at fifteen-cubit intervals. As Gabi had said, they glowed with ethereal blue light. Each was a circle with the Rook of Kievad Rus inside, about the size of her palm.

Kal drew a shallow breath. Time to find out if her kaldurite worked against *all* kinds of lithomancy.

"No risk, no reward," she muttered.

Durian's favorite dumbass motto.

Before she had a chance to chicken out, Kal threw herself at the ivy-covered wall, scaling it like a monkey and dropping down to the quiet street on the other side. She stood there for a moment, breathing hard, her fingers tingling.

The wards didn't change color or react in any way. Kal listened for shouts or running footsteps. All she heard was the chirp of night insects beyond the wall and the distant sound of a car horn.

A crooked grin split her face.

---

THE FIRST RUN went so smoothly Kal almost felt disappointed. The trendy, upscale neighborhood surrounding the school had late-night shops that carried every luxury her new clients desired. She returned with cigarettes, chocolate, some gossip rags, and four bottles of booze. Kal was treated like a conquering hero.

By the third week, word spread. Girls she'd never seen before approached her between classes, slipping her lists and money. She expanded her inventory to include books deemed too racy for the school library and spirits of every variety.

Beyond the wall, her makeup and pink hair gave an extra layer of disguise should anyone look too closely.

With each successful transaction, her escape fund grew. In the quiet moments before sleep, she would count her earnings and calculate how much more she needed to buy passage on a ship.

"Where should we go first?" Durian would ask, his voice fading as she drifted toward sleep.

"Anywhere," she'd answer. "Anywhere but here."

---

IT WAS A FINE, mild evening in Octaver, the month of the Hunter's Moon. Kal strolled along, pockets heavy with contraband. Perfume vials clinked against the miniature bottles of peach brandy the girls liked since they were easy to hide in school bags. She'd gotten quicker at these runs now that she knew exactly where to go for each item.

Her peacoat concealed the Lenormand School uniform of skirt and leggings. A few weeks of rest and good food had transformed her from the ragged, starving creature who had first arrived in Arjevica. No one looked at her twice.

After stopping at the confectioner's, she crossed off the last item on the list—dried apricots dipped in chocolate for Savina Agafia. Best get back over the wall before anyone noticed her missing.

Yet her footsteps dragged as she neared the school. She was tired of the same routine every day. A healthy breakfast of porridge and fruit, then hair and makeup classes, then a brisk walk around the sports field for exercise, then skincare and brow sculpting, then a healthy lunch, more classes, a bloody healthy dinner, studying for quizzes, and lights out.

So far, she'd bought nothing for herself, but she deserved a reward.

Kal paused before a shop window with rows of bottles that glowed amber in the lamplight. The sign above the door read *Falin's Fine Spirits* in gilded script. She'd been in there earlier, picking up a few things for her clients. It was almost midnight. On impulse, she pushed open the door, triggering a bell.

"Just about to close," the shopkeeper said.

"I'll be quick." Kal tried to smooth out her Pota Pras accent. "A small bottle of starka, please. Whatever brand is cheapest."

He rang it up. Kal paid from her profits and slipped out the door. She never drank at school, but a taste wouldn't hurt. She'd earned it.

"This is how it starts," Durian said, limping along at her elbow. "One sip of starka and next thing you know, you're passed out in an alley getting your pockets turned out by larcenous orphans."

"Oh, please," she muttered, unscrewing the cap. "There are no orphans around here."

Kal took a sip. It tasted like caramel and vanilla and dark summer plums, with a nice mellow afterburn.

"Speaking of bad ideas," Durian said, "remember when you tried to convince me to swim across that flooded wadi?"

"And I was right. There was a vein of argentite on the other side." She took another swig, wincing. Durian had balked and the Yun-Su sisters got there first. "If you hadn't been such a coward, we could have staked it."

"Bitch, you're crazy. The current was too fast! We would have both drowned."

"Then at least we'd be dead together."

His voice turned somber. "Don't say that."

The starka softened the edges of her thoughts. She took another big glug and veered toward a park with a marble arch at the entrance. It was covered with graffiti. On impulse, she reached into her pocket and pulled out a tube of purple lipstick. Standing on tiptoe, she scrawled across the white marble: *DURIAN LIVES*

Kal stepped back to admire her handiwork. Something about seeing his name writ large made her chest ache less.

"You're an idiot," Durian said, but she could hear the smile.

"I miss you," she whispered.

"I know."

She raised the bottle in a toast. "To all your terrible ideas."

A chill raised goosebumps along her arms—the same sensation she'd felt when the witches had tried to use lithomancy against her. She capped the starka, pulse leaping.

"Shit!" A blur of movement in the darkness resolved into a pair of long white coats. Kal looked around for a place to hide. Her own clothing was dark and she didn't think they'd seen her yet.

After a moment, she darted to a dry fountain and crouched behind the rim. She could hear voices, but couldn't make out the words. A quick peek confirmed that they'd stopped at the arch.

*Triple shit!*

The footsteps came closer, then halted a few paces away. The chill intensified, sliding across Kal's skin like a gout of ice water. She gripped the pistol in her pocket. She never went anywhere without her Bluekiller, but she wouldn't use it unless she had no other choice.

"Pardon me!" A new voice, male and slightly slurred. "Sorry, I didn't see you there."

"Watch where you're going," one of the witches snapped.

"Did you see anyone pass by?" the other added. "A young woman, perhaps?"

There was a long pause. Sweat slicked her palm around the pistol grip.

"Yes, actually. She went that way in quite a hurry. Dark hair, I think? Hard to tell in this light. But she was wearing a red jacket."

The freezing cold sensation faded as footsteps moved away from the fountain. Kal waited, barely breathing, until the park fell silent once more.

"You can come out now," he said.

Kal hesitated, then slowly rose from her hiding place. A young man leaned against the arch. He wore an expensive-looking cashmere coat with leather gloves dangling from one pocket. A university student, or just a rich boy. His hair was dark chestnut with a bit of wave to it. Eyes either blue or green, it was hard to tell.

His gaze traveled over her. "Snuck out, did you?"

Kal tensed. "What do you mean?"

"You're one of those Lenormand girls." He smiled. "The shiny shoes gave you away."

She crossed her arms. "What's it to you?"

"Nothing at all." He pushed off the arch with a feline grace that suggested he wasn't as drunk as he'd pretended to be. "It's your business. I'm just glad to be of service. But you should be careful. This neighborhood isn't as safe it looks."

Blue eyes, she decided as he came closer. But dark, like the deepest parts of the sea.

"I'll keep it in mind." She felt suddenly awkward. "But really, thank you. You saved me from . . . a good deal of trouble. Breaking curfew could get me expelled."

He studied her for a moment, his gaze intent as though she were a fascinating riddle. "Then why do it?"

Why indeed? Kal drew a breath, trying to think of a suitable reply. In the end, she settled on a partial truth. "Once you enroll, they don't let you leave, not until you graduate. They say it's for your own protection, and I do understand that, but . . ."

"You wonder what lies beyond the walls," he finished. "And you want more than what they give you."

She met his eyes. "Yes."

For a moment, he looked serious, as though he understood her perfectly. Knew what it was to be caged, to yearn for freedom. Then a wry grin curled his lips. "Listen, I don't usually chat up fugitives, but there's a pub around the corner that's open until one-thirty. Care to stop in for a quick drink? If you're on the lam, you might as well make the most of it."

His smile was disarming, but warning bells went off. "I wish I could," she said quickly. "But after that close call, I'd better get back."

He looked disappointed. On impulse, she rummaged through her pockets. Three strides later, she pressed a square wrapped in gold foil into his hand. "A small gift of thanks."

He stared down at the chocolate bar like he'd never seen one before. "You don't have to," he said.

Kal grinned. "I know. That's why it's called a gift."

His blue eyes widened in surprise as she leaned in and kissed his cheek. It was a little stubbly, but he smelled nice. Like rain-damp wool and a hint of soap.

"Stay out of trouble," she whispered with a wink.

Kal turned away, walking quickly out of the park. When she

glanced back, her savior was eating the chocolate. He gave her a wave.

Kal returned it with a mock salute, but her good mood soured as she remembered her own stupidity. Now the White Foxes knew she was in Arjevica.

She ran the whole way back. For once, she was glad to see the walls of the Lenormand School. What had felt like a prison was now her only safe haven. She grabbed a handful of ivy and started to climb, the bottles clinking in her pocket.

She kept thinking about her savior. Had he really taken her for a student sneaking out, or was the encounter not as random as it seemed?

"That's the problem," Durian whispered in her ear. "It's not paranoia when they really *are* out to get you."

His donkey bray chased her over the wall.

## CHAPTER 21
# CATHRYNNE

Her head throbbed like a second heartbeat. Memory returned in fragments. Leaving the Angel Tower. A car pulling alongside. The Jennies . . .

Cathrynne's eyes snapped open. She sat up too fast and pain lanced through her temples. She was lying on a four-poster bed with silk pillows and a goosedown comforter. Sconces cast warm yellow light across damask wallpaper. The windows were draped in heavy velvet curtains.

She was still in her cypher uniform, but her whip and cudgel were gone. So were the gem pouches.

Cathrynne swung her legs off the bed, gritting her teeth at a wave of dizziness.

She tried the door first—locked. When she opened the curtains, she saw a vast emerald lawn stretching toward a line of dark woods in the distance. No other buildings were visible, no roads, not a hint of where they'd taken her. The sky was overcast and a fine mist hovered above the grass.

She tried to open the window but it wouldn't budge.

"Have it your way," she muttered, picking up an antique chair. It was nice and heavy. She took three steps toward the central window and hurled the chair at the glass.

It rebounded off an invisible barrier with a sound like a struck bell and flew back at her. Cathrynne barely managed to duck as it crashed into an expensive-looking writing desk behind her, snapping one of its legs.

Abjuration magic. They'd left a shield in place.

She looked around, thinking. There wasn't a single scrap of metal in the room. Even the hinges and doorknob were wood. A room made to hold witches.

But not cyphers.

She picked up the broken chair leg, hid next to the door, and waited.

After an hour or so, she heard footsteps. They paused outside the door. There was a scraping sound as a bar was lifted on the other side. As the door swung inward, Cathrynne brought the chair leg down. It rebounded against another magical shield with such force that her wrist twisted and nearly broke. She cried out, half stunned by the pain.

"I do admire your spirit," said a cultured male voice, "but I'd hoped we might conduct ourselves with a bit more civility."

It was the dark-haired witch with streaks of white at his temples. He wore slacks and a tailored coat, and had the sleek, well-fed look of the very wealthy.

"Is it civil to kidnap someone?" she asked, cradling her throbbing arm.

"You left me no choice. I did invite you to come of your own accord."

She backed away as he entered the room. "Just tell me what you want so we can get this over with."

"Surely you can guess. I need to know everything Lord Morningstar has uncovered about the kaldurite."

She gave a mirthless laugh. "Well, someone tried to kill him with it. Was that you?"

The witch frowned. "No."

She bared her teeth. "See, I believe you. So you can believe *me* when I tell you I know nothing, except that Barsal

Casolaba was murdered for it and so was the boy from Pota Pras."

"Casolaba." He gave a dry chuckle. "Now that was a spectacular end. But I had nothing to do with him, either. What I need to know, what is of *paramount importance* right now, is where Kal Machena and Durian Padulski found the stones."

"I have no idea," Cathrynne said.

"You must grasp the urgency for both witches and cyphers in every province," he continued reasonably. "If we don't control it, the humans or angels will, and we'll lose what little power we still have."

He stopped at the writing desk to survey the damage, looking slightly amused. Cathrynne backed against the windows, but he didn't pursue her.

"Listen to me," she said tightly. "*I don't know.*"

He smiled. "I'd love to take your word for it, but I must ask for more concrete assurance. So you will give me a sweven of all you have done from the time you left Kirith until yesterday. Once that's over, you are free to leave."

Cathrynne's pulse leapt. A sweven used the ley to transfer memories from one person to another. It was done with a simple spell, but if she allowed it he would have access to *everything*, including her feelings for Gavriel, their kiss at Red Dog Camp— and even worse, her visions.

And if the White Foxes discovered that she was a seer, they would take her straight to the kloster and she'd never come out again.

"That's a ridiculous request," she said flatly. "I'm not letting you inside my head."

His brows rose. "Then I'm afraid we're at an impasse. I cannot set you free until you permit the sweven. It must be given voluntarily, as I'm sure you know. Swevens cannot be extracted against a person's will." His tone implied that this was a minor obstacle.

"Then you're out of luck," she said. "Sorry."

"I can make your problems in Arioch go away if you cooperate. Call off George Claymond and Audrey Hayes."

She laughed. "Lump and Crump? They don't scare me."

He regarded her for a long moment. "I know who you are, Cathrynne Lenormand."

It took all her fragile self-control not to react. "My name is Cathrynne Rowan," she corrected, though she could hear the lie in her own voice. The fear.

"And mine is Markus Viktorovich," he offered with a slight inclination of his head. "But we both know the truth of your lineage."

Something about him nagged at her. She studied his face but felt certain they hadn't met before. He was in his late middle years with tanned skin and thin lips. Attractive, in a ruthless way.

"Take some time to think about it," Markus said, walking to the door. "I'll come back tomorrow."

Once the bar settled into place behind him, Cathrynne resumed the search for weaknesses in her prison. There were none.

Darkness fell. Footsteps came, two sets this time. Markus's lackeys, Ash and Kane, opened the door.

"Stand back," Ash ordered. "All the way to the windows."

Cathrynne complied. They left a tray of food on the floor and retreated. Steam rose from a bowl of soup, alongside a chunk of dark seeded bread. She turned her back. Better to go hungry than be drugged. She curled up inside the footwell of the desk with the broken chair leg in one hand and fell asleep.

Morning light was filtering through the windows when Markus returned.

"Have you reconsidered my offer?" he asked.

She sat up. "I'm not giving you the sweven."

He eyed the untouched tray. "There's no purpose in starving yourself."

"I'm not hungry," she said, as her stomach betrayed her with a growl.

Markus stood aside as Ash and Kane replaced the tray with a fresh one. "It isn't poisoned," he said.

When Cathrynne didn't reply, he broke off a piece of bread and ate it, then sipped from the bowl. "Satisfied?"

She still said nothing, but once they'd all gone, she fell on the food and devoured every bit. It helped her think. Markus was careful. He wore no gems she could try to take away. The room was stripped of anything useful.

She would have to put him off guard, and then strike when he least expected it.

---

A WEEK PASSED. Each day, Markus brought her a breakfast tray, his manner unfailingly courteous as he asked the same question: "Will you give me the sweven?"

Each day, Cathrynne refused.

He never raised his voice. Never threatened. But she knew that wouldn't last forever.

However, she did figure one thing out.

On the third day of her captivity, she noticed a red squirrel darting across the lawn. It paused to unearth an acorn before bouncing away. The next day, she saw what appeared to be the same squirrel, digging in the exact same spot.

On the fifth day, she watched and counted: twelve seconds after the squirrel shimmied up a tree, a robin landed on the grass, strutted in a circle, plucked a worm from the ground, and flew to a low branch of the same oak.

This brief performance repeated itself every morning in a predictable loop.

She noticed other things, too. The way it always rained for about an hour after lunch. How the direction of the wind rustling the treetops never changed. The way the lawn remained pristine despite the lack of gardeners.

"Illusion," she murmured, pressing a palm against the misty glass.

The house could be anywhere. In the heart of a city or on an island in the middle of the sea. She had to consider the possibility that they'd forced with her while she was unconscious, so she could be in another province altogether.

When she escaped, she'd have to be ready for anything.

Cathrynne paced the confines of her prison—fourteen steps from window to door, nine steps from bed to desk. She grew desperate enough to consider trying to work the ley in her own blood. Only the knowledge that it would probably kill her stopped her from trying.

On the seventh day, desperate for any distraction, she turned to the stack of cloth-bound books Markus had left on the table. She'd ignored them thus far, but now she ran her fingers over the spines.

*Sinn of the Southern Provinces. An Evolutionary History of the Aquatic Sinn in the Lochs of Kirith. Taxonomy of the Great Northerns.* Et cetera.

Every single volume was about the Sinn.

Apparently, Markus's idea of a joke. Cathrynne opened one at random and studied an engraved illustration of a blue emperor. Its eyes and horns were golden, and so were the overlapping scales across its chest. It was elegantly built, long and serpentine, with blue claws tipping its six sturdy legs. Just like the one that had crawled out of a crevice in the Zamir Hills.

She idly paged through the books until her attention caught on a peculiar title. *A History of the Settlement of Eidanger, Years 430-450.* She opened the brittle cover and started reading. At first, she thought it must have been accidentally mixed in with the other books because it didn't seem to be about the Sinn. It was about a village in the far north of Sundland and had lists of names, all women, with the dates they had arrived.

After a few pages, she realized that the women were cyphers who had consorted with angels and born a draconic child, and the book was about what happened to them afterwards when they were sent into exile.

*Afterwards.*

Cathrynne re-read the passage several times, thoroughly shocked. She had been taught the offspring killed their own mothers. That cyphers never survived the birth. Clearly, she had been lied to.

It made her wonder what other lies she had been told, and whether this village still existed. The time period was over a century ago. But it meant that there were cyphers who had done the worst thing they could possibly do—and lived to tell about it.

Her stomach churned as she thought of the babies. Were they murdered? Or had the infants been spared? She flipped through the pages, trying to find out, but the slender volume didn't say—

"My father and uncle were killed by the Sinn," Markus said.

Cathrynne's head jerked up. She'd been so engrossed in reading, she hadn't heard the door open.

"It was a blue emperor." He came closer—but not *too* close. Markus Viktorovich wasn't stupid. "They were in the high desert surveying a new mine. I was seven and in school at the time. My mother survived, though she suffered extensive burns."

Cathrynne closed the book and casually placed it on the stack. "Well, I'm sorry about that."

"Thank you." He studied her, expressionless. "I need you to understand that I don't hate cyphers. Not like some of us do."

He was talking about the White Foxes.

"How reassuring," she said dryly. "Why don't you let me go then? I have rights, too."

Markus ignored this. "Many of you come from ancient, respected families. I believe your intentions are good. You are taught to protect the interests of the empire. To enforce its laws.

Just as it is my task to preserve the bloodlines from angelic cont-amination."

"I know what you do," she said. "Spare me the lecture."

He smiled. "Of course. But I'm sure you agree that we cannot allow any more Sinn to be born. They have the ability to repro-duce as a species. Left unchecked, I don't doubt that they will overrun the world."

His words hit a nerve. "What's your point?" she snapped.

"It is a fact that the Sinn are growing immune to lithomancy. I believe this might be an evolutionary defense mechanism." He reached into his pocket and held up a chunk of kaldurite. "This is one of the specimens Durian Padulski sold to the jeweler on my payroll."

"D'Amato," Cathrynne muttered, her eyes never leaving the stone. It was the first gem she had seen in over two weeks. It wasn't hot with ley, of course. But it was just what she needed to pierce the illusion, the shields, and get out of here.

"There are precious few samples to study," Markus contin-ued. "We must find the source, determine how it is forged—"

Markus cut off as she leapt up from the bed. She was inches from tearing the kaldurite from his grasp when a blast of projec-tive ley came through the open door. It was like being kicked in the chest by a mule. Ash smirked from the doorway as she flew backwards.

Markus gave her a disappointed look. "I hoped you might listen to reason, Cathrynne. Think about where your loyalties lie."

She made a rude gesture. "Give me the stone and we'll test your theory. I'll shove it right up your—"

The door closed. The bar came down.

---

TWICE A DAY, her brooding was interrupted by Ash and Kane. The routine never varied: a knock, followed by a curt order to stand against the windows. They never turned their backs, never stepped fully into the room. Kane watched while Ash set down a new tray and collected the old one.

When she asked them what had happened to Mercy, they ignored her.

But something happened on the tenth day. As Ash was bending down, Cathrynne had a vision of her standing on the Corniche in Kota Gelangi. A projective spell erupted from her palm. It struck a young man with sandy hair. His body flew over a stone wall and plunged into the river below.

Cathrynne only caught a flash of his face, but she recognized him. Durian Padulski, the boy whose house they had visited in Pota Pras. His body had been displayed, and although it had the disfiguring signs of someone too long in the water, she recognized the birthmark on his cheek.

Ash was the witch who had killed him.

The vision faded, but another followed as her gaze shifted to the male witch, Kane. This time she saw him standing in the hills, facing a young woman with springy dark hair and a lean, determined face. She held a pistol with both hands. Cathrynne heard the crack of the shot. He stumbled, blood blooming across his white coat like a crimson flower.

Kal Machena had shot him! Too bad the bastard wasn't dead.

The pair of White Foxes left, oblivious to her visions. The bar thudded down behind them.

Cathrynne sat still, the food forgotten. She always saw symbols—not actual events. Something was changing. She must be shifting into the later stage of foretelling. The one where you lost control.

Where you lost your mind.

Yet she felt a grim satisfaction. Kal Machena had fought back. And they didn't know where she was if they were reduced to interrogating Cathrynne.

*Run*, she thought. *Just keep running and don't ever stop*.

# CHAPTER 22

# KAL

S
he dug her fingers into familiar crevices, scrambling up the brick wall surrounding the Lenormand School. She'd made this trip a dozen times now, but the thrill of outwitting witches never got old.

Kal paused at the top to survey the manicured grounds. Moonlight silvered the grass and cast long shadows between the red-brick buildings. For a place that had once been a notorious reformatory, it looked peaceful. No guards patrolled the pathways. Why bother when magic detected any intruder?

The glowing blue wards set at intervals held steady, not even flickering as she dropped down to the street. As always, the kaldurite in her pocket made her invisible.

Thunder rumbled in the distance, but the sky above was clear and strewn with stars. With luck, the rain would hold off until she got back. Just a few more runs and she'd have enough money saved to leave for good.

Her main problem was getting a new identity card so she could cross the border into Bactra. Sardis had a busy port. From there she could buy passage on a vessel bound for anywhere.

Years ago, her brother Bastian had given her an old geography primer he'd won in a spelling bee. Kal didn't care much for school, but she and Durian would spend hours poring over the imports and exports of each province, plotting out their fortune. Hardwood timber from Bactra. Salt cod and freshwater pearls from Sundland. Fine porcelain and rare books from Kirith. Henna, frankincense, and silk damask from Iskatar.

Once their reputation was established, they would focus on luxury goods: textiles and ink, incense, oils and attars, spices like cinnamon, cassia, cardamom, ginger, pepper, nutmeg, and vanilla.

Lying in her bed at night, she'd dreamt of riding camels through the desert, trekking the snowy tundra south of Isai Minye, and watching the footraces in Lagash on festival days, which came every new moon. They would visit the Gulkishar, which meant Great Hall in Iskari, and drink sweet black tea with the palatine, who was the western equivalent of a consul.

Childish fantasies, yet she had believed they would come true. It was Durian's brash confidence, she realized that now. Without him, she wouldn't have imagined a life beyond the boundaries of Pota Pras.

Kal dragged herself back to the present, head down and hugging the shadows with the skill of someone who'd spent a lifetime avoiding notice. The white coats of the Foxes were easy to spot. Still, she didn't relax until she reached her destination.

Falin's Fine Spirits sat wedged between a bakery and a glove-maker. The shopkeeper, a balding man with spectacles perched on the end of his nose, gave Kal a nod of greeting. She grabbed a basket and began her usual circuit of the store, filling orders from her list. Seven minis of starka. Two of sweet red Gamay wine for the group who liked to drink on the roof. In the imported section, she scanned the shelves, hunting for anise-flavored arak from Iskatar.

She was vaguely aware of another customer but didn't pay much attention until she noticed the expensive cashmere coat. It was her savior from a week ago. He stood at the end of the aisle, studying bottles of zelas wine.

Kal shrank back, wondering if she could pay and vanish into

the night before he noticed her. Yet something made her hesitate. Curiosity—or just the chance to talk to somebody who wasn't dead.

"Bitch, I heard that," Durian said.

Before she could flee, he looked over. Recognition flashed across his face—which she had to admit was very attractive. She'd always been fond of men with light eyes. This one was pretty, but not *too* pretty. His nose looked like it had been broken once or twice and his hair was in need of combing. Though it was odd, she recalled his eyes as being a darker blue the last time they met.

"It's you," he said with a warm smile.

She raised a hand in greeting. "Hey."

He turned back to the shelf. "I was about to buy a bottle of zelas without having the faintest idea if it's any good. Maybe you could save me?"

"I don't know good zelas from bad," she admitted. "But I'm told the greener, the better."

"Ah, a vital piece of advice." He selected a bottle with liquid the color of spring grass. "This should suffice." He studied her heavy basket. "Throwing a party?"

"It's my birthday," she improvised. "And you? Special occasion?"

A shadow crossed his face before his smile returned. "Just a quiet evening." He hesitated. "I don't suppose you'd care to join me?"

She arched a brow. "You asked me that once already."

"And you turned me down." His grin turned rueful. "I have not forgotten."

"Well, I don't drink with strangers."

He walked up and held out a hand. "My name is Levi. Now we're not strangers anymore."

With no choice, Kal clasped his hand. It was strong and dry and very warm. He did have beautiful eyes, like a cool mountain lake.

"In a public place, of course." Levi gestured to the park down the street. "The benches there are quite nice."

Kal laughed. "Nice benches, eh?"

Oddly, he didn't laugh back. "You're making fun, but I can assure you that those are the finest benches in Arjevica."

"One drink," she said after a moment.

They paid for their purchases separately. She'd bought a backpack to carry her inventory when the list had outgrown her pockets. Outside, the night air had cooled. They walked together to the park fronting the ballet, its ornate columns gleaming white in the moonlight.

Levi opened the zelas and took a sip.

"Well?" Kal asked, watching his face.

"It's . . . truly terrible." He coughed and offered her the bottle.

Kal took a cautious sip. The wine was sharp and acidic, with a strange herbal aftertaste that lingered unpleasantly. She grimaced. "*That's* distinctive."

Levi laughed. "You should be a politician." He took the bottle back, their fingers brushing briefly. Again, she felt a pleasant tingle. They sat in silence for a moment, passing the awful zelas back and forth.

"You have me at a disadvantage," Levi said. "You know my name but I don't know yours."

"Oh! Right. Kyra Navarra."

She thought he would comment on her accent, ask where she was from, but he just took a swig from the bottle and tipped his head back to look at the stars.

"The world is a strange place, isn't it, Kyra?"

She studied his profile. The bold nose and sharply defined lips. A lock of dark hair tumbled across his brow.

"How do you mean?"

"Well, the way our paths keep crossing."

"Do you live in this neighborhood?"

"Now I do, but I come from another place. It's on the shore of the Southern Ocean."

Her interest piqued. The Southern Ocean was at the farthest border of the empire and she often wondered what might lie on the other side. "I've never seen it," she admitted. "But I've always wanted to."

"It's different from the Parnassian Sea. Wilder and bigger. After a storm, you might see waves as high as that roof." He nodded at the grand limestone building housing the ballet. "Everything depends on the winds and the currents. The tides, too, of course."

"Do you sail?" she asked eagerly.

"We have a dinghy. I've taken it out along the shore." He grinned. "It's hard to capsize, but I've managed it a few times."

"You're lucky," she said wistfully.

"That I was tossed into the ocean?" he asked with a note of puzzlement.

Kal snorted. "No, that you learned how to sail. I've always wanted to." She remembered her ship tattoo and decided to stop yammering. "Where's your hometown?"

"Niss. A bit outside, actually. It's all I knew until a couple of years ago. I guess you could say I had a sheltered upbringing."

"Do you have a big family?"

He nodded. "Lots of brothers."

"Me too."

He glanced over. "If you don't like the Lenormand School, where would you rather be?"

Kal sighed. "I'm working on that."

Levi watched two women walk through the park, arm in arm. "Not that it's my business, but if you keep sneaking out, they'll catch you eventually."

"It's *not* your business," she retorted, "and I know that. It's still worth it."

He offered her the zelas. Kal shook her head. She was angry, but not at him.

"I'm sorry," he said softly. "I say the wrong thing sometimes. You must forgive me. But don't you have anyone to help you?"

Kal was mortified at the sudden hot lump in her throat. "I do have a friend," she managed. "But he . . . well, he moved. To another province. I miss him."

Levi was silent for a minute. "I could be your friend, Kyra."

She exhaled a shaky breath. "That's sweet of you. But I'm sure you have better things to do with your time."

His unsettling blue eyes fixed on her. "I really don't."

Kal struggled to think of an offhand response. Something to deflect him. But he looked serious, like he actually cared about her even though they hardly knew each other. It made no sense, and yet she felt safe in his presence. More than she had in weeks.

She remembered kissing his cheek, and wondered what it would be like to kiss him properly.

Levi seemed to read her thoughts. His gaze softened, but he didn't lean closer. Just watched her, waiting to see what she would do next. Kal Machena never kissed strange men, but Kyra Navarra was considering it when a raindrop struck her cheek, followed quickly by another. The stars were vanishing behind a line of dark clouds.

"The storm's caught us," she said.

"So it has." He corked the bottle, and the moment broke. "I guess this concludes our impromptu party."

"I guess it does." Kal was suddenly aware of how late it had grown. "I should get back."

"Same time next week?"

She smiled regretfully. "To be honest, I doubt it."

His face clouded. "I'll be here. Come if you can, but I don't want to cause you more trouble." Before she could answer, he caught her hand and kissed the inside of her wrist. "Happy birthday, Kyra."

Her pulse fluttered as they said goodbye in the rain, then walked in opposite directions. Kal looked back once to see Levi's black coat disappearing around the corner.

# CHAPTER 23
# CATHRYNNE

O n the thirteenth day of her captivity, Markus didn't turn up. Breakfast came and went with no food, and then lunchtime.

Cathrynne mended the chair by stacking books about the Sinn under the missing leg. She sat and waited. The squirrel dug up its acorn and scampered to the oak tree. The robin plucked a worm from the ground. Clouds moved in and the late morning drizzle arrived.

She watched the illusion unspool with a growling stomach.

If he thought he could starve her into submission, he was in for a surprise. She'd often been sent to bed hungry in her first years of cypher training, not only for refusing to answer to the grace name "Serenity" but for other infractions as well. She could go without eating for days.

Surely someone must be looking for her by now. If Gavriel was awake, he would mount a search. Even if he was still recovering, Yarl would be trying to locate her. And Mercy . . .

Cathrynne drew a taut breath, forcing her fists to unclench. Mercy had the kaldurite stone. She would be safe from spells. It would take her a while to walk to Arjevica, but once she arrived at the chapter house and found Cathrynne missing, she would demand an investigation.

The only problem is that Cathrynne had no idea where in the world she was being held—

The creak of the wooden bar lifting was the only warning she had. The door was flung open by a witch with black hair cut ruler-straight to her shoulders. She had pale skin and broad, high cheekbones. Her onyx eyes fixed on Cathrynne with cold assessment, like a butcher eyeing a carcass. A moment later, invisible bonds pinned her arms to her sides. Cathrynne felt herself lifted up like a puppet on strings.

"Markus is too gentle with you," the witch said.

Her gaze sliced to the windows. Cathrynne struggled wildly, but the bonds only tightened, squeezing her ribs until black spots danced at the edges of her vision.

"I prefer more direct methods."

The windows flew open and Cathrynne floated toward them. The pressure around her chest eased just enough to allow her to draw a shallow breath before she was outside, suspended in midair.

The idyllic country estate vanished. She hung hundreds of cubits above a rocky gorge, the house clinging to the edge of a sheer cliff face. Far below, a river wound like a silver thread between stony banks. Icy wind tore at her clothes.

Slowly, the witch rotated her until she hung upside-down. Blood rushed to her head, pounding behind her eyes.

"The sweven," the witch said, her voice booming inside Cathrynne's mind. "Give your consent or I'll let you fall."

Her heart flailed against her ribs like a trapped animal. Cypher training had prepared her for many things—but not this utter helplessness. Yet she would rather die on the rocks below than spend the rest of her days looking through the bars of a kloster cell.

"No!" she screamed.

For an endless minute, she dangled there, gasping desperately

KAT ROSS

for breath. At last, the witch's bitter voice came again. "Then you're of no use to me."

The magical bonds released.

Cathrynne plummeted. A scream tore from her throat. The gorge walls blurred, the river rushed toward her—

She landed on something solid, knocking the breath from her lungs. Carpet ground into her cheek. She smelled the familiar scent of beeswax.

She was back in her gilded prison, sprawled on the floor, shaking uncontrollably.

"—extreme and counterproductive," Markus said. "I did not sanction this, Berti."

"She's wasting our time," the female witch—Berti—snapped.

"Torture doesn't produce reliable information," Markus countered. "And now you've ruined any rapport I had with her. Given more time—"

A scornful laugh. "There is no rapport! Your approach has yielded what, exactly? Two weeks of childish sulking? It does not matter what she believes. What matters is the gods-damned sweven in her head! Morningstar is beyond our reach now. The other cypher escaped as well. Until we find the Machena girl, Cathrynne Lenormand is our last lead to find the source."

"I'm not sure she knows anything," Markus said in a more subdued tone. "Why would she?"

"She spent time in Pota Pras. She and Morningstar went into the hills. Who knows what they found?"

"Kal Machena is still the primary target. She found the stone, she knows exactly where to find more, and we know she's in Arjevica."

"She *was* in Arjevica," Berti corrected, her frustration obvious. "But we've scoured the streets looking for her. Every damn hostel, alleyway, brothel, train station. The girl vanished into thin air—"

Neither of them paid any attention to Cathrynne, who lay motionless on the floor, digesting this new information.

Kal Machena was still alive, still free.

Mercy was alive, too, thank Minerva.

She didn't know what they meant by Morningstar being "beyond our reach." He could still be in the Angel Tower. Or he could be . . .

No. If Gavriel were dead, she would know. She would *feel it*.

Cathrynne slowly turned her head. Markus stood with his back to her, his posture rigid. Berti faced him, chin lifted in defiance, straight black hair framing her high cheekbones.

Seeing them together unlocked a door that had been shut for twenty years, sealed with complex weavings of liminal ley. But the spell was unravelling now, and her eyes glazed as memory returned.

---

YOU ARE eleven years old and sitting on the floor of your sunny playroom. Spread out on the carpet before you is the deck of cards your mother uses for party games. It has thirty-six pictures and you like to look at them and arrange them into patterns.

You glimpse the future sometimes, flashes that make little sense, but you know enough not to tell anyone about it.

You have seen the kloster and understand what it is for.

Today, you have made a picture with The Man, The Woman, and The Snake. Below them is The House and The Scythe, which you intuitively grasp means a sudden ending. Looking at the picture makes you uneasy.

"No," you say firmly, and cover it with the rest of the deck, then mix the cards up into a big messy pile.

You are alone on this fine spring day. Your sister Lara has gone to visit Lara's father Aleksandr, whom she calls Sasha. Lara is fifteen and not very nice. You were close when you were younger, but Lara never has time for you anymore. Sometimes you think she secretly hates you.

You have no father. You were adopted by Hysto Lenormand

after your birth parents died. They were witches, of course, just like your new family. You don't remember them because you were just a baby when it happened. Sometimes you feel jealous of Lara. Alexsandr Arco is rich and handsome, and he dotes on Lara.

Your mother is upstairs entertaining her seraphim friend, Alluin Westwind, and the servants have the day off, so when someone knocks at the front door, you go to answer it. Your mother told you not to let anyone in, but you are a dreamy child and you have forgotten the instruction. Sometimes your mother includes you in the visits with Alluin, who is kind and gentle, but not today.

Today, they told you to go amuse yourself in the playroom. It isn't fair.

You draw the bolt and open the door. Two witches in white coats are standing on the doorstep. The man is distinguished, with tanned skin and graying hair. His companion has tilted eyes of very light gray. Her gloves are red.

The man smiles. "Hello, little one. Is your mother home? We're friends of hers."

Your knees begin to shake. You grip the doorframe so you don't fall down. Darkness swirls around the two witches. It screams of loss and anguish. You try to close the door, but everything happens very fast. The man pushes his way inside and charges up the stairs, the woman at his heels. You're afraid, but you find the courage to chase after them.

You are old enough to know some lithomancy, and you draw projective ley from the emerald bracelet around your wrist, a present from grandmama. The spell is wild, inexperienced, but you have raw power and it knocks them down. The man spins back and hits you with a spell of his own. It feels like stepping under a cold waterfall. A strange sensation washes through you and you cannot feel the ley anymore.

Then you hear a scream, and you race to the top of the stairs, down the hall to the master bedroom, where your mother is naked and flushed with rage. It is a shock to see her undressed in front of strangers. She has full, pendulous breasts and a thatch of dark hair between her legs. She doesn't bother to cover herself. Alluin Westwind is gone, but the window is wide open, a draft fluttering the long white curtains.

Your mother notices you, your eyes lock, and then the witch with the red gloves takes your arm in a punishing grip and drags you back down the stairs, outside to a waiting car. More witches in white coats hold you still while she pricks your thumb with a needle. When she sees a drop of your blood well up, she gives an angry, satisfied nod. You don't know what it means, but you do know that your blood is purple, not red, which your mother said is because you have a rare condition but it's nothing to worry about.

Clearly, your mother lied to you.

You don't cry. You still believe this is some kind of mistake.

The witches drive away, and it is the very last time you see any of your family again.

---

TWENTY YEARS HAD PASSED, but Markus looked the same. So did Berti.

Rage burned away the last traces of fear, burned away caution and restraint. With a wordless cry, Cathrynne sprang to her feet. She crossed the room in three long strides. Berti's eyes widened as Cathrynne slammed into her, driving them both to the floor. She managed to land a flurry of punches before Ash and Kane came running in to drag her off.

It was the first thing you learned in cypher training. When you're fighting for your life, attack in a blitz. Keep the blows raining down faster than your opponent can react to them.

Berti was cursing a blue streak. Blood gushed from her nose. Cathrynne managed to break loose again and get a couple more kicks in. Then someone cast a projective spell, knocking her back.

"Close the fucking door!" Kane shouted.

The four of them bolted and the heavy door slammed shut. Cathrynne stood there for a minute, breathing hard. Then she started to laugh and cry at the same time.

---

AGAIN, they left her without food or water.

*Well worth it*, she thought, flexing her bruised knuckles.

When Markus returned, he looked unhappy. "You're being very difficult, Cathrynne."

He was impeccably dressed as always. A real dandy in pinstriped trousers and a red silk waistcoat.

"I know who you are," she said. "I remember everything. You took me from my family. Humiliated my mother!"

"I was doing my job," he replied. "Hysto shouldn't have fucked an angel."

"You're a monster."

Markus sighed. "Be reasonable. How long can you continue like this? Just give me the sweven and it will all be over. You can go home to Kirith and resume your duties without interference from the White Foxes ever again. I'll see to it. And you'll be doing a service to the empire." He gazed at her earnestly.

Cathrynne took a step forward. Markus braced himself but held his ground.

"I'll say this one more time," she spat. "You're never getting inside my mind. *Never*."

"So be it," a cold voice said.

Cathrynne turned as an older witch strode into the room. She wore weirdly heavy makeup and burn scars coursed across the left half of her body. The biggest caracal Cathrynne had ever seen prowled at her side.

"I have no patience for this," the witch snapped.

"Who are you?" Cathrynne asked.

"Veronica Viktorovich," she replied with disdain. "I have known your family a long time."

"Mother—" Markus began.

She cut him off with a sharp gesture. "I'm hardly surprised Hysto sired a half-blood bastard," Veronica said. "Nor that you are an ill-mannered, common creature."

The caracal bared its fangs in a hiss.

"My son is gracious," Veronica said, stroking the caracal's head with one scarred hand. "But I am not."

She snapped her fingers. Ash and Kane came trotting in like the obedient dogs they were. "Take her below," Veronica ordered.

Markus gave Cathrynne a look that was half pity, half reproach. *I tried my best. What happens next is your fault.*

Invisible bonds pinned her arms. They dragged her through the door and down a long flight of stone stairs. The light grew dim, the air cool and smelling of earth.

At the bottom of the stairs stretched a narrow corridor with heavy wooden doors set into the walls. Ash opened one, revealing a windowless cell with a ceiling barely high enough to stand upright. Kane shoved Cathrynne inside, sending her sprawling to the dirt floor.

"No!" she cried. "Wait!"

The cell door slammed shut, plunging the cell into darkness.

---

MINUTES STRETCHED INTO HOURS, hours into days. The absence of light was so complete that it made no difference if her eyes were open or shut. She had never known such darkness. Even on a moonless night in Arioch, there was faint lamplight through windows or the glow of embers in a dying fire.

Now she understood that the dark could be a living thing, pressing against your skin, filling your lungs with each breath.

Her stomach ceased its growling, settling into a hollow ache. Her throat felt like she'd swallowed sand.

Cathrynne was starting to believe they meant for her to die in this hole when a scraping sound came at the bottom of the door. A slot opened and torchlight spilled through. A metal cup slid across the dirt floor before the slot slammed shut, plunging her back into darkness.

She felt her way to the offering. Lukewarm water and what felt like a chunk of hard bread. She forced herself to eat and drink slowly, though every instinct screamed to gulp it down.

"Hello?" she rasped. "Is someone there? Markus?"

No answer. Never an answer.

She explored her cell, fingers tracing every inch of the stone walls. The door was thick wood, no metal hinges. When she finished, she began again. Anything to keep the panic at bay.

This must be what life was like in the klosters, although the seers had bars to look through. Some connection to the outside world.

———

THE SLOT OPENED. Food slid through. She ate mechanically, tasting nothing.

She prayed to Minerva for deliverance. Thought she heard a voice whisper to have courage but feared it was her imagination.

Felicity Birch used to say that where strength ends, faith begins. Cathrynne had never quite understood what that meant, but she thought she did now.

She recalled a day she'd been pulled off regular duties and given a senior class of cypher trainees in their final year whose instructor was down with the flu. She hadn't minded teaching, but she preferred the little ones. They were nicer to substitutes.

"I'd like to start with a prayer," she said.

It was a hot morning and the classroom's ceiling fan was

broken. The teenaged girls looked sweaty and hostile. One rolled her eyes.

"Do you have an objection?" Cathrynne asked.

They swapped glances. Then the eye-roller spoke up. She looked like she did two hundred pushups before breakfast every day. According to the seating chart, her name was Justice Holly.

"Cypher Aspen doesn't make us say a prayer. She goes right to lessons and then combat training."

"Huh," Cathrynne said. "Well, this one is dedicated to Minerva. Did you know she founded our order?"

A condescending smirk. "Yeah, we know."

"Did your teacher tell you what happened to cyphers back in the day, before they were even called cyphers?"

Justice faltered. "Before? I thought we were always shields."

Cathrynne leaned back against the desk. "Sadly, no. When it became clear that we were the ones responsible for the Sinn, and that our monstrous offspring were eating people, the witches created a special division to find infant cyphers and kill them."

She had the girls' full attention now.

"Anyone care to hazard a guess as to what this special division was called?" She looked around. "No one? Well, it was the White Foxes. Some babies were smothered. Others were left out for the wolves."

"Is that really true?" The cockiness was gone. Justice's voice was subdued.

"Go ask Felicity Birch if you don't believe me."

The girls looked shaken, but they deserved the truth. And they needed to learn the most important lesson of all: Never trust anyone except another cypher.

"The practice started in Sundland, but soon it spread throughout the empire," she continued. "Minerva finally put a stop to it. She declared that these despised byblows of witch and angel would be raised in the chapter houses and trained to protect humans. That the genetic curse was no fault of their own and they had a right to live. If it wasn't for her, none of us would be here. We shouldn't forget that. So I made up a prayer and I say it every morning."

Cathrynne closed her eyes. "Thank you, Minerva. You stepped in and saved us from the wolves and foxes, so I promise to carry out your will by arresting the guilty and shielding the innocent. I hope you come back someday. I hope wherever you are, you're happy."

When she opened her eyes, Justice and the rest were watching her.

"Would you like to say it with me?" Cathrynne asked.

The girls nodded and she went through it again, pausing so they could repeat the words. When they finished, she regarded them thoughtfully. "I was given a lesson plan, but I spilled jam on it. Honestly, it was rubbish anyway. Why don't you just ask me questions? Anything at all."

"Where *is* Minerva?" one ventured. "Like, where'd she go?"

"Wish I knew. Next?"

A skinny girl with brown hair named Remedy Alder raised her hand. "Why can't we learn anything except projective magic?"

"The witches don't trust us. If we knew abjuration magic—protective spells—they wouldn't have an advantage over us. Same with illusion. Next?"

"What if we accidentally use receptive ley?"

"Well, that wouldn't be easy since you won't be given receptive stones. But it's theoretically possible, if you drew from a gem or metal in the environment around you. Silver is receptive, for example. But that's why you do so many repetitive exercises. So you have complete control. Using both kinds of ley—projective and receptive—at the same time is very dangerous if you don't know what you're doing."

The girls stared blankly. Another thing their regular teacher had failed to mention.

"Okay, listen," Cathrynne said. "You know that every gem and metal has different qualities, right? The unique structure changes the focus of the ley vibrating within it. It causes a resonance."

This, they understood. The girls nodded.

"Since ley reacts to the mind, it's a matter of focus. Your will is the bridge to make things happen in the material world. It gives meaning and intent to the spell. But some kinds of magic break natural law, so be very careful what you draw from."

Another hand shot up. "Are all seers crazy?"

Cathrynne hesitated. "I don't think so. But they can't control their gift, and it disturbs them, so they have to be locked up. For their own good." Even as she'd said the words, she hated herself. It was a horrible thing to do to anyone, bricking them away like that.

"But isn't it useful to know the future?" the girl asked.

"You'd think so. But foretelling isn't like other branches of lithomancy. It's wild and uncontrollable."

"Have you ever seen anyone have a vision?"

Cathrynne was about to shake her head when Mercy's voice cut in from the doorway.

"I have," she said. "Once."

For such a big woman, she was light as a caracal on her feet when she chose to be. Cathrynne wondered how long she'd been standing there.

"The girl was about your age," Mercy continued as she entered the classroom, her red mane especially wild and frizzy that day. "We were in class, reading the resonance of different stones, when she suddenly went stiff."

Mercy's voice lowered. "Then the girl started to cry. I mean, hysterical. I couldn't understand her except for one word: *brick*. The teacher took her away to the infirmary. Well, an hour later, that same teacher was killed in a freak accident."

She waited until one of the girls whispered, "What happened?"

"She was teaching projective spells to an older class. One went wide and cracked the brick overhang. It fell on the teacher's head and crushed her skull. The next day, the girl was put in the kloster. I never saw her again. But you see, her warning did no good. And here we've wasted precious time talking about magic you'll never wield, if you're lucky."

Cathrynne shot Mercy a look of reproof that she ignored. "The thing to remember is that you'll never learn defensive magic," Cathrynne said, "so you have to be smarter and faster. But you're just as good as any witch. In fact, you're braver because you'll go out there every day with only your wits and a few gems. So have faith in yourselves." She eyed them seriously. "I do, by the ley."

"Now, who wants to go outside and throw me across the quad?" asked Mercy.

The tension had broken and everyone laughed.

"BY THE LEY," Cathrynne croaked in darkness, raising an icy hand to her forehead, the place where the will resided. After a moment, she touched her heart, too.

Time passed. She drifted in and out, seeking escape in the deeper places of her mind. Charmed memories of a happy and loving home. She had lived with her older sister Lara, her mother Hysto, and her grandmother Nestania. Three generations of women in a grand house with servants and a formal garden.

Hysto liked to throw lavish parties, and Cathrynne had a closet full of frothy silk dresses. Her mother enjoyed showing her off, the golden-haired orphan she had adopted after her parents died in a car accident. The guests would remark on Cathrynne's beauty and Hysto would smile with pride, though the moment no one was looking Lara would pinch her hard and hiss into her ear a single word that Cathrynne didn't understand: "*Changeling.*"

Lara wasn't always mean. Sometimes she was an indulgent older sister who let Cathrynne creep into her bed if she had a nightmare. They would spoon in the darkness and Lara would pet her hair and sing to her, old peasant lullabies she'd learned from Nestania.

Other than parties and social occasions, only two men visited the house on a regular basis. Alexandr Arco, who was Lara's father, and Alluin Westwind, the angel who had befriended their family. He came once a week, always bearing gifts for both Lara and Cathrynne.

Looking back, she recognized the lingering glances between Alluin and her mother, but at the time, she was an innocent child and never suspected a thing. They were discreet, always meeting at the house when the servants had the day off.

Nestania must have known about it. She *must* have. The affair had gone on for eleven years before the White Foxes caught wind of it.

Before Markus Viktorovich and Berti Baako caught wind of it.

Cathrynne knew who they were now, the witches who had dragged her from her home. She knew their *names*. It wasn't something you were ever told as a cypher. Most arrived as babies and never had a clue who did it to them.

But Cathrynne remembered everything. She'd broken through the block Markus had placed in her mind. And if she ever got of out here alive, she would make them suffer—

Rapid footsteps. The door swung open.

She scrambled back, raising an arm against the light. Before she could speak, a force yanked her into the corridor and hung her upside down. Cathrynne was eye level with Berti's face. Her jaw was swollen and discolored. A spectacular bruise spread across her cheek.

"Give me the sweven," Berti growled.

"No."

She was slowly lowered until she was staring at Berti's knees. The first blow caught her in the ribs. She gasped, trying to draw breath, but another kick followed, then another. She couldn't protect herself. Couldn't dodge. Could only endure as fists and feet rained down.

Just when she thought she'd pass out, the magic holding her aloft vanished. She crashed to the dirt floor, landing on her left shoulder. Fresh pain blazed through her. She curled into a ball.

Berti grabbed a fistful of hair and wrenched Cathrynne's head back. Her breath was hot and sour. "Give me the sweven."

"No." The word was barely audible.

Berti let her head fall against the dirt. "Then we'll be back," she said. "Next time, it'll be worse. And the time after that, and the time after that, until you break into a million pieces."

Kane and Ash threw her into the cell. The door slammed. The bar dropped into place. Darkness again. The iron tang of blood filled her mouth.

"No," she whispered, though the word sounded closer to a sob.

## CHAPTER 24
# GAVRIEL

H e woke to bright sunlight without warmth. Distant voices rose and fell in song. Their intricate harmonies washed over him, along with a gust of arctic wind.

He sat up, disoriented and weak. His last memory was of delirium and a cool hand on his brow.

*Cathrynne.*

A tendril of fear wormed through his belly, though he didn't know why. He was at the angelic stronghold of Mount Meru, in his own solar, an airy chamber with ancient mahogany furnishings and colorful tapestries of plants and animals. The doors to the balcony stood open. Beyond stretched the snow-clad Sundar Kush and, in the far distance where the gentle curve of the earth began, a glimmer of the Boreal Ocean.

The sky here was unlike anywhere else in the world: darkest indigo above, fading to cerulean and then pale blue at the horizon. Clouds drifted below the mountain peaks; such was the elevation of Mount Meru.

"You are awake, my lord!" a cheerful voice said.

Fenian Dawnsinger flitted through the arched doorway. The cherubim was a small, round man with flowing white hair. Prismatic colors swirled in his eyes. He was the seneschal who attended to the six archangels when they came home to visit. Gavriel had known him from boyhood and was fond of Fenian, but there was nothing he despised more than feeling ignorant and helpless.

"How long have I been here?" he demanded.

Fenian hovered above the foot of the bed, wings fluttering anxiously. "A fortnight, my lord."

"Two weeks!" Gavriel exclaimed.

The investigation into Casolaba's murder had gone cold by now. And what about Cathrynne? Had she returned to Kirith? Been reassigned to other duties? How would he manage to see her again if . . .

Gavriel tamped down this train of thought. "Where are my companions?" he asked, trying to sound dispassionate.

Fenian looked confused. "Your companions, my lord?"

"My secretary Edvin Yarl, for one," Gavriel snapped. "The cyphers Cathrynne Rowan and Mercy Blackthorn, for another. Where are they?"

Fenian quailed. "I'm afraid you must ask your father, Lord Morningstar. He will be pleased to hear you're awake."

Gavriel mastered his temper with effort. "It is not your fault. I apologize for my rudeness." He drew a deep breath, the frigid air clearing his head. "Who brought me here?"

Fenian brightened. "It was Lady Suriel. She sat at your bedside for the first week, but when you did not wake, she departed and asked me to keep watch over you."

"Did she say anything else?"

"No, my lord."

Gavriel sighed "Very well. Tell my father that I will come to him presently. I assume he is in the Chorale?"

Valoriel had always been a stern and remote figure, one to be obeyed without question and who rarely offered a word of praise. Naturally, this only made Gavriel want to please him all the more.

Then came the falling-out with the other two gods, Minerva

and Travian. Over the long centuries that followed, Valoriel withdrew from public life, often ordering Gavriel to stand as regent in his stead.

Music was the only thing his father cared about anymore. He would sit for months without moving, his gaze heavy-lidded and distant, listening to the choir. Once, Gavriel had asked him a question and received the answer a month later, with no acknowledgment that any time had passed.

He understood that despite Valoriel's physical form, he was not an angel but a god, and gods would always be unfathomable. Yet his father was no longer the energetic, decisive being Gavriel had once known. Secretly, he feared Valoriel was dying. Perhaps because the other parts of him—Travian and Minerva—had gone away.

"Ah, no," Fenian said. "He is at the Citadel."

Gavriel's brows rose. "Is he?"

"Yes, he spends most days observing the legions in their exercises."

"How long has that been the case?"

"Several years now, my lord."

Gavriel had not been to Mount Meru for two decades. Perhaps his father was improving. It gladdened his heart.

"Shall I bring food and wine?" Fenian asked.

Gavriel realized that he was very hungry, but he did not wish to delay seeing his father. He needed answers more than he needed sustenance. "Not just yet. Have my clothes been cleaned?"

"Indeed. You can find them in the wardrobe. I will summon seraphim to escort you." Fenian kept his expression neutral, but Gavriel knew what he was thinking.

*That I am too weak to fly on my own.*

"That won't be necessary," Gavriel said.

Fenian frowned. "Are you certain, my lord—"

"Perfectly." He managed a smile. "It is good to see you, old friend."

"And you, Lord Morningstar. We have missed your presence." The cherubim paused as though he might argue but changed his mind and flew away, wings humming.

Another arched doorway led to a bathing chamber with a sunken tub of rose quartz. Gavriel examined himself in the mirror. His face was thinner, the bones prominent. Angels were not immune to illness, but it was rare and usually mild.

He remembered feeling poorly the day after Barsal Casolaba's funeral. The healers coming from Angel Tower and finding nothing wrong with him. After that, his memories grew foggy. Haniel had visited, and a delegation of witches, though he could not recall speaking to them.

Whatever had laid him low must have been serious if he was brought to Mount Meru. Yet the purity of the mountain air and the healing power of the choir had dragged him back from the brink.

Gavriel bathed, pleased to find that he could flex both wings easily now. The break he had sustained falling from the rooftop was healed. He donned fresh clothing and stepped out to the open balcony. The drop plunged for thousands of cubits, but there was no need for a railing.

Angels didn't fall. At least, not accidentally.

Gavriel spread his wings, feathers ruffling in the updraft that perpetually flowed around Mount Meru's spires. A wave of dizziness swept him. But he could not appear weak, not here—and certainly not before his father.

Before he could doubt himself, Gavriel launched into the air, wings snapping open to their full span. For a few seconds, his own weight was too great for his wasted muscles, and he dropped like a stone. Panic clutched his chest. Then he remembered how to angle them to catch the thermals.

The fall arrested, he soared upward, heart racing. The exhilaration of flight raced through him. This at least had not changed.

Gavriel sped toward the Citadel of the Legions. It resembled a giant beehive, with dozens of open entrances into the barracks. The Citadel was not designed for defense since no army could launch a direct assault against Mount Meru. Any human—or witch, for that matter—would perish from the cold and the altitude before they were halfway up the mountain's flank.

Its main feature was the vast plaza that surrounded it, used for the drilling and training of the angelic host. As Gavriel approached, he saw them assembled, rank upon rank, their golden armor catching the sun, their movements perfectly synchronized.

On a high balcony overlooking the plaza stood a tall, solitary figure. He had dark hair and broad shoulders, with golden wing feathers. Even from a distance, Valoriel's commanding presence was unmistakable.

Gavriel spiraled down to land beside him. It took a great effort not to stumble.

His father's face—so like Gavriel's but for the grass-green eyes that had given him his other name, the Summerlord—registered approval, and Gavriel knew the risk had been worth it. Had he been carried by seraphim, he could picture the slight curl of disdain on Valoriel's lips.

"My son." Valoriel drew him into an embrace, a rare display of affection. "I am glad to see your strength restored."

Gavriel tried to steady the tremor in his thighs. "I am well enough." He turned to survey the host below. "Is there trouble brewing? Fenian tells me you spend your time here now."

Valoriel was silent for a long interval. Then he said, "We must be prepared for what is coming."

The words sounded ominous. "And what is that?" Gavriel asked.

His father's cool gaze studied the legions. "First, tell me what you remember."

"Not a great deal," Gavriel admitted. "I was told that Suriel brought me here. But last I recall, I was in Kota Gelangi. How did I end up in Arjevica?"

"She said a cypher brought you to her tower. And your secretary."

Valoriel's mouth thinned. He did not approve of Gavriel's penchant for associating with humans unless they were servants.

"They claimed that you were poisoned," his father continued, "with a gem called kaldurite."

Gavriel's quick intellect parsed the word at once. "Kal Machena," he murmured. "Durian Padulski. They're the ones who found it."

Valoriel nodded. "It has a unique property. It blocks the flow of ley entirely. A witch placed one among your wing feathers and kept it there with adhesive. It poisoned your blood."

Gavriel was stunned, but it fit with what Casolaba's mistress said—that the gem would change everything.

"Are you certain it was witches who tried to kill me?" he asked.

"Who else?" Valoriel replied. "They are the ones who murdered Casolaba over this gemstone. Clearly, the witches have the most to lose and are willing to kill to keep it secret."

"Has anyone spoken to the Morag?"

"What's the point? She will only deny involvement. No, the only course now is to secure the source of the kaldurite before the witches use it against us."

Gavriel exhaled, his mind racing. "I must speak to Cathrynne Rowan and Mercy Blackthorn."

Valoriel regarded him with a slight narrowing of his emerald eyes. "I imagine they have returned to Kirith, as you shall."

"Return to Kirith?" Gavriel stared at his father in disbelief. "But this stone is at the crux of it all. I cannot go home until I have proof of who murdered the consul—"

"Forget Casolaba," Valoriel said sharply. "Of far greater concern is the kaldurite and discovering where it came from." He looked suddenly intent. "Do you know?"

Gavriel shook his head. "I went to Pota Pras but never found the mine."

Disappointment clouded Valoriel's face. "I will set the seraphim hunting for this human girl, Kal Machena. In the meantime, you will go home and deal with all the pressing matters awaiting your attention there."

Gavriel opened his mouth to argue, but the beat of wings announced another arrival. Haniel alighted on the balcony in a flurry of white robes.

"Brother!" She came to his side and linked their arms. "I am so relieved to see you awake. We were all terribly worried. You must come to my solar and share a meal."

He did not want Haniel's company at the moment. There was too much to think about. "I will dine in my rooms—"

"Nonsense! The meal is already prepared. And you look as if you will keel over if you do not eat something."

In fact, he was ravenous. "Very well," Gavriel said. "Join us, father?"

A glance passed between them. Valoriel shook his head. "Food holds no appeal for me anymore. But you must heed your sister and take nourishment. We do not wish to see you take a turn for the worse."

———

CHERUBIM SERVANTS silently set out dishes of ashishim and karsu. The scent of pistachios, dates, and saffron rice mingled with a heady muscatel. Haniel was playing the gracious host, but her eyes—sharp, calculating—told a different story.

"More wine?" She lifted the crystal decanter.

One sip had set Gavriel's head spinning. "I prefer water," he said.

"As you like." Haniel took a sip. "It is from southern Iskatar. The humans there have a particular talent with grapes, if little else."

"You do them a disservice," Gavriel said. "The Iskaris are known for their poetry as well."

"Poetry that glorifies conquest and bloodshed," she retorted.

"That reflects their culture, not their nature." His gaze turned to the window of her solar. Night had fallen and a river of stars flowed through the sky above Mount Meru. A million suns, each with their own worlds. Had Travian and Minerva fled to one of them?

When he turned back, Haniel wore a cold smile. "You cannot deny the truth, Gavriel. Consul Casolaba's corruption is merely a symptom of the larger disease. The humans and witches cannot be trusted—certainly not with this new gemstone. They do not deserve the gift of free will."

A draft guttered the candles, casting shadows across her face. He had known Haniel for centuries. She was passive to a fault, never interfering in political matters. Now he wondered if that was a mask to conceal her own ambitions.

"The founding principle of Sion is free will," he reminded her.

She leaned forward, resting her alabaster arms on the table. "Travian and Minerva are gone, and it's clear they will not return. We must shape this world as we see fit, brother. Kaldurite—handled carefully—is the key."

"You knew about it all along, didn't you?" he exclaimed. "Yet you withheld that information when I first came to Satu Jos."

Haniel waved this away. "There were rumors such a stone existed, but no one had found one in centuries."

"Casolaba did," Gavriel said, "and it got him killed, along with the boy from Pota Pras."

"My point exactly! It is clear the witches were behind both deaths. They are desperate to find the source before we do." Her pink lips twisted. "The witches hoard power, while the humans squabble over scraps. And what do we do? We watch. We wait. We arbitrate petty disputes while the very foundation of our world crumbles."

Gavriel disliked agreeing with her, but some of what she said was true. "What exactly is your solution?"

"It is quite simple. Lithomancy is the foundation of the witches' power. Take that away, and they will have no choice but to fall into line. We abolish the chapter houses and place them under the direct authority of the archangels, to be deployed as we see fit. They will be a tool to restore order."

"Whose order? Our father's? Or yours?"

"*Ours*, Gavriel." Her tone grew honeyed again. "Would that be such a terrible thing?"

"What you're suggesting is tyranny. I won't be part of it."

A flash of anger crossed her face. "You have no choice. The decision has been made."

"By whom?" he snapped. "Have you spoken to the other archangels?"

"Some agree with me," Haniel said. "Others have grown complacent, attached to their pet humans." Her flat gaze suggested that Gavriel fell into this category.

"Like you've grown attached to fantasies of absolute power?"

Her hand moved like a striking snake. Gavriel caught her wrist, feeling the rage that trembled through her.

"You forget yourself, Light-Bringer," she hissed.

"And you forget what we *are*," he replied evenly. "We were created to serve, not rule."

She wrenched her arm free. "Naïve, as always. Do you imagine that your vaunted reputation means *anything*? That your judgments matter? You're a relic, Morningstar. Clinging to ideals that no longer serve us."

"Is that Valoriel speaking?" he asked bitterly. "Or is this ambition your own?"

Something dangerous flashed in her eyes. She rose from the supper table, her wings unfurling. "Be careful, Gavriel," she said softly. "Even those who stand highest among us can fall."

The door to the solar burst open. "Is that a threat, Haniel?"

Suriel stood in the doorway, looking elegant in a flowing dashiki of blue-green silk. Six seraphim flanked her, hands resting on their sword hilts.

"Sister." Haniel's stare cast daggers. "I don't recall inviting you."

Suriel stepped into the room, her dark braids adorned with gold beads. "I left explicit instructions that I was to be informed the instant our brother woke up, yet someone countermanded them."

Haniel scoffed. "I don't know what you're implying, but Morningstar is my guest, not my prisoner."

"Is that so?" Suriel moved deeper into the solar, her seraphim standing guard at the door. "Then you will not object if he returns to Arjevica with me."

"We were in the middle of a conversation," Haniel replied coldly.

"It sounded more like an argument." Suriel's smile was sharp as a blade. "Or perhaps I misheard?"

Tension crackled. His sisters had never liked each other. "My business in Satu Jos is not finished," Gavriel began.

"You have no say about what happens in my province," Haniel snapped. "Your investigation is closed. If you cross my border again, I shall take it up with Valoriel."

"We shall see," he replied. "Thank you for the meal, sister."

She glared as they left the solar, Suriel's seraphim guards closing ranks around them.

"You have excellent timing," he said wryly.

"And *you* have a talent for making dangerous enemies." Suriel's dark eyes were serious. "We need to talk, but not here."

Something in her face made him stop. "What's happened? Tell me now."

She pulled him into a crossing corridor. "You were brought to me in the middle of the night, at death's door."

"Kaldurite poisoning. I know."

"Yes, but what you don't know is that one of your cypher guards said it was Haniel who did it. And your secretary agreed with her."

Gavriel's brows rose. He was mildly shocked, but less so than he would have been an hour ago. Haniel had big plans for herself, and she would not suffer obstacles.

"What was their evidence?" he asked.

"Nothing conclusive, which is why our father doesn't know yet. Haniel has risen high in his esteem. She travels here often, far more than the rest of us. I think she whispers poison in his ear."

That would explain Valoriel's new habit of watching the legions rather than listening to the Chorale.

"The two cyphers can be trusted without question," he said. "And Yarl, too. I must speak with them."

"That is the problem," she admitted. "I sent Edvin Yarl back to Kirith for his own protection."

That worm of dread stirred in Gavriel's gut again. "And the cyphers?"

"They are missing. Both of them."

"How?" he managed, his throat suddenly dry.

"Mercy Blackthorn chose to remain behind when your coach was attacked in the forest. She may yet live, and I am searching for her. Cathrynne Rowan I met myself. She and Yarl brought you to the Angel Tower. After we spoke, she left for the chapter house in Arjevica, but she never arrived. She has vanished without a trace."

White-hot rage coursed through him. "Why wasn't I told this the moment I woke?"

"I'm telling you now," Suriel said, her tone sharpening. "Brother! Wait—"

Gavriel stormed back to Haniel's solar and threw the door open.

"Where is she?" he demanded.

Haniel's brow creased. "Where is *who*?"

"Cathrynne Rowan!"

"The cypher? Why would I know?"

"Because someone has taken her." He strode over to Haniel, fingers itching to seize her slender neck and hoist her into the air. "If you harmed her, I swear that you will regret it for the rest of your days—"

"I have no idea where she is," Haniel snapped, backing away. "How dare you accuse me?" She turned to the doorway. "Suriel, talk sense into him! What do I care about a *cypher*?"

Something in her voice brought Gavriel back to sanity. She sounded genuinely outraged.

"Listen, brother," Suriel said evenly. "If Haniel had entered my city, I would know it—regardless of her special powers. *It was not her.*"

Haniel arched a brow at him, her jaw tight.

"Just stay out of my way," Gavriel growled.

Her blue eyes grew even frostier. She raised her goblet. Her hand trembled slightly, whether from fear or anger he couldn't say. "As you wish, Morningstar."

He turned his back and joined Suriel in the hallway once more.

"We will return to Arjevica with the legions," he said. "They will go house to house—"

She seized his arm. "Valoriel will not deploy his elite soldiers for a half-blood cypher. And you will only expose your true feelings. Haniel is no fool. You have just given her more leverage over you! Take yourself in hand, brother."

He drew a deep breath. "Then *you* will help me find her, with every resource at your disposal."

"Of course I will help you," Suriel chided. "Why do you think I left your bedside? I have been trying to locate her. Calm yourself, Gavriel."

Icy wind struck his face as they launched from one of the platforms and flew toward the black tower called Sinjali's Lance, whose portals led to every province in Sion.

He would give Suriel a chance. But if she failed, he would tear her beloved city down with his own hands if he had to, stone by stone, until he found Cathrynne Rowan.

# CHAPTER 25
# CATHRYNNE

**W**hen the beatings failed, the White Foxes tried threats.

They said she would spend the remainder of her days in this dark cell, with a ceiling too low to stand and walls narrow enough to touch.

They said Gavriel Morningstar was dead. No one would come looking for her.

They said Mercy was being held in another cell, and she would die too if Cathrynne didn't cooperate.

But they were lying—about the last two things, at least.

She'd overheard them talking about how Mercy had escaped in the woods. And she knew Gavriel was alive because she dreamt about him. He was in a majestic city of snow and ice that could only be Mount Meru. He had been unconscious, but now he was awake.

Yet she saw a sword dangling above his head and knew the danger had not passed.

She *had* to get out of this prison. For herself, and to keep Gavriel safe from harm. She was still his bodyguard.

When she heard footsteps and saw the faint glow of a lantern under the door, she curled into a ball, muttering incoherently.

"Pick her up." Kane's deep voice.

From the corner of her eye, Cathrynne saw Ash crouch to enter the tiny room.

The White Foxes never wore projective gems. There was no metal in the cell, either.

But there was metal in Ash's face.

They thought Cathrynne couldn't use it. Cyphers didn't learn to wield receptive magic.

But they had forgotten that she'd been raised as a full-blood witch until the age of eleven. And she had nothing to do between beatings except comb through her early memories and dig out the things she'd been taught.

Projective magic used conscious *will*. Receptive magic used subconscious *need*.

Mastery was a far more complicated endeavor, but that was the gist.

Ash bent down and roughly grabbed Cathrynne's bruised arm. The moment she made contact, Cathrynne opened her mind to the resonance of the silver piercings.

She saw a moon reflected in water. Silver was connected with divination. It was also, as she had told the young cypher class, an element of protection.

*Mighty Minerva*, she begged, *please help me*.

Ash gasped as the ley flowed from her own jewelry into Cathrynne's shaky control. It flickered, then held steady, forming a shield. Cathrynne threw an elbow to her face, ducked past Kane, and got out the door.

She sprinted barefoot down the narrow corridor. Light flared ahead, and then someone unleashed a projective spell. It washed over her, but she could feel the protective magic dwindle. On the next blast, the shield wavered and popped.

Kane's huge bulk grabbed her from behind. Cathrynne screamed as they dragged her back to the cell and threw her inside. She lay there, panting. She knew they wouldn't come back for a while. Maybe days.

A heavy despair came over her.

But they did come back, only minutes later. As she heard their voices in the passage, the darkness faded and she saw . . .

. . . *the lid of a car trunk slams down. Ash is driving down a long gravel road, headlights spearing the fog. Marsh reeds whisper in the night wind. A splash and a bundle wrapped in chains sinks into black water.*

They were coming to murder her.

Cathrynne's eyes snapped open in the darkness.

Well, of course they were. She wouldn't give them the sweven and they couldn't let her go. Even cyphers had rights. Kidnapping and torture would bring trouble with the High Council.

A sick thrill of terror went through her. She stood, hunching awkwardly under the low ceiling. The door swung open. Light flooded in.

It was her usual tormenters: Berti, Kane, and Ash, who had taken out her piercings. Kane had also removed his silver bridge. There was a gap where his gleaming front teeth used to be.

"Turn around," Berti ordered.

"Listen," she said, licking cracked lips, "I changed my mind. You can have the sweven. Of my own free will."

Berti's expression didn't change. "Then give it to me now."

*And you'll kill me the moment it's done.*

She shook her head. "I'll give it to Markus."

"You have no leverage to dictate terms." Berti's gray eyes were pitiless. "Last chance. Give me the sweven."

"I swear I'll give it to Markus—"

Berti gestured to Ash and Kane. As the red-haired witch and her huge partner stooped to enter the cell, Cathrynne saw their hands around her throat. Saw the life drain from her eyes.

Blood trickled from her nose to her lip, but she barely felt it.

"Wait!" she cried. "I can be of value!"

Berti looked bored of it all. "How?"

Cathrynne swallowed hard, beyond terror now. Secrets meant nothing anymore.

"Ash killed Durian Padulski," she said in a rush. "I don't think she meant to. It was an accident. She was trying to stop him from running, but her spell hit him too hard. It stopped his heart. He was dead before he fell into the river."

Ash looked stunned. "How could you possibly—"

"Shut up," Berti said. She was watching Cathrynne intently.

"You're here to kill me," Cathrynne said. "Strangulation so it's cleaner. No blood. Then you'll drive my body to the marshes and let the tides take it."

The silence stretched, broken only by the sound of Kane's uneven breathing.

"We'll bring her to Markus," Berti said after a long moment.

Cathrynne started shaking. She thought her knees might give out and braced a hand against the wall. The three of them backed away to give her room as she crouched down and stepped out of the cell.

No one touched her. It was like she suddenly had a contagious disease. She walked with Ash in front and Berti and Kane behind. Just standing upright was a gift. She had no idea how long they had kept her in the cell, but when the cramped darkness gave way to wide, carpeted halls, tears blurred her vision.

They took her back to the bedchamber where she'd first been held, which now seemed like a palace.

"Sit," Berti commanded.

Cathrynne obeyed, moving stiffly to the bed and perching on the edge.

Ash and Kane watched her from their old post by the door. Berti left without another word. After a few minutes, she returned with Markus. He wore black tie like he was on his way to a party, not a silver hair out of place. He paused when he saw her, pity and disgust on his face. Never had she loathed him so much.

"You've been keeping secrets," Markus said.

"You didn't ask the right questions."

He studied her. "You're a seer, yet the madness hasn't consumed you."

Cathrynne smiled. "I've glimpsed the future and it isn't rosy, Markus."

"You mean the Dark-bringer."

She couldn't hide her surprise. "You know?"

"I know he will bring chaos, that is all. Have you seen his face?"

"No." She leaned forward. "But I can tell you this. When he comes, not even kaldurite will save you from him."

She sensed that Markus was unsettled, though he tried to cover it.

"The end of an age?" His tone was patronizing. "I heard the same from seers at the kloster in Arjevica."

So others besides Julia Camara were having the same vision. A chill went through her.

"But if you give me a name," Markus continued in the maddeningly reasonable tone he always used with her, "I promise to keep you under my protection."

Cathrynne didn't laugh aloud at the absurdity of this statement—only because it hurt too much to laugh.

"I want my freedom," she said.

"That might be possible, depending on what you know."

Berti stepped forward, her mouth an angry slash. "You can't seriously consider letting her go!"

Markus rounded on her. "And you went well beyond the bounds of what I approved for her interrogation," he snapped.

"Because you didn't want to know," Berti shot back, "but your mother approved it. She has more backbone."

His jaw tightened. "My mother is not the head of the White Foxes. I am, and you will do well to remember that."

The two witches stared at each other.

"She's doomed to go mad anyway," Berti argued. "It's obvious she knows nothing worthwhile. All this is just a ruse to postpone the inevitable. We'll be doing her a favor." She glanced at

Cathrynne. "Wouldn't you prefer a clean death now that you've had a taste of the kloster life?"

Cathrynne didn't bother to answer.

"I didn't mean for it to go this far," Markus protested, but his voice was weakening.

Ash watched her like a caracal about to pounce on a wounded rat. Kane stood slightly apart from the others. He was pale and sweating, as though he was in discomfort.

Maybe it was because she had just worked her first receptive spell, but Cathrynne sensed something. Muffled, but there. A faint resonance of metal.

Kane had removed his silver teeth. Ash had taken out all her piercings. Cathrynne knew there was not a single *pin* in this room. Neither Berti nor Markus would be so careless as to wear anything she could use to work lithomancy.

The vision flashed before her eyes. A silent gunshot. Red blooming against the white of Kane's coat.

Was it possible that Kal Machena's bullet was still inside him?

*Yes, it was.* She'd spent enough time at the infirmary to understand basic medicine. If the bullet had lodged near his heart or lungs, the doctors might have left it there rather than risk removing it.

That bullet was the last piece of metal she might ever touch.

Her last chance to walk out of this house alive.

But how to get hold of it? The bullet was inside him.

Cathrynne had been taught never to cast the ley in her own body. Doing so would kill her.

Well. She had nothing left to lose, did she?

She closed her eyes and felt the blood coursing through her veins—half from her angel father, half from her witch mother. She drew a thread of ley from it. Pain gouged her bones, bright and vicious.

Her focus narrowed to a single point: the bullet in Kane's

chest. It was composed of copper, lead, and antimony. The first two were receptive. But antimony was projective. Fire element.

"What are you doing?" Kane took a step forward, rage twisting his face.

Cathrynne *pulled.* A lightning bolt of agony made her eyes water—oh gods, it hurt!—but the bullet tore from his chest and flew across the room. She snatched it from the air, hot and blood-slicked.

Markus backed toward the door, eyes wide. "Now, Cathrynne—"

She ignited the antimony. Poured every lie, every blow, every moment of degradation into the spell. A shockwave blasted outward, exploding the windows. It threw Ash into a bookcase. Kane sank to one knee and gave a deep, terrible groan, one hand pressed to his chest. Blood seeped between his fingers.

Berti Baako sprawled on the floor. She looked like a fish that had just been slapped against a rock. Cathrynne walked over, grabbed her projective hand—Berti was a lefty—and snapped the bones like kindling. Berti screamed, a very satisfying sound. Then she broke the right one, too, for good measure.

"You little bitch!"

It wasn't Berti, who had fainted. Cathrynne spun around. Veronica Viktorovich swept into the room, gaunt and glittering in a sequined dress. Thick black makeup ringed her eyes. Markus stood behind his mother, the coward. Cathrynne knew she couldn't fight them both.

She ran for the broken window and flung herself into rainy darkness. She had no idea how far the fall would be. No idea where she actually was. But she would die before letting them take her again.

She felt a sharp sting along the sole of her foot as she cleared the jagged shards of glass. A stone terrace rushed up to meet her. She landed awkwardly, breath whooshing out. Her ankle twisted but somehow she rolled and gained her feet, too jacked up to feel much pain. She pushed on the terrace doors. Locked. *Dammit!*

Cathrynne glanced up at the floor above. Veronika's head appeared through the broken window. The smile on her face was terrifying.

"Stupid girl," Veronika called down. "Can you see your own death now? You should have taken the easy option, but it will be very hard, I can promise you that—"

Cathrynne rattled the door handle. This time, she heard a soft click and sobbed with relief. She yanked and it swung open. An empty bedroom lay beyond. There was a mirror in a gilt frame and she caught a glimpse of a wild-eyed, ghoulish creature that made her rear back until she realized it was her own reflection.

Another door, another hallway. Her vision tunneled as she broke into a fast limp. There had to be a way out. Just keep going, keep running—

She rounded a corner and slammed into a body. A white-haired man in a servant's uniform yelled something, but she couldn't make out the words over the buzzing in her head. She shoved him aside and flew down another flight of stairs. The pain in her foot was getting bad. And . . . damn, she was bleeding all over.

Shouts came from somewhere in the house, somewhere close. It was like a dream where you're trying to wade through quicksand with a monster at your heels. Cathrynne skidded across a foyer with a slick marble floor and nearly fell but managed to catch the edge of a table, the breath sawing in her throat.

*Running footsteps. They're coming down the stairs.*

She hobbled to the front door, trying to keep her weight off the foot that had been sliced to ribbons. It was locked so she grabbed a heavy umbrella stand and hurled it at the nearest window. Broken glass rained down on the front walk. She picked her way through the shards, no time to be gingerly about it, and then she was sucking in breaths of night air and cranking that limping run into high gear, leaving a trail of bloody footprints behind her.

The street was lined with neoclassical mansions behind iron gates, but no lights turned on at the ruckus. Apparently, the neighbors knew better than to get involved with whatever crazy shit went down at the Viktorovich residence.

If she hadn't chanced to look back, the cat would have had her. But she did and saw a lithe shadow padding silently down the center of the street. Veronica's caracal, its eyes gathering the moonlight like silver coins.

The fine hair on Cathrynne's arms rose up. It had fangs as long as her pinky finger and stood chest-high. A tufted ear swiveled as she wiggled through a hole in a box hedge and lay flat, the sweet, living smell of earth and grass making her heart clench after so long in sterile darkness. The caracal paused, head lifting to scent the air.

She held perfectly still, like a young rabbit in a field. After an endless minute, it padded away. She cut across a lawn and came out at another street, then paused to get her bearings. The houses were grand, with steeply peaked roofs and fanciful stonework. It was tempting to pound on a door and beg for sanctuary, but Cathrynne feared they'd hand her over—or be killed for harboring her. Not worth the risk.

She paused to tear a scrap from her filthy shirt and bind the deep cut in the pad of her left foot. When she looked up, Markus and his deranged mother were at the end of the street. They walked side by side, not even hurrying. They thought they had her cornered.

She ducked before they saw her and staggered through a stand of trees. The adrenaline rush was fading. A black tide of exhaustion threatened to drag her under. She'd been beaten and starved and lost a fair amount of blood. Not to mention working the ley in her own body, which should have killed her.

Angel Tower rose up in the distance, a white spire with a

gold cupola on top. It looked almost close enough to reach out and touch—and impossibly far away.

She was still in Arjevica. If she could just get out of this wealthy, too-quiet neighborhood, find somewhere with lights and people . . .

Cathrynne hurried around a corner and realized that she'd hit a cul-de-sac with no way out. At the end stood a house with a blue-painted door and gargoyles crouching below the turrets.

She froze, wondering if it was a hallucination. Twenty years had passed since she'd last seen that door.

"Cathrynne!" Markus's voice drifted through the darkness. "Don't make this harder than it needs to be. We can still work things out!"

All the pain she'd ignored came crashing down. She was pretty sure her ribs were cracked because every breath felt like she was being poked with a knife. Taking shallow, panting breaths, she unlatched the garden gate and limped up the path. The old familiar scent of a white rose variety called Polar Star perfumed the air. She felt delirious, as if it were all a fever dream and she would wake in that tiny room again.

There were no lights on at the house. Cathrynne's hand shook as she banged the owl-shaped knocker against the front door. She remembered that, too.

*Please be home, please be home.*

Were those shadows moving at the gate? She banged the knocker again, pounding it frantically until the door opened. A young servant in a nightcap stood on the other side. Her eyes widened.

"Who is it, Mary?" a voice called from within the house.

The door opened all the way, revealing a woman in her middle years with thick, straight brows and strong features. She wore a belted silk dressing gown, black hair streaked with gray loose around her shoulders. When she saw who had come to her doorstep, her face drained of color.

"Please, mother," Cathrynne pleaded, "let me in."

# CHAPTER 26

# KAL

It was almost the midwinter Caristia holiday and festive strings of white lights decorated the trees in Lavro Park. The air held a crisp edge that promised snow flurries, and a vendor did a brisk business selling hot cider with cinnamon sticks in paper cups. Couples strolled arm in arm along the gravel pathways, heads bent close. Everyone seemed to glow with happiness.

Kal envied them. She'd forgotten what it was like to lead a normal life. To be called by her own name and not be constantly looking over her shoulder. Her brother Bastian would be sick with worry by now, but without an identity card she was stuck in Arjevica.

Nerves made her low-heeled shoe jink a fast rhythm against the park bench. It was a risk meeting Levi again. She had everything to lose and nothing to gain. She *knew* that.

But something drew her to him. He dressed like a rich boy, but he didn't act like one. In a way, he reminded her of Durian when they first met. There was something different about Levi, like he didn't quite fit in with other people. She sensed a fierce intelligence, but also loneliness. He had secrets. Yet she felt safe with him and her instincts were pretty good.

"Plus he's gorgeous," Durian remarked. "Just saying."

Kal rolled her eyes. "You're so shallow."

He chuckled. "Takes one to know one."

Sadly, Durian had her number. Kal's heart beat a little faster when she saw Levi enter the park. He wore a gray wool coat and flat newsboy cap, his short-cropped chestnut hair brushing his nape. One arm cradled a bottle. He grinned when he saw her.

"You came," he said in that quick, musical accent she couldn't quite place. "I was bracing myself for rejection."

"Oh, really? But you're the one who's late," she teased.

"Only by three minutes," he protested. "And that's because the line at Falin's was out the door." He shook his head. "The Caristia crowds."

"How dare they have fun?" Kal said in mock outrage.

He frowned. "I suppose they have as much right to as we do."

She shook her head. Levi was very literal-minded. "I was joking."

"Ah." He took out a corkscrew and deftly twisted it into the bottle. The cork came free with a soft pop. His blue eyes twinkled. "Ladies first."

"Oh, I get it." She cocked a brow. "You're testing it out on me to see if it's as gods-awful as last time."

"Is it that obvious?"

Kal accepted the bottle with exaggerated reluctance and took a sip. She didn't know much about wine, but it was better than the cheap zelas. "Hey, that's pretty good."

He looked relieved. "The owner of Falin's said you like red Gamay."

In fact, her *clients* liked Gamay, but Kal wasn't about to tell him that. She felt touched at the effort he'd made.

"I think you splurged," she said, holding up her long blue nails, which sported fake diamonds. "That wine not only tastes expensive, but I bet it wouldn't even strip off my polish."

Levi laughed. "We can't endanger those nails. They look like they took a *long* time to paint."

"Oh, I don't do them myself. We practice on each other. It's all part of the exciting cosmetology track!"

Kal had planned to play the part of Kyra Navarra with all earnestness, but she couldn't keep the sarcastic edge from her voice. She could tell he picked up on it and quickly took a swig from the bottle. "Happy Caristia!" She lifted it in a salute, then passed it back.

"Caristia Eve," Levi corrected, taking a long swallow. "Which is even better because all the shops are still open. Have you eaten, Kyra? I'd love to take you out to dinner."

She glanced longingly at the row of cozy, elegant restaurants just a few blocks away. But it was too dangerous. What if she ran into a teacher from the school?

"Oh, I already ate," she said. "But thanks."

Levi nodded. Their first awkward silence fell.

"So . . ." she said. "You never told me what you do."

He leaned against the bench. One arm casually draped along the back, though he didn't touch her. "I work for my mother."

"What's she like?"

"She loves me. She loves all of us. But she isn't easy to please."

Levi offered the bottle. Kal passed. She hadn't eaten a bite since breakfast and the wine was going straight to her head.

"Doing what exactly?" she pressed.

His eyes met hers. "Mother has big plans for me. But right now, I fix problems."

She waited, but he said nothing more. "Well, that's not vague," she teased.

He thought for a minute. "Let's just say my mother has interests throughout the empire. When those interests are threatened, she sends me in to get things back on track."

The wine loosened her tongue. "Ah, so your mother doesn't always see eye to eye with the law, I take it."

"Human laws? Or angelic laws?"

"I don't know. Aren't they the same?"

"Not always. But my mother is a law unto herself, Kyra."

Across the street, the doors of the Orlov Theater swung open. A stream of ballet patrons spilled onto the steps, their voices rising like birds taking flight. Women in sparkling sheath dresses, men in black tie and long woolen overcoats. Sleek automobiles pulled up alongside caracal-drawn taxis, the drivers leaping out to open doors.

"Have you ever gone to the ballet?" Kal asked, thinking it looked nice.

Levi shook his head. "I'd rather be sitting here with you."

A group veered towards the park. Kal's heart stopped. Lara Lenormand walked arm in arm with a tall, auburn-haired witch. He said something and she threw her head back and laughed. A choker of emeralds and sapphires gleamed at her throat. Five seconds and she'd walk right past the bench.

It was too late to slink away. In desperation, Kal turned toward Levi. "Play along," she whispered. His blue eyes widened as she leaned in and kissed him. He tasted sweet like the wine, and he smelled even better. Some expensive aftershave that made her think of dark pine forests.

Levi stiffened. Then one hand cupped the nape of her neck, the other settling at her waist and drawing her closer. Kal was vaguely aware of the group walking past, but most of her senses were consumed with his firm lips and the way he kissed her, like nothing else existed in the world.

Lara Lenormand was long gone by the time she found the resolve to push against Levi's chest. He gently nipped her lower lip, then drew back to look at her face, his gaze heavy-lidded.

"That was . . ."

"A distraction," she said hoarsely. She peered over his shoulder. Lara and the other witches were halfway across the park.

Levi followed her gaze. "Who was that? One of your teachers?"

"Worse," Kal admitted. "The dean of the school."

"Then I'm glad she's gone," he said, adding softly, "but I'm not sorry she passed by."

Kal looked away, cheeks burning. "Let's go somewhere else. This is too public."

He corked the bottle. "I know just the place."

"Not your flat," she said quickly.

"Don't worry, Kyra. I don't expect anything from you. Not unless you give it freely."

She relaxed. "What did you have in mind?"

"A change of scenery. You won't run into any teachers, I can promise that. It's not far and the view is spectacular." He tilted his head toward the clocktower about a half mile away, its four illuminated faces marking the hour for all of Arjevica. "My cousin works there. I have a key."

She hesitated. "Just so we're clear. Don't think taking me somewhere private is going to get you into my pants—"

He frowned slightly. "If anyone should be worried about being taken advantage of, it's me."

"What?"

"Your gun pressed into my, ah . . . ribs when you grabbed me. You're not as subtle as you think."

She laughed despite herself. "No offense, but a girl needs protection in this town."

Levi's gaze darkened. "I'm your protection, Kyra. Nothing will ever happen to you while you're with me."

He looked dead serious. It was sweet. Maybe a little creepy, too, but still sweet.

"Fine." She smiled. "Show me this famous view."

They left the Beaux Arts district and walked through the hub of the provincial government. The buildings were closed for Caristia, but they had pretty wreaths and colored lights decorating the outside.

The clocktower stood just past the popular assembly. Levi unlocked the door and led her to a winding staircase.

"There are four hundred and twelve steps," he said. "Think you can make it?"

She snorted. "Of course I can."

Kal's legs began to burn around step two hundred. The spiral was relentless, winding ever upward into darkness, occasionally broken by small windows that offered glimpses of the city falling away beneath them.

The stairs ended at a wooden trap door. He pushed it open and climbed through, then turned back to offer her a hand. She took it, his warm palm sending little jolts across her skin.

The belfry was a forest of massive wooden beams, gears as tall as a man, and iron weights suspended on chains. Narrow catwalks wound between the mechanisms, leading to platforms positioned at each of the four clock faces. The air smelled of oil and dust.

He led her along one of the catwalks and stopped at a platform behind the eastern clock face. It was clear glass, except for the huge hands, and Arjevica spread out below in a sea of lights.

"I like high places," Levi said. "They give you a fresh perspective."

The soles of her feet tingled looking through the clock face. They had to be three hundred cubits in the air. A wave of vertigo swept over her.

"Not me," Kal said, trying to keep the panic from her voice. "I don't mind tight spots, but I don't like heights."

Levi frowned. "I'm sorry. If I'd known, I wouldn't have brought you."

"I didn't know until now," she admitted, hands shaking. "Damnit . . ."

He pulled her closer, resting his chin on the top of her head. "Just close your eyes and hold onto me. I won't let you fall."

His heart beat steadily against her chest. Kal's own pulse started to slow.

"I've made mistakes before," he said quietly, "but I don't want to make one with you."

"I . . ." She didn't know what to say. "Levi, I like you a lot. But I don't want to stay in Arjevica."

He didn't tense or push her away. All he said was, "That's obvious."

It felt so good to snuggle into his warm coat. "I"m sorry," she said. "I didn't mean to lead you on."

"Don't be sorry." His warm breath tickled her forehead. "I want you to be happy, Kyra. What's stopping you from leaving?"

She opened her mouth to lie, then reconsidered. He was the only soul she knew here besides the other students. She'd considered putting the word out among her client network that she needed a fake ID, but it was too much of a risk if one of the teachers found out.

Since that night at the park when she stupidly wrote *Durian Lives* in lipstick, Kal had sensed time running out. It wasn't a matter of whether she *wanted* to stay anymore. The only question was how long she could get away with this charade before the white witches found her.

And she had a feeling it wouldn't be much longer.

Levi might be her best hope. His mother sounded like she associated with some shady people. He'd kept Kal's secret about sneaking over the wall. It wouldn't be much of a stretch to admit that she wanted to leave the Lenormand School for good.

"I lost my identity card," she said, "and I can't go home for it. So I'm kind of stuck."

Levi pulled back to look her in the eye. His handsome face was grave. "I can help you with that."

"Really?"

"Sure. I have connections."

Her heart soared. "How much would it cost?"

"Nothing. Consider it a favor."

Kal didn't like owing people. "I can pay my own way. How much?"

His gaze lingered on her lips. "Virtue is its own reward."

She snorted. "You deserve a real reward."

A rumble like a purring cat came from his throat. "How about another kiss?"

Oh, it was tempting! "How about five draghas?" she countered.

His smile dazzled. "If you insist, I'll accept one dragha. *Reluctantly*."

"You can't buy a cup of kopi with one dragha!"

Levi sobered. "Well, that's all I'll take."

She didn't want to seem ungracious. "Thank you. It means a lot. How long?"

"Let me talk to some people. I'd say a week or so."

His arms were still firmly around her. She realized that her vertigo had faded. In the darkness of the clock tower, she could see the moon floating above the city, half in shadow, half in light.

"Why are you helping me, Levi?" she asked.

"Because it's the right thing to do," he said quietly. "I can tell you're scared of something. You put on a brave face, but you wouldn't be at the Lenormand School if you weren't running from something. If I had the power, I'd deal with whoever it was myself. But for now, I can make sure you keep a step ahead."

She absorbed this in silence for a minute. "That's it? You're not going to ask me who it is?"

"No. If you wanted to tell me, you would."

His shoulders tensed as three seraphim flew past the clock tower, their great wings beating hard. In the distance, Kal saw more angels speeding above the city. They were a common enough sight, but usually they were headed to and from the Angel Tower. These . . . well, the way they were quartering the streets below, they seemed to be hunting for something.

*It can't be me,* she thought with a shiver. *Can it?*

"You're getting cold," Levi said. "We should go down." He stepped back and held out a hand. Kal took it. They descended the long, twisting staircase, not speaking until they reached the street.

"Give me one week," Levi said. "I'll have your transit papers by then. Do you want to use the name Kyra Navarra?"

She shook her head. "Just make up a name. I don't care what it is." She bit her lip. "Can you buy me a cheap ticket on one of the ferries to Bactra? I promise I'll pay you back."

Once she crossed the wall for the last time, she didn't want to waste a minute getting out of the city.

"Of course. Let's meet at the docks. Say, nine o'clock." He tugged his cap on. "Can I walk you to the school? Make sure you get back safe?"

She smiled. "I'll be fine. Thank you, Levi. For everything."

In the moonlight, his face seemed both young and impossibly old at the same time. "It's my pleasure. Goodnight, Kyra." He flipped his collar up and walked away. Even his stride was athletic and graceful.

"You think he's too good to be true," Durian remarked.

Kal turned. He was leaning against a lamppost, the ember of a cigarette glowing in the dark. He wore the too-small brown suit from his wake.

"You don't even smoke," she muttered.

Durian flicked the butt into the gutter. "Tell me I'm wrong."

Kal sighed. Levi had vanished into the night.

"Not too good to be true," she said with a sad smile. "Just too good for *me*."

## CHAPTER 27
# CATHRYNNE

She woke to the smell of beeswax. For a bad moment, she thought she was back in Markus's house. She jerked to sitting, heart racing with the urge to run or fight, but the view out the window was of a garden, wild and overgrown yet familiar.

Beneath it was a toy chest with a snake made of green felt curled up on top, next to a tatty stuffed cat with stripes that were bleached nearly white on one side by the sunlight spilling into the room, as if it had not been moved in years.

Their names came to her instantly: Fang and Henry.

Cathrynne's pulse slowed as she realized that she'd escaped the monstrous Viktorovich family and was in her childhood bedroom.

It was too surreal.

She'd never expected to return. And once she'd gotten over the rage and betrayal and homesickness of a child who'd been given to strangers across the sea, Cathrynne had never wanted to. The girl who'd been driven away in the backseat of a Jentzen Mirage was a stranger. Nothing to do with her anymore. She was a cypher of Kirith now, and the chapter house was her family.

But chance had brought her back—and there was no escaping *that*.

She felt terribly thirsty and downed a glass of water that was sitting on the bedside table. Her feet were bandaged with fresh gauze. The rest of her felt like one big bruise. On the plus side, she still had all her teeth, and nothing seemed actually broken.

Voices murmured in the hall. For a moment, she was tempted to burrow under the covers and go back to sleep. Not face any of it. But that wasn't an option. Cathrynne rose stiffly from the bed and hobbled across the room, pressing an ear to the door.

" . . . three cracked ribs and multiple contusions. Her kidneys are likely bruised so she'll see pink urine. That should eventually stop on its own. The salve must be applied to her lacerations twice daily." A pause. "You understand that I have to report this. Assault is a serious crime—"

No. No, no. She jerked open the door. The three women in the hall turned to look at her. Her mother Hysto was still regal as a hawk, her face unlined though she was past sixty. Nestania, her grandmother, looked the same. Tall and olive-skinned, with white hair cascading to her waist. Gems gleamed at her throat and hands.

The third woman was younger and carried a black medical bag. She had brown eyes—not a witch. Her hair was cut short, and she wore a fashionable man's suit with perfect confidence. Cathrynne liked her, but she couldn't allow word to get out that she was here.

"No reports." The words came out a croak.

The doctor frowned. "You shouldn't be out of bed."

She gripped the door jamb. "I was in an accident. I'll be fine—"

"Nonsense," the doctor retorted briskly. "There are bruises upon bruises. It is quite obvious that these injuries were inflicted over time."

Hysto rushed to Cathrynne's side, guiding her back to bed. The raw look in her eyes made Cathrynne deeply uncomfortable.

"Tell the doctor I don't remember what happened," she whispered. "Make her go away. *No reports.*"

Hysto studied her for a moment, then nodded. She returned to the hall. They all spoke in low voices. The doctor came into the room.

"At least let me give you something for the pain," she said. "It will help you sleep."

"No sedatives," Cathrynne said firmly.

The doctor sighed. "Very well. But you must stay on bed rest for a week."

Cathrynne promised. She'd say anything to get rid of this woman. Hysto showed the doctor out, leaving Nestania, whose silver eyes seemed to see straight through her.

Please," Cathrynne rasped. "Tell no one I'm here. *No one.*"

"What have you gotten yourself into, child?"

"I'm not a child." Her voice hardened. "And you owe me this."

Nestania's gaze brushed the raven tattoo on her hand. A brief look of shame crossed her face. "Who did it?" she asked.

"I don't remember."

Cathrynne rolled over and shut her eyes. A moment later, she heard her grandmother leave the room.

---

FOR THE FIRST THREE DAYS, every time she slept, she had nightmares that she was back in the cell. The beatings were nothing compared to being trapped in that lightless place.

Someone must have heard her screams, because when she woke one morning, a big caracal was lying on the rug by her bed. She learned that his name was Tamar. His yellow eyes watched the window, and he rose to his feet whenever someone came inside the room. He let her scratch behind his ears.

When he left to do his business in the garden, or to eat chopped meat in the kitchen, Cathrynne felt anxious until he returned. But she trusted that he would alert her to any danger, and gradually she was able to sleep through the night again.

Markus and Veronica must know where she'd run to. She wondered if they would dare come here and try to take her back by force.

Perhaps not.

Hysto and Nestania were powerful witches. They would fight hard.

And Cathrynne's value was uncertain. Markus couldn't be sure she knew where the kaldurite source was.

The fact was, she *didn't* know.

Only Kal Machena did.

So the smart thing, now that the White Foxes had lost Cathrynne, would be to put all their resources into finding Kal.

Unless Markus decided that she needed to be silenced.

It was possible, but Cathrynne felt she knew him better than that. He was a cautious man.

They could both destroy each other. Therefore, the best option was to call a truce—for now.

A tiny smile curled Cathrynne's lips.

*I am learning to think like Morningstar.*

Hysto and Nestania brought trays of food. She pretended to be asleep so she didn't have to answer their questions.

Her half-sister Lara didn't turn up until the fifth day. As usual, Cathrynne closed her eyes the moment the door opened. The mattress shifted as someone sat on the edge of the bed.

"It's been a long time, but you're still my sister," Lara said fiercely. "I want you to know that I'm going to rain fire and fucking brimstone down on whoever did this."

Cathrynne opened her eyes. Twenty years had transformed the surly teenager into a poised witch with elegant clothes and glossy dark hair. Of course, Lara had grown up with all the wealth and privilege that came with the Lenormand name.

"I knew you were faking." Lara looked grim. "So who was it?"

Cathrynne regarded her stonily. Never had the gulf between them seemed so wide. "I don't remember."

"For Minerva's sake. We're blood." Her eyes narrowed. "You worked for Lord Morningstar. Was it him?"

She gave a pained laugh. "Gods, no."

"So you *do* remember."

"It wasn't him." She kept her voice carefully neutral. "Have you heard anything? He was ill. That's why I came to Arjevica. We brought him to Suriel at the Angel Tower."

Lara shrugged. "No idea. But there's been quite a commotion about *you*."

Cathrynne chewed her lip. "What about Mercy Blackthorn? She's my partner."

"Still missing. Who are you protecting? And *why* are you protecting them?"

When Cathrynne didn't answer, her eyes flashed. "You don't trust us."

Simmering anger tipped over to a boil. "Why should I?" Cathrynne retorted. "And don't give me that line about us being blood. You never came looking for me after I was taken away. Never gave a damn before."

Lara looked away. "I was ordered not to."

But they both knew she wouldn't have come to Arioch regardless.

"You don't know me, and I don't know you," Cathrynne said. "So as soon as I can walk, I'll get out of here. I don't need your help."

"Whatever." Her petulant expression reminded Cathrynne of the old Lara, who always threw a fit when she didn't get her way. "If someone did that to me," she snapped, "I'd kill them."

Her heels clicked against the hardwood floor as she strode from the room.

# CHAPTER 28
# GAVRIEL

H is wings sliced the air, each powerful downstroke carrying him in a circle beneath the domed cupola of the Angel Tower. Gavriel dropped abruptly, feet touching the polished floor just long enough to pace five steps before launching himself aloft again.

The waiting corroded his temper like acid.

The witches claimed that a note had arrived at the chapter house, in Cathrynne's hand, saying that she was returning to Arioch by ship. Yarl was back at Everfell. Gavriel had sent word to watch the docks, but he did not believe she had left Arjevica. Not of her own free will.

"She is *here*," he muttered. "I can feel it. Either hiding or being hidden."

"The witches deny involvement," Suriel said. "I have spoken to the Morag herself, as well as the heads of the chapter houses."

"What about the White Foxes? I don't trust them."

"They claim ignorance."

"Of course they do!" he erupted. "Someone is lying. And when I find out who it is . . ." He launched into the air again, aflame with restless energy.

If something had happened to her . . . No, he could not allow himself to think that way. Yet the prospect of losing her tightened around his throat like a noose.

"I will not remain here another hour," Gavriel said, striding for an open archway. "The witches can tell me to my face that they know nothing! And I will judge their honesty myself."

Suriel looked weary of his ranting. "Go, then," she said. "But I have asked the birds and rats for aid. If Cathrynne Rowan is in my city, I will know by sundown."

Communing with animals was Suriel's special talent. He nodded brusquely and launched into the air. He flew direct to the chapter house, alighting on the wide marble steps. The ornate Beaux Arts building rose before him, windows reflecting the overcast sky. A pair of witches at the entrance eyed him with hostility.

"I require an immediate audience," he said, not bothering with pleasantries.

One went inside. The other watched him in silence. After a moment, the first witch returned. "Come, Lord Morningstar."

She brought him to a tiny room with a wooden chair and a stack of broadsheets folded on a table. The message was clear: wait like any other petitioner.

He paced for a while, then scanned the gossip rags. With no fresh developments, Casolaba's murder was fading into the back pages. Levi Bottas, Casolaba's aide, had still not been found.

Gavriel threw the paper down, unable to focus. An hour passed, then two. He was about to go find someone and demand a meeting when the door opened. It was the same witch who had brought him there.

She led him up a staircase to a wood-paneled study. Another witch stood at the window. Her waist-length white hair glittered with jeweled pins, a testament to her age and authority.

"Lord Morningstar," she said crisply. "I am Nestania Lenormand. Please state your business."

He did not sit down, and she did not invite him to.

"I would like to know what you are doing to find Cathrynne Rowan."

"The cypher from Kirith?" Nestania's silver eyes revealed nothing. "Inquiries are being made."

"What sort of *inquiries*?"

"That is witch business."

"It is *my* business. She is from my province and was assigned to protect me. I am responsible for her."

"Then perhaps you should go home and see if she has returned."

"My secretary Edvin Yarl has already done so. She is not there."

Nestania clasped her hands. Each finger had a stack of rings. "I have spoken to Felicity Birch, the head of the cyphers in Kirith. We are doing all we can."

"Which is what exactly?"

Her chin lifted. "I do not answer to you, Morningstar."

"No, you do not," he agreed. "Yet you seem remarkably unconcerned that one of your own has gone missing. Is it because she is a cypher?"

Her eyes narrowed. "You go too far. I must ask you to leave."

Gavriel's patience, already stretched to the breaking point, snapped. "This is unacceptable. I demand to know what steps you are taking to locate her."

"*You demand?*" Nestania's eyes flashed. "We will handle this matter in our own way, in our own time."

"That's not good enough." Gavriel stepped closer. "What if she dies while you sit here doing nothing?"

"It would still be witch business."

"I will not accept that answer," he growled.

"It is the only one you will get."

"Then I shall take the matter to Mount Meru. Tell my father to deploy the legions."

He sensed ley gathering around her.

"You would not dare," she said with slow venom.

"Try me, witch," he snarled, all propriety gone.

"You have no jurisdiction here," she repeated, but there was a flicker of uncertainty.

"I am the chief magistrate of Sion," Gavriel said, his voice pitched low and deadly. "My jurisdiction is whatever I decide to make it."

A crackling silence followed. They traded glares, each measuring the other's resolve.

"Get out," Nestania Lenormand said at last.

Gavriel realized he would get nothing more from her. He strode from the study in a towering rage and flew in circles above the city. The more he thought about it, the angrier he grew. Either they did not care what happened to Cathrynne, or they were lying.

He would not stand for it. Gavriel sped for Angel Tower.

*If it is civil war the witches want, then they shall have it.*

# CHAPTER 29

# CATHRYNNE

The caracal stretched his lean body along the rug beside her bed, baring his fangs in a yawn. Tufted ears swiveled at every sound from the hallway, his gaze never straying from the door for long.

It had taken Cathrynne a week to gather the courage to explore her old bedroom. The armoire still had her child-sized clothes, brittle and moth-eaten like artifacts in a museum. A blue dress with silver piping. A gray cloak with pom-pom ties.

The sight triggered a flood of memories. Running through the garden as her mother called her in for dinner. Lara weaving her hair into intricate braids that were the latest fashion. Alluin Westwind, with his gentle smile, bringing her peppermint candies. She'd thought him a friend of the family. She'd had no idea he was her father.

She wandered to the writing desk and pulled open the center drawer. It still stuck halfway and had to be jiggled. There, tucked beneath a stack of yellowing paper, lay a deck of cards—the very deck she had been playing with the day the White Foxes came.

Thirty-six images, just as she remembered: The Ship, The House, The Fox, The Whip, The Crossroads . . .

The same ones that appeared in her visions, that haunted her dreams.

Tamar rose in one fluid motion. The door handle turned. Cathrynne grabbed a heavy glass paperweight, ready to smash Berti Baako's face with it. Or Markus Viktorovich. She wasn't sure which of them she hated more.

The door opened. It was her mother. Cathrynne set down the paperweight, surprised to notice her hand shaking. The adrenaline rush had been instantaneous. How long would she be jumping at shadows? She drew a steadying breath, though her mother didn't seem to notice.

"He likes you," Hysto said, eyeing the caracal, who had settled back on his haunches.

"And I like him," Cathrynne said. "How long have you had him?"

"Six years now. His mother was called Mereth. We got her after you . . . left." Hysto moved about the room, tidying things that didn't need tidying. "We kept it the same," she said, unnecessarily. "All your belongings."

"I noticed."

In the daylight, Cathrynne saw that her mother *had* aged. Besides the thick swathes of gray in her hair, the skin of her face looked thin and finely creased like crêpe paper. She wore a quilted jacket with colorful embroidery in panels down the front over a long white skirt and scuffed boots. A traditional Rus style that was very different from the modern, tailored woman Cathrynne remembered.

Now Hysto looked at her like a kicked dog. "I'm so sorry, Cathrynne."

Perhaps it was awful, but she felt a wave of disgust. "Don't be."

"Why not? Everything that's happened to you is my fault."

"I'm not some pathetic creature," Cathrynne said coldly. "I have a life. One I happen to like a good deal. So I'd appreciate it if you didn't make assumptions."

"You're right. I'm sorry—"

"You can stop saying that, too. It's been twenty years. I've done fine without you. So please, save the apologies." She had no idea where this cruelty was coming from, only that she hated her mother at the moment.

Hysto glanced at the door as if she might leave but didn't.

"I want you to know that we did not simply *go on* as if nothing had happened." Her hands kneaded each other. "After they took you away, I sank into a period of deep melancholy. You don't know what it is to lose a child."

"No," she replied evenly, "but I know what it is to lose everything else."

"May I sit?"

Cathrynne didn't want to do this, but she nodded. Hysto sank into a chair.

"We founded a school," she said. "For young women in need. Girls who might otherwise end up on the streets."

"That's admirable."

"I needed to help someone. It was the only thing that . . . I just needed to." She stared at Cathrynne for an uncomfortable moment, her expression haunted.

"What?"

"It's just . . . you look so much like your father."

She already knew that. She certainly didn't look like her mother and half-sister. "What happened to him?"

"I don't know." Hysto dabbed her eyes with a sleeve. "He fled when the White Foxes came. Alluin was arrested and I never saw him again." Bitterness tinged her voice. "Mount Meru disciplines its own. I sent a plea for any information to the Angel Tower, but no one would tell me." She looked out the window. "I was ostracized for a time, but the Lenormand name still carries weight and I have friends on the Council. Eventually, the scandal blew over."

"Well, I'm glad for you," Cathrynne said, her tone still cool.

"I'd hate for you to be punished for the rest of your life. That would be unfair, wouldn't it?"

Hysto went pale. Before she could respond, the door swung open and Nestania entered. "I have word of Lord Morningstar," she said.

Cathrynne's pulse leapt. "Has he recovered from his illness?"

"Fully."

She couldn't keep the smile from her face. "I would like to see him."

Nestania looked regretful. "I'm afraid that's impossible."

"Why?"

"He has returned to Kirith."

Cathrynne frowned. "He's gone home?"

Her grandmother's eyes were pitying. "Did you expect any different? His reputation for coldness is well-earned."

*But he is not cold,* she wanted to shout at them. *He is not cold at all!*

"He doesn't know I'm here," she muttered. "I know I swore you to secrecy, but I would make an exception for him—"

"I saw him myself today," Nestania said. "He is aware."

Her heart clenched. "Did he leave any message for me?"

"I'm afraid not. Best forget about him," Nestania said briskly. "He has clearly done the same about you. Now, your mother and I have decided to move you to our dacha in the countryside. The fresh air will speed your recovery."

"I'm not a child." Cathrynne locked eyes with her. "You can't simply make decisions on my behalf."

"Don't be difficult," Nestania retorted. She seemed surprised to find that the pliable young girl she'd known two decades ago had grown into a headstrong woman.

Hysto stepped in, her voice soft and coaxing, which was equally irritating. "We only have your best interests at heart. Surely you remember the summers we spent there, swimming at the lake and playing tennis?"

Cathrynne gave a grudging nod. Those were the long, lazy golden days of her childhood.

"You were born there, darling," her mother admitted. "I left the city when the pregnancy was too far along to hide anymore. I'm sorry I lied to you." She shared a look with Nestania. "But we had no other choice—"

"I don't want to talk about that," Cathrynne snapped. "Please, just leave me alone."

Hysto recoiled. "Very well. But I beg you to consider it. All we want is to keep you safe. It is a great gift that you have been returned to us."

They left. Cathrynne stared into space.

Gavriel was gone. Back to Kirith without a word. She tried to make sense of it. Would he leave without saying goodbye?

He would if he felt something for her. In that case, a clean break would be best.

She swallowed the knot in her throat. Maybe some time in the countryside would do her good. She needed to recover physically before she tried to find Kal Machena. But there was no way she'd leave the young woman to the mercy of the White Foxes.

Suddenly, the room felt horribly stuffy. She needed fresh air. Cathrynne opened all the windows. A cool breeze blew in and she inhaled the scent of roses.

A starling landed on the sill, eyeing her with a bright, quizzical gaze.

"Hello, pretty thing," she said. "I wish I had some seed for you."

A tawny flash from the corner of her eye was all the warning she had.

"No, Tamar!" Cathrynne threw herself into the path of the leaping caracal. The starling took flight, and his paws raked along her arm. She winced. A little blood oozed from the scratches, but they barely hurt and it was worth it to save the bird.

"I won't scold you," she said to Tamar, "since it is your nature to hunt. But I think you are well-fed enough, my friend."

He gave her a reproachful look, then laid his paws on the windowsill and watched the bird speed skyward. Only a single purple-green feather remained. Cathrynne picked it up and presented it to Tamar. He sniffed the feather, growled, then took it delicately in his jaws and lay down by the bed again.

CHAPTER 30

# GAVRIEL

He landed on Suriel's private balcony, visions of retribution thundering in his head. He no longer cared about the empire's delicate balance of power, nor about the laws he had spent a lifetime enforcing.

He did not care that Nestania was entirely correct in claiming that Cathrynne's disappearance was "witch business" and none of his.

He did not care that Arioch wasn't in his province, and he had no jurisdiction here.

All he cared about was getting Cathrynne back. If that meant storming the chapter house and extracting answers by force, so be it.

Gavriel's sister was waiting for him in her personal chamber, wearing a green silk turban and serene expression.

"The witches know something," he snarled before she could speak.

"Gavriel—"

"If our father won't intervene, we'll do it ourselves. Summon your seraphim guards. Put them under my command—"

"Calm down," Suriel said with exasperation. "I have found her."

The world stopped. He drew a ragged breath, fear and hope warring within him. "Alive?"

"Yes."

His wings trembled. "Where is she?"

Suriel's brown eyes were grave. "You will not like what I've discovered, brother."

"Just tell me," he pleaded.

"She's with her birth family. The Lenormands."

Gavriel's brow furrowed. "The Lenormands? I just spoke to Nestania. She denied any knowledge!"

That cunning old witch.

"Cathrynne is Hysto Lenormand's daughter." Suriel watched him carefully. "Her father was an angel named Alluin Westwind."

The memory surfaced with agonizing clarity. A disgraced seraphim kneeling before him, convicted of breaking his oath with a witch lover. Gavriel himself had wielded the Rod of Penance, had spoken the words of exile.

"Oh, gods," he whispered.

Suriel nodded grimly. "I didn't make the connection myself until one of my birds saw her at the Lenormands' home. Then I dug a bit deeper." Her voice gentled. "You couldn't have known, Gavriel."

But he should have remembered. "Does *she* know?" he asked.

"That you sentenced her father? Of course not, how could she? No one outside Mount Meru is privy to the details of angelic trials. As you're well aware." Suriel laid a hand on his shoulder. "I fell in love with a mortal once. It only led to heartbreak."

"I never said I loved her."

"You don't need to."

He drew a ragged breath. "She's with her family now? Safe?"

"Yes."

Gavriel studied his sister's face. "You're withholding something."

"Promise to remain calm."

"Just tell me."

She sighed. "Someone mistreated her."

Blind rage returned, swift and hot. "Who?"

"I don't know."

Gavriel moved to the archway, wings unfurling.

"Brother!" Suriel called after him. "Think before you act. The Lenormands are powerful. And whatever is between you and this cypher—"

But he was already gone, his wings carrying him into the darkening sky.

———

THE LENORMAND MANSION stood in the oldest and grandest part of the city, a testament to centuries of mining wealth. Gavriel pounded on the door. He was soaked to the skin from a sudden cloudburst, and a chill settled into his bones. He was still weak, though he would not let them see it.

His pounding was answered by Nestania herself. "How dare you come to my home?" she hissed.

"How dare you lie to me?" he countered. "I've been out of my mind with worry and she's been here all along!"

Nestania's eyes narrowed. "And what claim do you have on her, Lord Morningstar? Your kind has brought nothing but heartache to this family. I'm only protecting my granddaughter from further suffering."

Her dart hit home. Yet he could not leave without seeing her.

"I have no intention of causing Cathrynne pain," he said tightly.

"You already have," Nestania snapped.

They stared at each other.

"Let me inside," he said, trying hard to master his temper, "or I will take this matter to the Morag—"

"Who's at the door?"

Another witch appeared. She had long dark hair and looked too young to be Cathrynne's mother.

"Go back inside, Lara," Nestania said irritably. "Lord Morningstar was just leaving."

Lara arched a brow. "That's funny, he doesn't look like he's going anywhere to me."

"This is not your concern, Lara—"

"Maybe I should tell Cathrynne. Let her decide."

Nestania looked furious, but Lara seemed weary of her meddling.

"She's a grown woman. You have no right, grandmother."

"She swore me to secrecy—"

"Not from him."

Nestania looked as though she would rather cut off her own hand, but she stepped back. "You can have ten minutes," she said.

"I'll take you to her room," Lara offered.

He gave her a grateful look. "Thank you."

The Lenormand home was spacious and adorned with treasures from across Sion—artwork, statues, vases—but the decor barely registered. They climbed a flight of stairs. Lara opened a door at the end of the hall.

Cathrynne lay on a narrow bed, a quilt pulled up to her chest. Her face was bruised, and she looked terribly thin. Their eyes met. She said his name, and then he was rushing forward to kneel at her bedside. The way her face lit up was like stepping into sunlight after years of darkness.

"Gavriel," she exclaimed, "you came! I thought you'd gone back to Arioch."

"What?" He frowned. "Of course not. I've been searching for you for days!"

He had a powerful urge to to take her in his arms and carry her home to Everfell. Nurse her back to health. And then tear whoever had done this limb from limb.

"Ten minutes," Nestania reminded him. "She needs her rest."

Cathrynne scowled. "I'm fine."

"Let them be, grandmother," Lara said firmly.

Nestania huffed. The door closed behind them.

Gavriel carefully took her hand. "Who did this, Cathrynne?" *So I can return payment to them tenfold.*

She looked away.

"You can tell me," he said gently. "Whoever it is."

A struggle played across her face. "Promise me something first," she said.

"Anything."

"You won't act unless I allow it. Swear, Morningstar! Upon your father's name. I know your word is unbreakable."

His wings tensed. "You have my solemn oath that I will do nothing without your permission. Was it Haniel? I will see her cast down into a pit so deep—"

Her hand on his arm stilled him. "It wasn't Haniel. But they know something dangerous about me. And if I accuse them, they will reveal it to the High Council."

Her face was desolate. Gavriel thought of their visit to Gia Andrade, Casolaba's mistress, and remembered how Cathrynne had stood, staring intently down the street, at least ten seconds *before* the coach came careening around the corner. Her uncanny ability to predict that it was meant for *him*, and to shove him out of the way. The nosebleed afterwards.

The knowledge was sharp and bitter. "You are a seer," he said.

A flash of terror crossed her face. Gavriel did not blame her. He could scarcely imagine a worse fate. She seemed to be in control of the gift, but he wondered how much longer that would last.

"I had my suspicions after the coach," he admitted. "But Cathrynne, I would never, ever tell anyone. You don't need an oath for that."

Her breath was taut. "I had to use my ability to escape. There was no other way. They were going to kill me. I saw it." Her eyes lost focus, and a blade twisted in his heart.

"Who?" he asked.

"Markus Viktorovich. Some of the other White Foxes in Arjevica."

"Do the witches know?"

"No one knows. You're the first person I've told." She met his eyes. "Markus will deny everything, of course. He's the one who took me away twenty years ago. Him and a witch named Berti Baako. He'll say I'm lying to get revenge. The only way to prove what he did to me is to give a sweven to the High Council. If I agree, it would ruin the Viktorovich family . . ."

"And you, as well," he said in disgust. "They would know you're a seer and entomb you in the kloster."

Cathrynne gave a humorless laugh. "I would rather see him get away with it than accept that life. Markus knows it. So he'll keep his mouth shut if I do."

The injustice of it sickened him. "I made you a promise and I'll keep it," he said. "But someday, we will find a way to bring them down, Cathrynne. And I swear before all the gods, I will not let them take you away again."

*Tell her the truth now. Tell her what you did. The role you played.*

Yet he couldn't bring himself to confess. Not just yet. Gavriel told himself that she had suffered enough, but the truth was that he couldn't bear to see the trust in her eyes turn to hatred.

"What about you?" Cathrynne studied him. "How are you feeling?"

He set his guilt aside and told her everything that had transpired since he woke at Mount Meru. Cathrynne looked troubled.

"Does your father support Haniel in seizing control of the kaldurite?" she asked.

"Yes. They are claiming the witches poisoned me. An obvious pretext. I fear this could lead to civil war."

Cathrynne stared out the window, her brow creased with worry. "We have to find Kal Machena. She's the key to it all. If the White Foxes get her first, they'll torture her until she leads them to the source, and then they'll kill her."

He exhaled slowly. "I fear Haniel would be no more gentle. But the girl could be anywhere."

"No, one of the White Foxes said she was in Arjevica, but they couldn't find her. That she'd vanished into thin air—"

A knock came. A few seconds later, the door opened and Lara came in. "Your ten minutes are up," she said dryly. "Grandmother has been watching the clock."

Gavriel stiffened, ready to argue, but Cathrynne cut him off.

"Lara," she said, "if I tell you what happened to me, will you do as I ask?"

Her sister gave a fierce nod. "Whatever it is, I'm in."

"Good. Because we need your help."

# CHAPTER 31
# KAL

A pea bounced off her forehead.

"Are you even listening?" Gabi demanded with a teasing smile.

Kal looked up from her uneaten casserole. The dining hall's background noise surged back; clinking silverware, loud conversations, the occasional burst of laughter. "Sorry, what?"

"I was saying," Gabi continued, "that Professor Haddad is sleeping with the history teacher. They were making eyes at each other all through assembly."

"Scandalous," Kal said. She chewed and swallowed, tasting nothing. Darkness pressed against the bay windows. It was almost time. Levi should have her new identity card and ferry ticket to Bactra. They were meeting at the port at nine o'clock.

Now that the day she'd dreamt of had arrived, Kal felt an unexpected bout of nostalgia. She liked her roommates, and the other girls in her classes had finally warmed to her. Even the cosmetology track wasn't so bad. Truth be told, she'd grown to enjoy it a little bit. She was just starting to feel like she might belong here.

"But you don't," Durian said from the bench next to her. "We have to keep moving, Kal. Keep running until we find Travian. He's the only one who can protect you now."

Durian had been saying a lot of weird stuff like that lately. Cult of the Bard stuff.

Elena leaned forward, sympathy in her eyes. "You look tired, Kyra."

In truth, she was both exhausted from barely sleeping the night before and keyed up for the night ahead.

"It's been a long week," she said. "I think I'll turn in early."

"It's not even eight. We were going to study in the library, remember?"

"Oh, right. I'll catch you there later." Kal felt bad lying to them. Worse that she couldn't say a proper goodbye.

Gabi—always the intuitive one—gave her a searching look as if she suspected something.

"I swear," Kal insisted, "I really am okay. Just a little strung out. All those late night runs."

That made sense. Gabi nodded and turned back to Elena.

Kal bussed her tray. She was nearing the exit doors when another student intercepted her. Petra from Brock Hall. She was tall and quick-witted, with a dry sense of humor and a weakness for licorice candy.

"I'm not making a run tonight," Kal said in a low voice. "I don't know when the next one will be, so keep your money for now."

"It's not that," Petra whispered back. "Lara is looking for you. I saw her twenty minutes ago. She was crossing the quad and I heard her mention your name."

"Lara Lenormand?"

Petra cocked a brow. "You know any other Laras? I think she might be onto your little side business."

Kal's heart stuttered. "Did she say that?"

Petra just shrugged. "She wasn't alone. She had a cypher with her, and a man. He's a real looker."

Kal swallowed bile. "Are you sure?"

"Yeah, he had black hair and—"

"I don't mean the guy," Kal snapped.

Petra looked annoyed. "You better get your story straight. Just a heads up." She quickly walked away.

Kal pushed through the doors into the rainy dark. Every instinct screamed *run for the hills*, but she needed her stones to get past the wards.

And her Bluekiller pistol, just in case.

Once she got away from the dining hall, Kal broke into a sprint. The dormitory loomed ahead, windows glowing yellow in the gathering darkness. She was almost there when a figure stepped into her path.

"Hey, Kyra." It was Manij, the teacher who had found Kal on a park bench and brought her to the Lenormand School. She stood under an umbrella, her glasses fogging in the rain.

Kal smiled, hoping she didn't look as guilty as she felt. "Hi, professor. Just turning in early to study."

Manij smiled back. "I'll walk you to the dorm. We can share my umbrella."

"Oh, no, I don't want to hold you up."

"Don't be silly." She stepped closer, forcing Kal to shelter under the umbrella. It was too small, and rain pelted her back.

"What a night!" Manij said cheerfully. "Of course, we need the rain. Everything's been so dry. So, are you getting on well with your roommates? Making friends?"

Kal wanted to scream. "They're all so nice."

"And your cosmetology studies? I'm glad to see you're working hard. Assessments are coming up soon."

"Oh yeah, I love it. I decided I want to be a hairdresser. Um, I'm sorry but I have a test tomorrow, actually. So I can just, you know, run over to my dorm, it's right there . . ."

"Don't let me keep you." Manij finally moved aside. "Good luck!"

"Thanks," Kal mumbled, hurrying past.

She glanced back once she reached the Zayla Khan Residence Hall. Manij still stood there, staring after her.

Kal took the stairs two at a time. The halls were empty—everyone was at dinner or in the common rooms. The triple she shared with Gabi and Elena was the last door on the left. She paused, listening. Silence on the other side.

Hopefully, Lara had already checked and saw she wasn't there.

Kal cracked the door, ready to bolt, and was relieved to find it empty. She slipped inside and hurried to the wardrobe. Carefully pressed skirts and blouses hung in a row. She shoved them aside to reveal the heavy peacoat hidden at the back. The kaldurite stones were hidden in the lining. The pistol was under her mattress, along with all the money she'd earned from her contraband shopping trips.

Kal peeled off her sodden school jacket and changed into her old mining outfit of shirt and trousers. Then she tugged on the peacoat. It was too warm to wear inside and she started sweating instantly, but Lara couldn't mess with her now.

She took a last glance around, whispered the word *bye* to no one, and flew back down the stairs. The grounds were deserted. Kal kept to the shadows, skirting the pools of light spilling from windows. She was almost at the wall when she heard the scuff of a shoe behind her. Before she could turn, a hand clamped over her mouth. She struggled wildly as her attacker pulled her into the shadows.

"It's me," a voice whispered in her ear. "Stop fighting."

*Levi.* He let go and Kal spun to face him, nerves jangling. Rain plastered his dark hair to his forehead.

"What are you doing here?" she demanded. "We're supposed to meet at the docks—"

"Shhhh!" He raised a finger to his lips and pointed.

A group of three was moving along the path toward the dining hall. Kal recognized Lara Lenormand and the pair who had crashed Durian's remembrance. She grabbed Levi's hand and dragged him against the wall of the engineering building.

"Shit, that was too close," she breathed. "I was just having dinner in there."

She turned to Levi, hoping he wouldn't question her about who they were, but he wasn't watching them. He was watching her.

"The ferry won't sail in this weather," he whispered. "The departure was delayed until tomorrow. So I bought you a train ticket instead."

"A train? To where?"

"Sardis. You can make a fresh start." He handed her an envelope. Kal quickly checked the contents. As promised, he'd brought a legit-looking identity card . . . in the name of Kayla Jentzen.

"Like the car?" she said with a frown.

Everyone knew about Emil Jentzen, even in a backwater like Pota Pras. He was a famous inventor whose company manufactured several models of luxury automobiles.

Levi shrugged. "It's a name, isn't it?"

"Well, yeah. But it's an *unusual* name. One that people might remember."

His face fell. "I'm sorry, Kyra. I should have thought of that."

"It's okay." She bit back her annoyance. "We can talk at the train station. But we need to get out of here before the dean comes back." Not to mention the other two, who were probably worse.

Levi nodded and they jogged through the grounds, steering clear of the residence halls. The rain hammered down, turning bare patches in the grass to mud. They were almost to the deserted section of wall that she liked to climb over when a thought struck her.

Kal stopped abruptly. "How did you get through the wards?"

"What?" Levi turned.

"The wards." She took a step back. "This place is wrapped in enough protective magic to stop an army. How did you get inside?"

His expression hardened. "We don't have time for this, Kal."

The name landed like a gut punch. Her hands went cold. "What did you just say?"

"I said, we don't have time, Kyra!"

But she saw in his eyes that he *knew*. He'd messed up.

She drew the pistol from her pocket in one fluid motion, backing away. "Who are you?"

Levi stared at her in disbelief. "You're seriously going to shoot me?"

Her finger tightened on the trigger. "How did you get through the wards? Don't lie again!"

He raised his palms. "Do we have to do this now?"

"Yes, motherfucker, we do!" She stopped well out of reach, holding the pistol steady.

"I brought you what I promised, didn't I? I would never hurt you, Kal. And I never lied to you, not once. You have to believe me. Our deal is still on. Just tell me where you found the stones. You can keep whatever you have. I think it's a fair trade."

In an eyeblink, Kal was back on the Corniche, watching her best friend die. The muddy smell of river water filled her nose.

"You people are all the same," she said tonelessly.

"That's not true," he argued. "I'm really sorry about your friend. I had nothing to do with that. But we can help each other. You get your freedom, we get the source—"

"Walk away," Kal said. Her heart slammed against her ribs. Cold sweat pooled under her arms. "I *will* shoot you, I swear to Travian. So walk away."

Levi held up his hands, eyes calm. Too calm. What was wrong with him?

"Stop," she said, steadying the grip with both hands.

He took a step toward her. "I know you won't do this, Kal—"

She pulled the trigger.

The report was lost in a cannonroll of thunder. Levi grunted, dropping to one knee. He pressed a hand to his side. When he pulled it away, blood dripped from his fingers. It was a bright, metallic silver.

*What the fuck?*

"Kalisto Machena!"

She turned to see Lara Lenormand running toward her. Behind her were the cypher and the man from Pota Pras. But he wasn't a man. He was an angel with great black wings, like some terrible bird of prey.

## CHAPTER 32

# CATHRYNNE

She was grateful beyond measure to find Kal alive, but the girl wasn't alone.

Levi Bottas—the dead consul's bumbling aide—knelt in the grass before her. Kal held a pistol at her side, its barrel pointed down. She stared at them blankly and seemed to be in shock.

"I didn't intend to kill you on the rooftop, Morningstar," Levi called out as Gavriel strode up. "Only to scare you off."

Everything about him was different. His voice, his gaze, the set of his shoulders. Even kneeling—and, apparently, shot—he gave off natural confidence and charisma. Bottas was a phantom, Cathrynne realized. And they were all his cat's paws.

"Then you don't know me at all," Gavriel replied icily.

Levi winced in pain. "No," he agreed with a touch of weariness. "It was a mistake. One of many."

"You lured Casolaba up to the spire," Gavriel said. "Why?"

He laughed softly. "You never met the man, but I promise you, he deserved it. Working for him was like stepping on a slug in bare feet. Slimy, unpleasant, and hard to scrape the ooze off. He wanted me to kill everyone who knew about the kaldurite." Levi's blue eyes flicked to Kal, then back to Gavriel. "I knew that when I refused, he'd simply add me to his death list and get someone else to do it."

The amiable mask slipped and something darker crossed his face. "So I made the first move. I told him I had a buyer willing to pay a king's ransom for the stones, but he was an eccentric fellow and wanted to meet at the top of the dome. Casolaba would have followed me into the jaws of a blue emperor for the right price."

"But really . . ." Cathrynne put in. "*Impaled?*"

"A little present for everyone he screwed over in his long and shitty career." Levi's smirk died as he turned to Kal. "Come with me," he said in a low urgent voice. "I'll keep you safe, I swear. They just want to use you."

"*You* just want to use me!" she retorted.

"No. I could have taken you by force, but I didn't. I wouldn't do that to you, Kal—"

"Shut up," Lara snapped. "You're not going anywhere and neither is she."

Levi gave her an amused smile. "Whatever you say."

One hand was pressed to his shoulder to stanch the wound. There was something wrong with his blood, Cathrynne realized. Something very, very wrong. It looked silver in the moonlight.

"What are you?" she asked.

Levi Bottas looked down, a lock of dark hair falling across his face.

"Answer her," Gavriel snapped.

He made a guttural sound of pain. The lamps along the pathway flickered.

"What in Minerva's name . . ." Lara said slowly.

Levi lifted his head. His eyes glowed an unearthly blue, as if they held pure ley. He gained his feet in one graceful motion. Cathrynne unleashed a blast of projective magic an instant before Lara did the same. Their combined spell struck Levi with enough force to level a building, but he merely staggered back a step. Then he began to *grow*. Taller, wider, muscles bulging in thick cords along his arms and neck.

"What's happening?" Kal squeaked, scrambling back.

When his massive shoulders caught in the branches of an oak tree, forcing him to duck his head, Gavriel voiced what they were all thinking. "Run!"

Cathrynne's cracked ribs protested, but she gritted her teeth and took off. Lara and Kal ran ahead, but Gavriel slowed his pace to stay at her side. They ran between a pair of buildings as the giant who called himself Levi Bottas stomped through the grounds, bellowing Kal's name. Cathrynne hoped it was an illusion until she glanced back and saw one hand swipe at a roof, sending slate tiles cascading down.

They ran until they reached a stone fountain filled with wet leaves. Everyone crouched behind it, fighting to catch their breath.

"What by the three gods *is* he?" Gavriel panted, looking grim.

Kal hunched her shoulders as everyone looked at her. "I have no idea! I thought he was human."

"How long have you known him?" Cathrynne asked.

"Not long. A few weeks." She glanced sidelong at Lara. "He promised to help me get out of Arjevica."

Lara snorted. "You should have come to me. I could have protected you—"

"Yeah, everyone keeps saying that," Kal snapped. "But I don't want your protection. I just want to be left alone!"

Lara opened her mouth to argue but Cathrynne cut in. "So you shot him?"

Kal looked on the edge of tears. "I didn't want to, but I found out he was lying. Just using me to get the stones." She swallowed. "I only shot him once. I'm not even sure where I hit him. I wasn't aiming to kill. Then I saw his blood. It's *silver*. What does it mean?"

"I've never seen that before," Cathrynne said quietly. "Have any of you?"

The others shook their heads.

"We need to get out of here," Lara said. "I'll force us to the chapter house."

Kal's face hardened. "No."

"Be reasonable," Lara hissed. "We're trying to help you!"

Her gaze unfocused. Cathrynne sensed the stones in her bracelet lighting up. Some projective, others receptive. The hair on her arms rose as Lara expertly braided the flows together. Liminal spaces opened where they made contact with each other, like tiny wormholes. A box began to form, and now she could see that the outlines of it were made of violet liminal ley.

Lara was forcing them all, whether Kal liked it or not.

Except that when she tried to extend the box to include the young woman from Pota Pras, the whole construction popped like a soap bubble. Lara looked astonished.

"That's never happened before," she muttered. "What's going on?"

Cathrynne noticed that Kal had one hand jammed in her coat pocket. She'd assumed it was the gun, but now she realized that Kal must be clutching a lump of kaldurite. Which meant she couldn't be forced—not against her will.

If she told Lara, the argument would get ugly. Better to handle the situation another way.

"There's no time," Cathrynne said urgently. "Levi needs to be contained before he hurts a student or staff member. I'll stay here with Kal while you gather more witches to deal with him."

Lara looked torn, but she gave a hard nod. She pulled off her rings and pressed them into Cathrynne's palm. "Topaz, sunstone, and sugilite," she said. "Set in copper and gold."

Then she was gone, sprinting into the darkness. In the distance, Levi continued his search, his lumbering form blotting out the lamps along the pathways.

Cathrynne turned to Gavriel. "Can you fly with her to Suriel?"

He considered it, then shook his head. "I won't leave you here alone. And two will be too much weight."

"I can handle myself," she assured him. "It's the girl he wants."

"I'm right here," Kal said. Her chin lifted. "I am *not* getting toted around like a piece of luggage. In fact, I have a train ticket in my pocket and I intend to use it—"

Cathrynne tensed as she spotted movement. Two figures approached at a jog—Lara and Hysto. She felt relief, followed on its heels by guilt at the way she'd treated her mother the last time they spoke. Hysto had saved her life. Risked the wrath of the High Council that said cyphers could never see their birth mothers again. She deserved civility at least.

Yet their arrival seemed way too quick. Something wasn't right . . .

Their faces shimmered, wavering like a heat mirage. The illusion slipped. Cathrynne felt an electric jolt of terror. It was not her sister and mother, but Markus Viktorovich and Berti Baako.

Gavriel stepped into their path. He clearly knew who they were because he looked furious. "How dare you come here?" he demanded, hands fisting. "I suggest you turn around this instant before—"

Markus hurled him aside with a contemptuous flick of one finger. Gavriel slammed into a thick oak and fell to the earth, groaning. Cathrynne ignited a chunk of brown agate, but Markus easily deflected the attack. He unleashed another battering assault, forcing Cathrynne to duck and roll.

Everything happened so fast. A knife glinted in the moonlight. Kal yelled. Cathrynne feared she'd been stabbed. Then she saw that Kal's wool coat had been slashed open, the lining hanging in flaps. The cold shine of kaldurite stones glittered in the grass. Kal scrabbled for the stones on hands and knees, but Berti got there first. She kicked Kal hard in the side, then grabbed her hair and dragged her back, kicking her again.

Ash's candy-red hair materialized out of the darkness. She wore thick leather gloves. She quickly swept the kaldurite stones into a pouch.

"Those are mine!" Kal bared her teeth. "Give them back!"

Berti slapped her across the face. "Shut up!"

Markus regarded Cathrynne. The bastard didn't look smug, of course he didn't. He was too refined for that. Too self-righteous. No, he looked regretful, like she was a bright student who had wasted her potential and was about to get expelled.

"You should have accepted my offer when you had the chance," he said. "Now it's too late. But we have the girl. She'll give us what we need."

In the rainy night, Cathrynne's scalp prickled. Three symbols appeared, hovering in the air, just as they had weeks before at the Nilssons' home.

A golden key, a sailing ship, and a coffin.

A witch was about to force—either Berti or Markus, it didn't matter who—but this time the coffin wasn't for Mercy, it was for Kal Machena.

Cathrynne felt the painful pressure shift in her ears. She knew firsthand what the White Foxes would do to Kal once they had her alone in that house of horrors. Her fingers closed around Lara's rings. Topaz and sunstone, projective. Sugilite, receptive.

Cathrynne had never been taught to force, that dangerous art of bending reality to create a portal, but she'd seen the witch Ninnoc do it, hurling her and Mercy from Arioch to Kota Gelangi in an eyeblink.

And she'd just watched Lara make a box—although not all the way.

Passivity and surrender were the keys to working receptive magic. The problem was that Cathrynne wasn't good at either of those things. Her training had focused on offensive magic, which was all outward-flowing. Directing one's will to manifest a specific outcome.

She quickly jammed the topaz ring on her left ring finger, the sugilite on the other, and tried drawing on them both simultaneously. The projective magic flowed well. But the other was like trying to push water back into a faucet. It only ran one way.

Markus's eyes narrowed. "What are you doing, Cathrynne?"

*Bloody hell!* It wasn't working. Why wasn't it working?

She was an ambi, able to use both hands for projective magic . . .

But maybe . . . maybe not for receptive?

Cathrynne tried to focus, tangentially aware that Kal was struggling with Berti Baako. Gavriel had dragged himself to standing and was delivering a series of dire threats to Markus, distracting him long enough to buy a few more seconds.

But that's all she had. Because Ash was coming her way with a look of implacable hatred, and she had kaldurite stones so Cathrynne couldn't touch her with ley.

She quickly switched the rings. The projective topaz was now on her right hand, the sugilite on the left. *Please, Minerva, I'm surrendering to your will. Help me save them.* She felt the topaz flare, and this time, the sugilite flowed inward, its cool, healing energy racing through her veins, through her heart and mind, reading her emotions, and then flowing back out again to join the threads of fiery topaz.

A sheen of sweat broke across her brow as she braided the opposing forces together, just as she'd seen Lara do. They fought each other tooth and nail. She feared they'd tear her apart. Perhaps tear the whole world apart.

"To me!" she cried through clenched teeth. "Hurry!"

Kal wrenched herself free of Berti's grasp. Gavriel was near enough to take the girl in his arms, folding his wings around her.

"Stop!" Markus strode forward, his face white. "You'll all die—"

Cathrynne staggered to Kal and Gavriel as the lines of the box joined together. Then came a clap of silent thunder, a deep vibration that made her cracked ribs ache. *Wait,* a panicked voice in her head screamed. *Where are we going?*

The warp and weft of reality folded, and Cathrynne felt the sickening lurch of falling, again and again, through the spaces between.

## CHAPTER 33

# KAL

S he gasped for breath, panic clawing at her throat.

Kal had gone from the rainswept grounds of the Lenormand School to a cold, clear night in what looked like the Zamir Hills, which wouldn't be so bad except that she was buried up to her neck in hardpan. She tried to wiggle a single toe. Nothing budged.

"Help! Anyone!" The plea emerged as a barely audible wheeze. A gibbous moon cast hard-edged shadows across the cracked earth.

She remembered groping through the wet grass for her kaldurite stones after the White Foxes slashed open the lining of her coat, spilling them everywhere. After that it got blurry. She'd felt a strange shockwave ripple through her. Then the sensation of free-falling but with no *up* or *down*.

A jarring impact and she was here, only a head sticking out of earth hard as granite, like she'd materialized in the middle of it. She could turn her face and not much at that, but in a sense she'd gotten lucky. A little lower and she'd be dead of suffocation. It was hard to imagine a worse way to go.

Something moved at the edge of sight. Kal's head jerked

toward a pile of rocks. Her mouth went dry as a scorpion sidled into a patch of moonlight. One of the big desert queens with claws like wire cutters. From ground level, it looked even bigger.

*Well, maybe there were worse ways after all.*

Kal licked her dry lips. Scorpions had poor eyesight. The way they hunted was by sensing the tiny vibrations of prey through their eight legs. Of course, Durian had told her that.

The scorpion crept forward a few steps, then stopped. She tried to sink deeper into the earth, but it was pointless, she couldn't move anything below her neck. The forcing spell must have woken it up.

"Actually, they're nocturnal," Durian said. "It was probably awake."

He squatted to her left, so she could only see him from the corner of her eye.

"You're not helping," she hissed.

"What can I do? I'm a figment of your imagination." Never had his donkey bray been more irritating. "They only attack when they feel threatened. I doubt it will mess with you—"

The scorpion skittered closer. Close enough to count the armored segments of its body, the jointed legs picking delicately across the sand. It was about as long as her forearm, with a shiny black carapace.

Kal tried not to appear threatening. She was, after all, only a head. But the scorpion must have been riled up by the spell that had planted her in the ground like a fence post. Its tail lifted, preparing to sting. The barb at the tip carried enough poison to kill a pack mule. Kal squeezed her eyes shut—

And heard a solid *chthunk* a few inches away. She opened her eyes. A knife pinned the scorpion to the earth, where it twitched weakly. She let out an undignified sob.

"Are you okay?" It was the blonde cypher.

"Can't move," she rasped.

"We'll get you out," she said. "I'm sorry, the forcing went wrong."

*No shit.*

"It was the first time I ever tried it," she continued. "I guess it could have been worse."

"For who?" Kal croaked.

Dark wings unfurled against the sky, blotting out the moon. She thought it was a Sinn and resigned herself to death yet again. Then she saw the gold-green eyes of the angel.

"There's an old mine in the hillside," he said. "Maybe we can find some digging tools there."

The cypher nodded. "You stay with her."

She returned a few minutes later with a pick. She didn't waste time talking, just started hacking away at the hard-packed earth. The pressure eased around Kal's shoulders, then her chest. She gulped in a full breath, dizzy with relief.

The pick rose and fell in a steady rhythm. When her right hand came free, Kal flexed her fingers, wincing at the pins and needles. The angel took a turn digging, and soon they were hauling her out of the hole, covered in red dirt.

"Nothing's broken?" the cypher asked anxiously. "I really am sorry I lost you. But the White Foxes were about to force you someplace else, and trust me, this is still the better option."

Kal hadn't known that. She suppressed a shudder. "I believe you. And I'm okay. Just stiff."

Now that she was free of her earthen tomb, Kal took a more serious look around. She realized with a sinking heart that she was back where the whole awful thing had started—Clear Creek Mine.

"What are your names?" she asked. "I don't even know who you are."

"Cathrynne Rowan," the cypher said with a smile.

Kal had been a bit afraid of her, but she had an honest face. Her eyes were kind, not dead like Ash and Kane.

"Gavriel Morningstar," the angel said. "From Kirith."

*Morningstar* . . . Kal froze. Everyone knew that name. He was the Light-Bringer. "You're an archangel," she stammered.

Not even seraphim came to Pota Pras except to conduct the census. She never thought she'd speak to an angel, let alone the son of Valoriel himself. *Funny*, she thought with bitterness, *how everyone suddenly has such a great interest in me.*

"I believe the ley brought us here for a reason." Gavriel Morningstar fixed her with an intent gaze that made it impossible to look away. "Show us where you found the kaldurite. Once the source becomes public, you'll lose your value to the witches. Levi will stop hunting you. You'll be free to live your life."

All that was probably true, though she took the "free to live your life" part with a good dose of cynicism.

"And if I say no?"

"We won't coerce you," Cathrynne said quickly. "I promise."

"But we can't just let you go," Gavriel added. "It's too dangerous. I will take you to my sister, Suriel. She can protect you for now."

That option did not appeal to Kal at all. She believed they meant well—certainly more than the others hunting her. But she instinctively distrusted anyone who wasn't human. Which now apparently included Levi, the one person she'd thought was on her side. The betrayal still hurt.

Kal sighed. "And if I say yes?"

"Then you'll take us to the exact place you found the stones," he said. "Once that's confirmed, you can do as you like."

A sandy-haired figure appeared behind the archangel, lounging against a boulder with his ankles crossed.

"Take the deal," Durian advised. "But don't be stupid. Get more stones while you're down there. Then lose these two in the tunnels."

Kal pretended to think it over. "I *am* sick and tired of running," she said to Gavriel with the right note of reluctance. "And maybe you're right about the ley bringing us here, because the source is in there." She pointed to the abandoned entrance of Clear Creek Mine.

Cathrynne Rowan drew a deep breath. "How far down is it?"

"Don't like tight places, huh?"

A shadow crossed her face. "No," she admitted, "I don't."

Kal tried not to stare at the woman's bruises. She felt a stab of pity.

"It's not far. Less than half an hour, I'd say, and most of it's pretty easy walking."

Cathrynne gave a taut nod. "I can manage that."

Kal led them to the mine entrance. Boards crossed the opening, plastered with faded warning signs, but she and Durian had pulled most of them off. She ducked inside and lifted the edge of a canvas tarp. Their stash remained untouched. Two electric torches and a few extra waterskins. She handed one torch to Cathrynne and kept the other. Kal drank deeply from a skin, then offered it to Cathrynne.

"It's clean," Kal said.

Cathrynne drank, then passed the water to Gavriel.

Kal used the chance to turn her back and quickly check the pistol wedged in her belt. It had been under her shirt, pressed against her body, and didn't seem any worse for the premature burial. Kal slid it back into her waistband and switched on her torch. The beam cut through the darkness, illuminating the tunnel entrance. Rusted rail tracks disappeared into the blackness. Timber supports held up the ceiling, warped with age. Cathrynne stared into the tunnel mouth, her skin ashen.

"You stay up here," Gavriel said. "I'll go."

"You can't," Cathrynne replied. "Look what a single stone did to you."

He frowned. "I won't touch anything."

"Even so, just being near so much kaldurite could kill you." Her voice hardened. "I can do this. Wait for us here."

Gavriel Morningstar looked like he would rather die than let her go into the mine alone. Kal wondered if anyone would ever look at *her* that way. It must be nice. Although judging by the cypher's grim expression, she wasn't thinking about that at the moment.

"You're too big to carry if it makes you sick," she said. "And I'm not letting you die down there."

A muscle in his jaw feathered, his expression mutinous, but in the end he deferred to her. "If you're not back in one hour," he warned, "I'm coming after you."

They shared another look that seemed to say a great deal without words. Cathrynne's face softened. "Fair enough," she said, turning to Kal. "Lead the way."

Kal switched on her torch and ducked into the tunnel. The familiar mix of stone dust and rotting timber made her want to sneeze. But there was another faint smell this time, wasn't there? A hint of burnt toast. Or something like it. Her nose wrinkled.

Durian's braying chuckles faded as she followed the tracks into darkness.

---

"WHO DID THAT TO YOU?" Kal asked as they passed a rusted-out hulk of machinery. "The bruises, I mean. If you don't mind my asking."

"I don't mind," Cathrynne replied. "It was the White Foxes. They took me captive. They thought maybe I knew where the source was. Of course, I didn't, but they wouldn't believe me."

"Those people are evil," Kal said quietly. "You're lucky to be alive."

"I almost wasn't. But your bullet saved me."

"Huh?"

"I escaped by pulling it from Kane's chest and using the bronze casing to cast a projective spell. The surgeon left it there after you shot him."

"Seriously?" Kal said, impressed. "I'd hoped he was dead, but . . ." She barked a dry laugh. "I'm glad it worked out for you."

"Let's hope he's really dead this time." Cathrynne was silent for a minute. "I *am* sorry about the forcing. It was an insane risk. But I didn't want what they did to me to happen to you."

Whatever it was must have been pretty bad, but Kal didn't want to know the details. "How'd you find me?"

"Lara Lenormand remembered your description. She's my sister."

"Ah." Kal frowned. "But you're from Kirith."

"I was born in Arjevica."

Her voice sounded breathy and tight, like she was trying to pretend she was fine. Distracting herself from the claustropho-bia. Kal understood. She'd had her own little freakouts before. Talking about something else always got her through them.

"I saw you," Cathrynne said. "On the riverboat from Kota Gelangi. You had a ship tattoo."

Kal touched her neck. The rain and dirt had rubbed away the makeup. "I got it a couple of years ago. Stupid."

"No, I like it. What's the significance?"

*Just keep talking.* "My friend and I were saving up to buy a boat. Figured we could be traders, sailing up and down the Parnassian Sea."

"That sounds nice."

She glanced back. Cathrynne's torch bobbed along behind. "Well, it beats living in Pota Pras. Anyone in that town who catches a break moves somewhere better. It's the hope of a lucky strike that keeps people going. But my friend grew up moving constantly, he's been everywhere. Ask him what they eat for breakfast in Iskatar and he'll tell you. He made traveling all over sound like fun, even though I know he and his mom had some rough times, too. Before all this, I'd never been out of Satu Jos."

"So your family are all miners?"

"Not exactly. My parents investigate claims for bigger compa-nies. Drawing up maps, certificates of location, that kind of thing."

"That doesn't sound so bad," Cathrynne said.

"Yeah, well, you spend most of the time clawing your way to

the top of some nameless hill in the middle of nowhere and taking survey measurements. It's fucking exhausting and it doesn't pay a lot, but I guess it beats wasting your life underground."

Kal paused for breath. She hadn't meant to say so much—or quite so bitterly—but it felt good to tell the truth. Cathrynne knew who she was. Where she came from and why she was running. Maybe it *could* all be over, once everyone knew where the source was.

She pushed ahead before the cypher could respond, ducking through a narrow gap where part of the ceiling had collapsed. They'd reached the section where the new tunnel branched off. The rock walls were no longer rough-hewn by human tools but smooth and glassy.

Cathrynne stopped walking. "Why is it different?"

"Sinn fire melts the rock like butter," Kal explained. "It leaves behind tunnels like these. They use them to move around underground."

She had to give the cypher credit—she didn't turn and run. But she did look green.

"How do you know they're gone?" she asked.

"I mean, I don't. But you can usually feel the vibrations if one is close."

"Usually? But not always?"

"Yeah, that's right." Kal could tell from the rapid rise and fall of her chest that she was struggling. "You don't have to go any further."

"I'm fine," Cathrynne said tightly.

Kal shrugged. "Whatever you say."

They walked in silence. Unlike the straight mining tunnels, this one twisted and turned, following some logic only the Sinn understood. A few times they passed offshoots that plunged into darkness. Kal didn't remember seeing those the last time. She felt certain they were new but didn't want Cathrynne to panic, so she kept her mouth shut. The burnt toast smell grew stronger.

A small voice—not Durian, this one was all her own—suggested that maybe they should turn back. The area was clearly more active than it had been. But Kal had nothing to start her new life. Once again, the witches had taken everything she had of value. But that cavern was full of kaldurite. Just a few would make her fortune.

*No risk, no reward.*

"How much farther?" Cathrynne asked. "I feel like we've been down here forever. You said it was a short walk."

"The cavern is just ahead," Kal replied. "But we'll have to crawl."

Cathrynne swore under her breath. "You didn't mention that before."

Kal turned to face her. "Sorry, you didn't ask."

The cypher's jaw clenched. "How far is the crawl?"

"About twenty cubits. It's really not so bad."

She grappled with this for a long moment. "I'll go first. I want to be able to see the end."

"Fine by me."

They splashed through the shallow river that marked the crevice. Cathrynne eyed it with trepidation, then dropped down to shine her light through.

"I can see the other side," she said with a touch of relief.

"You don't have to go in," Kal said again. "I promise the kaldurite is there."

The cypher sat up on her haunches. "I believe you. But I still want to go. I need to . . ." She trailed off.

"Prove that you can?" Kal finished.

Cathrynne nodded.

"Believe me, I get it," Kal said. "I've crawled into some seriously funky places for the same reason." She smiled and Cathrynne smiled back. At that moment, Kal decided that she couldn't abandon this woman in the tunnels. She just couldn't do it.

"The Light-Bringer," she said in a rush. "I've heard his word is unbreakable. Is that true?"

"It's true. Integrity means everything to him."

"So when he said I'd be free, he meant it?"

"He did, and you have my word, too." She paused. "I'm so sorry about your friend, Kal. He didn't deserve that."

She thought Durian might appear and crack a joke, but he didn't. A hot lump tightened her throat. "Thanks," she managed. "You'd better go first. We only have an hour before the angel comes looking for us, remember?"

The crawl turned out to be easier than last time since neither of them was wearing a pack. Cathrynne slithered through the low tunnel faster than Kal could believe, then bent over with her hands on her knees, breath rasping. It opened into a vast cavern that their lamps couldn't fully illuminate. Stalactites hung from the ceiling like icicles, matched by stalagmites that rose from the floor. In some places, they joined to form columns thick as old trees.

"Hey, you did it," Kal said, patting her back.

"Hated every second, but . . . *Minerva's luck*," Cathrynne breathed, looking around in awe.

Hundreds of kaldurite stones in varying sizes were scattered across the cavern floor. Blues deepened to violet, reds flashed like glowing embers, all changing as the light of the electric torches moved across their facets.

Cathrynne crouched, watching the colors shift. She used her sleeve to pick up a stone. "Amazing, isn't it?" she said. "Like a void in the ley. How is that even possible?"

While she was preoccupied examining the stone, Kal discreetly scooped handfuls into her trouser pockets. When they were full to bulging, she returned to Cathrynne.

"You know where it is now," she said. "So let's get back—"

The stones on the cavern floor began to wobble and jitter,

sending sparkles of light across the cavern walls. Cathrynne stiffened. They stood motionless, barely breathing. The tremors came again, stronger this time. Rhythmic quakes that sent dust sifting down from the ceiling. Then came a sound that turned Kal's blood to ice: a dry scrape like a dozen knives being sharpened at once.

She extinguished her torch with a quick twist. Cathrynne followed suit a second later, plunging them into darkness.

A glow appeared at the crevice. Not the steady light of a torch but the flickering orange-blue of living flame. It brightened, throwing distorted shadows across the cave wall. The air grew forge-hot. Sweat erupted across Kal's body. She pulled the Bluekiller from her belt. Subtract the bullet she'd fired at Levi and she had seven left.

"Get back!" Kal cried.

They scrambled out of the way as a gout of white flame shot from the crevice. That burnt-toast smell scorched her lungs and coated her tongue. Through wavering lines of heat, she saw that the narrow shaft they'd crawled through was now a full-fledged Sinn tunnel.

She grabbed Cathrynne's hand, gripping the pistol in the other. They backed away as the head appeared, roughly the size of a mining tram, with a crown of six silver horns. Its gaze found them. The blue emperor opened its jaws, revealing teeth like ivory daggers.

The Sinn unleashed a deafening roar. It bulled into the cavern, moving with the speed and power of a fright train. They retreated to the rear wall, where another smooth-walled tunnel wound into darkness. Kal switched her lamp on, flashing the beam into the gloom.

When she turned, Cathrynne was staring at the Sinn in fear and wonder. Kal paused, transfixed by the creature's monstrous beauty. It was a thing of heat and shadow, shifting like a bed of live coals, all burnt orange and bloody red except for the eyes, which were a rich golden hue.

Then she yelped as a torrent of flame licked the cavern wall to their right.

"Go!" Kal shoved Cathrynne into the tunnel. Then she turned and pulled the trigger until the hammer fell on an empty chamber. "I hope I hit it," she panted. "I mean, it's too big to miss, right?"

A furious roar answered as they fled into the tunnel.

# CHAPTER 34
# CATHRYNNE

S
he chased the wildly bobbing light of Kal's torch. The tunnel was high and wide with slick walls like volcanic glass. Her chest felt as if a fist was insistently pounding on it, and there wasn't enough air to fill her lungs. Seeing a blue emperor out in the open had been bad enough. But down here, deep underground . . .

When she glanced back, a fiery shape filled the passage from floor to ceiling. There was no way to outrun the creature. Her only hope was to distract it so Kal could get away. Cathrynne slowed and turned to face it. She still had Lara's rings. They were mostly depleted, but the sunstone held enough ley for one good blast. She ignited it just as the blue emperor's snout came around the bend.

Her attack seemed to have no effect other than enraging it more. It thrashed in a frenzy, head swinging back and forth. Cracks skittered down the tunnel walls. Cathrynne looked up to see chunks of stone crashing down. She threw herself to one side as a wave of dust billowed outward.

The torch was knocked from her hand. Darkness closed in. Coughing, she scrambled away from the collapse. When the dust settled, a wall of fallen rock blocked the tunnel. And she was on the wrong side.

The Sinn crawled backward a short ways, its blue claws scraping against the fallen rocks, then stopped. Its stare, illuminated only by the eerie flickering light of its mane, was deeply unnerving.

Kal's muffled voice came through the rubble. "Are you hurt?"

"No! Are you?"

"Some scrapes. Not too bad."

Cathrynne dug a tiny hole near the top of the rubble. She poked her fingers through and felt Kal grip them. For a dizzying instant, she remembered holding Julia Camara's fingers through the bars of her cell in much the same way.

"Run!" she urged. "Tell Gavriel what happened. I'll find another way out."

"I'll help you dig," Kal protested. "We can widen the hole—"

"There's no time. It'll take hours. Just go!"

Kal squeezed her fingers.

Cathrynne turned to face the Sinn. Its head was draconic, with a ridged crest and crocodilian nose. But its eyes were what riveted her. They were deep and ancient, and they studied her with clear intelligence.

The creature stalked closer, its body flowing like molten metal, muscles rippling beneath the shining scales. She couldn't help searching for some hint of its origin. Some sign that it had come from a cypher like her. But the creature seemed utterly alien. It was born of a curse—or some genetic throwback to the cosmic dragon that was the first avatar of the triple god. What stood before her was nothing like witch nor angel.

Its nostrils flared, taking in her scent. The flames along its spine burned brighter, shifting from blue to violet. Its jaws parted, exposing curved teeth. The Sinn's chest expanded. Cathrynne recognized the tell.

You learned to spot them in combat training. A foot coming

forward, an arm swinging back. In animals, it might be a lashing tail or low growl. There was always a tell when something was about to attack, and the Sinn were no different.

She threw herself behind a pile of rubble as heat cooked the air. The flames missed her by inches, though the smell of burned hair filled her nostrils. Ethereal blue fire licked along its spine, casting the tunnel in fey half-light. It seemed to be studying her, head tilted slightly to one side. What thoughts churned behind those ancient eyes?

Cathrynne forced her breathing to slow. Instead of giving in to panic, she focused her senses outward, reaching with the part of her that was fully witch. *There.* The cave-in had exposed something buried in the granite ceiling. A seam of quartz ran through the rock above. Cathrynne slammed her palm against the wall and reached for the ley trapped within the crystals. It surged through her, hot and electric. She drew deeply, and deeper still, shaping it into a lethal arrow of force.

The projective magic struck the Sinn like a battering ram. Its massive body skidded backward down the tunnel, claws carving furrows in the stone. The impact knocked more rock loose from the ceiling. When the air cleared, she spotted the huge form of the Sinn halfway down the tunnel, partially buried under debris.

Coughing, she staggered toward it. The beast lay stunned and unmoving, though its mane still flickered with flames. She could see its blue tongue between the fierce ivory teeth. It was panting, its eyes closed. She found a rock, ready to bring it down on the monster's skull if it showed signs of attacking again.

The cave-in was at her back. She could try to dig through, but that would take a long time. The only other way out was past the Sinn. There might be room to squeeze along the tunnel wall if it didn't wake—

She was a few cubits away when eyes the size of dinner plates opened. The Sinn blinked twice, its gaze sharpening at the rock in her hand. Cathrynne froze.

"Won't you kill me, witch?" The words rumbled from its throat.

She stumbled back in shock. *Did it just speak?*

"Well?" the Sinn repeated with a touch of impatience. "Are you deaf?"

"No," she managed, lowering the rock. "I don't kill helpless things."

It growled, a sound that raised the hair on her arms. "I am not a thing." It shifted, rocks falling away from its body. "Nor am I helpless."

It stared down at her. A silky white beard sprouted from its lower jaw. She had not noticed that before.

Cathrynne drew a deep breath. "Then perhaps I should ask if *you* plan to kill *me?*"

It studied her in silence for an interminable minute. When it opened its mouth, she tensed, unsure if words or fire would emerge.

"Why are you here, witch? Your kind never comes below."

Cathrynne hesitated, then decided on honesty. What did she have to lose? "I was seeking a stone. One that repels the ley."

A low rasping came from its golden-scaled chest that might have been laughter. "What would you do with this stone?"

"I don't know," she admitted. "But a lot of people are looking for it."

The laughter grew louder as the creature rose up on thick legs. It shook off the rock dust like a bear after a swim, scaled hide twitching as it whipped its body to and fro as much as the tunnel would allow. Cathrynne coughed and covered her nose. When it was satisfied, it stopped and peered down at her. She was near enough for it to snap her head off with a single bite.

"The stone of which you speak is a bezoar," it said.

The word was unfamiliar. "What is that?" she asked.

Its eyes narrowed, slits of gold in the darkness. "I will not explain it to you, witch. But they are our defense against your kind."

Cathrynne's mind raced. "The stones are made by the Sinn? Then why do you keep them in the cavern?"

"When they grow too large," came the grumbling reply, "we must eject them or they will cause indigestion. The cavern is for old bezoars, witch."

She bit her lip. "I am not a witch. I am a cypher."

Its eyes widened slightly. "Mother of our species."

She swallowed, her throat terribly dry. "Yes. Do you have a name? Mine is Cathrynne." She paused. "Cathrynne Rowan Lenormand."

"I am called Borosus," it replied. "Since you spared me, I will spare you."

They regarded each other warily for a long moment. It occurred to Cathrynne that she might be the first person to speak with a Sinn in centuries—or ever. How little they really knew about their enigmatic enemies.

Something about the creature's name seemed masculine, as did the timbre of its voice, but she didn't want to make assumptions.

"You are a *he?*' she asked cautiously.

"I am a he," Borosus agreed with a purring rumble that might have been amusement. "And you are a *she*. All cyphers are *she*."

Cathrynne nodded. "That's right."

It shifted its bulk, nostrils flaring. "My brothers and sisters come."

Fresh fear prickled along her spine. "Will you show me the way out, Borosus?"

He grumbled agreement and backed down the tunnel, gesturing with a claw for her to follow. She spotted her torch and blew off the dust. For a wonder, it turned on, though the glass lens was cracked. When they reached the cavern with the kaldurite, Borosus pointed her to the tunnel she and Kal had come through. The rock still glowed a fiery red.

"I can't go out that way," Cathrynne explained. "I'll roast."

Borosus's tail thumped against the rocky ground. It reminded her of a person idly tapping their fingers as they considered a problem.

"There is another way," he said at last.

They returned to the dim recesses of the cavern, where a narrow crevice broke the wall.

"Take this path," he said, "to the third tunnel. Turn left, then take the second right after the stream. Follow the draft of fresh air to the fifth crossing and up the shaft with the iron rungs. It leads to the surface."

Cathrynne repeated the directions under her breath. "What about my friend?" she asked. "The human girl? Can you help her?"

Borosus snapped his jaws. "You ask too much. If she is wise, she will find her own way out. Now go, before my kin arrives."

Without another word, he turned and crawled away, his flaming mane casting dancing shadows on the walls until he disappeared around a bend. Cathrynne repeated the directions to herself once more, then started down the passage he had indicated. Third left, second right. She repeated the directions again and again as she walked.

She hoped Kal had made it out safely, but there was nothing she could do to aid her now. Not with a ton of rock between them and more Sinn on the way. The torch flickered, its light shrinking. She quickened her pace, counting the turnings. Third left. Second right. Follow the draft.

She managed the first part just fine, and whispered a prayer of thanks when a faint whiff of fresh air brushed her cheek. But the draft seemed to come from multiple directions, swirling and changing. She hesitated at a four-way junction, trying to recall Borosus's exact words. Fifth crossing? Or was it the fourth?

She chose a path at random, moved forward with less certainty. The torch dimmed, casting barely enough light to see the ground before her feet. Wrong turns looked the same as right ones in the near-darkness. The air grew still. No draft at all. This wasn't right.

She turned back, but the junctions all looked identical now. Cathrynne stopped, her pulse quickening, as the torch gave a final sputter and went out.

# CHAPTER 35
# GAVRIEL

The instant he felt the tremor, he knew they were in trouble.

It came as a faint vibration beneath his feet. If he had not been still and silent, he wouldn't have noticed. But he remembered the sensation from the night at Red Dog Camp. Sinn moving within the tunnels.

Fear gripped him—not for himself but for the two women down there in the dark. There was nothing he could do to stop a blue emperor, but he could warn them. If it wasn't already too late.

He had no torch, but there were ways of making light. With a pained grimace, he tore out one of his covert feathers and used the barb to prick a thumb. Blue blood welled up, imbued with enough ley that it shimmered in the darkness, giving off just enough light to see by. Then he set off, marking the wall with a smear of blood every twenty cubits. The main shaft sloped gently into the hillside, its low roof supported by timber beams. Twenty minutes of walking brought him to a cave-in where a horizontal shaft bisected the first. It was too round and smooth to be part of the original mine. There seemed to be no other way down.

For a moment, the weight of the rock felt crushing. He was a being of air—of open sky and cool wind and lofty heights. This place was solid and stale and deep, and he did not belong here. A visceral sense of wrongness invaded his gut. Or was he nearing the source of the kaldurite?

Gavriel squeezed his thumb and left a mark at the juncture. Then he delved into the tunnel.

His wings were tucked tight against his back, but the Sinn-bored shaft was large enough to allow him to walk upright. He didn't sense more vibrations. Perhaps the creature was just passing through. When he reached another junction where three tunnels branched off, Gavriel closed his eyes and listened.

There—a scrape on stone. He moved toward the sound, the dark trying to devour his weak pool of blue light. "Cathrynne!"

A dust-coated figure appeared from the blackness. It was Kalisto Machena—and she was alone.

"What happened?" he asked, hurrying up to her.

The girl looked distraught. "We found the cavern, but a blue emperor came along. It attacked. We ran and the ceiling came down—"

"Where's Cathrynne?"

She gestured behind her. "Back that way, but you won't be able to reach her." The young woman's voice wavered on the edge of tears. "She was trapped on the other side with the Sinn—"

"Go up and wait for us at the exit," Gavriel said, his mind racing.

Kal started to protest, but she looked exhausted. Gavriel reminded himself that she had been chased by a giant, buried up to her neck in the desert, and now attacked by a Sinn. He would not ask more of her.

"Go," he said gently. "I'll find her."

Kal gave a weary nod and stumbled down the tunnel. Gavriel pressed onward. "Cathrynne!" he shouted. "Answer me if you can!"

His own voice echoed back. Gavriel delved deeper into the maze of tunnels. He met several cave-ins and numerous branchings. Each time, he chose randomly and marked his passage with a smear of blood. He called her name again and again, uncaring that something else might be drawn to the sound of his voice.

In one of the smooth Sinn-bored tunnels, a dull boom echoed, followed by a strong tremor that sent loose pebbles skittering at his feet. Gavriel braced himself, but the shaking finally stopped. Another collapse somewhere in the labyrinth of tunnels. The mountain was shifting, settling. Time was running short.

He had almost given up hope when he caught a whiff of vetiver and almond blossoms. Spirits lifting, he followed it through an empty cavern, past several smaller tunnels, and into a place where a shallow lake of still water had gathered. There, on the rocky shore, sat a slight figure with flaxen hair. Her head lifted.

"Gavriel?"

Relieved laughter spilled out. He ran up and pulled her into an embrace, inhaling the smell of her hair. "Thank the gods! Are you hurt?"

When he pulled back, her eyes were wide. "I met a Sinn. Gavriel, it spoke to me . . ."

She took a step and stumbled.

Gavriel caught her. "Spoke to you?"

She nodded. "They are not what we think. They're *intelligent*."

He lifted her in his arms. She made a weak protest, but her head rested against his shoulder. Gavriel retraced his steps through the tunnels. Faint tremors shook the rock walls every few minutes, speeding his footsteps. They emerged just as dawn broke over the Zamir Hills. Gavriel swore softly.

Kal Machena was gone.

He could see a trail of faint scuff marks in the dirt, ending at a gravel road. She could have gone in either direction. She had an hour head start, and he knew how skilled Kal was at hiding—especially in the hills she'd grown up in.

He glanced down at Cathrynne, at the fading bruises on her face, the blue shadows beneath her eyes. She was in no condition to help him search for Kal. And the girl clearly did not want to be found. Perhaps she deserved to be left alone, as he had promised.

*Free will.* Travian's greatest gift to his children.

"Hold tight," he ordered. Cathrynne hesitated only briefly before her arms slid around his neck, fingers locking at his nape. He secured her against him, one arm behind her back, the other under her legs.

His wings extended to their full span, fourteen cubits of midnight velvet catching the last rays of sun. He crouched slightly, then pushed upward with his legs as his wings swept downward in a powerful stroke. They shot skyward, the ground falling away. Cathrynne's arms tightened, her face pressed against his shoulder.

Gavriel angled east, toward the sea. Toward Everfell.

---

He flew through the night. The stars wheeled overhead as Cathrynne slept in his arms, her body warm against his chest. Dawn approached from the east, a pale line dividing sea from sky.

First gray, then pink, then a fierce orange that painted the underside of scattered clouds. The Parnassian Sea stretched below them, dark waves tipped with gold. Her weight was nothing to him. Still, he felt her presence like an anchor—not a burden but a tether to something he'd never allowed himself before.

The sun breached the horizon. Light spilled across the water, a path of fire leading to Arioch. The city appeared in the distance, white stone walls rising from rocky cliffs, the towers and spires of the colleges catching the new day's light.

Gavriel banked north toward the wild coastline where Everfell stood alone on its promontory, a mound of gray stone against green hills, brambles twining along its walls. He landed on the veranda that extended from the eastern wing, opened the glass doors with one hand, and strode inside.

Edvin Yarl was coming down the staircase. His face lit up.

"Lord Morningstar! Thank the gods you found her," he said with feeling.

"There is much to tell you," Gavriel said, "but we must get her settled first."

Cathrynne stirred in his arms. "Where are we?" she asked groggily.

"Home," he replied.

The guest rooms were located on the third floor, rarely used but meticulously cleaned and aired. Yarl followed them upstairs and opened the doors, then rushed to turn down the quilt. Gavriel laid Cathrynne on the bed.

"Rest," he said gently, tugging her boots off and pulling the covers up.

She smiled at him, then snuggled into the pillow. "Just a quick nap," she said.

He retreated to the doorway where Yarl waited, his face carefully composed.

"She stays until she is well enough to return to the chapter house," Gavriel said. He glanced at the bed. Cathrynne's eyes were closed, her breathing even. Something tightened in his chest. "Until then, tell no one she is here."

Yarl nodded. "Of course. Shall I have some tea brought round?"

"Yes, please. And food. I'm starved."

After passing on these orders to the cook, Yarl joined him in the dining room, where Gavriel ate a quick meal of soup and cheese and sketched out the broad strokes of all that had happened in the last few days.

"I'll keep my ear to the ground regarding events in Kota Gelangi and Arjevica," Yarl promised. He shook his head. "I cannot believe it was the young aide who murdered Barsal Casolaba!"

"We must discover his true identity," Gavriel said. "But I am too tired to think more on it just now."

"You should retire, sir."

"In a while." He gave a weary smile. "If you need me, I'll be in the library."

Gavriel sought the peace of his inner sanctum and the comfortably familiar scent of cold ashes, leather, and parchment. Correspondence had piled up during his absence. Letters and entreaties from across the empire. He broke the wax seal on an official-looking missive from the Collegium in Andar Jeyla and read the opening lines.

Then read them again.

Something about a complaint over new tariffs on nutmeg and lentils, but he found it impossible to focus on the particulars. His thoughts drifted to Cathrynne and the feel of her in his arms. The *rightness* of it, despite his father's laws and the harsh punishments he himself had doled out to others.

Gavriel leaned back, Valoriel's stern, slightly contemptuous voice echoing in his head. *You are an archangel of Kirith, not some lovesick boy.*

No, of course he wasn't. He had brought Cathrynne Rowan to Everfell for her own safety, nothing more. She had endured enough suffering on his behalf. She needed time to heal and recover before she resumed her duties. Everfell was the ideal place for that, peaceful and secluded, with a dozen servants at her command.

*I am a shepherd, not a wolf.*

Yet the words of Alluin Westwind returned to him unbidden.

*I love this witch with all my soul. With every breath and thought and deed. Have you never loved someone thus?*

## CHAPTER 36
# CATHRYNNE

Everfell sat atop a windy hill a short walk from cliffs that plunged down to the sea. The light had a bright, dazzling clarity and the air was never still, with a perpetual salt breeze blowing off the waves.

Cathrynne opened all the windows of her bedchamber and soaked in a copper tub filled with piping hot water. One of the maids was about her size and had kindly lent her two dresses suitable for the warm spring weather, one white with yellow flowers, and one forest-green with a square neckline. She chose the green one, which was a little loose in the bodice but otherwise fit perfectly. Her ribs were still tender, so she was glad for the extra room. The gathered skirt fell just below her knee, comfortable for walking and sitting.

Her room had a four-poster bed with a soft, faded quilt patterned with stars in varying shades of blue. A hope chest sat at the foot, while the other half of the chamber nearest the windows held a pine armoire smelling of mothballs and a vanity with a wavy three-paneled mirror.

Cathrynne sat down and studied her reflection. It had been over a week since she escaped from Markus and the bruises had healed to faint shadows. She looked more like herself again—on the outside. But so much had happened, she needed time to process it all.

The strange powers of Levi Bottas. Seeing her mother, sister, and grandmother after twenty years. *Actually speaking to a blue emperor named Borosus* . . . The last part still felt like a dream. And the flight across the Parnassian Sea! It had been exhilarating and terrifying at the same time. Much of the trip had passed in darkness, and she had drifted off for long parts of it, but the sensation of being carried by an angel was not one she would soon forget.

Cathrynne liked Gavriel's home immediately. It was quiet and peaceful, with simple, sturdy furnishings. The only sounds were the calls of birds and chirps of insects. She untangled her damp hair with a silver comb from one of the vanity drawers. It had terrible knots from the wind whipping it about, and she worked through them slowly and patiently, watching the barn swallows swoop and dive beyond the window. It made her think briefly of the illusion at Markus's house, of the robin and the squirrel and the vast green lawns. She wondered if the spell was drawn from a real place somewhere in the world. It had been so perfect, so detailed . . .

A knock came. Cathrynne opened the door. It was the apple-cheeked maid, Mia, who had lent her the dresses.

"You look lovely, miss," she said with a smile. "Breakfast is ready, and the master sent me to ask if you'll join him on the veranda."

"Oh yes, I'm famished. I'll just get my boots on." She looked around the room. "Er, if you know where they are."

Mia's blue eyes twinkled. "They were in quite a state, miss. The master took the liberty of ordering a new pair from the cobbler down at the village. You can wear these in the meantime."

She handed Cathrynne a pair of stout walking shoes that looked to be about the right size.

"Ah, thank you." She took the shoes and sat on the edge of the bed. "I'll be right down."

Mia smiled. "It's nice to have company at the house. Lord Morningstar so rarely invites guests."

Cathrynne thanked her again and laced on the shoes. Then she drew a deep breath and composed herself. Now that Gavriel had brought her home to Kirith, she should leave straight after breakfast for the chapter house in Arioch. There was so much to tell Felicity Birch, who must be worried about her. Yet she felt dread at facing the interrogation that surely awaited. Mump and Crump would demand to have a go at her, and she needed to come up with a *very* convincing story about where she'd been during the time at Markus's house.

A thrill of fear went through her. If they found out she was a seer . . . No, there was no reason they'd ever find out, not so long as she managed to lie convincingly. Which was the problem. She had never been good at deception. Cathrynne chewed her lip. She decided to eat breakfast before making a decision. It was always easier to tackle one's problems on a full stomach.

***

A long stone veranda faced the sea and that is where she found Gavriel, with his legs stretched out and his black wing feathers ruffling in the gentle gusts that came across the moor. He wore gray trousers and an open-necked linen shirt with the sleeves rolled up. He looked distractingly handsome, even scowling at the broadsheet in his hands.

"Bad news?" she asked, sitting down at the table.

It was laid with an array of platters that made her nose twitch appreciatively. Poached eggs, savory potatoes with onions and paprika, thick-sliced toast and pots of strawberry jam, black tea with cream and sugar, and what smelled like heavenly cardamom scones. A proper Kirithi breakfast.

Gavriel glanced up, his face softening. "How do you feel this morning?"

She slathered butter on a slice of toast and took a big bite. "Much better. Tell me what you're frowning at, Morningstar."

He sighed and folded the broadsheet. "The witches have declared the Casolaba case to be solved. They are blaming Levi Bottas."

"Who confessed that he did it," she reminded him, adding a heaping spoonful of jam to the toast.

"Yes, but I still don't know the exact nature of his relationship with the consul, who else is involved—"

"Or how he managed to turn himself into a giant," Cathrynne finished. "Oh, I think this is the best jam I've ever tasted! So where is Levi Bottas now?"

"No one knows. Yarl keeps a network of informers throughout Sion. They say he's vanished. A team of witches searched every inch of the Lenormand School and found no sign of him."

Cathrynne swallowed the last bite of toast, her appetite fading. "Do you think he'll go after Kal?"

Gavriel shook his head, clearly troubled. "I don't know. But I'm certain she escaped the Clear Creek mine. I met her in the tunnel only a short distance from the exit, and I saw her footprints when we came out. She took one of the roads."

"I worry about her, Gavriel."

"So do I. But I don't think she wants to be found."

Cathrynne stared out at the beaten-silver waves in the distance. She thought of Kal's sailing ship tattoo, the dreams of adventure she shared with her friend Durian. "She's tough and resourceful. And she pocketed more of the kaldurite stones. They'll give her some protection."

Gavriel nodded, studying her with an intensity that made her self-conscious. "And you? I worry about you, too, Cathrynne."

She piled her plate high with eggs and potatoes. "I'm fine."

"How can that be true?" His voice grew rough. He was angry, she suspected, though not with her. "After what the White Foxes did?"

She set her fork down. "Which time? Last week, or twenty years ago?"

"I mean Markus Viktorovich." Gavriel practically growled the name.

"We do seem destined to keep crossing paths," she said. "And I still owe both him and his mother. But thanks to them, I faced my worst fears and survived."

Gavriel leaned forward. For a moment, she thought he might reach for her hand, but then Mia bustled over and he sat back. The young maid seemed to sense that she was intruding, for she quickly refilled the teapot and left.

"Ever since I was taken from Arjevica to Arioch by carriage at the age of eleven, I've had a fear of closed spaces," Cathrynne admitted. "Even being confined to barracks was an agony. It's funny, because I can sit and read a book for hours with no difficulty, but if I'm told I *can't* leave a room, I become terribly restless—"

"Aha," he said with a half smile. "And you claimed you didn't read books."

"You remember that?"

"I remember everything." He noticed her hunting for the salt cellar and pushed it closer. Their fingers brushed as she took it, and Cathrynne felt a little jolt. "But please continue."

She gazed into his green-gold eyes, trying to gather her train of thought. "I don't like the dark, either. Funny for a cypher, I suppose, but I dislike feeling helpless. That was the worst part of my captivity. At first, Markus held me in a spacious room, but I kept trying to escape, and I wouldn't give them what they wanted, so his mother had me moved to a tiny cell under the house."

"That's barbaric," Gavriel muttered. "I had no idea the Foxes were still so brutal."

She forked potatoes into her mouth. "Then you don't know them very well. But my point is that I endured it without losing my mind. If I had not done that, I never could have gone down into the tunnels with Kal. I wouldn't have met Borosus. I wouldn't have seen the source."

He nodded. "They tried to break you," he said. "But they only made you stronger."

Cathrynne liked that. "Yes." She drained her cup of tea, feeling pleasantly restored. "Do you ever walk on the moors? I wouldn't mind a spot of exercise."

Gavriel grinned. "Every day, when I'm home." He stood, tossing the broadsheet aside. "Come, I'll show you the estate."

A flight of stone steps led down to a kitchen garden with early spring lettuce and a few cabbages, and then to a track leading across the moor. Cathrynne followed him down, glancing back to admire the manor house behind her. Everfell had a pleasingly wild, untamed appearance. Seven chimneys rose from its slate roof, and dense brambles covered its stone exterior. Prickly on the outside, she thought with amusement, just like its master. Yet like Gavriel, it also made her feel safe and wanted.

Spring had taken firm hold and the heather was in bloom, vast swathes of purple against the green meadow grass and fescue. Gavriel shortened his stride to match hers and they hiked in easy silence for a while.

"How long have you lived at Everfell?" she asked.

"About five hundred years. I've tried to keep it as it was when I first came. We light the hearths for warmth in the winter, and use candles and oil lamps rather than electricity. I hope it's not an inconvenience."

She shook her head. "Not at all. My family's dacha in the countryside was much the same. I like the simplicity of it."

A shadow crossed his face at the mention of the Lenormands.

"I'm sorry for the way my grandmother treated you," she added quickly. "It was unfair."

Gavriel looked uncertain—which was not a quality she'd seen often. "I don't blame her. It's my fault . . . " He paused and drew Cathrynne to a halt. "There," he said softly, pointing to a russet shape in the heather. They watched the fox trot past, its bushy red tail almost as large as its body, and disappear into a stand of gorse.

"She's hunting voles," Gavriel said with a smile. "Spring means new litters and hungry kits."

Whatever he'd been about to say regarding Nestania, he seemed to change his mind. They rambled along dirt tracks that wound through the rolling hills, meeting more denizens of the heath. A startled chocolate-brown hare with black feet zigzagged across their path, running so fast it was a blur. A few minutes later, Cathrynne exclaimed over a nest with three speckled eggs hidden in the grasses until a pair of irate skylarks harried them onward. Gavriel pointed out golden plovers and merlins, a distant roe deer in a copse, and the tracks of a badger along a muddy section of road.

It was so different from the streets of Arioch where Cathrynne had spent her entire adult life. The city had its charms, but she began to understand Mercy's yearly trips into the mountains to hike and camp. There was a peacefulness in the wilds, a calm solitude that healed the soul.

They reached the cliff edge in late morning. The inland sea stretched to the horizon, sunlight fracturing on the waves. Wind gusted stronger here, blowing salt spray amid the cries of gulls. They stood side by side in silence, watching the waves heave against the rocks below.

"Sometimes I launch from the cliffs," Gavriel admitted, "and fly with the peregrine falcons."

"For fun?" she teased.

He donned a scowl. "I am unfamiliar with that term, Rowan."

"Oh, stop. Do you really fly with falcons?"

"I do. And we race." He preened. "I usually win."

She shadowed her eyes with one hand, scanning the sky. "Aren't they the fastest thing in the world?"

"They are the fastest *animal*," he said. "A falcon's heart can beat up to nine hundred times per minute. They are extraordinary. My father borrowed some of their traits when he designed the angels." His lips curved. "I don't hunt small birds, but I do have the ability to tuck my wings and dive at tremendous speeds."

Cathrynne had seen falcons perform this feat from the top of the astronomy tower in Arioch. "It makes me dizzy just thinking of it. Aren't you afraid of crashing into the water?"

"Of course." The wind tugged a lock of raven hair across his forehead. "That's why it's fun."

"I won't ask for a demonstration," she laughed.

He grinned and gazed out to sea. "None of my friends are here today. They are probably tending their fledglings." He leaned over the cliff until the soles of Cathrynne's feet began to tingle and she reminded herself that tumbling over the edge was not a concern for him. "You can't see it from above, but they nest on the ledges."

She took in the wide panorama of rolling hills, distant woods, and sun-kissed waves. "This is a beautiful place. Thank you for showing it to me."

"I suppose we should head back," Gavriel said with reluctance.

As they turned to the path, he bent to pick a bouquet of buttercups. He presented it to her with solemn formality, the sunlight burnishing the flecks of gold in his eyes. "I'll have a vase with water brought to your room," he said.

She grinned and held the bouquet under her chin. "Well?"

He looked befuddled. "Well, what?"

"If my chin turns yellow, it means I like butter. Haven't you ever tried it?"

He shook his head, a wry grin tugging at his lips. "I must say, your chin is *very* yellow."

"Then I shall have scones for dinner, with extra butter and jam," she declared imperiously.

"As my lady desires."

She flushed and covered it by tickling his chin with a buttercup. "Does the lord of Everfell like butter?"

"Only if it comes from the local pasture," he said loyally. "The cows are happy, so they make the finest butter in all of Sion."

"And do you commune with these happy cows?" she asked, as they started walking back to the house.

"I do. They are part of the estate and thus under my personal protection." He glanced at her. "As you are, Cathrynne."

She arched a brow.

"Not part of the estate," he added hastily. "You know what I mean."

"I do," she said. "And I'm glad you brought me here. It's a good place, and I needed that. But I should be getting back to the chapter house. I must tell them about the kaldurite."

"Of course," he murmured. "I have considered the matter, and I believe that under the law, it belongs to the witches. Haniel would only work mischief if she had control of it." He paused. "It's getting late though. One more night before you leave would do no harm. I shall miss your company, Cathrynne."

She tried to ignore the small thrill that went through her. He meant nothing by it. And she could not . . . would not . . . *Ugh*. Why did her thoughts tangle so when she was near him? Flustered, she bent to add some sprigs of meadowsweet to the bouquet. The white blossoms complemented the yellow, but it also gave her a chance to gather herself.

She could not say that she would gladly stay for weeks, taking long walks with Gavriel across the moor, eating divine food, and pretending that they could be more to each other than cypher and angel.

"One more night," she agreed. "I confess, I like it here very much."

He looked boyishly happy. They walked back to Everfell, trailing short noonday shadows across the moor.

\*\*\*

A delicious lunch had been laid out when they reached the house. Fresh lemonade with just the right amount of tartness, chilled tomato soup, cucumber and cheese sandwiches on the same soft, chewy white bread she'd had for breakfast, followed by little cakes dotted with just-picked blueberries. Cathrynne stuffed herself and regarded Gavriel's trim waistline with envy. How on earth did he manage to eat like this every day? If she had his cook, she would end up very plump—and too content to care a whit about it.

The only thing to do after a long walk and leisurely three-course lunch was to take a nap. She retired to her bedchamber, leaving him in his study (where else?) to go over the heaps of correspondence that had piled up in his absence.

She drifted off to the cheerful warbling of robins in the birch trees. At first, she dreamt of Borosus. He was soaring above the sea, blue scales shining in the sun. A smaller Sinn with silver and green scales flew beside him. Somehow Cathrynne knew it was a female.

She stood on the cliff edge, watching them perform an intricate dance together, plummeting toward the waves in a tight spiral and then rolling away at the last moment. For such large creatures, they were graceful and acrobatic. Cathrynne felt a profound sense of awe. The Sinn were not mindless predators as she had been taught. They were thinking, feeling, intelligent beings who had been persecuted for hundreds of years.

She was about to call to Borosus when the ground beneath her feet crumbled. Dirt and pebbles skittered into the void below. She scrambled back but it was too late. The cliff gave way and she was falling, the walls racing past as she plunged to her doom on the jagged rocks—

As often happens in dreams, there was no impact. A moment later, her pulse still thundering, she stood on a vast plain of ice and fire. The sky was as black as the bottom of the ocean. But a cold gray light, like dawn on a bitter winter's morning, illuminated the barren landscape.

At the rim of the horizon was a smudge that might have been hills, or possibly a city, but it was obscured by the steam rising from pits in the frozen earth. Cathrynne closed her eyes and tried to wish herself back in her bedchamber.

When she opened them, nothing had changed—except that a figure was walking towards her. It had reddish skin and wore no clothing besides a loincloth around its hips. Its head was bald as an egg. The features were blandly androgynous, but as it drew closer, two small, high breasts became visible and Cathrynne revised the pronoun to *she*.

"Greetings!" the woman called with a toothy smile. Her head cocked in appraisal. "I am surprised to find a witch here." She chuckled. "But all are welcome!"

Cathrynne looked around with trepidation. "Is this the Plain of Contemplation?"

"It has many names. I call it Char'azul." Her eyes had a reddish cast as well and they fixed on Cathrynne with alert interest. "I am Merric. What is your name?"

Her voice was honeyed, but Cathrynne sensed danger in the question. "This is only a dream," she said firmly. "And you are not real."

Merric laughed. She gazed at her hands, flexing the long, slender fingers. "Funny, I feel quite real. I think it's *you* who have come here only in spirit. That does happen every now and then." Her voice sank to a sultry whisper. "But you have power. I can smell it. Perhaps a bargain can be made."

Cathrynne frowned. "What kind of bargain?"

"That depends on what you want."

"I see. And what do *you* want?"

Merric grinned. She had pointy eyeteeth like a caracal. "Many things . . ." She trailed off, head tilting back. "Ah. He comes at last!"

Cathrynne turned to follow her gaze and spotted a tiny spark in the black sky. It grew bigger by the moment, trailing flame like a comet.

"The time of exile and penance is here. You must not interfere, Cathrynne Rowan Lenormand."

She startled at the new voice behind her. The red-eyed woman had vanished and Julia Camara stood in her place. This time, the light of madness flickered in the seer's eyes.

"If you try, the gods will die and you will join me in the kloster for the rest of your days—"

"Stop!" Cathrynne covered her ears. "Just stop!"

Julia threw her arms wide to the heavens, an expression of mad exultation on her face. "He comes!"

Icy fingers gripped Cathrynne's heart. It was the angel of her dreams, approaching at a terrible velocity like a star falling to earth, except that this time she could almost see his face—

Cathrynne sat up in bed, trembling. It had grown dark outside. A sob escaped her just as the door burst open and Gavriel rushed in holding a candle. The bed creaked as he sat on the edge of the feather mattress.

"I heard you scream," he said, his brow furrowed with concern. "Are you well?"

She wordlessly shook her head. He set the candle down, and then his strong arms circled her, drawing her close. He murmured words of comfort and reassurance against her hair and she relaxed against his chest, the warmth of his wings enfolding them both.

"Just a bad dream," she said, pulling back to look into his eyes. "I . . . I can't remember it now."

He tenderly brushed a lock of hair back from her face. "You're safe here, Cat."

Once he had called her by her cypher surname, Rowan. Then Cathrynne. But the distance between them was melting away. She didn't care to examine what it meant—especially the dream, which she recalled in vivid detail. She knew she should tell Gavriel about it. Warn him . . .

And she would. But right now, she wanted to kiss him. So that is what she did.

## CHAPTER 37
# CATHRYNNE

Gavriel's lips were warm and yielding and tasted of mint tea. He allowed her to kiss him for a few seconds, but she sensed that he was holding himself in check.

Frustration boiled over. Cathrynne released his shoulders and sat back. "I wish you would make up your mind, Gavriel Morningstar. If you want me to leave, I will. But don't give me flowers and come uninvited into my bedroom if you feel nothing for me!"

He blinked, then gave a low, bitter laugh. "Feeling nothing is not the issue, I can assure you. Quite the opposite." He searched her face. "Is this truly what *you* want?"

She nodded, her pulse beating wildly. "I'll make sure no child comes of it. There are potions I can take. But . . . yes. Just once."

He released a taut breath. His wings spread behind him, black as a raven, as she pulled him down, rolling to her side so they lay face to face. The window was open and she could hear the distant roar of waves against the cliff. Gavriel did not touch her for an agonizing minute.

"I was married twice," he said softly. "Once to a human, once to an angel. They both died long ago. I could not bear the pain of losing another wife, so I hardened my heart. But you have cracked it open, Cathrynne."

She stroked the silky hair at his nape, ignoring the stab of jealousy at the mere thought of him with other women. Dead ones, no less!

"We can never have more than this night," she said.

His eyes darkened. "Then I must make sure you never forget it."

Gavriel's hand slid beneath the hem of her cotton shift, lightly tracing the curve of her hip. She arched against him, a soft sound of pleasure escaping her lips. His reserve cracked and he kissed her, his heart beating against hers, but much swifter. His hand found the swell of her breast.

Cathrynne closed her eyes, surrendering to the fever heat of his skin, the rasp of his beard as he trailed kisses down her throat. She tentatively found the juncture where his wings met the blades of his shoulders. They were covered with soft down. Gavriel shivered against her and she felt him stiffen . . .

Suddenly, he pulled back. Embarrassment sent a hot flush up her neck. So he'd come to his senses after all. She should have expected it. Why was she torturing herself like this?

"It's not you," Gavriel said hoarsely. "I would give anything for us to be together. It's all I've been able to think of for days. You consume me." He sighed. "But there's something I've been keeping from you. It's about your father."

Cathrynne sat up, wary. "What about him?"

"After Alluin Westwind was arrested, he was brought to Mount Meru to await my father's judgment. But Valoriel was in one of his melancholy moods. He got that way sometimes, not speaking for months, delegating his responsibilities to me or my brother Michael."

She listened in silence, nameless dread burrowing into her heart.

"On the day your father was brought to the Censura,"

Gavriel continued, "Valoriel had ordered me to stand in as regent. I was the one who passed judgment on him."

Her hands felt cold. Cathrynne pulled the quilt to her chest, drawing her knees up. "Have you known all along?"

Gavriel shook his head. "Only since Arjevica, when I realized the Lenormands were your birth family. I . . . I had forgotten the incident."

"Forgotten," she repeated tonelessly. "I see. And what was his sentence?"

Gavriel looked away. "Two hundred years on the Plain of Contemplation."

She inhaled sharply. "That is severe."

"I see that now." He looked miserable. "But at the time, I did what I thought was right. What the law called for. I do not defend myself, Cathrynne." He drew a shaky breath. "Your father begged me to show leniency. I refused. Worse still, I knew that no angel has ever returned from the Plain of Contemplation."

The heat she'd felt moments before was steadily building, but she didn't want to feel his hands on her, or to kiss those perfectly shaped lips.

No, she wanted to hurl him through the window.

"I wielded the Rod of Penance with little thought for those your father left behind," Gavriel admitted. "Nor for the nature of his crime, which arose from love not hate—"

"Get out," she said.

The words came out calm—far calmer than she felt. His forlorn expression only made her angrier. The dream must be of her own father as he was cast into perdition by the very angel she had nearly fallen for. She felt tricked, used, and heartbroken at all once.

Gavriel nodded as if he'd expected as much. "I don't blame you for hating me. But Cathrynne, please, I want you to know that—"

"Just go!"

His face went blank as though she'd slapped him. He strode to the balcony doors and threw them open. Cold air rushed in. Gavriel looked back at her once, his face a mask of pain and regret, then stepped off the edge. Dark wings carried him up and out of sight.

Cathrynne stared at the fluttering curtains. She felt gutted, yet why should she be surprised? He was Sion's chief magistrate, notorious for his strict adherence to the letter of the law.

And he had lied to her about it. Lied for days.

A small voice reminded her that Gavriel had only done what he believed was right at the time. Yet the fact that he had not even *remembered* her father—that was the worst part. He must have sent a great many angels to their doom to be so cavalier about it.

Cathrynne's jaw clenched. Her first assessment had been spot-on. Gavriel Morningstar was a complete prick!

Her gaze fell on the vase filled with cheerful yellow buttercups, the bouquet he had picked for her on the moor. Cathrynne gripped the iron bed frame, drawing deep on the fiery red ley contained in the metal. An instant later, the flowers burst into flame and the vase exploded.

Cathrynne instinctively threw up a shield, using receptive magic from Lara's ring. It deflected the flying shards. *I'm learning,* she thought with grim satisfaction. Luckily, the water that spilled on the floor doused the smoldering embers. She stared the mess, drawing deep breaths.

It reminded her of the nightmare. The endless plain of ice and fire. Once again, Julia Camara's prophesy came back to her.

*"When he falls from grace, you must not interfere. You must let him serve his penance, even if it lasts forever."*

*"Penance for what? And why would I interfere?"*

*"Because you love him."*

Now Cathrynne wondered if she was speaking about Alluin Westwind. Was her own father destined to be this Dark-bringer? Because she *certainly* didn't love Gavriel Morningstar.

Cathrynne's hands knotted in the quilt. She felt a sudden urge to be gone from Everfell. She could not stand to be there another minute! She didn't belong here, and she certainly didn't want to face Gavriel in the morning. Didn't want to hear his pleas or excuses—or worse, his frosty silence.

She lit a fresh candle and quickly donned her trousers, jacket and bodice, which Mia had laundered. Wearing the uniform of the cyphers made her feel calmer, more in control.

She'd make up a story. No one need know she'd been here. And Gavriel would never risk his precious reputation, so she could count on his silence.

Cathrynne left Everfell through the unlocked glass doors to the terrace and strode down the drive for a mile or so until she reached the road leading southwest towards Arioch. She did not look back.

\*\*\*

The walk into the city was long and tedious, with plenty of time to think. Did her mother and grandmother know what Gavriel had done? Cathrynne thought not. They would not have allowed him through the front door if they did. No, they disliked Morningstar on principle.

Yet now that she'd cooled down, Cathrynne had to admit that he had another side to him. Playful, kind, passionate, protective. She would be with *that* man in a heartbeat. But it was impossible. At least he had the decency to come clean before they slept together. Gavriel did have honor. She could not fault him that.

Now it was time to face the witches of Arioch. A guilty warmth spread through her as she recalled his ardent kisses, but they would never know about that. *Never.*

She firmly shoved Lord Morningstar from her thoughts and mentally reviewed what she would tell Felicity Birch. She decided to stick to the truth as much as possible, especially about the kaldurite. The stones had caused at least two deaths that she knew of, but maybe some good could come of it. If seers had a way of blocking the ley, they might not go mad—or at least they would have more control over their gift. And cyphers could protect themselves against the magic of full witches!

Cathrynne grew excited as she thought of all the ways that kaldurite could save lives. She'd never had a say in important decisions before, but they would have to listen to her this time. She was the only person besides Kal who knew exactly where the source was. She could speak for the voiceless, for those with no influence. Cathrynne bit her lip. Would Gavriel tell his father about the Clear Creek Mine? If so, she needed to act fast.

The sun was high by the time Cathrynne arrived at the chapter house. She went straight to Felicity Birch's office and rapped on the door, eager to hear the advice of her trusted mentor. The familiar voice came from within, crisp and commanding: "Enter."

Cathrynne pushed the door open and froze. Felicity sat behind her desk, but she wasn't alone. Marvel Yew, head of the Satu Jos cyphers, sat in a chair opposite. Her hair was braided tight to her head, and the burn scars along her neck and jaw were clearly visible in the bright daylight. The flame and forge of her province was emblazoned on her jacket. Silver eyes locked on Cathrynne, a vivid contrast to her dark skin.

"Rowan," Marvel said grimly. Her whip-thin frame uncoiled from the chair. "You have impeccable timing. I just came to deliver a warrant for your return to Kota Gelangi."

Felicity frowned. "Where have you been? I heard about the incident at the Lenormand School, but then you disappeared again—"

Marvel cut her off with a sharp gesture. "She can save her explanations for the High Council."

Cathrynne had expected punishment, but not this fast. "What have I done?" she asked in a subdued voice.

There were many, *many* possibilities. Best to determine exactly how much they already knew.

"We have witnesses who saw you abduct the Machena girl," Marvel replied, her features stern.

The "witnesses" could only be Markus Viktorovich and Berti Baako. The prospect of facing them again sent a spike of ice through her belly.

"I didn't abduct Kal," Cathrynne protested. "I was trying to save her!"

"Then where is she now?"

"I don't know. The forcing went wrong and she got away."

Marvel's expression hardened further. "Forcing? You aren't supposed to even know how to do that!"

Cathrynne opened her mouth, then closed it again.

"This will not weigh in your favor," Marvel said in an ominous tone. "Come, we return to Kota Gelangi at once."

Cathrynne threw a desperate look at her boss.

"She just arrived," Felicity said reasonably. "I'll debrief her first, and then she can go pack—"

Marvel gave a humorless laugh. "Coach her on what to say, you mean? I think not. We'll have the full story out of her with no interference." A look passed between the two women. "She won't be harmed, but as we just discussed, the importance of the Machena girl cannot be overestimated." Her gaze flicked to Cathrynne. "Whatever you know, you must give it to the Morag."

Cathrynne swallowed, her throat dry. "A sweven, you mean?"

"Perhaps. Unless your story is *very* convincing."

A threat? Or a subtle warning? "Yes, mum," Cathrynne muttered.

The office suddenly felt too small. Airless. Her chest tightened. What if all this ended with her being handed over to Markus again? He'd put her back in the tiny dark cell in his basement. She was a nobody and he was the head of the White Foxes in Arjevica. He could do whatever he wanted with her.

She heard his cultured voice whisper in her ear: *Give me the sweven.*

Sweat broke out on her palms. She felt a panic attack coming on and forced herself to take a long slow breath.

"Are you alright, Rowan?"

Marvel Yew was staring her with a concerned expression. Her voice was not unkind.

Cathrynne forced a nod, clasping her hands to hide the shaking. "Yes, mum."

Marvel eyed her for a moment more, then gave a brisk nod. "Then let us depart, the Morag awaits."

They left the office and took the path toward the forcing ground, Marvel marching ahead. Felicity fell in beside Cathrynne. "The High Council is in an uproar over this new gemstone," she whispered. "If you have knowledge they can use, save yourself with it."

Cathrynne nodded distractedly. She drew several more deep calming breaths and her galloping heart began to slow. Yes, that's just what she would do. She was *not* powerless, not anymore. She had leverage. And if things went badly, she would tell the High Council what Markus and his mother had done to her and let the chips fall as they may.

They were approaching the kloster, where the seers gathered to watch through the bars of their cells. They ranged in age from teens to white-haired elders. She met the eyes of Courage Hazel, the young cypher who had been sent up a few weeks before.

Courage deserved her name. Despite her circumstances, she appeared calm and unbroken. Yet her gaze was so knowing, so *pitying*, Cathrynne could not look away. She twisted her head as she walked by the kloster, and so she saw Courage Hazel's lips move. Too far to hear, but the words were clear.

*He comes.*

A cold hand gripped her heart. So her parting with Gavriel Morningstar hadn't changed the future. Cathrynne decided that once the Morag was done with her, she'd seek out Julia Camara and demand answers. Of course, she might end up being entombed in a cell herself—

"Are you listening?" Felicity demanded.

Cathrynne jerked her gaze back. "Yes, mum."

"Because you don't look like you are." Felicity harrumphed. "I have one piece of good news for you. Mercy turned up at the chapter house in Arjevica. A bit worse for wear but alive."

Cathrynne's spirits leapt. "Truly? Thank Minerva! I had faith in her, but still . . . I was starting to worry."

"As we all were," Felicity agreed with a smile. "The Morag ordered her brought back to Kota Gelangi, so you will see her there."

That she would not face the witches alone was another great relief. Felicity squeezed her hand, then dropped it when Marvel glanced back at them with a slight frown. But Cathrynne walked with her head higher now. Whatever happened, she planned to go down fighting—and she could count on Mercy to have her back.

The forcing ground stood at the far edge of the chapter house compound, surrounded by an iron fence plastered with yellow caution signs. The gate creaked as Marvel pushed it open. A male witch awaited them, his thick black hair pulled back into a knot. Cathrynne recognized him—the same one who had met her and Mercy in Kota Gelangi when they first arrived.

He reached into the pouch at his waist and took out two stones, one black with veins of scarlet, the other clear with a blue heart.

"Wait!"

The shout came from beyond the fence. George Claymond and Audrey Hayes ran up the path, their white coats flapping behind them. "You cannot take Rowan," Audrey shrieked. "We must question her first!"

Cathrynne glanced at Marvel, who wore the barest hint of a smile. "Proceed, Jareth," she said to the male witch.

Mump and Crump were at the gate now, George red and wobbly, Audrey's thin face cinched into a scowl. "You can't—"

Jareth brought his hands together. Receptive and projective

ley joined in a crackling ball of energy. George's furious shout faded as if it came from a great distance. The ground fell away and the world spun sideways.

*Farewell, Gavriel Morningstar*, Cathrynne thought sadly, as the roaring current of liminal ley seized her.

# CHAPTER 38

# KAL

S imão Gomes D'Amato nested his best set of jeweler's loupes in a box of black velvet and secured the bundle with twine.

The tools represented thirty years of his life. Now they, like him, were fleeing. It was only a matter of time before someone came to silence him for good.

His throat tightened as he tucked the box into a shabby cloth suitcase. Don't look rich, his mother always told him. People will try to cheat you. But don't look poor, either, or they'll think you're a failure.

Not an easy woman to please, his mother, but she was right about that. He'd always kept a low profile. Prosperous, but not *wildly* prosperous.

He never went looking for trouble.

It found him nonetheless.

He regarded the brass scale, the set of testing acids, and the ledger—no, not the ledger. Damning evidence. He'd burn it.

"Idiot," he muttered to himself. "Greedy fool."

It had started innocently. A man claiming to be Consul Casolaba's aide had visited Simão's shop a year ago. Would he be interested in providing information about what gems were moving through the market? Nothing illegal—just early alerts about major finds, who was selling what, which rockhounds had struck it lucky.

The arrangement was easy and profitable. Every month, an envelope of crisp dragha notes would come through the mail slot. He listened to gossip, watched the trends, sent weekly reports through a courier. It was most agreeable.

Then the witches turned up.

One morning he'd arrived to find two of them waiting inside his locked shop. He'd nearly pissed himself. Not just witches. White Foxes. The man was huge with silver teeth, and the woman wore a dozen studs and hoops in her face. She looked a bit crazy.

"You have an arrangement with the consul," the woman said. "You'll give us the same deal for half the price. And you'll keep your mouth shut about it."

He had nodded fervently. "Of course, of course. I am happy to be of service to the chapter house."

She leaned in. "You don't serve the chapter house. You serve *me*."

"Yes, yes." He wiped the sweat from his forehead. His hand came away sticky with pomade.

"Good," she said. "We're looking for a gem that resembles serpent's eye. It'll be cold. No ley. Understood?"

"Sure. No ley."

She dropped a wad of bills on the counter. Her gray eyes reminded him of the fish on ice at the market.

He hadn't had a choice. Not really.

For a while, it had gone smoothly. The White Foxes demanded little, and their payments supplemented what he got from the consul's office. He moved from his small flat in a lousy neighborhood on the city's outskirts to a larger apartment within walking distance of the shop. Feeling flush, he sent money to his sister in Old Sarpedon, who had too many kids and a no-good husband.

Life had been good. Until those kids walked into his shop.

Simão closed his eyes, feeling sick. He should have turned them away. Said nothing.

But he'd been scared. What if they took the stones to another jeweler, and it got out that they'd been in his shop?

"Then it would have been me floating in that river," he muttered.

The shop bell tinkled, jerking Simão from his thoughts.

"We're closed!" he called. "Come back tomorrow!"

No answer, just footsteps. He shoved the acid kit into his suitcase and snapped it shut. He'd have to leave the scale behind. It was too bulky.

"I said we're closed!" he called again, emerging from the back room.

His heart stopped.

The girl from Pota Pras stood there. She held a gun, pointed at his chest.

"Please," he gabbled, raising his hands. "I had nothing to do with—"

"With what? Selling us out?"

The look in her eye made his bladder feel heavy and full.

"I didn't know what they would do!" he squeaked. "I just passed along information. That's all I ever did. I'm nobody!"

His eyes darted to the front door. The street beyond was busy with late afternoon shoppers. If he shouted, someone might hear.

The gun lowered to his crotch. "Run and I'll blow your dick off." Her laugh was wild. "Maybe I will anyway."

"I have money!" he blurted, glancing at the cash drawer. "Take it all! It's yours."

She stepped closer, the gun steady on his left eye now. "I'm not a dumb hick. I know you've got a safe in that back room."

He swallowed hard. "Okay," he said, keeping his hands where she could see them. "Okay."

"Slowly."

He led the way into the workroom, painfully aware of the pistol aimed at the back of his skull. The safe sat behind a false panel in the wall, concealed by a heavy cabinet. He moved the cabinet aside. It slid silently on hidden rollers.

"Open it," she said.

His fingers shook as he dialed the combination. He had to try three times before it opened. Inside sat stacks of dragha notes, bound with paper bands marking their denominations. Hundreds, mostly, with a few bundles of smaller bills. A year of payments, plus the large bounty he'd received from each of his clients when he gave them the stones.

The girl inhaled sharply. It must be more than she'd expected.

"Stand back," she ordered.

He retreated to the corner. With her free hand, she pointed to his suitcase, sitting on the workbench.

"Dump it," she said.

He hesitated. "My tools—"

"Dump it *now*."

He unlatched the case and upended the contents.

"Lie on the floor and start counting."

Simão sighed and sank to hands and knees. His belt dug into his generous belly.

"All the way," she barked.

He awkwardly lay face down. He heard the rustle of banknotes filling the suitcase. The snap of the latches.

"Didn't I tell you to count?" she said.

He sneezed. Dust filled his eyes. "How long am I counting?"

"To a thousand. I'll be back to check, so you better not stop."

She poked him with the barrel on the back of his neck. He began counting aloud, his voice weak. "One. Two. Three. Four . . ."

He heard her footsteps retreat, then the tinkle of the bell. Still, he counted.

" . . . ninety-eight. Ninety-nine. One hundred."

Simão paused. He strained to listen. Just the distant sounds of the street.

Cautiously, he pushed himself to his feet and crept to the door. It stood ajar. He peered out, looking both ways. The girl from Pota Pras was gone.

He hurried to the back room, stomach churning. He had to leave town before someone else came. Someone without mercy.

The face of the White Fox with the silver rings in her face came immediately to mind.

But how could he run now? He had nothing—

Simão drew up short, blinking in surprise as he peered into the depths of the safe. He couldn't believe it. She'd left him about a third of his stash.

And that wasn't all.

He picked up the stone. Watched it turn blue, then red, then violet.

"Thank you," he whispered, filled with shame once again.

---

KAL SHUFFLED FORWARD with the crowd waiting to board the ship. A port official moved down the line, checking identity cards. She handed hers over with a smile.

He glanced at the forged documents, then at her face, then back to the papers. Sweat gathered at the small of her back despite the cool breeze coming off the water.

"Purpose in Iskatar, Miss Jentzen?" he asked.

"Family visit," she replied with a smile. "My cousins live in Lagash."

The official handed back her papers with a disinterested nod and moved on to the next passenger. She exhaled and crossed the gangplank with a bounce in her step.

The steamer was a workhorse with peeling paint and a barnacle-crusted hull. Not the elegant cutter she dreamed of, but it would get her to Iskatari capital. From there, she planned to buy her own ship, hire a crew, and set sail for the corners of the map. Someplace beyond the reach of witches and angels both.

Kal found a spot at the rail and set the suitcase between her feet. She scanned the docks, looking for a young man with dark hair and eyes that had a habit of subtly changing color. Who had blood like quicksilver. She still didn't know who Levi worked for. Didn't even know what he *was*. But the forged papers he gave her were good enough to fool a customs official.

Of course, she didn't see him. Levi would be searching the docks and train stations in Arjevica, not Kota Gelangi.

She felt a pang and berated herself for a fool.

The deck vibrated as the steamer pulled away from the wharf. The gap of dark water widened. Kal looked back at the sprawling city of Kota Gelangi, at the distant smudge of the Zamir Hills. She wondered what D'Amato was doing right now. If he was smart, he'd take the money she left him and run. The funny part is that the gun wasn't even loaded. She'd used up all the bullets shooting at the blue emperor.

Kal slid a hand into her pocket, folding her fingers around the clay disk stamped with mining license 009-735-021. And under that, in fading letters, *D. Padulski*.

She would gladly trade the contents of the suitcase at her feet for a chance to go back and do things differently. Pick a different jeweler this time. Or better yet, figure out what they'd found before it was too late.

But she couldn't. So she'd do the next best thing and make all of his schemes come true. Travel the world and build a fortune to beggar the queens of old.

"You did it, bitch."

She turned. Durian stood beside her, the wind ruffling his hair. His eyes were fixed on the open sea beyond the harbor mouth.

"We did it," she corrected.

He grinned. The unrepentant smirk of a scapegrace. Of a poor boy from nowhere whose dreams were as big as the Southern Ocean. He winked at her.

And then he was gone.

## CHAPTER 39
# GAVRIEL

He threw open the balcony doors. Wind gusted into the library, scattering the neatly sorted papers like autumn leaves. Letters on trade routes and tariffs, legislative updates and economic forecasts. The latest census data and what it meant for each province. All the minutiae that kept the empire running smoothly.

Once Gavriel had relished his lofty position, steering the course of this great ship of state with a steady hand. A stroke of his pen and laws were overturned, treaties renegotiated. All for the higher good—or so he had told himself. Yet he'd worn blinders when it came to Sion's unspoken caste system.

The White Foxes had abused Cathrynne with impunity because they knew the word of a cypher would not be taken seriously. And Gavriel had played no small part in upholding this injustice. How would her life have been different if she was never taken from her family? If she had grown up with both mother and father in a safe and loving home?

Seeing the light in Cathrynne's eyes cool to contempt had been wrenching but no more than he deserved. It was why he had put it off until the last moment. By the three gods, it had taken all his willpower to stop and tell her the truth. Just the memory of her in his arms lit a fire again.

Gavriel drew a steadying breath and flexed his wings, testing them for long flight.

"Leaving again so soon, sir?"

Edvin Yarl stood in the doorway, a sprig of purple thistle livening the buttonhole of his black morning coat.

"I made a mistake," Gavriel said. "I must put it right."

Yarl tilted his head. "I have never heard you admit to an error," he said dryly. "Not once in forty years."

"I fear I have been too proud." Gavriel studied the man who had given him unwavering loyalty and wise counsel, who had foregone a wife and children for stuffy conference rooms and irregular hours. "I know I have not been the easiest employer."

"Sir?"

Sentiment had never been Gavriel's strong suit. His father had rarely given praise, or even thanks. "I only wish to tell you that your service has been exemplary. And that your friendship means a great deal to me."

Yarl looked alarmed. "That sounds like a farewell."

"No." Gavriel forced a smile. "It is simply an overdue thank-you."

Yarl stood straighter. "The pleasure has been mine, Lord Morningstar."

Gavriel felt a twinge of regret. For what exactly, he could not say.

"I shall return," he said. "But it might be some time. Good-bye, Edvin."

He strode to the balcony and launched himself into the night. Misty rain swirled around him as he skimmed above the heath, then banked northwest.

He'd sent Alluin Westwind to the Plain of Contemplation without an instant's hesitation. The seraphim had violated the first edict of Sion and his punishment must be swift and harsh—

or so Gavriel had believed at the time. Now Westwind's words returned to haunt him.

*I would die for her. Perhaps that means nothing to the law, but you are a man. You must have passions and desires.*

Gavriel had rejected the argument out of hand, but he could not honestly do so now. After seven centuries of life, he finally understood what it was to love another being. To yearn for someone so completely that the world seemed empty and cold without them.

The wrong he had committed against Cathrynne and her family was a festering wound that would never heal until he found a way to correct it. She might not forgive him even if he made amends, but he would do it anyway. He would do anything for her, even if it meant defying his father. Twenty years of exile was long enough. Justice without compassion was no justice at all.

Of course, no angel had ever returned from the Plain of Contemplation. Alluin Westwind would be the first.

* * *

The stars came out, hard and bright. Gavriel followed the rugged coastline of Sundland where land met sea in a clash of rock and foaming waves. The Wick of Aith spread below him, a wide bay dotted with isles of black granite where seabirds nested in countless numbers.

His wings found a thermal rising from the sea and he soared higher, conserving strength for the final push. After some hours, the coastline gave way to boreal forest. Pine and spruce, broken by the occasional frozen lake. Smoke rose from isolated villages tucked into valleys.

Sunset painted the landscape gold as he passed over Isai Minye. The capital of Sundland gleamed below, alabaster stone and rose marble, its avenues laid out in symmetrical geometric patterns. His brother Michael ruled here, extending Valoriel's will with rigid obedience.

Beyond Isai Minye, the green foothills of the Sundar Kush

shouldered up from the valley floor, gradually rising to alpine tundra and at last the death zone of nearly vertical peaks that marked the northern rim of the empire. Ice tried to form at the edges of Gavriel's wings, but the heat of his blood melted it before the weight could drag him down.

Full dark had claimed the sky by the time Mount Meru appeared. The mountain soared impossibly high, dwarfing the nearby peaks like a giant among mortals. Thousands of lights twinkled across its face.

Gavriel aimed for the Censura, a windswept platform hewn from the black rock of Mount Ogo. To his relief, it was empty. Sometimes his father or his brother Michael presided over trials here, but neither was present. Gavriel alit upon the icy ground, his feet sliding a pace before he regained his balance. Snow caught in his dark hair as he carefully made his way to the rear wall and pressed a small depression in the stone.

A hidden panel swung open. Heart beating faster, he withdrew an oblong box from the recess. For a moment, he hesitated. Other than loving Cathrynne Rowan, this was the first openly rebellious act of his life. He knew that his father would not condone bringing Alluin Westwind back from the Plain of Contemplation. Gavriel was not even certain such a thing could be done, or if Alluin still lived. But he had to try.

He opened the box and gazed upon the sinister black wand that lay within. The Rod of Penance. He didn't know where it had come from. If his father had made it, or if it was, perhaps, even older than the gods themselves. But when he touched it, the rod seemed to recognize him, coming alive in his hand. It grew warm and Gavriel sensed power gathering.

The words of banishing always included the name of the accused. Gavriel hoped he could summon Alluin back to Mount Meru in the same way. He turned to the great double-doors set into the wall, both carved with dark runes. The outline of the archway blended with the rock and was nearly invisible to the naked eye—until he raised the rod and spoke the ancient word of opening. A flickering light appeared along the cracks. It gave scant illumination, like weak starlight. As one, the doors silently swung wide, revealing the abyss beyond.

He stared down at the roiling clouds. If he succeeded, Valoriel need never know what he had done. He would quietly bring Alluin Westwind back to Arioch. He could stay at Everfell while Gavriel found a way to contact Cathrynne . . .

A soft sound made him turn. Gavriel scowled as a small figure with hair and wings the pure white of an egret landed on the platform.

"What are you doing here, brother?" she asked innocently. "I thought you had gone home."

Annoyance surged through him. He quickly hid the rod behind his back. "I might ask the same. We are far from your solar, Haniel."

She gave him a cool smile. "I happened to be passing. But since I am here, we should talk, brother."

"Yes, let's," he snapped. "We can start with how you tried to kill me."

A delicate brow arched. "Such melodrama," Haniel retorted. "If you were less stiff-necked and an ounce more sensible, we could have worked together to find the source of the kaldurite. I only wanted you confined to your bed while my agent found the girl from Pota Pras." She gave him an apologetic frown that he felt sure was feigned. "I didn't realize how potent the stones were. But you are fine now, and there is no permanent harm done, is there?"

Gavriel's eyes narrowed. "Your agent? You mean Levi Bottas?"

She sighed. "Levi took matters into his own hands. I never would have killed Casolaba in such a stupidly spectacular manner. He meant it as a warning to the witches, but it only resulted in them calling for your aid."

"And the first attempt on my life?" Gavriel said acidly. "Also an unfortunate accident?"

She ignored this. "I gave Levi one last chance to redeem himself with Kal Machena. Unfortunately, he bungled that as well. The girl is gone again, as you must know."

Gavriel shook his head. "What is he? Some kind of weirdling?"

Humans and witches had mingled their bloodlines for centuries. The unions were not forbidden, but they did occasionally result in people with odd powers.

Haniel studied him for a long moment, her face impassive. "Leviathan is nephilim," she said at last.

"Nephilim?" Gavriel frowned. "What is that?"

"The offspring of witches and angels," Haniel said evenly, "if the mother is angelic."

Gavriel had been told that those unions never produced offspring. He thought of the boy's blue eyes and stared at her in shock. "*You* are Levi's mother."

She gazed back with quiet defiance.

"Who is the father?" Gavriel demanded.

"That is not your concern."

The hypocrisy of it stunned him. "Does Valoriel know about this?"

A gust of wind carried the faint sound of singing from the Chorale. Haniel closed her eyes, her soft, youthful face tipped back to listen. "Exquisite, isn't it? Hundreds of voices blending with not a single sour note. I understand why our father spent all his time at the Chorale. It allowed him to forget the ugliness in the world below."

"Answer the question," Gavriel snapped, losing patience with her rambling.

Haniel regarded him with bland indifference. "Cyphers are abominations," she said. "They have the capacity to birth Sinn, our age-old enemies. But my son is different. He is sterile."

"How can you be so sure?"

"There are ways of testing it," she replied evasively. "My point is that he has immeasurable value. He can move in elite circles with no one the wiser. Leviathan is loyal to Mount Meru, but he appears human."

"Loyal to Mount Meru?" Gavriel echoed. "Or to you, dear sister?"

Haniel ignored the sarcasm. "It doesn't matter. My aims are the same as our father's." She took a step forward. "The mortals and witches will make kaldurite into a weapon against us. They are too greedy and corrupt to be allowed to govern themselves anymore. They have proven time and again that they don't deserve free will. Fear is the only thing that seems to keep them in line."

Her gaze turned to the distant silhouette of the Citadel. "The legions have been idle for too long," she added softly. "It is time they were put to good use."

A chill swept him. When had Haniel's thinking become so distorted? He had to talk her out of this before it was too late.

"Not everyone is like Barsal Casolaba," Gavriel protested. "Some of our cousins are loyal and generous, with little thought for themselves. Others make beautiful works of art and music, dance and literature. Take my city of Arioch. It is a hub of learning and enlightenment. If you would deign to leave your tower and actually speak to the people who live in your own province, you would find that they are not much different than we are—"

Her shrill laugh of incredulity cut him off. "You can't be serious. Our father took great care when he made us. But humans were *created* to be flawed. Travian's twisted sense of humor, I suppose."

"Just because a thing is flawed does not make it worthless," Gavriel said firmly. "Can you not see, Haniel? It is humanity's very imperfections that allow them to grow and change for the better, while we remain static. Worse, afraid to admit that we are wrong because such a thing is supposed to be impossible."

He thought of all the angels who had been condemned to Plain of Contemplation for minor infractions. The trials were conducted swiftly and secretly, but it must be thousands by now. What had happened to them all?

Haniel shook her head. "I admit that a few humans do rise above the herd, but most spend their lives competing to fulfill primal urges for food, shelter, and procreation. They are industrious and even quite clever at times, but they are also cruel and selfish."

She sniffed. "The witches *think* they are superior, more civilized, but that is only because they wield the power of lithomancy. Look at what they have done with that power! They pay lip service to the elected assemblies, but in reality Sion is ruled by an oligarchy that feeds off the blood of the mines." She studied him with an obstinate tilt to her chin. "Tell me that is not true."

"Some of it might be," he conceded. "But it is far more complicated than you present it to be. I suppose you will claim the angels are perfect."

"Not at all. But they hate us for it anyway, brother. And you can be assured that they will use this new stone to pull us down and destroy us." Her face hardened. "We *must* control the source of the kaldurite, and you will show me where it is."

Haniel's utter confidence rankled his pride. How dare she presume to issue orders? She had no authority over him.

Before he could think twice, Gavriel withdrew the Rod of Penance from behind his back. "Or," he growled, "I will send you to the lower plane to *contemplate* the wisdom of your actions, sister."

Her sapphire eyes flashed. "You wouldn't dare."

"Wouldn't I?" Righteous fury filled him. "I have every right. You ordered the death of Barsal Casolaba. You tried to kill *me*—twice. And your reckless union with a witch has produced offspring with dangerous and unsanctioned powers." He strode forward, blood heating. Haniel retreated, nearly tripping over her gown in her haste. "As chief magistrate of Sion, I judge you guilty."

Haniel bared her teeth like a cornered animal as he raised the Rod of Penance. She stood at the very edge of the platform, her wings tensed to take flight.

"Your sentence is . . ." Gavriel drew the thin, frozen air deep into his lungs. He thought of Alluin Westwind. Reminded himself of why he had come here in the first place. With a supreme effort, he mastered his anger. "To return to Kota Gelangi and call off your hunt for Kal Machena. The kaldurite does not belong to us." Weariness came over him. "I cannot judge you for loving a witch. But I strongly suggest you leave before I change my mind."

Haniel eyed him warily. "Gavriel Morningstar showing mercy? No one would believe it."

"I have changed." His voice grew stern. "But I cannot allow your son to walk free. Levi is a murderer and will be brought to account for it."

She stared at Gavriel for a long moment. "If you can find him," she retorted, eyeing the Rod of Penance. "Now put that vile thing away before—"

"What is going on?"

Gavriel's heart sank at the new voice. He turned to see their father alight on the Censura's platform. The bright gold of his wings emitted a warm light as he strode forward, hand extended. "Give it to me," he said in a peremptory tone.

In his presence, Gavriel was a callow youth again, chastised for watching the legions drill when he was supposed to be studying his law books. That small act of rebellion was the farthest he'd ever gone in defiance of his father—until now.

"Did you not hear me?" Valoriel demanded impatiently.

Gavriel's arm moved of its own accord, surrendering the Rod of Penance. Haniel watched them both, her expression inscrutable again.

"Why are you here?" Valoriel asked. His eyes, green as fern moss, studied Gavriel intently.

"I have come about Alluin Westwind," he admitted.

His father looked surprised. "The seraphim guard?"

"Yes. His sentence was too harsh. I intend to grant a commutation."

Valoriel's expression cooled. "I hoped you wanted to speak of greater matters." He glanced at his cunning daughter and Gavriel realized that Haniel had long been whispering in his ear.

"You mean the kaldurite," Gavriel said, trying to hide his disgust.

"We *must* control the source before this corruption spreads. It is already happening. Even the angels are changing, becoming like their flock. Look at you, Gavriel."

"I uphold your laws," he replied warily.

"It is too late to dissemble. You think you love this cypher. Why else would you be here pleading on behalf of her father?"

Pride flared. "Because it is the right thing to do. The sentence was unjust." He cast a mutinous look at Haniel. "If *she* can love a witch, I can, too."

"Careful now," Valoriel warned. "I am the one to decide such things."

His mind reeled. His father knew everything—and didn't care. "Why aren't you punishing her? How is this tolerated?"

"Leviathan will be a great asset in the days to come."

"What about Minerva and Travian?" Gavriel demanded. "Do you honestly believe they will allow this coup?"

Valoriel did not appear concerned. "Minerva lives like an anchorite, distant from the workings of the empire." He gestured at the sea of darkness stretching to the horizon. "Travian is out there somewhere, gambling and whoring no doubt, but I have not sought his counsel in centuries. He is a child, preoccupied with whatever shiny new bauble he holds in his hand, with no thought beyond gratifying his own desires. It is up to us to preserve the peace."

"What you describe sounds more like war," Gavriel protested.

"Then choose a side," Valoriel growled. His gaze narrowed.

"Let us speak of your cypher. Cathrynne Rowan is the most powerful seer in generations. We could use her gift." He gripped Gavriel's shoulder. "You may have her as a consort if you persuade her to serve Mount Meru."

Gavriel stiffened. "She is not a slave to be traded for favors."

A spasm of irritation crossed Valoriel's handsome face. "Very well, I shall keep it simple. Do your duty and all will be forgiven. Bend the knee and swear allegiance. I will set you and Haniel above all the others to rule Sion as you see fit."

*To rule.*

Long ago, Sion had kings and queens. Some were good, some bad. The last ones were very bad indeed, which is why they'd been violently overthrown and the dynastic system changed to one of popular assemblies.

Yet it was a seductive offer. For a minute, Gavriel's head spun with the possibilities of limitless power. He could punish the White Foxes for their brutal excesses—and even disband them completely.

He could divert resources to Pota Pras and the countless hardscrabble towns like it. Build schools and decent housing and hospitals. Enforce the ban – widely ignored – on child labor in the mines.

He could end the barbaric practice of cypher infants being taken from their parents.

Perhaps his father was right. The empire needed a firm hand at the tiller. And who was more suited to the task than Gavriel Morningstar?

He looked up and saw Haniel watching him with glittering eyes, a slight smile of triumph on her lips, and Gavriel understood in a flash that the reality would be different. Valoriel only wanted a henchman to enforce his diktats with an iron fist. By the end, Gavriel would have no honor, no integrity.

Yet for once it wasn't fear for his reputation that swayed him. It was the millions who would lose what freedoms they had. He knew what Cathyrnne Rowan would say. She had more heart, more soul, more courage than a hundred of his kin.

Haniel had to be stopped. He needed to get his father alone, make him see reason. But now was the not the time.

"I must return to Kirith," Gavriel said evenly, "to think it over."

Valoriel looked displeased. "What is there to think about? I will have your answer now."

His tone was confident, assured. Gavriel would obey as he always did. They might disagree over minor matters, but his son would not dare to say—

"No." Gavriel straightened his spine. "This course of action is immoral and ill-advised. I cannot in good conscience be part of it. Nor should you, father."

Valoriel stared at him, as if he could not quite fathom what he was hearing.

Haniel laughed. "So be it, Light-Bringer. As I warned you, even the highest among us can fall."

Eight armored seraphim dropped down from the night. In their hands dangled chains of adamantine, bright as diamond and heavier than lead. Gavriel spread his wings and leapt for the edge of the platform. A chain caught his right wing, grinding against the bone. Another caught the left. He was hurled to the icy stone.

"Your sister warned me that you would rebel against my authority," Valoriel said with a deep scowl. "I did not want to believe it, but she was right. You have grown arrogant and prideful, Gavriel. Too certain of your own judgment."

The Rod of Penance pulsed with fey power. Black ley leaked from the tip, curling like smoke in the frigid air. The seraphim seized his hair and dragged him to kneeling.

"Some time in exile will remind you of your place at my feet," Valoriel continued. "Perhaps after a millennium or two, you will see reason."

Anger and shock turned to disbelief. This couldn't be happening. He was Sion's chief magistrate. An archangel!

"I have the right to a trial," Gavriel cried, his voice hoarse.

"So you do," Valoriel agreed. His face was a pale moon in the darkness. "I accuse you of treason and find you guilty."

He raised the rod. The air thickened. The clouds churned, black and angry. Lightning flashed within their depths. Gavriel's heart raced with terror, shame, and other nameless emotions. Alluin Westwind must have felt the same as he stared through the portal at the unknown fate awaiting him below.

"What a great disappointment you are," Valoriel added bitterly.

Gavriel's gaze lifted to his father. When had his eyes grown so cloudy? His chin so weak?

All of Gavriel's life, he had believed Valoriel to be a paragon of virtue and reason. But now he saw him clearly—an aging god who had become as morally bankrupt as those he planned to subjugate.

"You will regret this," he snarled. "That I vow."

"Your vows mean nothing," Valoriel retorted.

"Then hear me now, *father*," Gavriel spat. "You corrupt all you touch. You rail against mortals' greed and ambition while scheming to shed the blood of innocents. You punish angels for loving witches while breeding half-blood nephilim in secret."

Valoriel looked down at him, lips tight. "I do what I must to preserve order."

"You do what feeds your own power," Gavriel said with contempt. "Nothing more."

For an instant, he thought his father would strike him. But then Valoriel nodded to the seraphim. A silver gauntlet flashed, and white-hot pain exploded along Gavriel's right shoulder, radiating down his back. He clenched his jaw to trap the scream, too proud even now to show weakness. A biting gust of snow stung his eyes as the seraphim dragged him to the edge of the platform. His right wing dangled useless; the heavy chains of adamantine held his left wing fast.

"I renounce you, Gavriel Light-Bringer," Valoriel intoned. "I cast you down and strip you of all titles and offices."

The lights of Mount Meru blurred behind him like jewels cast across the velvet firmament. Haniel stood at their father's right hand wearing an amused smile.

"Goodbye, brother," she said sweetly.

He gritted his teeth against the agony. "I'll be back. You can count on it."

*I'm sorry, Cathrynne*, he thought. *So sorry*—

The seraphim hurled him headlong into the abyss.

# AFTERWORD

Dearest Reader,

I hope you enjoyed *Dark Bringer* and I apologize for leaving you on a cliffhanger (not even a cliffhanger, really, since he went straight over the edge). Rest assured, the story of Cathrynne Rowan and Gavriel Morningstar doesn't end here, and I have SO much more to tell. The next book in the series is titled *War Witch*. It will come out in 2026, so keep an eye out—or better yet, join my list, *The Sorcerous Pen*, and never miss a new release.

My ravens will also deliver a free ebook, along with early access to sales, giveaways, diabolical potions, and arcane lore.

Until next time, happy reading!

# ACKNOWLEDGMENTS

A huge thanks to Carol Edholm for catching lots of silly errors (though of course, any that snuck through are mine entirely).

And for Laura Pilli, who saved me from a badly timed kiss, as well as sundry other mishaps and tediously written action scenes. Grazie, cara!

# ABOUT THE AUTHOR

Kat Ross worked as a journalist at the United Nations for ten years before happily falling back into what she likes best: making stuff up. She loves to hear from readers, so drop a line anytime! She lives in Connecticut with her son and lots of rescue cats. Stop by her website for maps and playlists and other goodies!

www.katrossbooks.com
kat@katrossbooks.com

instagram.com/katrossauthor
facebook.com/KatRossAuthor
pinterest.com/katrossauthor
bookbub.com/authors/kat-ross

# Also by Kat Ross

*The Fourth Element Trilogy*

*The Fourth Talisman Series*

*The Fourth Empire Series*

*Nightmarked Series*

*Lord of Everfell Series*

*Lingua Magika Trilogy*

*Gaslamp Gothic Collection*

*Some Fine Day (dystopian YA standalone)*